Mary Howitt, Margaret Howitt

An Autobiography

Mary Howitt, Margaret Howitt

An Autobiography

ISBN/EAN: 9783337011451

Printed in Europe, USA, Canada, Australia, Japan

Cover: Foto ©Raphael Reischuk / pixelio.de

More available books at **www.hansebooks.com**

MARY HOWITT

An Autobiography

EDITED BY HER DAUGHTER

MARGARET HOWITT

"Confide to God that thou hast from Him; oh thou soul weary of wandering! Confide to the Truth, that which is from the Truth within thee, and thou shalt lose nothing."

ST. AUGUSTINE

IN TWO VOLUMES

VOL. II.

LONDON

WM. ISBISTER LIMITED

15 & 16 TAVISTOCK STREET COVENT GARDEN

1889

CONTENTS.

CHAPTER I.

AT CLAPTON.

1843-1848.

CHAPTER II.

IN ST. JOHN'S WOOD.

1848-1852.

CHAPTER III.

THE HERMITAGE.

1852–1857.

CHAPTER IV.

WEST HILL LODGE.

1857–1866.

CHAPTER V.

THE ORCHARD.

1866–1870.

CHAPTER VI.

IN SWITZERLAND AND ITALY.

1870–1871.

CHAPTER VII.

ROME AND TYROL.

1871–1879.

CHAPTER VIII.

THE HOME IN MERAN.

1879–1882.

CHAPTER IX.

IN THE ETERNAL CITY.

1882–1888.

LIST OF ILLUSTRATIONS.

MARY HOWITT.

CHAPTER I.

AT CLAPTON.

1843–1848.

On our return to England in April 1843 I was full of energy and hope. Glowing with aspiration, and in the enjoyment of great domestic happiness, I was anticipating a busy, perhaps overburdened, but neverthless congenial life. It was, however, to be one of darkness, perplexity, and discouragement.

Just before our departure from Heidelberg we made a pedestrian excursion into the remnants of the ancient Hardt Forest. There, seated at the foot of a mighty pine-tree, Frau von Schoultz, the niece of the Royal Academician, Thomas Phillips, sang so splendidly, in Swedish, Tegnèr's "Old Gothic Lion," an heroic national air greatly beloved in Sweden, that some peasant-girls cutting an early growth in the glades of the wood came forth, and with brandished sickles kept time to the strain.

It was a lovely day and a beautiful scene, yet marked by an unspeakable sadness, which was afterwards to dim the brightness of our lives. Our handsome, nimble little Claude, then in his tenth year, and called by his preceptors, for the sweetness of his disposition and his brilliant attainments, *der goldene Junge*, was perceived to be lame. He said, "It was nothing." But when we insisted on an explanation, he confessed to his right knee being tired. "It hurt him just a little; nothing to speak of."

He continued to limp, and we, naturally troubled, to ask, "What did it mean?"—"He fancied it was sprained. He had felt it ever since —— (mentioning an English youth), following him up the staircase, had, for a joke, lifted him up by the collar over the balustrade, which was not much more than a yard above the pavement. Somehow he had slipped out of his hands and dropped, but he had lighted on his feet. He had not been hurt. He only felt his knee when he was tired."

Poor Claude! He seemed so bright and cheerful, that, by some strange chance, although shocked by the disclosure, we accepted his explanation. The entire party returned home weary; and he seeming not more so than the rest, we forgot, in the stir and occupation of leaving Heidelberg, our momentary anxiety.

But after my husband and I, with the younger children, had arrived in England, and we were busy settling in a house we had taken at Upper Clapton, we received a letter from our daughter, Anna Mary, that filled us with dismay and anguish. Claude's knee had developed the most alarming features of disease. The English physician at Mannheim, who had seen him, desired that his parents might be immediately apprised, and he taken home. With scarcely the delay of an hour, therefore, William set off to Heidelberg, and brought back the dear child from the first-rate private school where we had left him with his eldest brother.

To Anna Harrison.

"*The Grange, Upper Clapton, July* 23, 1843.—My week consists generally of seven working days, or, speaking more correctly, perhaps, because my employment is very much to my mind, my week is made up of seven active Sabbaths. The first day, however, is distinguished from the other six as the day when I mostly write to those I love best.

"I do not know whether dear mother has told thee of poor Claude's sad accident, and of his being now at home perfectly lame. Oh! it has been the saddest trial we ever had in our lives! Never was my heart so wrung; never did I shed such bitter tears as I have done over this poor child! William fetched Claude from Germany. He then took him to Mr. Liston, one of the most eminent physicians in London. He could counsel nothing but amputation. We could only consent to this as the very last means. William thought then of taking him to Sir Benjamin Brodie; but that kind, excellent man, Joseph Pease, of Darlington, a very particular friend of William's, begged him first to ask the advice of Dr. Bevan, a Friend, a very clever and conscientious man, whom, supposing Claude were his child, he should employ.

"Dr. Bevan recommended Mr. Aston Key, and under his care, accordingly, Claude was put. He, like Liston, thought the case was most serious. He would not give us hope, but said there was a chance of his regaining the use of the limb. He advised bandaging, and accordingly that has been done. Thou canst believe, dear sister, what an awful trial this is. You have had experience of a similar affliction, and can sympathise with us. Alas! I was proud of Claude, who, I fancied, would make a figure in life. I am humbled now. I throw all on the mercy of God, and hope and trust that He may bless the means which we make use of to restore him.

"Poor Claude has a nice little invalid - carriage, with an inclining seat, so that he lies in it, and in it he passes nearly the entire day. Charlton, who is as sturdy as a little pony, draws him about the garden, and one of the servants when we go out all of us together. I am impatient to get the other two dear children home, for, till they are with us, I do not feel sure but that some other trouble may be impending over us. Among the many blessings that I have, I must not forget dear William. He has the heart of an affectionate woman, with all the solidity of judgment and the firmness of the most masculine mind. Night and day is he always ready to help, to comfort, to suggest, and, what is more than all, to do. He carries Claude in his arms up and down stairs. He thinks nothing a trouble; he is never out of temper. I grumble, despond, and am petulant; he is none of these.

"And now, what do I mean to do with regard to 'the Society'? Nothing, dear Anna. If they will let me alone, I shall let them alone. We shall occasionally go to meeting, but shall endeavour to find some place of worship near us, which may suit us better than Friends' Meeting. Our children would derive no benefit from going there, and for their sakes we must find some place of worship where we may take them regularly. I fancy in religious opinion I differ from thee, because mere creeds matter nothing to me. I could go one Sunday to the Church of England, another to a Catholic chapel, a third to a Unitarian, and so on; and in each of them find my heart warmed with Christian love to my fellow-creatures and lifted up with gratitude and praise to God. But indeed each day, each passing hour almost, preaches some sermon to me ; and if I never entered an acknowledged place of worship, I should believe that, in my way, my worship would not be unacceptable to Heaven. Nevertheless, we feel it right that the children should be brought up with some little religious discipline as to mere outward form ; and, please Heaven, we will endeavour, in the home-life, to instil into their souls the spirit of Christian love."

"*Sunday, Oct.* 8, 1843.—With the exception of Claude, we are all quite well. Little Meggie is now in the room with me. She is a regular girl, a tidy little body, who never is so happy as when she is doing some kind of woman's work. Her great delight is to arrange my things. She is as still as a mouse, and turns out my drawers and boxes and lays everything in again in the neatest way; and I never know where to find what I want. But it amuses her and gratifies her love of order.

"We have just now a great cause of annoyance, and which will be a cause of loss to us. A publisher in London, a low fellow, has brought out the remainder of Mdlle. Bremer's works for one-and-sixpence each, the very books we are now translating. It is very mortifying, because no one knew of these Swedish novels till we introduced them. It obliges us to hurry in all that we do, and we must write almost night and day to get ours out, that we may have some little chance. Though many persons will no doubt buy this cheap edition, we still hope that the circulating libraries will take ours. It made me quite poorly last week."

"*Sunday, Oct.* 15.—How art thou, beloved sister, this fine, fresh autumn morning? Oh, how lovely everything looks! It has been a stormy week, rain, mist, and wind; but all now is calm, bright, and fresh. It does one good, for it reminds one of such periods in one's own experience. This morning, as I went into the garden, there was a sound of church bells, a murmuring as if the very air was full of them. Now and then there dropped noiselessly a dead leaf from the trees above. There is nothing much to tell in all this, but it impressed my heart with a feeling of love and assurance that made me happy. I loved every one connected with me, and my heart sprang towards thee.

"We have apprehended for some time that the system of bandaging was not applicable to Claude's case. A friend of ours, whose son suffered from a similar accident, confirmed our opinion, and we have now put Claude under the great homœopathic practitioner, Dr. Epps. I hope thou art not one of those who look on homœopathy as quackery."

To Elizabeth Bennett, Daughter of Imm Trusted, of Ross.

"*Upper Clapton, Oct.* 19, 1843.—Many thanks for your kind letter. We have indeed been most intensely anxious, and have had cause for deep sorrow in the case of our poor dear Claude.

"How truly did we sympathise with you in your bereavement you will believe, and had I known where to address you, should certainly have expressed it. Let me assure you how great the pleasure would be, if it suited your convenience, to call upon us and renew the personal acquaintance which began so agreeably in

summer weather, and, as it were, among the flowers in
Surrey.

"I take great interest in your children, and shall
always be glad to observe how your system of education, which appeared to us so excellent and wise, answers
its end in developing their characters and minds. We,
who cannot devote so much time to ours as you can,
have an excellent and learned young German as tutor.
We hope, with the blessing of Heaven, that it may
answer, and that we may in the end make them wise,
good, and happy."

To ANNA HARRISON.

"*Sunday, Oct.* 22.—Thy last interested me deeply, and
awakened in all our hearts the deepest sympathy. We are
quite sure that nothing but the most sincere conviction
would have induced thee to take so decided a step as joining the Church of England. We all think that thou hast
done quite right; and we admire and love Daniel for his
kindness and co-operation in it. I shall not, of course,
write anything to our mother about thy change of opinion;
but when she comes to us, as I believe she will shortly,
I shall then have a talk with her, and can no doubt
make her quite satisfied with it. I am sure that she
will be reconciled, and most likely think, as I do, that
sincere conviction is of far greater worth than an
educational belief. May God give thee peace, as I do
sincerely believe He will, in this step which thou hast
taken.

"I am a little uneasy how we are to manage when
dear mother comes, for it is our bounden duty to make
her visit as pleasant as we can; and I am afraid that
she will see much of which she will be inclined to dis-

approve; yet I hope, in the spirit of love and good sense, she will bear with us.

"We have Eliza back, and to-day dear little Meggie has been with her to meeting, and for the first time. Charlton and Alfred go to church with Herr Müller. Charlton went to meeting one Sunday. When he came back he said, 'I shall always go to that meeting, I like it so much!'—'And why, Charlton?' we asked. 'Oh! because there is a dog-kennel there.' Poor fellow! what a reason for going to meeting! Meggie would say she liked to go because all the people were so good to her, and smiled at her so kindly!"

"*Oct.* 29.—Our dearest mother seems troubled rather by our making use of homœopathy for Claude. She has an idea, I fancy, that it is in some way connected with the spread of the Catholic religion. It is true that it was introduced by a German, and he might be a Catholic, but it is not peculiar to that body of people. Dr. Epps is almost a Friend in many of his opinions. He is a most remarkably kind person, and has something almost apostolic in his manners. We knew him first in Nottingham, after William had published his 'History of Priestcraft.'"

"*Sunday morning.*—Dearest sister, send me, as thou sayest, a chronicle of thy home. Tell me what thy children say and do, that I may have some knowledge of them. For myself, do not I always write the most egotistical letters in the world? Thou must know my children well; and I seem always to extol them, just as if they were the most perfect creatures in the world; whereas they are not so. Anna Mary, however, is good beyond words.

"We are now more than ordinarily busy. We have embarked a great deal of money in our publication of the Swedish novels, and the interference of the upstart London publisher, of which I have told you, is still most annoying. Mdlle. Bremer, however, has written a new novel, and sends it to us before publication. We began its translation this week, and hope, by beginning to print immediately, to be able to publish it at the New Year; about the time it will appear in Sweden and Germany. . Thus we shall have a great advantage with a fair field to ourselves. We are writing as fast as possible, and with such an invalid as Claude in the house, every moment is taken up.

"I shall be able to send thy children a book at Christmas which they will like, I hope. It is 'The Child's Picture and Verse Book,' which I have translated from the German work commonly called 'Otto Speckter's Fable-Book.' William will send them 'The Marvellous History of Jack of the Mill,' a story told to our children three winters ago by their papa—literally told night after night, like an Arabian tale, and afterwards written down for them. It was a present to them last Christmas in manuscript, and whatsoever profit it produces will be their own property.

"How true is what thou sayest of the Church prayers! I always feel it so; and because the Church service is so good, so beautiful, and so applicable to all hearts and all states, the sermon itself is of less consequence.

"I think this letter of Emma's will please and interest you all. It is a delight to see how entirely they seem to be in their right place in America; nor could I, even for the selfish pleasure of near intercourse, wish them back. When I write to Emma I shall speak of the change in thee, in the manner in which we think it ought to be regarded. I have never written of it to our mother, but I have spoken to her of my own views very freely, and I fancy that she takes it all now much more easily. I have told her not to trouble herself about the commotions in the Church of England, &c., &c.; and she has written more cheerfully on that subject. I imagine, nevertheless, dearly beloved sister, that thou and we should differ, not *quarrel* remember, about some points. Thou would find us desperate Radicals, Corn-Law League, universal-suffrage people. But what would that matter? We could agree heartily to differ."

" *Sunday afternoon.*—Poor dear Claude! It is one of his bad days. His leg is painful to him, and keeps him sadly fretful and uneasy. He has shed many tears, and that is by no means usual with him. We have, however, an invitation out for to-morrow evening, where we can take him; and, poor child! it is such a pleasure to him to go out now and then to see fresh people, and lie on a fresh sofa; thus I feel quite obliged to any one who will let us take him with us. This will do him good, will make him to-morrow forget his pain. He has a great quantity of books in his little carriage, and we have a boy to attend upon him, who draws him about all day long. Were he not my child, how interested should I be in the pale, sweet-countenanced boy who is always reading, let one meet him in his carriage when one may! Mr. Tegg, the publisher, has been most kind in sending him books—several pounds' worth. Oh, how grateful to Mr. Tegg I am!

"'The book by William of which thou speakest is, I suppose, 'Peter Schlemihl,' by Chamisso, which he translated for a publisher at Nuremberg. We will send you a copy with the other books. The story is clever in its earlier part, but will not, I fancy, greatly please thee as a whole. It is very popular in Germany, Claude is now in bed. The rest of the family are going to tea. Later we shall have a little music, and the Lord's Prayer chanted in German ; a piece of music which contains the whole soul of devotion, and which makes a part of our Sunday evening pleasure. Then the day will be done, and to-morrow comes thy letter."

"*Sunday afternoon, Feb.* 25, 1844.—I have very little news of any kind to send thee, for I have hardly been out of Claude's room the whole of this week. I will, however, tell thee an anecdote of Charlton which pleased me. He had practised very nicely on the piano, and kind Herr Müller said he would play him something pretty as a reward. It was a little song about summer, which he had set to music.

" Charlton listened evidently in a dream. 'What are you thinking of, Charlton?' asked his tutor. 'I was thinking,' he replied, ' how I once was so happy. I should like to live that day over again. I was by myself in the field ; all was so still ; the sun was shining, the grasshoppers were jumping in the grass, and I was so happy. I should like to live that day over again !' 'You shall live again many hundreds of such days,' said good young Herr Müller. I was pleased, dear Anna, for it was a glimpse into the mind and experience of a child, and I saw how happy his life may be. Many and many a time has he gone wandering by himself about the field, when I never thought how full of gladness it was to him, but have said, perhaps, 'Look at that poor

little solitary thing wandering by himself; do somebody
go to him.'

"What thou sayest about Friends tying themselves
so much down to drab I understand perfectly. I, however, have long ceased to do that. I have a perfect pleasure in colour, and indulge myself in it. For instance,
what dost thou say to the two little children having scarlet
coats trimmed with fur! Eliza takes Meggie regularly
to meeting in hers. She goes to call on Friends dressed
in it. I was greatly amused at one visit she made.
There was a grave old woman-Friend in the house.
She seemed charmed with Meggie, who, in her black
velvet bonnet and scarlet cloak, looked, I suppose, somewhat regal. She admired and talked to her, and said
to Eliza and the Friend of the house, 'I should
fancy the little Princess-Royal such a child as this.'
Presently it came out that she was William Howitt's
child—the child of a Friend! The old lady, on hearing
this, put her away from her, and said, 'How thou art
dressed! See, thou hast frightened the dog out of the
room!' 'Art thou a Friend, too?' she said to Eliza,
and on hearing that she was, she turned herself round
and said not another word to her. But, after all, Friends
are becoming more liberal in regard to colours; for
instance, many plain Friends have crimson curtains to
their dining-rooms, and very handsome carpets, chosen
with good taste."

"*March* 3, 1844.—Anna Mary, Alfred, and I have been
this morning to the Unitarian chapel, and have heard
a sermon, which pleased us greatly, on religion being
a thing of every-day use and application. Dear William's
prepossessions are all very strongly in favour of Friends,

and he would like each of us to attend meeting; but then he is obliged to confess how very little instructive or beneficial it is. He goes himself now and then, and would go oftener, could he leave Claude; and for him, who can, as Friends say, 'centre his mind down,' it may be right, but for me it very rarely is so. A Friends' Meeting is only good for me when I am tired, mind and body, and want perfect quietness.

"Do not be shocked, dear sister, at our attending a Unitarian chapel; for they are the people, after all, with whom we seem to have most unity of feeling and opinion. If, however, we lived in a village where there was a good clergyman, I should go to church. But here, where all are Puseyites and a proud congregation, sitting in luxuriously cushioned pews, I should hardly like, nor could I in conscience join them. I do not, by any means, call myself a religious woman in the common sense of the word. Love and Faith make up the perfect Christian. Love I have, but, alas! I want faith. When I think of William's mother, with her deep religious feeling, her faith, which was strong enough to remove mountains, how short do I see myself! I sometimes could almost wish that I were a good Catholic; for they, of all people, have faith; and it is faith that gives to the soul its strength and assurance."

"*March* 10, 1844.—A week of great anxiety and painful watching almost by night and day has brought us round to Sunday again. Poor Claude has had a bad week. Oh Anna! if he recovers, I shall believe that the Almighty has spared him for some great and good work. I used to wish that Claude, with his keen, clear

intellect, should be a lawyer. I now would wish for him
to be a preacher of the Gospel, to show forth to all how
good and powerful and rich in love God is. But the
Lord's will be done, and so that His will be accomplished in and for Claude it will be right, and far better
than we, with all our love for him, could bring about."

WILLIAM HOWITT TO ANNA HARRISON.

"*March* 12, 1844.—Mary's letters, I know, have made
you aware by what a frail thread our dear Claude held
possession of life. That slight filament gave way this
morning. At twenty-five minutes past eleven o'clock
he breathed his last most easily and peacefully. I
think you never knew the dear lad, with his extraordinary powers, great wit and humour, and of a loving
disposition. He has been taken from us exactly on the
day twelve months on which the youth who occasioned
his injury came to Heidelberg."

Here may be added, that once, when his father, in great
distress of mind, suddenly exclaimed to him, "I wish
the lad who dropped you had to undergo all this, dear
Claude," raising his eyes with an expression of sorrow
and surprise, he replied, "Oh papa! don't say that; I
cannot bear the thought of it. Please let my love be
given to him, for I remember him with nothing but kindness." And the message was sent.

"*March* 19, 1844.—My dearest sister, we are to myself
a sort of riddle. We all feared and dreaded that the
poor dear child never could be restored to us, yet we
hoped and deceived ourselves to the last. I did not
realise that he was actually going till within a few

hours of his death. Yet he had, I now can plainly see, been stricken by the hand of Death for several days. He has been like an angel, whom we entertained unawares. I hope and trust the blessing of his presence will not soon depart from us. It seems to me that he has fulfilled his mission, which was to draw our hearts upward to God.

"For him, dear child, I can have no fears. There was nothing but love in his soul. No rancour, no bitterness. Oh, what a consolation it is to us now to remember this! He opened his heart two or three times to us, and how beautiful and consolatory a view it gave us! He confessed the little sins that lay heavy on his conscience, and seemed comforted when we could assure him that the Almighty would forgive them and much more.

"But still, dearest Anna, could I but have realised to myself the near approach of his end, I would have had more conversations with him on such subjects, and I earnestly hope and trust that the sin of omission may not be attributed to me. He was ten and a half, yet his mind seemed matured in these twelve months of sickness. We shall not remember him as the child, but as the friend, the beloved companion of so many sorrowful months. May it only please the Almighty that we may be worthy to meet with him, where there is no more sorrow, no more suffering, and no more parting!

"He was buried yesterday afternoon in the Friends' burial-ground at Stoke-Newington. Many Friends met us at the grave, and three ministers spoke. It has knit my heart to Friends, for I believe they all sympathised with us."

"*April* 2, 1844.—Thy letter, my dearest sister, was

indeed like the voice of the truest and sweetest affection.
I have turned to it again and again, and I feel that,
among the many blessings which I enjoy—and I enjoy a
great many—is that of having a sister like thee. I have
received several letters on this sorrowful occasion, which
are precious to me, and which I shall keep among my
valued things.

"Yes, dearest Anna, I will believe that whom 'the
Lord chasteneth He loveth.' I am sure that there is
much good in affliction, and my present, most earnest
prayer is, that the good which we all feel in this sorrow
may not soon pass away. I dare not make covenants,
lest I should break them, else I would covenant with
God and with myself to make this great grief useful to
myself and to others. How can we indeed be teachers
of others in any way, more especially in the best of all
ways—that of guiding them heavenwards—unless we
have been baptized in sorrow? We cannot see the
beloved of our souls taken from us without longing to
follow after. We are linked, as it were, to heaven, and
minds of a high and pure character are permitted also to
have glimpses into heaven, where they are; and thus
what we have known and felt we can speak of.

"Do not suppose, however, dearest sister, that I am one
of the favoured who are permitted to have the heavenly
visions. I am like the women sitting by the sepulchre,
who love much and sit in their sorrow, for they know
not yet that their Lord is risen. I cannot tell thee how
I long, however, to comfort mourners like myself. Oh,
how I love them! How I long to sympathise with them!
And I have, in my weakness, besought of the Almighty
that the good results of this affliction may be in me the
power to soothe and to strengthen such as mourn.

"I see how beautiful is resignation, but this can only be perfected by faith. May God, in His mercy, give it to me. 'Lord, I believe ; help Thou my unbelief !' Such is the cry of my heart, and happy beyond all worldly possessions is it to dwell in the light of faith undoubtingly, unquestioningly.

"How true it is that in the midst of life we are in death ! To us it seems as if our dearest Claude was the only one who had died, as if death had only visited our house. But if we walk out, or go to a place of worship, or where many persons are assembled, we see almost every third person in mourning like ourselves. I cannot tell thee how my heart warms to such. Their hearts have been wrung like ours. Their eyes have wept bitter tears. I long to sit down with them and talk to them of their dead. It is so pleasant to me to talk of Claude that I fancy they would like it too. I could listen for hours to mothers or loving sisters who would tell me of beloved and long-waited-upon invalids. And oh ! dearest sister, I think if there be one blessing greater than another, it must be the recovery of such an invalid, the watching the beloved one gaining strength, advancing from one stage to another towards health. How little do people think of these things ! and yet they are among the best blessings of life.

"To-morrow I intend again to commence my regular avocations. Poor dear Claude ! at this very moment I see the unfinished translation lying before me, which was broken off by his death. Alas ! I could have shed burning tears over this. How often did he beg and pray of me to put aside my translation just for that one day, that I might sit by him and talk or read to him !

I, never thinking how near his end was, said, ' Oh no,
I must go on yet a page or two.'   How little did I
think that in a short time I should have leisure enough
and to spare!   Oh Anna! of all the agonising feelings
which I know, none is so bitter as that longing for
the dead.   Just one day, one hour of their life, that
one might pour out the whole soul of one's inextinguish-
able love before them, and let them feel how dear, in-
expressibly dear, they are.   My very heart at times dies
within me from this deep and agonising longing.   But,
dearest, when we have angels in heaven, does not death
seem robbed of its terrors?

"I wonder how it is with families in heaven, for there
must be different degrees of worthiness in the different
members.   Some must have lower places than others.
I would be content to sit on the lowest footstool might
I only be permitted to behold the glory and the bliss of
my beloved ones, and to make compensation to them in
some way for my shortcomings on earth."

"*April* 17, 1844.—The Friends have been most kind
to us.   They permitted us to choose the spot where
dear Claude should lie.   They did not even wish him
to be buried among the children, and they will allow
us to plant shrubs and flowers on his grave.   He lies
near Charles Lloyd, the poet, on whose grave some
friend has planted a cypress.   It is no use telling one
that the resting-place matters nothing to the dead.
That is true, but it does matter to the living.   Jesus
wept at the grave of Lazarus.   The women wept at
the tomb of Jesus, and hearts that love truly and sorrow
deeply want the same indulgence.   I am sure that it
is pleasing to God that they should have it.   I do not

see exactly how Friends' minds can be operated upon, but I am sure that if this question could be fully discussed, very many among them would feel the same."

"*June* 16, 1844.—Only a very few words to-day, my dearest sister, and all because I am working hard to be at liberty to make my long-talked-of journey. I set myself last week to finish my story, and by great industry I am happy to say I did, having been three weeks over it. I have laid the scene of it at Uttoxeter, so if it is read there, the little town will wonder at my *impudence.*"

The story to which I thus refer was called "The Two Apprentices," and belonged to a series of tales which I had been writing, at various intervals, for several years. A simple, somewhat affecting little story, called "A Night-Scene in a Poor Man's House," having appeared in my friend Mrs. Alaric Watts's "Juvenile Souvenir" at Christmas 1838, it was read by the publisher, Mr. Tegg, of Cheapside. He immediately wrote and proposed that I should furnish him with a series of books to illustrate household virtues. He wished the number to be thirteen—a baker's dozen, as he said. My husband, the best literary friend and critic that I ever had, induced me to agree; and Mr. Tegg, a very peculiar man, who, from arriving in London a poor Scotch lad with a few halfpence in his pocket, had now, by his quick wit and industry, amassed a fortune, behaved through the whole transaction in the most straightforward, satisfactory manner. He punctually paid for each MS. as he received it, never advertised the works, and yet one edition succeeded the other; this large, silent sale being perhaps accounted for by his extensive connection with the Colonies. The first of this series, which appeared under the general title of "Tales for the People and their Children," was called "Strive and Thrive," and was followed by "Hope On, Hope Ever." From my earliest childhood I possessed a most keen sympathy, together with a deep interest, in lives and experiences different from my own, and which often caused my parents to censure my inquisitiveness. Yet this did not check the promptings of my heart, and my retentive memory thus acquired a store of incidents chiefly connected with poor people, their small joys and great sufferings.

In my married life at Nottingham, Alice Cheetham, a monthly nurse, had become, by her goodness and general efficiency, an established friend of the family. She was always a pleasant figure in the house, wearing nice, old-fashioned dresses, and possessing the tidiest, daintiest ways. On one occasion she stayed with me at Uttox-eter. It was no case of serious illness, and these few weeks in the real country were a delight to her. I had much earlier learnt her life's history, and sympathised with her. I knew the fates of her various children, and especially her sorrow about her wild son, Samuel, who had almost broken his mother's heart many years before by enlisting as a soldier. Where he was she knew not; he had been in India, he might now be dead. It was a terrible grief, of which she seldom spoke.

However, here she was now, very happy for the time being, in the remote country town of Uttoxeter, which had been exempted by the Duke of Cumberland, when on his way to Culloden, from ever henceforth having soldiers quartered in it. One night they might remain, but no longer. Therefore, Uttoxeter would be every now and then put into a state of excitement by the marching in of one or two regiments, with their heavy waggons piled up with baggage, soldiers' wives and children. The men were billeted for the night at the various public-houses. The baggage-waggons remained in the market-place. Should it, however, be a market-day, they were brought into our street, which, opposite to our house, was the widest in the town. Thus all the stir, bustle, and interest of that strange family life of common soldiery would be in part revealed to us children. I watched each detail with intense interest, and had no unfrequent opportunity of doing so, during the terrible years of the Napoleonic war.

An incident of this kind, with the events that might easily accrue, is introduced in my little story of "The Two Apprentices." Now, however, it is simply what befell my poor friend, Nurse Cheetham, that I wish to narrate. The weather was fine, and as I did not require her attendance, I desired her to take a walk. In so doing she met the soldiers of a regiment from Ireland, who were dispersing to their night-quarters; and amongst them, came upon her own son, the long-lost, long-lamented Samuel. Although he had been absent for years, mother and son both recognised each other in the street. Her intense joy may be imagined. For the moment every desire of her heart was satisfied. He was a fine-looking fellow, in good health, who, lazy or thoughtless, had let the years roll on without writing. Of course, she was up at four the next morning, once more to see her boy, to give him a parting kiss and blessing, and, doubtless, all the money she had. It was one little ray of light and love, which made that poor faithful mother so unspeakably happy. I had my pleasure in it also. She never heard from him, much less saw him again, at least not while we were at Nottingham.

Here I may mention, in connection with literary engagements, that I edited, in 1839 and the two following years, "The Drawing-Room Scrap-Book," published annually by the Messrs. Fisher. I was not proud of the work. It had been carried on for some years by L. E. L., until her marriage with Mr. Maclean in 1838, and I was her successor. The agreement was personally to furnish poems to the engravings chosen by the publishers. The payment was £100 per annum, and in that period of mental activity I could often write a poem in a day. Some of my pieces were English renderings of German poetry by Freiligrath and Clemens Brentano. Heine's exquisite lines on a mother taking her sick son to be cured by the Virgin Mary at the holy shrine of Kevlaar I translated in 1841. My successor was Miss Sarah Stickney, originally a Friend, who especially devoted her pen to the enunciation of moral truths, addressed principally to her own sex. She married the Rev. William Ellis, also an author, who had been a Nonconformist missionary to the Sandwich and South Sea Islands. They carried on a successful girls' school at Hoddesdon, in which they sought to combine scholastic and domestic teaching, the boarders taking it in turn to assist in cooking, &c.

We had not long been at Heidelberg, when a new realm of mental wealth unexpectedly opened to my husband and me. Our excellent and highly-accomplished friend, Madame von Schoultz, had derived much alleviation from the study of Scandinavian authors in a time of terrible suspense, caused by the mysterious disappearance of her Swedish husband, who, it was

subsequently discovered, lost his life in the Papineau
rebellion in Canada. With her we commenced Swedish,
a delightful employment, which might be called a relaxation rather than a labour, for here were no puzzling
terminations as in German, but a similarity of con-
struction with the English, which made it and its
cognate Danish of comparatively easy acquisition.

Fredrika Bremer's novels of Swedish family life delighted us by their originality, freshness, and delicate
humour, and we determined to introduce them to the
English reading public. My husband and I translated
"The Neighbours" and "The Home" from the German
versions, but in the new editions which speedily followed
we compared and revised them with the Swedish. In
England and America they immediately met with wide
recognition, although, when we first translated "The
Neighbours," there was not a house in London that
would undertake its publication. We printed and published it and others of the Bremer novels at our own
risk, when such became the rage for them, that our
translations were seized by a publisher, altered, and
reissued as new ones. The men in our printer's office
were bribed from America, and in one instance the
pirated sheets appeared before those we ourselves sent
over. Cheap editions ran like wildfire through the
United States, and the boys who hawked them in the
streets might be seen deep in " The Neighbours," "The
Home," and " The H—— Family."

The first of very many letters which I received from
Fredrika Bremer expresses her pleasure at the English
publication of " The Neighbours," and is dated Stockholm, February 21, 1843. She speaks modestly in it
of her productions, and is surprised that her common-

place delineations of every-day life should suit the fastidious taste of England. Nevertheless, she hopes still to write more worthily of the life in her native land, saying in conclusion, "Sweden is a poor but noble country, England is a rich and glorious one; in spirit they are sisters, and should know each other as such. Let us, dear Mrs. Howitt, contribute to that end."

To the best of my ability I united with her in so doing.

The far-famed citron-*soufflé* of the estimable Louise in Mdlle. Bremer's novel, "The Home," also procured for me a most agreeable and lasting friendship with an estimable gentlewoman, Miss Eliza Acton. In perusing "The Home," the *soufflé* had not escaped her observation, and she was anxious to obtain the exact receipt from Mdlle. Bremer for the second edition of "Modern Cookery." She was also desirous of information about "sweet-groats" and other preparations of grain mentioned in "The Neighbours" as forming part of the national food of Sweden; for she was much troubled by the culinary inaptitude of the English people. She had found that amongst the lower classes not one in ten could even make a loaf or boil a potato as it should be.

In the summer of 1844 I had the delight of visiting my beloved sister, Anna Harrison, and her family. At the end of July I was taken a charming little trip of five days from Liverpool to Llanberis and back by my brother-in-law, Daniel, in the company of Anna, their eldest son, Charles, their uncle, Richard Thompson, who was a most delightful old Methodist, and Mary Harris, an agreeable young woman-Friend of independent means. We had a rough but amusing voyage to the Menai Bridge, where there was an excellent inn. Telford's marvellous erection did not then pair with the Britannia tubular bridge, but uniquely spanned the strait in airy sublimity. We walked to it, viewed it on all sides, and knew not how sufficiently to admire. We ascended a hill to obtain a peep at the mountains, and how lovely they looked, lying calmly and magnificently in the repose of the late evening, with Snowdon in their midst! Enraptured by the view, and the thought that I was actually in the land which had been the object of my childish desires and fancies, I kept silently repeating what my parents had often said when I was young: "We really will, some time or other, take a cottage in Wales, and spend a few summer months there."

On leaving my kind relatives at Liverpool, I went, accompanied by my dear niece, Margaret Ann Harrison, to see my mother at Uttoxeter; and both accepting an invitation to Clapton, journeyed with me to London.

On September 8, 1844, I say, writing to my sister Anna :—

"I am sure thou wilt be glad to know that at length the troublesome duty of house-hunting is over. We have taken a house a short distance from the one where we now live. It is almost strange that, after seeking all round London, we come back at last to our own neighbourhood.

"I shall be very sorry to leave The Grange, notwithstanding its disadvantages; for it is endeared to me from many causes. Poor Claude liked it so much. It was his only home in England after our return; and the whole house and garden are full of memories and traces of him. The tracks of his carriage-wheels are still on the garden-walks. There is a shady path, which he called, 'The Vault,' where he liked to be drawn in the heat, and an

apple-tree that seemed especially his own. It is foolish,
but I feel as if he would still think of us as living here.
I am glad that we do not leave the neighbourhood, for
my heart is drawn towards the spot where he lies. His
memory is one of the sacred and precious things, over
which is a halo of love. Thank God for a hope of re-
union with the dead."

The house which we had taken was one of a couple
of well-built, substantially finished residences of the last
century, situated in Lower Clapton, and called "The
Elms," from the row of noble old elm-trees in their front.
It contained ample wainscoted chambers and a broad staircase of polished oak, leading to spacious reception-rooms.
The windows at the back looked into the pleasant garden,
with its creeper-festooned walls, long lawn, and flowering
shrubs; and beyond to quiet meadows, through which
flowed the river Lea, to vast marshes and the woodland
line of Epping Forest.

We had for our next-door neighbours, and thence for
life-long friends, Mr. Henry Bateman and his family. He
was the brother-in-law of the Rev. Thomas Binney; on
the Committee of the Religious Tract Society, and deservedly esteemed in Nonconformist circles for his active
benevolence, promotion of religious freedom, calm, out-
spoken denunciation of evil, unflinching adherence to
duty, and faithful trust in God under all circumstances.

The earlier portion of our residence at The Elms was
very pleasant. I recall it with a tender regret as worthy
and befitting in every way. The house was commodious,
the children well cared for and happy. Their chief and
favourite companions were Arthur Bateman, the children
of my beloved widowed friend, Mrs. Todhunter, and

the five little granddaughters of Dr. Southwood Smith.
Octavia Hill, the third of these sisters, often stayed with
Charlton and Meggie. She was their chosen playmate
and counsellor, and devised, even in their games, schemes
for improving and brightening the lot of the poor and
the oppressed.

The retiring and meditative young poet, Alfred

THE ELMS, LOWER CLAPTON.

Tennyson, visited us, and charmed our seclusion by the
recitation of his exquisite poetry. He spent a Sunday
night at our house, when we sat talking together until
three in the morning. All the next day he remained
with us in constant converse. We seemed to have
known him for years. So, in fact, we had, for his poetry
was himself. He hailed all attempts at heralding a
grand, more liberal state of public opinion, and con-

sequently sweeter, more noble modes of living. He wished that we Englanders could dress up our affections in a little more poetical costume ; real warmth of heart would lose nothing, rather gain by it ; as it was, our manners were as cold as the walls of our churches.

Pastor Carlson, the agreeable and intelligent minister of the Swedish church, frequently came to us. On a delightful summer afternoon, he brought with him Fahl-crantz, Professor of Theology at Upsala, the Sydney Smith of Sweden. He possessed a marvellous play on words, which is more difficult in Swedish than in fuller, richer languages. We sat on the lawn in the most cheerful good-fellowship.

Here too the Catholic priest, Dr. Willson, whom my husband had learnt deservedly to respect in Nottingham, came to see us. He had just been made first Catholic Bishop of Tasmania, and was on his way to the colony, where he so greatly ameliorated the condition of convicts.

My husband, on the announcement of his intended " Visits to Remarkable Places," received, in 1838, a letter from Manchester, signed E. C. Gaskell, drawing his attention to a fine old seat, Clopton Hall, near Stratford-on-Avon. It described in so powerful and graphic a manner the writer's visit as a schoolgirl to the mansion and its inmates, that, in replying, he urged his correspondent to use her pen for the public benefit. This led to the production of the beautiful story of " Mary Barton," the first volume of which was sent in MS. to my husband, stating this to be the result of his advice. We were both delighted with it, and a few months later Mrs. Gaskell came up to London, and to our house, with the work completed. Everybody knows how rapturously

it was received ; and from that time she became one of
the favourite writers of fiction.

My husband had translated a curious little book from
the third German edition, the real "Wanderings of a
Journeyman Tailor ;" P. D. Holthaus, who had trudged
through Europe and a part of Asia Minor, supporting
himself by his needle in Constantinople, Rome, and
elsewhere.   It appeared in 1844.   In 1845 he was busily
engaged on his "Homes and Haunts of the Poets."   I
wrote "The Author's Daughter" for "The Edinburgh
Tales," and in 1846 collected my ballads, chiefly written
some ten or fifteen years earlier, my miscellaneous poems,
and four poetical translations.   These were published in
one volume in 1847.

I had also turned my attention to Danish literature,
which my knowledge of the Swedish and German languages made me easily understand.   H. C. Andersen's
"Improvisatore" I first translated from the German
version, but after mastering Danish I made my work,
as far as possible, identical with the original.   It appeared
at the beginning of 1845, and gave great pleasure and
satisfaction to the author, who felt himself gracefully
and faithfully reproduced in English.   He begged me
to continue translating his works ; he longed to be known
and to be loved in England, as he was on the Continent,
where, from the prince to the peasant, all were so good
to him ; appreciation, fame, joy, followed his footsteps.
His whole life was, in consequence, a beautiful fairy-tale,
full of sunshine.   It was in this strain that he wrote to
me from Denmark and Germany.   I translated his "Only
a Fiddler," "O. T., or Life in Denmark," "The Constant
Tin Soldier," and other of his "Wonderful Stories," his
"Picture-book without Pictures" and "A True Story of

my Life." The "Improvisatore" was the only one that went into a second edition; the other books did not pay the cost of printing. Nevertheless, Andersen, having been assured in Germany and Denmark that my husband and I had made a fortune out of his translations, came himself to London in the summer of 1847, to make an advantageous monetary arrangement with us. He felt, he wrote me, that I had always acted as a sister to him, and was deeply grateful to me; and as he could not bear the thought of our discussing money together, Herr Hambro, his banker and countryman, would do so in his stead. My husband saw Herr Hambro several times on the subject, and from him heard of the exaggerated ideas that Andersen had of our gains. The worthy banker undeceived his friend, and although disappointed of his hope, Andersen wrote to me on August 28, 1847, the day before he left England, begging me to translate the whole of his fairy-tales. His Leipzig bookseller had brought out a German edition, beautifully illustrated, and the woodcuts could be procured for a small acknowledgment. I was then deeply engrossed in other literary work, and foolishly, it now seems to me, let the proposal drop. Unfortunately, the over-sensitive and egotistical nature of this great Danish author much marred our intercourse.

I may give, as an example, an incident that occurred on July 31, 1847. We had taken him, as a pleasant rural experience, to the annual hay-making at Hillside, Highgate, thus introducing him to an English home, full of poetry and art, of sincerity and affection. The ladies of Hillside, the Misses Mary and Margaret Gillies —the one an embodiment of peace and an admirable writer, but whose talent, like the violet, kept in the shade; the other, the warm-hearted painter—made him cordially welcome. So, too, our kind and benevolent host, Dr. Southwood Smith, who was surrounded at this merry-making by his grandchildren, Gertrude Hill and her sisters. The guests likewise were equally anxious to do honour to Andersen.

Immediately after our arrival, the assembled children, loving his delightful fairy-tales, clustered round him in the hay-field, watched him make them a pretty device of flowers; then feeling somehow that the stiff and silent foreigner was not kindred to themselves, stole off to an American, Henry Clarke Wright, whose admirable little book, "A Kiss for a Blow," some of them knew. He, without any suggestion of condescension or of difference of age, entered heart and soul into their glee, laughed, shouted, and played with them, thus unconsciously evincing the gift which had made him earlier the exclusive pastor of six hundred children in Boston.

Soon poor Andersen, perceiving himself forsaken, complained of headache, and insisted on going indoors, where Miss Mary Gillies and I, both most anxious to efface any disagreeable impression, accompanied him; but he remained irritable and out of sorts.

Some passages in my letters may now deserve attention. To my sister I write in December 1844 :—

"Yesterday Richard Howitt was here. There is something so quiet, patient, and melancholy about him, as quite touched my heart. Anna Mary's affection for him is perfect devotion; as a little child she loved him, and he is happy in her love."

In July of 1845 I tell my sister :—

" William has now been from home a week. We are too busy to miss him much; and his pleasant letters are a most agreeable diversion to our solitude. His last have been from Sheffield. He has been with James Montgomery and Ebenezer Elliott, and has obtained from them information which will make his 'Homes and Haunts of the Poets' extremely interesting. He is to-day at Newcastle-on-Tyne; from there he goes into Cumberland, and will visit Wordsworth."

To Miss Margaret Gillies.

" All the time William was in the neighbourhood of Rydal it poured with rain. He was one whole day a prisoner with the Wordsworths; but the day was pleasant indoors.

" He says both Mr. and Mrs. Wordsworth are tolerably well; and dear Mrs. Wordsworth sat mending her shoe, while the room was full of strangers, who had called to honour the poet. There was, among others, an American general there, an advocate of slavery, with whom William and Mr. Wordsworth had a great argument. All the day afterwards Wordsworth kept rejoicing that they had defeated the general. 'To think of the man,' said he, 'coming, of all things, to this house with a defence of slavery! But he got nothing by it. Mr. Howitt and I gave it to him pretty well.' The Latrobes, I think from Africa, were there to dinner. In the evening the Bishop of Salisbury was expected, but he did not come. Some Friends came, however, and it seems to have been a right pleasant time.

" Poor Dora had gone to Portugal. She was in a very sad state of health. Her husband's brother was there; and they thought that a voyage out and a stay of some

time might be of essential benefit to her. On the contrary, she had been taken with a very serious illness,
and they had been much alarmed. This is very melancholy. They talked in the very kindest manner of Miss
Gillies. This last bit is what I wanted most to communicate to you. They who love us truly will not lightly
change."

Letter to my sister, written in 1845, but without a
date :—

"I seem to have done very little this year. I have
translated nothing, written nothing of any length, yet I
never in my life felt so completely occupied. Sometimes,
indeed, I have been so sick of writing and of the sight of
papers and books that I have had quite a loathing to
them. But these are unhappy times always to me, and
only arise from over-weariness ; my delight is working.
I thank a good Providence, Who has enabled me to do a
little, I hope, towards diffusing sentiments of love and
kindness.

"I am just now deeply interested in the Anti-Slavery
question, the real, thorough Abolitionist view, which
would cut up this crying sin root and branch, and
spare none of its participators. Our friend, William
Lloyd Garrison, is now in London, with one of the most
interesting men I ever saw, a runaway slave, Frederick
Douglass. The narrative of his life, written by himself,
is most beautiful and affecting. William met with him
first in Dublin, and now that he is in London, we have
seen a good deal of him. I wish I could lend you some
of the very interesting and heart-rending Anti-Slavery
books that have been given to us, and which have so
wholly absorbed my thoughts, that now, like many a

good old Friend, I can talk of nothing but 'the dear
Blacks.'

"Ferdinand Freiligrath, the German poet and our dear
friend, has been now for some time an exile from his
country, on account of what we English should call very
innocent writings, but what the Germans term seditious.
He is a fine poet and a noble, good man. We have
induced him to come to England and try his fortunes
here in this land of commerce. He was brought up a
merchant, understands many foreign languages, and is
thus a most desirable person in a counting-house. He
came here rather more than a fortnight ago, and was with
us two weeks. On Saturday he went to Rotterdam to
meet his wife and child. Now I am expecting them to
arrive any moment. We shall thus have for the present
our house very full. We wish extremely for him to
settle in London, because we like him and his wife so
much, that it is a pleasure to have some of their society.
If London fails us, we must try elsewhere."

"*Nov.* 1845 (*after a visit to the seaside*).—Thou
inquires, dear sister, who our friends the Smiths are,
who contributed so much to make our Hastings sojourn
agreeable. The father is the Member for Norwich, a
good Radical and partisan of Free Trade and the abolition of the Corn-Laws. Objecting to schools, he keeps
his children at home, and their knowledge is gained
by reading. They have masters, it is true, but then
the young people are left very much to pursue their
own course of study. The result is good; and as to
affection and amiability, I never saw more beautiful evidences of it. There are five children, the eldest about
twenty-two, the youngest eleven. They have carriages

and horses at their command; and their buoyant frames and bright, clear complexions show how sound is their health.

"Every year their father takes them out a journey. He has had a large carriage built like an omnibus, in which they and their servants can travel, and in it, with four horses, they make long journeys. This year they were in Ireland, and next year I expect they will go into Italy. Their father dotes on them. They take with them books and sketching materials; and they have every advantage which can be obtained for them, whether at home or abroad. Such were, and are, our friends the Leigh Smiths, and thou canst imagine how much pleasure we were likely to derive from such a family."

"*Nov.* 30, 1845.—The Freiligraths have been living in lodgings near us, and found it very expensive; and as he is now in the office of Messrs. Huth, German merchants, we advised them to take a house and furnish it. They did so, going by our recommendation to the cabinet-maker and upholsterer of whom we bought our furniture, and they were to have from him six months' credit. I went with them on Saturday, and we chose their furniture, and it quite delighted me to see what pleasure they felt in having a house of their own. Later on the same day, when Freiligrath returned to the office, one of his employers asked him what he had done, how much he had bought, &c. 'Well,' said good Herr Huth, 'I shall now pay for this furniture, and I sincerely wish you well in your new home.'

"Poor Freiligrath was greatly overcome, and I can assure you that we were all quite affected when we heard of it. It has made our friends so happy. He says he shall serve the merchants now with *heart*-service. What a glorious world this would be if every one did all the kindness that was in his power!"

"*Dec.* 13, 1845.—Dear mother is now an accepted member of this meeting. Two of the most respectable Friends, in a worldly point of view, called on her this week to announce to her the fact. She was much pleased by it. The one thing that is wanted to complete her full comfort is more free intercourse with Friends, who are afraid of us. The story of 'Johnny Darbyshire, a Country Quaker,' which was published lately in the 'Edinburgh Tales,' has scandalised them greatly. William has been written to about it, and as they fancy we are sarcastic and inclined to ridicule the Society generally, they avoid us.

"I cannot tell thee how much interest we all feel in the certainty of the repeal of the Corn-Laws. We have tickets promised for the monster meeting at Covent Garden Theatre on Wednesday, when all the great heroes of the League will meet. It is a noble battle that they have fought. And now, thank Heaven! they are just on the eve of their great, glorious, and bloodless victory."

My mother was at this period residing with us, and I am struck with affectionate admiration at the remembrance of her great tact and forbearance under circumstances not readily assimilating with her convictions, and of her keen observation and good sense, which would have preserved us from sundry pitfalls, had we been willing to profit by them. She chiefly employed herself

reading or knitting in her own room, and merely saw
our intimate friends, who were very favourably impressed
by her peaceful exterior and unsectarian utterances. But
whilst she highly approved of our literary productions
and general sentiments, she took exception to our advocacy of the stage, from the persuasion that virtuous
persons, assuming fictitious characters, became ultimately
what they simulated. She consequently eschewed some
exemplary actresses—our familiar associates—terming
them "stage-girls, whom she pitied, but whose accom-
plishments she abhorred."

All Friends, however, were not so severe as my excellent mother in their condemnation of actresses, for
Charlotte Cushman met with just appreciation from the
son of the plain ministering-Friend, William Forster,
of Tottenham. This was the celebrated William Edward
Forster, who had not yet been disowned for marrying
out of the Society, or taken any prominent part in the
government of his country, being chiefly known as a
staunch Liberal and joint-proprietor with Mr. Fison in
the Greenholme worsted-mills, near Burley, in Wharfe-
dale. On one occasion, when Charlotte Cushman, with
her intimate friend, Eliza Cook, was staying at Mr.
Forster's Yorkshire residence, she received from him
an entire piece of alpaca of his manufacture, and of a
new dark colour called steel-blue. It was worn by both
ladies with no little pride. Miss Cook, who dressed in
a very masculine style, which was considered strange at
that time, with short hair parted on one side, and a
tight-fitting, lapelled bodice, showing a shirt-front and
ruffle, looked well in her dark, steel-blue alpaca; and
Miss Cushman, who possessed a strongly-built, heroic
figure, not the less so.

Many enlightened Friends saw nothing to take offence at in "Johnny Darbyshire." Samuel Gurney's daughter, Chenda Barclay, made inquiries, thirty years later, how she could once more procure "the delightful story," saying, "when she was a child, she used to make all the Quaker worthies roar with laughing by reading it to them." Her friend, Mrs. Alfred Tylor, who, as a girl at Stoke-Newington, felt for us deeply in the loss of Claude, long remembered the calls she made on us with her excellent father, Edward Harris, as well as, in happier days, their spending an evening with us. A French lady was present, who sang comic songs, which some of the Friends thought rather too gay for their principles, but which charmed and delighted her less Quakerish heart.

We had at that time become constant attenders at the Unitarian chapel in Hackney, the minister being the much-beloved Dr. Sadler, who later edited the Life of Crabb Robinson. There was also a Unitarian chapel at Stoke-Newington, where formerly the husband of Mrs. Barbauld had preached. My husband and I went on one occasion to this chapel to hear a remarkable man, Joseph Barker. He came from Yorkshire, and preached powerfully in racy dialect. So great was his reputation, that all the Unitarian ministers of London and the neighbourhood were assembled to hear him. His sermon depicted the Saviour, not as the mighty, omnipresent Son of God, but the Son of Man, the friend and fellow-sufferer of the human race, the great Teacher, the lover of each individual man, woman, and child, and Who was, as he expressed it, "a loomp o' luv." Barker, who had been a Methodist, never remained steadfast in his opinions. He next wandered on from a humanitarian belief into infidelity.

In 1846 my husband, at first merely a contributor, became one of the editors and part-proprietor of a new cheap weekly periodical, *The People's Journal*, which we hoped to make a good work, that would help to better the moral and intellectual condition of the working-classes. In the course of the year I write to my sister :—

"What canst thou mean by thinking that *The People's Journal* is not Christian in spirit? Of all things has it been our aim from the first, and will be to the end, to make it the organ of the *truest Christianity*. The bearing of all its contents is love to God and man. There is no attempt to set the poor against the rich, but, on the contrary, to induce them to be prudent, sober, careful, and independent; above all, to be satisfied to be workers, to regard labour as a privilege rather than a penalty, which is quite our view of the case.

"It does not, to be sure, cry up Church and State. It does not say that the present social institutions are perfect. But it endeavours to have all reforms made in the spirit of Christianity and for the purposes of Christianity. No living beings, dearest sister, can estimate Divine Revelation higher than we do. It is the greatest boon to man under all circumstances, be his station in life what it may. Nevertheless, it is in the spirit of Christianity to raise man in the scale of being, to enlighten and enlarge his understanding, to ennoble and purify his heart. It is his greatest ornament in prosperity, his best consolation in adversity. It is the poor man's safeguard and friend. No one, however poor in this world's goods, can be abject who has the light and comfort of the Gospel within his soul. This, dearest sister, if it be sound

and true, is the foundation on which this little journal
is built; and please God, with His benediction, it
shall be made an instrument of good and of blessing
in a thousand ways."

"*Oct.* 12, 1846.—We are more than ordinarily occupied with many things, among others the *Journal*, in
which we are striving to make some very important
changes, but which require an amount of labour and
painstaking for which I was quite unprepared. However, we hope that we shall be well repaid for all our
endeavours, and then we shall never begrudge them, or
remember them other than with satisfaction. I trust you
have all liked my memoir of that good man Garrison. I
did not say all I felt, because I feared many readers would
think me extravagant. To my mind there is no impro-
priety in comparing to Christ men who have striven to
follow His example. All do not see it so, and as we
write for the many, I have been contented to mention
facts and leave them to speak for themselves. Did thy
dear children attend any of the meetings of the New
Anti-Slavery League, which have been held latterly in
Liverpool, in which Garrison, H. C. Wright, and Frederick
Douglass have taken part? I hope they have, and that
their hearts are concerned in the cause. I have admired
dearest mother's zeal in this great question of humanity.
She has seen and talked with these good men here; and
she has knit such a quantity of nice things for the Anti-
Slavery Bazaar in Boston as is really quite amazing in
one at her time of life."

"*Dec.* 18, 1846.—This comes to tell you that William
will sleep at your house on the night of January 5.

He is to attend a soirée of the Mechanics' Institute on the 6th, and from there goes to Leeds, where he takes the chair at a soirée of the Co-operative League, of which he is a sort of father. We are very, very busy, as on the first of January comes out our *own Howitt's Journal.* We have discovered that the manager of the *People's Journal* has kept no books, and has mismanaged the whole thing dreadfully. I hope we shall get out of the business free of loss. William has attended many public meetings in London latterly, and speaks splendidly. It is the very time for us to establish our paper. Do not be anxious about us; we are all in high spirits; and it is perfectly cheering to see how warm and enthusiastic people are about our journal.

"We have had Tennyson with us a good deal lately. We quite love him."

My husband, considering the remedy for the wrongs of labour to be the adoption of the co-operative principle or the combination of work, skill, and capital by the operatives themselves, had written "Letters on Labour," which led to the foundation of the Co-operative League. Its object was to supply the industrious classes, both male and female, with gratuitous information on the great social questions of the day, unfettered by sectarian theology or party politics, with the motto, "Benefit to all, and injury to none." He was asked to preside at co-operative meetings, and to lecture on the subject in different towns of the kingdom. In complying, a series of disappointments, however, soon proved to him that it would require years of active, steady effort before any practical success could be attained; the millions being quite unprepared calmly and wisely to consider great principles.

The Leeds Co-operative League, called also "The Redemption Society," and which was exceptionally prosperous, held its first anniversay in January 1847. It was during William's absence to preside at this meeting in Leeds, where the interest displayed in co-operation by the entire population formed a cheering contrast to the general apathy, that I was subjected to a peculiar experience, whose awful reality has never passed away from my mind. I had retired to rest in good health and spirits, when suddenly a strange, alarming sense of perplexity, of impending, all-embracing darkness and evil, overwhelmed me. My terror made the heavy four-post bedstead shake under me. I was not ill or faint, nor did I think it requisite to call assistance. I knew the power which controlled me was either mental or spiritual. Surely I must have cried to God for help, as slowly the horror of great darkness passed away, and all was tranquil within me. It was, I am willing to believe, a token permitted by Divine love and wisdom to warn and prepare me for the discipline required to loosen my trust in the creature, and to place it wholly in the Creator. It preceded a time of calamity. We had speedily severe monetary losses and mortifications, and gained new and sad revelations of human nature.

Assisted by Samuel Smiles, a most able defender of the rights of industry and the benefits of self-culture, and other gifted and popular writers, we sought in the pages of *Howitt's Journal*, in an attractive form, to urge the labouring classes, by means of temperance, self-education, and moral conduct, to be their own benefactors. Unfortunately for ourselves, the magazine proved, like its predecessor, a pecuniary failure; and Ebenezer Elliott remarked to us in a shrewd, pithy letter :—" Men engaged in a death-struggle for bread will pay for amusement when they will not for instruction. They woo laughter to unscare them, that they may forget their perils, their wrongs, and their oppressors, and play at undespair. If you were able and willing to fill the journal with fun, it would pay."

In August 1847, in a letter to my sister, I remark :—

"Thou wilt be glad to hear that we have drawn up our resignation of membership, signed it, and when thou readest this, it will be noised abroad that we are no longer Friends. Strange as it may seem to thee, I have an old love of the Society. I know that the majority of Friends are narrow-minded, living as much in the crippling spirit of sectarianism as any denomination whatever; and I know that they and I never could assimilate; yet I do love them all, with an ingrained sentiment, which makes me feel as if somehow they were kindred to me. It is strange, perhaps, but there is not one so-called religious body that I could conscientiously connect myself with. There is, to my feelings, a want of real spirituality, a want of a real, child-like, loving trust in them all. I am not quite sure whether I should not find in the writings of Swedenborg what best accorded with my views and feelings. Anna Mary has been reading a good deal on these subjects lately, and from what she and others tell me, there is more truth in Swedenborgianism than one commonly finds out of the New Testament."

In the first days of January 1848 I communicate to Anna the sorrowful intelligence of the death of our beloved sister in America; and in the following May, that our dear mother had peacefully breathed her last. She was interred in the Friends' burial-ground, Stoke-Newington, at the side of Claude.

CHAPTER II.

IN ST. JOHN'S WOOD.

1848-1852.

AT Michaelmas 1848 we left Lower Clapton and settled near Regent's Park. To this removal allusion is made in the following letters :—

To MISS MARY GILLIES.

"The last note in the old home I write to you. I am just on the point of leaving it, but I do so without regret. I expect A. M. has written to you about the new home, where she now is. In a note she wrote yesterday she says the house improves on acquaintance. It is 28 Upper Avenue Road ; quiet and pretty, we think, and with a garden. I am frightened at the expense of this moving. It lengthens itself out, as the Germans say ; and I can see no end to it. However, I was told last night by Mr. Henry Bateman, that I was likely to be employed to write by the Tract Society, which pays well ; that has pleased me, although how I am to be *orthodox* enough I cannot tell. I am to send in a *sample*. Can you help me to a good idea? I must be a little religious, and I mean to have a death in it ; as the readers of tracts, I have been told, always ask for ' a pretty tract with a death-bed in it.'

"Do you know a very delightful American book, called ' A New Home ; or, Who will Follow?' The lady who wrote it, Mrs. Kirkland, is in London. She called on us yesterday, and is a bright, clever, kind-looking woman, who has greatly taken my fancy. She will come to us at the new home on Sunday next. Can you drop in to tea? Do, dear creature, and as many of you as can."

"*Upper Avenue Road.*—My dearest sister, I have been very busy. Besides that, I am so deadened and stupefied often, that I can hardly rouse myself to get out of the regular jog-trot routine of the day. I sit down after breakfast and work, work, work; then when the usual stint is done, I only want to be quiet and sleep. Tell me about your new house, and let me know how you arrange your furniture, for I have a sort of upholsterer's genius in me, and I take great interest in furnishing. We like our new house very much, though we find it is much colder than the old one. It is much slighter built, and what is called a single house, so that the rooms have many outer walls, which makes a great differ-ence. The greatest want to me is the not having a little working-room to myself. I am obliged to do my writing in the dining-room, and thus I am exposed to constant interruption. But even this has its bright side, because I can bear interruptions better than either William or Anna Mary. It would drive them mad; the poor mother of a family learns to be patient; that is one comfort.

"Times are so bad that publishers will not speculate on books; and when I have finished the work I am now engaged on, I have nothing else certain to go on with. Heaven help us all! Yet what is our case to that of thousands besides? I dislike going outside the door, because I am met by such pale, appealing countenances of begging women and children ; whether it is that I look kind and sympathetic, or that the poor feel an affinity to the poor, I know not, but they follow me as I go along like dogs, and I cannot get rid of them. I see other people pass them by, and they take no notice ; but they fairly fasten on me like leeches. What is to be the end of all this poverty and distress God only knows ! "

"*Jan.* 1, 1849.—Accept, my dearest sister, my best and kindest wishes for your happiness through the coming year. May God abundantly bless you, and may it please His infinite mercy to spare you suffering and sorrow.

" I should like my dear niece, Mary, to be here when the hawthorns are in bloom in Regent's Park, because they are so inconceivably beautiful. She could, even at the worst, walk every day into the park, sit on the benches under these trees ; then walk on to the Botanic Gardens or the Zoological Gardens, and really enjoy herself.

" We have just become acquainted with a most interesting young man, Edward La Trobe Bateman. He is a decorative designer and illuminator. He brings us the most exquisite things to see ; work out of missals, and out of fine old illuminated books in the British Museum and in grand old libraries. He has taken a house not far from us. He and a friend of his, a young man of similar tastes, are going to fit it up with furniture of their own designing and making. They have loads of old china, the most gorgeous thou canst imagine. We are to be consulted about the fitting-up of this place ; and we promise ourselves, in a small way, a great deal of pleasure.

"I want to send you, as soon as I get a copy, 'Our Cousins in Ohio,' which will interest you, because it describes dearest Emma and her children; and is, I think, such a beautiful picture of her in the midst of her home."

I had in 1846 completed a little book, "The Children's Year;" being the true history of my two younger children for the space of twelve months. It was very simple and true to Nature; and I wished all children to read it, except those described therein, as I considered it would give them a notion that all they did or said was of importance. My sister Emma was so pleased with the idea, that she sent me a similar journal, a faithful narrative of her children's life for a year. At her request all the names of people and places were changed in " Our Cousins in Ohio."

" *Midsummer*, 1849.—I have had my pen in my hand many times, thinking, 'Now I will write to dear Anna,' but something or other has always prevented me. I have been busy in various ways; for thou must bear in mind that now I have not only to do what I can, but that I must also sew for the family.

"I have just finished a story, in one volume, for the opening novel of what I suppose is to be called, 'Bradshaw's Railway Library'—a set of shilling books, to be sold at all the railway stations in the kingdom, for railway travellers. The publishers did me the compliment to ask me to write the opening volume. I have chosen the title, 'Mr. Elworthy and his Heirs,' * and

* This same tale, called "The Heir of Wast Wayland," was brought out by Messrs. Simms & M'Intyre, 1851.

used the incident of that young woman of Uttoxeter—
I forget her name—who married John Fox, many years
her senior; and then, after his speedily occurring death,
all his relations and the heirs-at-law trying to get the
property from her and her unborn child. Of course,
I have laid it in another scene, and altered the characters; but the main facts are the same. I have taken
as the locality one of those lovely Yorkshire dales, of
which I retain so pleasant a memory. After my story
was constructed, I spoke with Birket Foster's father
and his aunt Sarah about the Yorkshire scenery, and
they told me I was not far wrong.

"Now I am going to see if I can write some tracts,
but I do not think I shall succeed; still, as a kind friend
will introduce them to the Tract Society, it is worth
while to see what I can do.

"We were yesterday at a very pleasant soirée; an
entertainment given to all the men, women, and boys
in the employ of John Cassell, the proprietor of the
Standard of Freedom newspaper, to which William
contributes. It was the anniversary of the establishment
of the paper; and this day, therefore, was celebrated
by a great temperance entertainment in his vast warerooms in Fenchurch Street, for John Cassell is likewise
a dealer in coffee and tea; and all the people thus
employed were there also.

"There are about fifty boys in the coffee business and
the newspaper and printing office. I had the agreeable
task of making tea for these little fellows. All were
dressed so neatly, their faces were so clean, and they
looked so happy, it was perfectly delightful. After tea
a very nice band of musicians played, and all who liked
danced in one of the great warerooms. Then came

a course of interesting chemical experiments, ending
with the administering of laughing-gas to several of the
young men and boys, which occasioned a great deal
of merriment.   I observed that its effects were very
similar to a short mesmeric trance; in many cases the
subjects being affected by music in the same beautiful
manner.

"There was then a short lecture on Scottish song, in
which several lovely pieces were sung.   Next came a
series of beautiful dissolving views, with which everybody was delighted.   The shouts of the young people
were charming.   While this was going on in a great
room, decorated with green branches of oak, birch, laurel,
and such-like, and with flowers, an abundant supper
was preparing in another: such piled-up dishes of sand-
wiches and of cake; such heaped-up dishes of splendid
strawberries, and jugs of excellent milk, with fruits and
lemonade.   The people ate, drank, talked, and laughed,
and were as well-behaved as the politest party in
London.

"A gentleman sang the well-known song, 'We'll
speak of man as we find him;' after which William
proposed the health of Mr. Cassell.   He spoke about
the beauty and excellence of such entertainments as the
present; in which all were happy, all were improved, all
were refreshed in body and mind, yet not one drop of
intoxicating liquor had been drunk.   He then spoke of
the wonderful merchants and tradesmen of London, who
had begun life poorer than the men who surrounded
him, and had, as in the case of Mr. Cassell himself,
risen by their own industry to be as rich and powerful
as princes; not forgetting, however, that the true use of
money was the diffusion of happiness and the means of

moral improvement in those around us—such was the use made of it by our entertainer.

"It was then midnight, and so ended the pleasant festival. I hope this time next year we may all meet there again ; for we too, like the poor people, are servants, in the best sense of the word, to John Cassell. Long life and prosperity to him, says my heart in deep sincerity."

With regard to the attempt at tract-writing, the sample sent, and entitled "Woodnook Wells," was returned by Mr. Henry Bateman as quite ineligible. It was then submitted to John Cassell, who, greatly admiring it, had it immediately appear in the pages of his periodical, *The Working-Men's Friend*.

In the July of 1849 we went with our children for some weeks into the Peak of Derbyshire, among the scenes which my husband and I had visited together after our marriage, twenty-eight years earlier. We all spent a real holiday amongst the grey hills and green valleys. It remains in the memory as a season of bright sunshine, soon followed by a heavy, passing cloud.

On Friday, November 9, I was surprised by receiving a call from a respectable woman, who, introducing herself as Mrs. Copeland, of 11 Upper Stamford Street, Blackfriars, demanded the rent due to her from September. How still greater my consternation when she, with equal amazement at my ignorance, exclaimed, "A gentleman named Youl had taken the rooms for poor Mrs. Howitt, who was in such destitution that she was compelled to make private application for relief to the nobility;" adding, "I was very sorry for you, ma'am, I am sure, but when letters evidently containing money, and sealed with coronets, kept coming, and I never got my rent, I made so bold as to learn your address at the British Museum, and was surprised to find you living in so good a house."

A Mr. Edward Youl we certainly well knew, through his becoming a very clever contributor to *Howitt's Journal* in the spring of 1847. He was then about thirty, with abundant black hair, and being, he said, very short-sighted, wore spectacles. He mentioned that he was a Cambridge graduate and a classical tutor, but having just finished the education of his late pupil, he resolved to seek no other engagement, but devote himself to literature. Later, he told us in confidence that he was struggling with poverty for conscience' sake. He was the only child of a pawnbroker, who had amassed a large fortune, and died intestate; but he was determined to die of starvation rather than claim such ill-gotten wealth; and had married a lady in straitened circumstances connected with the Society of Friends. We believed the romantic story, which was in keeping with the spirit of his high-toned writings. We permitted him to come to our house, introduced him to several of our friends, and procured him, amongst other literary employment, a permanent engagement with John Cassell, who gave him a salary of £200 per annum for what amounted to about three days' work a week on the *Standard of Freedom*. In this situation he displayed remarkable efficiency; but when he had been about a year with Mr. Cassell, he became very lazy, and consequently, after repeated warnings, was discharged in the summer of 1849.

We did not wish to abandon Mr. Youl, and as his wife (who had never attracted us) manifested an insatiable desire to go on the stage, our friend, Charles Kean, very obligingly obtained her an engagement with a manager at Hull; and Mr. Linwood, a Unitarian minister, who had become a Congregationalist, and the purchaser of the *Eclectic Review*, consented to meet Youl at our house on Sunday, November 11, to secure him as a regular contributor.

On the previous Friday, however, Mrs. Copeland made me the above-mentioned extraordinary disclosure, and on the next day my husband, after obtaining a warrant for Youl's apprehension, and a detective to put on his track, proceeding along Stamford Street, recognised him approaching at a great distance. Youl, although without spectacles, suddenly dived down a by-lane and entirely disappeared. He must instantly have gone to Hull, as his wife wrote to me on the morrow, Sunday: "My husband will make every explanation if you will forgive him. Dear Mrs. Howitt, pray think of our prospects; mine will be sacrificed with his, and they are just opening so bright."

The ensuing day Youl, from York, wrote a begging-letter in my name to Macaulay, and received £10 by return of post. The detective traced him to Leeds, where he seemed to sink into the ground; for, impatient of the stigma lying upon me in many unknown quarters, I insisted, in spite of the entreaties of our legal adviser, on sending a statement of the fraud to the daily papers. We had immediately instituted an extensive inquiry, and found that, amongst other persons of rank and influence, he had forged my name to Lords John Russell, Lansdowne, Denman, Mahon, and Brougham. The latter, writing in explanation from Cannes, stated that on receiving an application from me speaking of great pecuniary difficulties, and requiring immediate assistance, he had instantly sent it to Lord John Russell, with a strong recommendation to settle a pension on me, applied on my behalf to Miss Burdett - Coutts, and himself forwarded £20. He would, if needful, return from Cannes to give evidence. Sir Robert Peel had generously remitted £50. The forged letters returned to me were written in a crawling, exaggerated strain. In acknowledging a donation from the Bishop of Oxford (Wilberforce), I was made to say: "I went down on my knees and thanked God, Who had moved his lordship's heart to such noble kindness to me."

In December, Mr. Justice Talfourd sent us word that an individual who had in the previous summer extracted £20 from him under the assumed name of Thomas Cooper, author of "The Purgatory of Suicides," had written to him from Liverpool, and was certainly our man. The same evening our eldest son and the detective went to Liverpool, put themselves into communication with the police, the post-office, and the owners of the American packets ; but Youl eluded their vigilance.

In the following April 1850 Mrs. Youl called, in Liverpool, on the wife of the celebrated manufacturing chemist, Dr. Muspratt, and sister to Charlotte Cushman, saying, "her husband was the person who had made use of my name to obtain money. It was only lately she had learnt what he had done." "I never saw a poor creature in such affliction," wrote Mrs. Muspratt ; "she has pawned everything, even her wedding-ring. I gave her the money to go to London, where she hoped she might find some assistance."

Some years afterwards John Cassell encountered Youl sitting opposite him in a New York eating-house.

Although differently disguised, he recognised the voice
and features, and accosted him by name. Youl, how-
ever, most coolly denied ever having been in England.
In March 1870 one Robert Spring, *alias* Sprague, *alias*
Redfern Hawley, and a host of other *aliases*, was tried
and convicted in the Court of Quarter-Sessions in
Philadelphia for false pretences. Experts believed this
man and Youl to be identical. He had been, in America,
"The distracted father of a large family;" "A poor
widow with a few autographs of the distinguished dead;"
"The orphan daughter of Stonewall Jackson;" "Maggie
Ramsay under religious convictions;" "The kind Dr.
Hawley," &c. We were assured by a gentleman in the
Department of the Interior, that "the various dodges
he was discovered to have originated and successfully
played; the versatility of character he had assumed; the
systematic mode of keeping his accounts (for his ledger
had been captured); the very extraordinary manner in
which he had shaped his frauds to avoid the penalties of
the law if caught; and the success with which he had for
years foiled all efforts to trace him out, would, if given in
a narrative form to the public, present them with the
picture of the ' Prince of Swindlers.' "

I had earlier often said, and honestly thought, that it
was a fine thing to combat with one's self and stand
victor; and when residing in St. John's Wood, rising
above many anxieties and disappointments, I determined
to be strong and joyful. Life, under the most adverse
circumstances, was full of riches, which I would neither
disregard nor squander. Thus treasuring up all the
simple elements of beauty around me, I still remember
the charm of a suburban spring morning. Up and down
the Avenue Road the lilacs and tacamahacs were coming

into leaf, the almond-trees were full of blossom, and the
sun shone amid masses of soft silvery cloud. Then,
again, there was rural Belsize Lane, delightful at all
seasons, with its lofty elms and luxuriant hedgerows of

BELSIZE LANE, ST. JOHN'S WOOD.

rose-bushes, elders, and hawthorn. How green, too,
were the sloping fields leading from the St. John's Wood
end of Belsize Lane to Hampstead!

My eldest daughter, who desired to devote herself to
art, had never forgotten the profit and delight which she
had derived from our visits to the German capitals and

their works of art. Our visit to Munich and the studio of Kaulbach had especially impressed her mind and imagination. We had, after passing through the field of long waving grass, by which flowed the rapid Isar, entered the large, half-neglected-looking building used by the great artist as his *atelier*. There we had seen not only the cartoon of his famous "Destruction of Jerusalem," but the inimitable illustrations to "Reineke Fuchs." On an inner door were painted a boy and girl, as if done in the very exuberance of fancy, and of such loveliness, that they would enrich the walls of any house whatever. Kaulbach, then scarcely middle-aged, had received us with great courtesy in the midst of his work. When we asked him if he conversed in English, he replied, "I speak no language but German, and *that*," pointing to his painting! Indeed, what more eloquent and universal tongue need be spoken?

Anna Mary felt that Munich and Kaulbach would afford her the most consonant instruction, and in May 1850 went thither, accompanied by a fellow-votary, Miss Jane Benham. They were most generously received as pupils by the famous painter, who assigned to their use one of the rooms in his picturesque studio by the Isar.

A few days after their departure for Munich, Henry Chorley—then leading a somewhat luxurious, literary, bachelor life at the West End—came to tell me he had accepted from Messrs. Bradbury & Evans the editorship of *The Ladies' Companion;* and he wanted Annie, as we all now called my daughter, to go to a great miracle-play of the Passion, performed that year by the devout peasants of Ober-Ammergau, and who would, at its termination, thank God on their knees that He had once more permitted them to perform the sacred drama in His honour. There would be *Stellwagen* to the place from Munich; and he begged her to write for him a description of the whole thing, from the setting-out in the morning to the end of the play. She willingly complied, and thus first made known this remarkably striking, pathetic, but now trite subject to the English public. Other descriptive letters from her pen appeared in *Household Words* and the *Athenæum*. They were much admired, and Henry Chorley encouraged her to collect and publish these scattered "bits," which, under the title of "An Art Student in Munich," formed a fresh and charming book, because so genuine.

On February 20, 1850, I received the following from Charles Dickens, written from Devonshire Terrace :—

"I address this note to Mr. Howitt no less than to you. You will easily divine its purpose, I dare say ; or at all events you would, if you knew what companions of mine you have ever been.

"You may have seen the first dim announcements of the new cheap, literary weekly journal I am about to start. Frankly, I want to say to you, that if you would ever write for it, you would delight me, and I should consider myself very fortunate indeed in enlisting your assistance.

"I propose to print no names of contributors, either in your own case or any other, and to give established writers the power of reclaiming their papers after a certain time. I hope any connection with the enterprise would be satisfactory and agreeable to you in all respects, as I should most earnestly endeavour to make it. If I wrote a book, I could say no more than I mean to suggest to you in these few lines. All that I leave unsaid, I leave to your generous understanding."

Thus, from the commencement of the *Household Words*, we became, most willingly, contributors to its pages.

To my Daughter at Munich.

"*June* 1, 1850.—I have sent off my first little note to you hardly four hours since, and now I begin to write again. Charlton has asked me what day in the week I like best, and I tell him, henceforth the day on which I receive a letter from you. I must not omit to mention that one of Charlton's hens has laid an egg. You can imagine his felicity. He has cackled more than ten hens, and could not tranquillise himself until the egg had been boiled for his father. The other event of the morning is, that Alfred has been told that 'The Miner's Daughter' in *Household Words* was either by Currer Bell or Mrs. Gaskell. He was much amused, knowing it to be his father's.

"Walter Cooper and Gerald Massey, the two leading co-operative tailors, come here on Sunday, and go a stroll on Hampstead Heath with your father. Gerald Massey is a young poet, a really eloquent writer, very good-looking, and, I hear, quite a gentleman."

"*Sunday, Aug.* 18, 1850.—Do you remember that long lovely field by the side of Caen Wood, which is reached from the Lower Heath at Hampstead and through a brickfield? I have an uncommon affection for it. There is a mound in it like an ancient barrow, and on which grows a group of picturesque old fir-trees. The view thence is most lovely. On the left lie the wooded heights of Hampstead, with an opening to the distant heath, over which the sun sets splendidly. In front is all the mass of wood of Lord Mansfield's park, and on the right the village of Highgate, with its church on the hill, its scattered woods and villas; and between us and them the green slope of the field and the reservoirs below. Yet, to show you how ridiculously things fall out in this world, Miss Meteyard and your father went with me last evening to my favourite mound. There, hanging from one of the old branches of a scathed fir-tree, was a man's shirt. Some beggar must have stripped himself of his under-garment, and, with a sense of the horrible and comic combined, suspended it by the neck. It looked, at a distance, like some shocking suicide. We sat down on the mound, your father and Miss Meteyard very wittily parodying Shakespeare and Hood's 'Song of the Shirt.' A lady and gentleman with a blue-coat boy came up. We agreed to listen to what they said. The shirt aloft waved its ragged arms, it shook its ragged tail at them. They neither said a word nor made a sign. Was the shirt a mere spectral imagination of ours? No, there it surely was. Yet they would not or could not see it. We left them seated on the hill, with the old shirt aloft seeming to make fun of them.

"Your father has entirely finished his 'Madam Dorrington of the Dene.'"

"*Filey, Yorkshire, Sept.* 2, 1850.—Here we are," I write to my sister, "at a small fishing-village, which is attempting to convert itself into a bathing-place. The coast is beautiful; very wild by places; and the sands to a great extent as smooth as a marble floor. It is a

favourite resort of people who prefer quietness and seclusion. Strange to say, we prefer Scarborough, and are
going to remove there in two or three days.

"When first we came the weather was stormy. The
wind was high, and the surging, roaring sea gave a
character almost of savageness to the coast scenery. This
we greatly enjoyed. Now the weather is bright and
genial as midsummer, and the sea as calm and smooth
as a mirror. We bathe and ramble about the shore, and
lie with our books on the tops of the breezy headlands,
looking out over miles and miles of sea; with the gulls
and sea-birds wheeling and screaming about us; listening to the never-ceasing murmur of those restless waters,
from whose depths seem at all times to come forth such
wonderful and mysterious voices. I can listen to them
for hours.

"We have Charlton and Meggie with us. His holidays at the London University School fall at this time.
Miss Eliza Meteyard ('Silverpen'), too, is with us. She
is now a sufficiently old friend of ours for us all to feel
perfectly at ease one with another. She has her work as
well as we. Poor dear soul! she is sitting by me at this
moment with her lips compressed, a look of abstraction
in her clever but singular face, and her hair pushed back
from her forehead, while she is busy over a story about a
Bronze Inkstand, which she hopes to make a very fine
one. A good creature is she! She has just published
a most interesting juvenile book, called 'The Doctor's
Little Daughter.' It is her own early life. Out of the
money thus obtained, she has provided for and sent out
a young brother to Australia; while for another she is
striving in another way. Indeed, she is both father and
mother to her family; yet she is only seven-and-twenty,

and a fragile and delicate woman, who in ordinary circumstances would require brothers and friends to help her.
How many instances one sees almost daily of the marvellous energy and high principle and self-sacrifice of
woman! I am always thankful to see it, for it is in
this way that women will emancipate themselves."

To MY DAUGHTER.

"*Scarborough, Sept.* 17, 1850.—We have now Mrs.
Smiles and Miss Wilkinson with us. You may remember, my dear Annie, your father speaking of the latter,
when he came from Leeds. She is very bright, agreeable, full of spirit. The children perfectly adore her.
Friday.—The Smileses have gone. Dr. Smiles came on
Wednesday. We have greatly enjoyed their visit. He,
full of mirth and playfulness, walked about with the
children, helped them to make mounds and canals in
the sands, and found as much fun as they did in watching the sea come up, assault these constructions, and
lay them waste. He would ask little boys and girls,
much to their astonishment, whether they were married;
to the amusement of Charlton and Meggie, who enjoyed
the blank looks, especially of one little fellow of about ten,
who said simply, 'No, he was not married, but his father
and mother were.' He also greatly diverted our children
by answering a group of juveniles, who asked him what
o'clock it was, that 'he did not carry a clock about with
him. He could only tell them what o'watch it was,
which would perhaps do till they got home.'

"We are reading a wonderful book, 'Alton Locke, Poet
and Tailor: an Autobiography'—an extraordinary production, very, very fair, and exceedingly clever. It will
make a great stir. It is written by Mr. Kingsley, a

clergyman of the Church of England, brother-in-law to Mr. Froude."

"*Nov.* 1850.—We have been very busy this week in getting ready articles for Christmas. Your father is writing a beautiful story for the Christmas number of *Household Words.* I am also writing a fresh ballad for the same journal. It is a sort of fellow to 'Richard Burnell,' which earlier appeared. I have got desperately absorbed in it. It is curious to me to see how very much these ballads are a reflection of my own being and my especial interests. The great ballad-writing time with me was when you were a girl, and those earlier productions are very much about children, and beautiful spiritual-minded young maidens. Then for many years I wrote no ballads at all. I fancied that I never should write any more. But a new inspiration has come over me. The joys and sorrows of one poor friend have found utterance in my 'Richard Burnell,' and those of another will come forth in my dear 'Thomas Harlowe.' I am also asked to write a ballad for the Christmas number of the *Illustrated News,* and to give Henry Chorley one for *The Ladies' Companion.*

"I work always in your painting-room, in which I have made no alterations. I venerate the old things and the old memories. But I am getting over my intense longing for you. I can take up beautiful thoughts of you and lay them down again at will, and not be ridden, as it were, by them, driven by them, haunted by them till they become like a nightmare. Oh! that was dreadful. If I were a painter, I should paint a Ceres mourning for the lost Proserpine. I understand that mother's heart so well, that I should not fail in making a countenance

befitting.   I can see the wonderful head of the maternal
Ceres, with her heart, not her eyes, full of tears, revealing
inexpressible love, and yet desolation.   Don't imagine
that I am such an one now.   I am very happy ; nor would
I wish my Proserpine to be here."

" *Nov.* 30, 1850.—I shall copy your account of the
consecration of the Basilica for the *Athenæum*, but I am
afraid it is too gloriously papistical for the present time
in England.   You can have no idea what a tide of popular feeling has set in against everything Catholic.   ' No
Popery' is written over all the walls of London.   Public
meetings are held everywhere, and petitions and protests
are got up by all parties against Papacy.   There never
was so anti-Catholic a nation as this.   However, your
account is very beautiful and picturesque, and they may
give it as news, though your father thinks they will probably remove some of its glory."

" *Dec.* 9, 1850.—I asked your father what there was
to tell you.   He said, 'Tell her that the King of Prussia
has ordered Freiligrath out of his dominions ; that the
Catholics at Hampstead have put up within these few
weeks a grand, new, and rather beautiful Madonna and
Child, as large as life, over their chapel-door ; and that
the people have pelted it with mud and stones ; and that
the other day, when he passed, two men stood and cen-
sured the image, saying, ' it was idolatry in a plain
form,' whereupon your father thought that he had
seen idolatry in a much plainer form.   Tell her that
there is so little news, that the *Times* has nothing
to write about but Papal Aggression ; but that, spite
of the *Times* and all the saints, Cardinal Wiseman

has been installed, and that we have now an English Cardinal in London.'"

"*Dec.* 19, 1850.—You ask what people think about the state of French politics ; they are amazed, confounded, indignant. The *Times* writes gloriously about it, and for that reason is not permitted to enter France. I expect Napoleon will be elected to-morrow, and that despotism will raise its head and lord it over the nations for a time. But the day of reckoning, when it does come, will only be all the more terrible. The end of the tragedy is not yet ; we are only in the first act.

"Poor dear Miss Meteyard is in some trouble just now because people are beginning to discover *popery* in her little book. Some influential person warned her publishers, Hall & Virtue, against her as a Jesuit in disguise ; and she so rationalistic ! Her publishers are therefore hanging back about accepting her collected tales, and they had been so earnest about them just before."

"*Christmas Day*, 1850.—Last night Eliza Fox wrote proposing for them and Mrs. Gaskell to come to us this evening. Meggie suggests that we should not be grand and intellectual—but ghost-stories and capital tales should be told, and that we should even play at blindman's buff. We may be merry and tell tales, but I doubt the playing at blindman's buff."

"*Thursday.*—The first thing I do this morning is to tell you that last evening went off very well. We had only the Foxes, Mrs. Gaskell, the Garth Wilkinsons, Mr. Doherty, Miss Meteyard, and Mr. La Trobe Bateman.

"On Christmas Eve, Miss Meteyard, having written to

Messrs. Hall & Virtue to know the name of 'the influential person' who had charged her so falsely, received from them, in reply, one from her saintly enemy. It was a most pious letter from the Honourable Mr. Finch, brother to the Earl of Aylesford. He expressed satisfaction in her assurance that she was no Catholic, but he still maintained the dangerous character of 'The Doctor's Little Daughter.' He had taken it, with the offensive passages marked, to a noted Church of England publishing firm. After this letter Messrs. Hall & Virtue said they must decline her tales. It is the loss of £250 to poor Miss Meteyard, while I suppose that Mr. Finch, surrounded by creature comforts, would go to rest on Christmas Eve feeling that he had done God service.

"Mrs. Gaskell is much pleased with your writings. She says you do not make the reader see the things with your eyes, but you present the scene itself to him. She hopes, on your return, you will collect and publish your letters in a volume—a sort of 'Art Life in Munich.' Her praise was quite gratuitous. She is going to remain in London and in Essex till February, the air of Manchester not agreeing with her.

"I must now tell you Mr. Doherty's ghost-story, if so it may be called. He was a very intimate friend of the late Lord Wallscourt, an excellent and enlightened nobleman, who had large estates in Ireland, and wished above all else to promote the best interests of his Irish dependents. Part of the year he lived in that country, devoting himself to his people; the rest of his time he spent with Mr. Doherty and other social reformers in Paris. He took it into his head that if Mr. Doherty would go and live on his Irish estates, he could bring about the most wonderful reformation amongst the population. He urged his going very much, offered him every inducement, entreated him by his grand philanthropic nature, by his friendship to himself. In vain. Mr. Doherty said, in short, that he was so importunate as to become to him a bore; that Lord Wallscourt teased him, just as a wife often teases her husband, by her well-meant zeal, till he will not, perhaps, do that which it would be well for him to do. On May 28, 1849, Lord Wallscourt died suddenly of cholera in Paris. Then a deep remorse and self-reproach fell upon Mr. Doherty's mind. For aught he knew to the contrary, his friend had died feeling anger towards him, feeling wounded, disappointed. One day, as he sat full of bitterness against himself, he saw, in broad daylight, Lord Wallscourt walking with two gentlemen. They seemed to be in deep discourse, when he appeared suddenly to say, 'There is my dear good friend Doherty. I must tell him how much I love him.' He gave him a look of the tenderest, most joyful affection, and was gone. The nobleman had appeared as if attired in full Court suit; and had he come in the flesh, he could not have restored more peace and assurance to Mr. Doherty's mind than was given by that *ideal* look."

"*Feb.* 10, 1851.—The catkins are out on the hazels, little buds are forming on the hawthorn-hedges, and the gorse is in blossom. We, Miss Meteyard and the children, have been a most beautiful walk to Hampstead Heath. While your father and Miss Meteyard talked politics and abused Harriet Martineau for her new *infidel* book, 'Human Nature,' or some such title, by herself and Mr. Atkinson, the children and I strolled on together and talked of the good and happy time,

when you would be at home again. We agree that you
will not be back till the *end* of May."

"*Feb.* 24, 1851.—Ah! yes, my own beloved, all you
say of the chapel-going is true enough. But somehow
I felt as if this non-observance was becoming perfect
neglect; for the want of form as naturally degenerates
into neglect, as observance can into mere form. We
say, 'We will walk out with the children into God's
Temple and worship there; and in the evening we will
read a beautiful chapter in the Gospels, or some other
noble, glorious book. Thus we will make the Sunday
holy and attractive.' But it is not so. Six times at
least out of ten some cause or other makes the walk
commonplace and secular. When we come back, either
somebody drops in, or else 'Pendennis' or 'David Copper-
field' or some other attractive book is read; Charlton
falls asleep, and so the day is done. Then, the influence
one's outward example has on the servants. To them
it appears as if worship so-called, which perhaps in
them is sincere, has no value with us. In this way our
good works—that is to say, the true worship within us—
is not seen of them, and so they cannot in us glorify our
Father who is in heaven. Again, I sometimes think
there are things which are approved of God, and which
bring His blessing, though we may be apt to undervalue
them. Of this kind, I am half-inclined to consider these
regular religious observances. They have their subtle
influences. They are among God's commands to us;
and although we do not altogether see the reasonable-
ness of them, we should try to reach the blessing through
obedience. It is in this spirit that I have taken these
sittings in Dr. Sadler's chapel at Hampstead.

"You can have no idea what an excitement Harriet Martineau's book is making. It is always out when we send to the London Library for it. I want to see it, for I cannot help fancying it less terrible than people affirm. Dr. Carpenter says that 'she does not declare that there is no God, but she does not *believe* there is one. If there is one, however, then she does not believe Him to be any mechanical genius, that He has nothing to do with the making of the world, and that she feels so very happy to be independent, and to have nobody to domineer over her!' Douglas Jerrold's last is on this subject; he says, 'There is no God, and Harriet Martineau is his Prophet.''

"*Feb.* 28, 1851.—Before I begin my day's work, I must, as usual, have a little bit of talk with you. Oh, what a lovely morning this is! I walked round the garden before breakfast with Charlton, and went with him into his poultry-yard. While we were there an egg was laid; then Charlton put it into another nest, to show me what one of the hens would do. She walked in, tucked the egg under her *chin*, carried it out a little way, set it down, and looked at it. Charlton says they carry them out in this manner sometimes into the middle of the yard. I wonder what queer thoughts are in their brains when they do so."

"*Friday.*—We have read Miss Martineau's book. It is, to my mind, the most awful book that was ever written by a woman. She and this wise Mr. Atkinson dethrone God, abuse Christ, and prefer Mahometanism to Christianity. It made me sick and ill to hear them talk of Jesus as a mere clever mesmerist. To me it is blasphemy. To show you how evil the book is, I must tell you that Alfred wanted the Inquisition for its authors, and I sympathised with him. It will make good people devilish in their indignation and anger, and it will set all the poor infidels crowing like cocks on a dunghill. And only think, in their large appendix, in which they support themselves by such authorities as Hobbes, Lord Bacon, Sir James Mackintosh, &c., I should see a long article with the innocent name of Mary Howitt to it! It is the account of the Preaching Epidemic in Sweden. Curious as it is, it proves nothing, and seems merely introduced to make me out an infidel. I think this has provoked your father more than anything else.

"Yes, dearest, Joanna Baillie is dead. I am glad you had that kiss from her, for she was a good woman."

Throughout the year 1851 my husband and I were working together at a history of Scandinavian literature. It was a perfect delight to me to translate old Norse ballads. They were to me most fascinating, rude and bloody as many of them are, and possessing a forcible simplicity such as we had earlier met with in the German ballads of Uhland. The Danish literature we found richer than the Swedish, both in quantity and variety. The pristine lore of Iceland and Norway was especially collected and translated into Danish. We were enchanted with the fable or *saga* literature, and found again almost all our ancient nursery tales: the little old woman whose petticoats were cut shorter, "Jack the Giant Killer," the pig that would not go over the brig, and the rest. We thus gained quite a respect for those familiar tales, which the wild, stout old Danes brought to Britain from the far North. Then the grand, quaint wisdom of the *Eddas*, reminding us of Ecclesiastes, such as the sayings—"It is hard leaning against another man's doorpost;" "I clothed the wooden figures in my garments, and they looked like heroes; whilst I, the unclothed hero, was of no account;" or, "Go often to the house of thy friend, for weeds soon choke up the unused path." Finally, how worthy of perusal the modern dramatic masterpieces of Oehlenschläger, and the charming historical novels of Ingemann, the Sir Walter Scott of Denmark! But while we found the Danish richer in graceful, poetic, original productions, the Swedish bore off the palm in history, epic poetry, and modern fiction. What, indeed, can be grander than Tegnér's "Frithiof's Saga" or Runeberg's "Hanna," and his other pathetic poems of austere Finland, and its brave and patient children?

In our domestic circle we were greatly interested in the new development of the English fine arts. The taste of the age, into the fourth decade of this century, had been for what appealed as pure, noble, and harmonious to the mind rather than to the eye or ear. The general public was wholly uneducated in art. By 1849, however, the improvement due to the exertions of the Prince Consort, the Society of Arts, and other powers began to be felt; a wonderful impulse to human ingenuity and taste being given in the preparation of exhibits for the World's Fair, to be held in London in 1851. In this important æsthetic movement Mr. Owen Jones was a prominent teacher. He was most ably seconded by his assistant, Edward La Trobe Bateman, our young friend, who was endowed with an exquisite feeling and skill in decorative art, extremely rare at that time. He maintained there was no excuse for ugliness,

as beauty properly understood was cheap. He was
an intimate associate of the P.R.B.'s, for so the pre-
Raphaelite brothers termed themselves.

This famous band of art-innovators had now arisen,
and were startling the world by the novelty and oddity
of their composition and colouring, combined with a marvellous fidelity in detail. Connoisseurs shook their heads,
and refused to believe they had power or originality,
and that they would, in the end, come out all right;
declaring if they had real genius they would walk in
the steps of their great contemporaries, not in those of
painters belonging to an early ignorant age. Besides,
if their avowed principle was correct, then authors
should write in the language of Chaucer.

When Millais, in 1851, exhibited at the Royal Academy his "Mariana in the Moated Grange," "The Dove
returned to the Ark," and a quaint picture of two
children from a poem by Coventry Patmore; and Holman Hunt some works equally strange and naïve in
treatment, the then recently-appointed President of the
Royal Academy, Sir Charles Eastlake, privately said it
was the last year he and the Hanging Committee would
admit this outrageous new school of painting to their
walls.

It was the day of small things to those now world-
famed, highly-appreciated artists, and I remember one
of the most distinguished asking us, as he had no
banker, to cash a cheque of £14, given him by a Manchester gentleman for a small oil-painting.

Earnest and severe in their principles of art, the
young reformers indulged in much jocundity when the
day's work was done. They were wont to meet at ten, cut
jokes, talk slang, smoke, read poetry, and discuss art till

three A.M. They spoke of *The Germ*, their magazine, which unfortunately met with a speedy end, as if pronounced with a "g" hard, making it sound like the "g" in girl, and found endless amusement from outsiders saying to them, "Why do you call germ thus? But of course you are right," and then adopting the wrong pronunciation.

In July 1850 an American poet and painter, named Buchanan Read, then on his way to study art at Düsseldorf, Munich, and Florence, spent an evening at our house in the company of some of our friends. He had earlier sent us his first volume of poems by the American publisher, Mr. Fields, and now brought us the second. But in spite of this kind attention, he seemed such a timid nonentity that I had continually to jog my memory to prevent his suffering from neglect. A few days later the very clever and intelligent young Irish poet, William Allingham, who had been present, told Holman Hunt and Dante Rossetti he had recently met a number of Americans at our house. Upon this Rossetti replied, "By the bye, some of those Americans write glorious things. I have come across some lyrics in the *Philadelphia Courier*, signed 'A Miner,' and written from Hazeldell, on the Schuylkill, as fine as any I know. I first met with one specimen, and was so delighted with it that I sent to Philadelphia for all the papers containing the poems from Hazeldell, cut them out and pasted them in a book with other gems of poetry."

Rossetti forthwith produced a big book of poetry, and began reading some of the lyrics, and as he expressed the deepest obligations to the unknown writer, Allingham volunteered to call on a little American, who had asked him to do so, and try to learn from him who

was the splendid poet of Hazeldell. Accordingly, Mr.
Allingham went to Mr. Buchanan Read, and told him
what had passed. As he proceeded, the stranger's face
became crimson and his entire frame agitated. "I am
the writer of these poems," he replied, with tears in his
eyes.

There was, of course, nothing to be done, after this
marvellous discovery, but instantly to carry off the prize
to Rossetti. They found him in his studio, quite absorbed, working from a model. He just looked up as
they entered, gave a sharp little nod, and went on
painting. Allingham, however, walked up to him and
said, "I have brought you the poet of Hazeldell bodily."
Rossetti dropped his brush, and with a face glowing
with excitement, cried, "You don't say so!" He quite
overwhelmed the bashful stranger with his joyous ac-
clamations, adding, "How delighted Woolner will be,
for he prizes your poems as I do!"

In the midst of the jubilation Holman Hunt entered.
Now, Read had a most intense desire to see Leigh Hunt,
and this being divulged to the two pre-Raphaelites, who
were busy, they deputed Allingham to carry their visitor
to Leigh Hunt, and see that he was treated with due
honour. Leigh Hunt, however, was out; so they returned to Rossetti and Holman Hunt, and spent a grand
evening together.

The next time Buchanan Read came to us, we had
perused his fresh, invigorating poems, and were delighted to see him again. And now the ice being
broken, we found him to be a very generous, grateful
young man, possessing much original power and fine
discrimination of art. He had been painting in Rossetti's studio, and in constant intercourse with his host,

William Rossetti, Holman Hunt, and Woolner. As the day for his departure to Düsseldorf approached, a great gathering of all the P.R.B.'s took place, to commemorate his last evening in their midst. They read aloud his poetry, made much of him, and told such capital stories, that some of them rolled on the floor with laughter. But although they remained together until four or five in the morning, they could not part with him. He prolonged his stay, and as he absented himself in their company from his lodgings at Mr. Chapman's, in the Strand, it was reported that the pre-Raphaelites had carried off Read in a chariot of fire.

At the close of 1870 we met him once more in Rome, where he was then residing with his gentle and wealthy wife, and dispensing hospitality with a most lavish hand. We were present at a grand entertainment which he gave in honour of General Sheridan, whose bard he might justly be called, from his very spirited and popular lay, "Sheridan's Ride," having heightened the hero's fame in America. The task upon his vital powers in his character of poet, painter, and most sociable host led to the constant use of strong stimulants, which ruined his health. It caused him, in 1872, to quit Rome for his native land, where he breathed his last the day after stepping ashore.

One brilliant Sunday morning, in the spring of 1851, my husband and I, walking down the fields from Hampstead, with all London lying before us, suddenly saw a wonderful something shining out in the distance like a huge diamond, the true "mountain of light." It marked the first Great Exhibition in Hyde Park, a new feature, not only in the fine view, but in the history of the world. We met a humble Londoner

evidently on his way to Hampstead Heath.   William
said to him, "Turn round and look at the Crystal
Palace shining out in the distance." He did so, and
exclaiming, "Oh! thank you, sir; how wonderful!"
stood gazing as long as we could see him.

Some reader has, without doubt, still fresh in his
recollection the gay, animated appearance of London
in this spring of 1851. The evidence of the approaching Exhibition was apparent on every side: houses and
shops cleaned and repainted, hotels for "All Nations"
and coffee-houses of the "Great Exhibition" opened
right and left; huge waggons, piled with bales, slowly
moving along to Hyde Park; and, standing in bewilder-
ment at the corners of streets and by omnibuses, were
foreigners, with big beards and moustachios, in queer
felt-hats and braided coats; whilst elegant French-
women, in long cloth cloaks with picturesque hoods,
and plain drab bonnets with rich interior trimmings (a
new style of dress, beautiful from its severity), might be
seen in Regent Street and Piccadilly, acting as a foil
to Oriental magnates in gold embroidery, flowing silk,
and gorgeous cashmere.

How crowded, that spring, was the private view of the
Portland Gallery by lords, ladies, artists, priests, and
distinguished foreigners!   J. R. Herbert, R.A., grave and
thin of countenance and spare of form, walked bareheaded
at the side of the portly, benign Cardinal Wiseman,
and with reverence pointed out various pictures to him.
Then came a low buzz and movement of excitement in
the throng, which contained the Archbishop of York
and the Bishop of London, when Cardinal Wiseman,
Dr. Doyle, Roman Catholic Bishop of Carlow, Father
Gavazzi, and Mazzini were seen grouped together

examining the same painting. "How very odd!" was the general remark; and my husband added, "The fine arts may truly be said to form neutral ground!"

"*April* 3, 1851.—I should like you, my dear Annie, to bring such things as you particularly covet to have, with you from Munich; of course, a statuette of Kaulbach and a crucifix. Talking of a crucifix reminds me of what that young Catholic lady, Miss McCarthy, a niece of Cardinal Wiseman's, told Miss Meteyard. Herbert, the painter, who also lives in Church Row, Hampstead, has taken a large room in Hampstead for some great fresco-paintings he is about. He requested Miss McCarthy to pray to the Virgin and to some good saints for his success. There is a beautiful religious spirit in this that I like. While writing this last sentence the dear little blind canary, which has not sung a note for ten days, has suddenly burst out singing like a small Jenny Lind. How delighted I am! and so will the children be."

"*May* 15, 1851.—We are very glad," I write to my sister, "to hear of the various visits in prospect. The Crystal Palace is a wonderful sight. There is more poetry in and about it than the human heart can conceive. We were there all yesterday. If I denied myself other pleasures, I could not deny myself this. I mean to go once a week at least, while we are in London. I can understand how you, away from the scene, should not perhaps feel the enthusiasm and excitement of it. But remember that such a meeting of the ends of the earth has never before occurred.

"I expect Anna Mary the first week in June. William

goes as far as Heidelberg to meet her. When she arrives
I shall be almost out of my senses with joy."

To MY HUSBAND IN HEIDELBERG.

"*May* 27, 1851.—Our Cambridge day was wonderful.
At half-past six in the morning I was at the Leigh Smiths'.
The Pulskys, Professor Kinkel, and a good number of
Hungarians with various outlandish names were at breakfast. I had already taken mine. At seven we set out in
the open carriage and omnibus, full inside and out, to the
Shoreditch station. There we met the remainder of our
party, excepting Freiligrath, whom I had been expected
to bring, and did not know it; Lord Dudley Stuart, who
is ill, and Monckton Milnes, who is either just married
or going to be, I don't know which. We were a party of
twenty-one. What introduction there was of one bearded
and moustachioed man to another, and of these to the
ladies! What a jabber of French, German, Hungarian,
and English! At length Mr. Smith, who seemed as
happy as a boy, and Willie Smith had paid the fare of the
whole party; the tickets were handed to every one, and I
was asked to make all the foreigners about me understand that these tickets were to be kept, as they were
our credentials for a free return. We took our seats in
carriages especially appropriated to our party. In mine
were the Pulskys, husband and wife; Professor Kinkel;
a Herr Kroff from Prague, who has lived sixteen years
in London, a nice old fellow, to whom I took a great
fancy; Mrs. Parkes, and myself. We were as merry as
so many larks. We flew past the stations, and only
stopped for about three minutes at Bishop's Stortford.
Before ten we were at Cambridge, and there were met by
a Trinity College omnibus and carriages, sent, as we were

informed, by 'Mr. Smith, of Jesus, to take us to the
"Bull."'   At the 'Bull' we found Ben, who in the first
place, led us through some of the College courts, and gave
us a hasty glimpse of beautiful mediæval buildings, lovely
avenues of limes, picturesque cloisters, gateways, halls,
and chapels, with smooth lawns, fountains, glimpses of
meadows golden with buttercups, and lines of drooping
leafy trees, till we were all wild with admiration and
delight.   All I wanted was you and Annie!   Well,
having had these glimpses of Cambridge, part of us went
to Ben's rooms in Jesus College, and the remainder to
the 'Bull' to have breakfast.   What a breakfast we had!
Ben's friends were still all at church; but presently, just
at the right moment, when he was gone to look after the
folks at the 'Bull,' and when we had drained his big
coffee-pot and wanted more, in came three young fellows
in caps and gowns, Chinnery of Keys (Caius), Mullins
of John's, and Cowan of Trinity.   Then there was an
increase of life and activity.   'Oh! you want coffee,
do you?' and away flew Mullins, and brought down
somebody else's big coffee-pot.   Then in rushed a
new undergraduate with his coffee-pot, and there was
plenty.   Next water was wanted; Herr Kroff must
have a glass of water.   Water was not to be had, but
Barbara knew where her brother's soda-water was.   So
down she delved into a cupboard, and up came bottle
after bottle; some was soda-water, some was ginger-
beer.   The gentlemen drank both out of a huge silver
tankard with a glass bottom.   Oh! if you could have
seen the fun, freedom, and jollity of those bearded,
moustachioed men, who had been students up and down
in Germany, it would have delighted you.   Pulsky put
on Ben's gown and cap, and enacted a respectable

English student, 'Smith, of Jesus.' Every one was full of fun, and what roars of laughter there were! When full justice had been done to the pickled salmon, ducks, fowls, tongue, and pigeon-pie, we joined the rest of the party in the court of 'King's,' and went the round of every college; each being alike, yet different; all beautiful, all rich; a union of architectural grandeur and picturesque effect with the verdure of lawns, meadows, and lovely trees. At half-past three we went to afternoon-service in King's, the finest chapel in Cambridge. I cannot tell you how exquisite it is. Then all assembled at the 'Bull,' and our one-and-twenty, with six handsome young undergraduates added, sat down to a table covered with excellent and delicious dishes. You can imagine the talking, laughter, and wit. After this came a little speech from 'Uncle Adams,' who, in the absence of Mr. Smith and Ben, returned thanks to the German and Hungarian ladies and gentlemen who had honoured his brother and nephew with their company that day, making an allusion to the struggle for liberty, which, though defeated, was not lost, and so on. Pulsky acknowledged the compliment in a little speech, in which he entangled himself, and was helped out by his wife. She laughed very merrily, and with tears in her eyes, for he was speaking of poor Kossuth. As she had laughed at her husband's break-down, she must, as punishment, make a speech. Therefore the 'Ladies of Hungary' was proposed. A crimson flush came over her face. She took her glass in her hand, and in a very few words expressed her thanks, and called upon the ladies of England to demand the liberation of Kossuth. Very soon the carriages were announced. So, with many most cordial farewells to the group of friendly undergraduates, we took our seats again in the vehicles—a little varying the arrangement of people, of course. We reached London a quarter before eight. Again the Smiths' omnibus and carriage, and as many cabs as were needful, were in waiting; and all who did not incline to go to supper in Blandford Square were sent home to their own doors.

"Barbara came yesterday to know how I felt after 'all the fatigue.' She says it seems to have put new life into her father. What a fine thing it is to be able to give pleasure on a magnificent scale !

"Kinkel could not imagine much hard study in rooms 'so comfortable' as we saw at Cambridge. No doubt he contrasted them in his mind with the bare floor, wooden chairs, the high-standing wooden desk, and the bed in the same room of the foreign university student."

I had soon the bliss of having my art-student home from Munich. With her we doubly enjoyed the sight of the productions, wealth, workmanship, and of people of all regions of the world assembled in the Crystal Palace. It was to us the veritable "House of Fame" foreseen by Chaucer four hundred and seventy years before.

On the last day of September I returned home, in advance of my family, from Southend, where we had been spending our autumn holiday. On Monday morning, October 2, 1851, I write to "My beloved ones all ! greeting.

"What a getting on board we had ! The boat tossed and heaved ; everybody was sick ; it poured with rain ; it blew ; there was such a crowd of people. Yet I enjoyed it all.

" When we came to Greenwich an old grandmother and
a little lad, who had been seated next me, left the boat.
'Why don't you go too?' I asked a little girl in a blue
veil, with a red bundle, who had seemed to belong to
them, and yet remained. 'I belong to nobody here,' she
said. 'I am going to London.'—'Where do you come
from?'—'From Sheerness; but I came from Portsmouth
last week. I have come to be with some relations at
Sheerness for twelve months.'—'And so now you are
going to London?'—'Yes; to stay at my uncle's till
Monday.'—'Where does he live?'—'I don't know.'—
'How, then, will you find him?'—'He will meet me.'
—'Where are you to get out?'—'At London.'—'But
it must be some particular place; is it Blackwall?'—'I
don't know.'—'Is it Hungerford?'—'I don't know; it is
London! Are you going to London?'

" I cannot tell you how my heart pitied this little forlorn
creature. 'Yes, I am going to London,' said I. 'But
now tell me about your uncle. What is he, and what is
his name?'—'He is a painter, and his name is Bustle.
I know he will meet me. He made an appointment.'—
'Well,' said I, 'we'll see. You shall stay near me, and
I will inquire at the different places as we stop if Mr.
Bustle is waiting. So you come from Portsmouth. Do
your parents live there?' (I was so afraid of this question lest they should be dead, but she was not in mourning.)—'Yes, they live there. My father is a dentist, and
my name is Ellen Tarrett.'—'And is your uncle a kind,
good man? And are you sure he will meet you?'—
'Quite sure; he came down to Sheerness and made an
appointment.'

" Poor, small, trusting child! It seemed frightful to
me that she should thus be turned adrift amongst

strangers. She was so pale, thin, and meek-looking, I was full of anxiety for her. Still, she seemed to have faith in Mr. Bustle, though she did not know where he lived. I thought it was no use distressing her with my fears, for if by the. end of the journey she was never met, I should take her home with me. It was now quite dark; we were entering London; it poured with rain. The whole fore-deck was crowded with hop-pickers, many of them Irish; such a dismal, squalid, wet crew. I thought, if this poor child fell into their hands they might steal her bundle and murder her. I went and found a good fellow belonging to the boat, told him about the little girl, and begged him at every place where the boat stopped to shout out an inquiry for Mr. Bustle. Poor little Ellen and I stood together under my umbrella looking out. Presently we came to London Bridge. Down went the steam-chimney. 'Oh!' she exclaimed, 'this is London. My aunt said I should see the chimney go down.' I wish I could give you an idea of the miserable hop-pickers that were now thronging out of the boat—the smell of wet rags, the squalling children on the women's backs, the shouts, the swearing, the jabbering in Irish, the calls for 'Mrs. Baker,' for 'Betsy,' and for 'Jim.' Little Ellen and I were driven on by this crowd. 'Is Mr. Bustle there?' shouted the trustworthy sailor. No reply. The throng of Irish was getting thinner. I was growing quite desperate. 'Is Mr. Bustle there?' again shouted he, and a voice from under an umbrella replied, 'Is Miss Tarrett there?' I felt such a thrill of joy. 'Yes, she is,' I said. 'Now, go, little dear; I am so glad!' The good sailor led her along the plank, and I saw her carried off, red bundle and all, under a big umbrella."

To Miss Wilkinson, on her Marriage.

"*Nov.* 1, 1851.—I meant to have sent an epistle of family greeting to meet you at your new home on October 10; but, unfortunately, a whole crowd of visitors—relatives and foreigners—among whom is Miss Bremer, kept me so wholly occupied the earlier part of the month, that I neglected everything, excepting the immediate duty of the hour and the day. Then, when the crowd had a little dispersed, I was obliged to turn all my thoughts and give up all my time to prepare what was needful for my daughter's return to Munich. She is now gone. Everybody, I believe, is gone with the exception of Miss Bremer; and I begin to atone, if possible, for all my apparent neglect and actual shortcomings. It was, my dear Mrs. Gaunt, only apparent neglect, for indeed we all thought and spoke of you, and wished you as much happiness as we felt you merited; that is a large share, we assure you.

"Accept our best wishes, therefore, and let me congratulate Mr. Gaunt on having, according to my ideas, taken into his house a spirit as bright and as cordial as daylight itself. May you long live together, and be able, with every passing year, to say that your lives have been made still better and happier through each other. Our most kind remembrance to Dr. and Mrs. Smiles, when you see them."

In September 1849 Fredrika Bremer first stayed with us, on her way to the United States and Cuba, whither, seized by the spirit of an old Viking, she was journeying at the age of forty-seven. She was short and plump in figure, and simple in her attire, which was made picturesque by a cap of a conventual shape, trimmed with deep lace; and she won our affection by her warm-heartedness and freedom from ostentation.

From America she wrote to me that the "sun of the Western world had developed in her many germs, that had been lying snow-covered for dozens of years, but which, under its influence, began to grow and expand, making her feel that her remaining span of life would barely suffice for the ripening of what then filled her soul."

In the autumn of 1851 she again passed through England. Her religious and social views had, in America, been materially influenced. An intense desire animated her to aid in the liberation of every oppressed soul; above all, to rescue her country-women from the dark and narrow sphere alloted them; and Sweden listened to her pleadings for woman.

To my Daughter in Munich.

"*Nov.* 1851.—It is quite true that Miss Bremer's beloved sister Agatha is dead. It was yesterday in the Swedish papers. She does not yet know it. We were at her evening party last evening, and the Swedes present were speaking about it amongst themselves. Some of them wanted me to give her an intimation of it before she leaves for Sweden; but I cannot. I do not wish to be in any way a bird of ill omen to her. But how sad it is! Jenny Lind's secretary, a very upright young Swede, travels with her; and the thought of the sorrow awaiting her makes him quite miserable."

In the self-same year of the Great Exhibition in Hyde Park, gold was found in Australia. The marvellous gold-romance of California had now begun in our own colonies. It seemed, in a period of over-population and misery in Europe, that gold, the great lure of the human heart, had been revealed in vast continents to call out people thither with a voice against which there was no appeal. Nothing was talked of but Australia, and the wonderful inducements offered to emigration.

My husband, who was a good sailor, and needed a real change from his hard brain-work, suddenly resolved on a trip to the new El Dorado, where he should once more see his brother, Dr. Godfrey Howitt, who was successfully established with his family in Melbourne. He should also learn what opening there might be on the Australian continent for our two sons, who were to accompany him. Anna Mary permanently returned from Munich to see our beloved ones off. They left us in June 1852, R. H. Horne, the author of "Orion," sailing with them in the *Kent*. We should have felt the separation appalling but for the wholesome panacea of work.

CHAPTER III.

THE HERMITAGE.

1852–1857.

OUR first occupation after the departure of my husband and sons for Victoria was moving from the Avenue Road to Highgate. I had once hoped that Andrew Marvell's half-timbered, very picturesque cottage there might have been our home. It proved, however, at the time to be too dilapidated to be rented with economy or prudence.

In the meanwhile Edward Bateman had taken, on lease, The Hermitage, situated at Highgate, on the West Hill, a little above Millfield Lane. The premises consisted of a small three-storeyed house and a lesser tenement, The Hermitage proper, containing a room on the ground-floor, and an upper chamber reached by an outside rustic staircase and gallery; the whole covered with a thick roof of thatch, and buried in an exuberant growth of ancient ivy. It and the dwelling-house stood in the midst of a long sloping garden, and were hidden from the road by palings, fine umbrageous elms, and a lofty ash which retained the name of "Nelson's Tree," from the famous admiral having climbed it as a boy. When to let, the landlord, in order to beautify the place, had painted the interior woodwork of the house dark green, and introduced bad stained-glass and grotto-work into the cottage. Notwithstanding these gimcrack attempts at rusticity, Mr. Bateman, perceiving the capabilities, had immediately secured it, and

then, under his skilful hand and eye, transformed it
into a most unique, quaint and pleasant abode, the fit
home for a painter. He had temporarily located Dante
Gabriel Rossetti in The Hermitage, when, determining to
go to Victoria, where his cousin, Mr. La Trobe, was Gover-
nor, he transferred the lease to us. Woolner and Bernhard
Smith were his fellow-travellers, and it was agreed that on

ANDREW MARVELL'S COTTAGE AT HIGHGATE.

the following 12th of April the P.R.B.'s in England were
to meet together to make sketches and write poems for
the P.R.B.'s in Australia, who were simultaneously to
meet and forward a Mercury of their proceedings home.
  Whilst The Hermitage was being transformed, and the
voyage of the pre-Raphaelites still in embryo, I remember
walking one March evening, at six o'clock, with Woolner
along Millfield Lane. After we passed the house once occu-

pied by Charles Mathews, the comedian, but later much enlarged, we witnessed a splendid sunset effect. The western sky was filled with a pale, golden light, fading into violet, then blue, and just in the violet hung a thin crescent moon, with one large star above her. Woolner could not sufficiently admire this exquisite poem of Nature, and I perceived that he was not only a sculptor, but a poet.

CHARLES MATHEWS' HOUSE IN MILLFIELD LANE.

For upwards of two years my daughters and I dwelt alone at The Hermitage, busily occupied in writing, painting, and studying ; our anxious hearts filled with the deepest solicitude for our dear absent ones, who were bravely encountering deprivation and toil. We could only remember that God was with them as much in the Bush as in a civilised land. It is not hard work, but the gnawing pain of the mind that kills ; and the memory of those days of suspense, aggravated by the very defective postal communication with Australia, brings with it a most grateful sense of the extreme kindness and delicate consideration of our opposite neighbour, the Baroness, then Miss Burdett-Coutts. She constantly invited us to Holly Lodge, and thus afforded us change of thought and relaxation in her highly cultivated circle.

Some of the chief incidents of this period are given in the subjoined extracts from letters.

To my Husband.

"*Sept.* 3, 1852.—I drive on with my work like some thing blind and deaf; listening, and seeing nothing but the one object, work. Sometimes Annie and I sit together in the same room, each at our table, for an hour or two, never speaking. Then we say, 'How quiet and pleasant it is, and what a holy and soothing influence there is in this blessed work!' I have not yet finished the first volume of Miss Bremer's travels in America.

"We have had quite an incursion of people here of late, and a whole American family are coming to drink tea with us to-morrow. We were just going to bed one night at our usual hour of ten, when a ring came at the gate. The dogs barked ferociously, and behold! it was William Allingham. He had heard we were ill from the Brownings, and so was come to inquire after us. We sat talking with him till half-past twelve. We enjoyed it very much, and asked him to come to us the next day. So he came. It was just in the midst of the terrible thunder and lightning that we have had here of late, and this led him to tell us what was just then deeply interesting a number of people in London; the Brownings among the rest.

"There is in Holborn a respectable tradesman, who is a firm believer in spiritual influences, in astrology, mesmerism, &c. This man has known for long that the house in which he lives is haunted by evil spirits and doomed to an ill end. He discovered that, many years ago, a murder had been committed in it. He consulted clairvoyants about it, and all foresaw that a fearful explosion would take place. He had six or seven letters from clairvoyants in different parts of the country, warning him of the impending danger, that the house would fall and burst the gas-pipes, the gas would explode, and terrible loss of life ensue. The man, who is apparently most sensible and intelligent, is personally known to Robert Browning, but his name is not to be revealed, because it would injure him in his business. During one of the last storms, this tradesman and a friend of his saw from a distance the lightning apparently concentrate itself over the house, and a red tongue as of fire rise up from the roof. They believed it must be burning. However, no harm was done. William Allingham asked me to note down that it was generally foreseen that the explosion was to occur between midnight and four o'clock the following Sunday morning. That was a fortnight ago to-day, and nothing has occurred. It was, however, a curious circumstance, which, when told us, interested us much."

"*Dec.* 3, 1852.—The Queen has read 'Uncle Tom's Cabin,' as well as all her subjects; she and the Duchess of Sutherland, and others of the good and great about the Palace, have determined to make a demonstration in favour of the slave. Her Majesty in her own person can do nothing; therefore this movement comes from the

Duchess of Sutherland. From her I received an invitation to meet a number of distinguished women at Stafford House, to take into consideration an address from the women of England to the women in America on the subject of slavery. I was quite appalled, and felt I had not a bonnet fit to go in; however, I got a new bonnet, and went.

"People were all most kind and polite. Lady Shaftesbury told me that her children had my juvenile books; and the Duchess of Sutherland and her daughter, the Duchess of Argyll, were particularly friendly. To my surprise, I found my name put down on a committee of women, which consists of Lady Shaftesbury, the Hon. Mrs. Kinnaird, myself (I give the names as they stand), Mrs. Sutherland, and Mrs. Grainger.

"The Duchess read a very interesting letter from Mrs. Stowe to the Earl of Carlisle. She seems delighted at this movement in favour of the slave; and certainly it is very fine, originating with our Queen, as it does, no doubt.

"Speaking of 'Uncle Tom's Cabin,' I must not forget to tell you that the sheets of this work, I believe before its publication in America, were offered for £5 to Charles Gilpin. He would not buy them. Then they were offered to Mr. Bogue, then to Mr. Bohn, and rejected by both. They were bought in the end by Routledge. Now there are at least twenty different publishers' editions, Bohn's and Bogue's among the rest; and it is supposed that upwards of one million copies have been sold in England alone."

"*Dec.* 8, 1852.—Charles Gilpin and George Alexander have come over to me in solemn deputation from the Anti-Slavery Society to remonstrate against the Duchess of Sutherland's Address to the American Women. But though I regret one or two expressions in the Stafford House Address, I yet adhere to it and its party."

"*Feb.* 22, 1853.—I was yesterday at our Committee for the Ladies' Address to their American Sisters on Slavery. There will be 400,000 signatures, it is expected.*　I had a good deal of talk with Lord Shaftesbury. He is one of the kindest, strongest, most agreeable of men. 'Uncle Tom' is being translated into Russian by order of the Czar; it is said preparatory to an abolition of serfdom. I went to the Committee with this news, but all thought it too good to be true. Then came Lord Shaftesbury and confirmed it. Miss Bremer writes beautifully on slavery. She seems to think that a spirit of emancipation is growing up in the South itself. This seems proved by three large slaveholders having—it is said in consequence of 'Uncle Tom'—emancipated all their slaves.

"How wonderful is the effect of that book! Lord Shaftesbury, who is just returned from France and Italy, said that 'in Italy it is devoured; but that the Jesuits, to make it suit their purpose, have introduced the Church instead of Christ. Thus poor Uncle Tom, the best Christian almost that ever lived, is made to preach for the Jesuits!' He also mentioned that the great prize ox in Paris this Christmas was called 'Uncle Tom.' What people will do with Mrs. Stowe, when she comes in May, I cannot tell. I expect she will be welcomed as no crowned head ever was."

"*March* 1, 1853.—The P.R.B.'s are most anxious for news of their Australian travellers. Rossetti was up here on Sunday, and very desirous to learn whether we had

---

* They amounted to 576,000.

received tidings, as neither the friends of Woolner nor of Bernhard Smith have received any. You may imagine with what eagerness after Australian news and news of vessels the *Times* is consulted each evening.

"We are now busily correcting the proofs of Enne-moser's 'History of Magic.' What industrious people you and Alfred were to translate all that mass of MS. on your voyage. What a curious work it is! M. Reclus, a French acquaintance of Miss Acton's, was here the other evening. He knows much about magic and occult things, and is acquainted with many French and German books on the subject. Is it not singular the widespread belief in such agencies? Rossetti told us the other evening some most remarkable ghost-stories."

"*March* 14, 1853.—I had a dream three nights ago, which has made me very unhappy; and yet, in a manner, I can account for it. I was thinking on Friday night of dear Claude's death—the next day being my birthday, and his into the better life. In the night, then, I dreamed that a letter came from Alfred. It seemed to contain three bills of credit, but the only words I saw in the letter were, '*My father is very ill.*' I woke in an agony of heart such as no words can describe. The misery of the dream has not ceased yet. I do all I can to reason with myself, to say that it was caused by my thinking of poor Claude's last hours. And I hope it was. God help us and preserve us to each other! I know that you all are exposed to hardships and dangers of many kinds. They rise up before my imagination and make me very un-happy. I can do no more than keep a prayer in my heart, which is uttered many, many times a day: 'Oh God! protect my beloved ones."

"*March* 20.—What a dreadful time we have had! Yesterday was the last grand meeting at Stafford House. On arriving I had only spoken to the Duchess of Sutherland and Lord Shaftesbury, when Mrs. Carpenter came up to me and asked, 'What is this about Mr. Howitt in the *Times?*' All the strength went out of me. I said, 'I do not know; what is it?' She then told me Dr. Carpenter had read something about an accident to your cart. I sat and listened to the proceedings of the meeting, hardly hearing a word. The Duchess talked to me most kindly, singling me out, as it were. I had no pleasure even in such kindness. The people were allowed to see the rooms after the meeting; but I did not care for it, and sat down in a window, amid all the grandeur, sick with apprehension.

"Annie was as much alarmed as I was when I came home and told her. Long and dreadful were the couple of hours that went on till the paper came. We read then the letter from an Australian correspondent. He says that your cart broke down on the way to the Ovens, and that he fears you are suffering from the climate. Somehow that letter took the sting out of our wounds. We had not, however, seen Willie Howitt, who came up to-day with his Australian home-news. Now we know that you are ill. Willie, however, assures us that all who go to Australia suffer at first from the climate."

"*March* 29.—No letters from you yet! We have regained a little composure after the terrible blow. Never in the whole of my life, with all our anxieties, have I passed such a time of suspense as this has been since that awful night of my dream. Oh! may it please our Heavenly Father to protect and restore you to us. I should really go out to you, were it not for Annie and Meggie. These partings are awful things. Think, only your last letter to us was written in October, and Alfred's on November 7. God help us! But I will hope and trust, as I have hitherto done. Yet I somewhat dread the *Great Britain* coming in. She is expected every hour.

"Mr. Green, the blind gentleman who lived nearly opposite to us in Avenue Road, has made a most kind arrangement for us. He will send our letters once a fortnight free of charge by his line of vessels; thus we need no longer trust to the mails. Yet it is sad to think that you will not receive this till the beginning of July."

To Alaric Watts.

"*April* 5, 1853.—You and dear Mrs. Watts will be pleased to know that we have had very long and interesting letters from William. They came by the *Great Britain*, and are dated December 23, when they were all three hundred miles up the country. They had encountered many adventures by the way, and all had been ill, William seriously so. Their illness was caused by camping in a swampy situation, at a time when, their cart having broken down, they were detained by its being repaired.

"God, however, always sends His Angel in some form in one's sorest affliction. So it was now. They found, when poor dear William was at his worst, that at seven miles' distance there was a large sheep-station. There they sent to ask for something they needed, and when Mr. and Mrs. Forlonge, the owners of the station, heard that it was William who lay sick, they sent down everything in their power for his comfort; then, when he was able to be removed, had him conveyed to their house in a spring-cart, took the entire party and all their belongings under their roof; and though utter strangers, treated them with brotherly kindness. They proved to be not only true Samaritans, but intellectual, highly cultivated Scotch people.

"This illness is an affecting passage to us in the narrative of their two months' journey; still, it is cheering to know that even in the wilderness kind hearts are to be met with. For the rest, nothing can be more Robinson-Crusoe-like than the whole expedition. They seem to enjoy it. It is impossible for William to speak too highly of Alfred, who has not only resources for all difficulties and a brave spirit, which nothing can subdue, but so much tenderness, sympathy, and devoted affection in sorrow.

"Charlton is in his element among birds and duck-billed platypuses, flying squirrels and opossums. Edward Bateman is with them, and was one of the best nurses to dearest William in his illness.

"A great load is lifted off our hearts; and more than ever now we feel that we must and may confide them to God."

To WILLIAM HOWITT.

"*April* 10, 1853.—It has been most pleasant to meet the Boothbys again before their departure for Australia. You will have learned already that Mr. Boothby is going out to Adelaide as second Supreme Judge. All his sons are eager about Australia. Who would have imagined that, when he and you, years ago, were members of the Nottingham Town Council, you would meet once more in the Antipodes?

"While writing, Dr. Sutherland has called. He is

delighted with your letter in the *Times*. Just as he was leaving, who should come in but Dr. Smiles. He intends now to settle in London. He too was full of your letter, the first description that had ever made him see Australian scenery. After he was gone, Meggie and I set out for our walk, and soon we met Barbara's father, who stopped the carriage to speak to us. He is very anxious that the dredging-machines in use on the Thames should be introduced in Australia, to scoop up the gold in the creeks.

"Now I must try to think over what news there is. The great topics seem to be :—In the political world, the proposed new scheme of Property and Income Tax, which would make everybody pay something ; the proposal of paying off a portion of the National Debt with Australian gold. In the literary world, the International Copyright, which some expect will be in force within three months. In society in general, the strange circumstantial rumour of the Queen's death, which, being set afloat on Easter Monday, when no business was doing, was not the off-spring of the money-market. Mr. and Mrs. Charles Kean, who were here the other day, spoke of it, saying truly that for the moment it seemed to paralyse the very heart of England. The Keans, by the bye, send the very kindest messages to you.

"I forget whether I told you of the invitation to Stafford House of not only our Ladies' Committee, but of the Committee of the old Anti-Slavery party. The latter were invited to see the result of the labours of the noble duchesses, ladies, and all the rest of us, in twenty-six large volumes. The Committee of the Anti-Slavery party consisted of twelve Quaker ladies. When they received their invitation to Stafford House, they wrote back to ask if they might each be allowed to bring a sister or a friend.

The Duchess very graciously consented, and their number grew to four-and-thirty. There they were when we entered; all sorts of Friends, plain and smart, old and young, grave and gay, sitting as if in meeting, round the room. We were invited to meet Mrs. Stowe at Stafford House, but whether all the thirty-four or only the original twelve Quakeresses will go I know not. She has arrived at Liverpool, and her ovation has begun."

"*May* 4, 1853.—The great talk now is Mrs. Stowe and spirit-rapping, both of which have arrived in England. The universality of the phenomena renders it a curious study. A feeling seems pervading all classes, all sects, that the world stands upon the eve of some great spiritual revelation. It meets one in books, in newspapers, on the lips of members of the Church of England, Unitarians, even Freethinkers.

"Poor old Robert Owen, the philanthropist, has been converted, and made a confession of faith in the public papers. One cannot but respect a man who, in his old age, has the boldness to declare himself as having been blinded and mistaken through life; and who, upon the verge of human life, sends forth the concealed yearning of his soul after a spiritual world and an immortality. Yes, indeed, is not the greatest proof, after all, of an immortality the innate longing after it, and the belief in it existing within each human being, whether encased in external intellectual pride, worldly joy, or hardness of heart, and that too throughout all ages and shining forth from all mythologies?

"Especially are the aristocracy interested in these rappings, which become contagious; a medium of spiritual communication may in some cases be developed by the laying

on of hands.   There is a singular resemblance between it
and mesmeric power.   The old hobgoblins and brownies
seem to be let loose again, for all the spirits appear to be of
a singularly *low* order, frequently lying.   Mr. Beecher, the
brother of Mrs. Stowe, has delivered in America a series
of lectures to a vast assembly, demonstrating that these
phenomena are the work of the devil.   Well, perhaps,
they may be.

"Barbara, who is now investigating these strange
glimpses into an occult power of nature, told us last
night a singular circumstance connected with Lady
Byron's mother.   Lady Milbanke had discovered, as a
young woman in Switzerland, that she was endowed, like
many of the natives, with the power of discovering water
by means of the divining-rod.   When Dr. Wollaston had
written a most learned treatise upon the superstition of
the divining-rod, he was surprised to receive a letter
desiring an interview with him on Wimbledon Common
by the writer, who possessed the power he so severely
denounced.   Dr. Wollaston went to Wimbledon, and
great was his surprise to perceive a carriage approach
the spot of appointment.   An elegant lady, accompanied
by some equally fashionable friends, alighted, and declared
herself the writer of the letter, and ready to test her power;
and she still more astonished Dr. Wollaston when, taking
a hazel-rod, she pointed out again and again concealed
springs of water.   This anecdote of Lady Milbanke had
been told Barbara, I believe, by Lady Byron."

"*May* 8, 1853.—Mrs. Stowe has arrived in London.
She is come with husband, brothers, sister-in-law, and
nephew.   She is a simple, kindly creature, with a face
which becomes beautiful from expression.   We spent an

evening with her at the Binneys' on Friday. It was a
sort of open house, hundreds of people coming and going.
When we reached the front-door we were struck by the
crowds which had gathered round it; we heard some
one say he had come to get a peep of 'the composer of
" Uncle Tom's Cabin." ' Wherever she goes, and it is
known that she is there, a crowd gathers. It is something like the enthusiasm in America for Jenny Lind.

"I was yesterday at Stafford House, with some hundreds
besides, composed of the aristocracy and many distinguished people. Mrs. Stowe and her relatives had taken
luncheon with the Duke and Duchess of Sutherland, and
the dukes, duchesses, lords and ladies of their family. In
the grand gallery the reception took place, the Duchess
of Sutherland and Lord Shaftesbury introducing interesting personages to Mrs. Stowe. Then the principal persons
took seats in the middle of the room, and the company
stood round. Lord Shaftesbury read a very nice address
of welcome to Mrs. Stowe, which was handed her; and
her brother made a tedious speech, and read a rather
stupid letter from an American who had emancipated his
slaves. This was the first part of the day's proceedings.
People walked about and conversed together, and were
introduced to Mrs. Stowe, if they had patience to wait for
an opportunity. Tea and coffee were handed round by
footmen in drab and scarlet or in Highland costume.
Then the Duchess and Mrs. Stowe retired to a smaller
apartment, where the ladies were invited to follow.
Here, after a good deal of amusement in separating the
ladies from the gentlemen, Mrs. Stowe made a capital
little speech, or rather talked to us in a very simple
manner; her countenance beaming, and a merry smile
at times playing over it, till she looked to my eyes as

beautiful as the splendid and gracious lady, the friend of Queen Victoria, seated beside her."

"*June* 29, 1853.—Dined the other day with Sir David Brewster at Lord Shaftesbury's. Later in the evening a servant being ordered to bring a hat from the hall, it was made to spin round by some of the family and guests assembled in the drawing-room. It was very odd. Dr. Braid of Manchester says the phenomenon is produced by the power of mind over matter; and that if the mind is fixed on matter long enough, and with sufficient intensity, it will inevitably operate upon it. The effect which all this table-turning, hat-moving, and spiritual intercourse is producing on all kinds of people is marvellous. Robert Chambers, the Alaric Wattses, the T. K. Herveys, are all believers and operators."

"*Aug.* 20, 1853.—Only think, last Saturday we actually went to the Camp at Chobham; and that through the politeness of the S. C. Halls. We found Mr. Fairholt at the station, and travelled together. Mr. and Mrs. Samuel Lover, Mr. Ansdell, and some other guests of the Halls' were also in the same train. At Addlestone station was Mr. Hall, who conveyed the party to Firfield, that wonderful abode, which so confounded good Dr. Förster by its magnificence; its urns, vases, busts, pictures, its Sèvres, Dresden, and Wedgwood, and so forth. After partaking of an elegant breakfast, all the party entered carriages and rolled away to the Camp.

"It was quite exciting, when we came out on the main road, to see all the vehicles hastening on towards the Camp, mail-coaches, omnibuses, cabs, and carriages crowded with people; the footpaths also crowded with pedestrians.   Vehicles, people, horses, trees, hedges, and grass were all powdered with thick dust for the four long miles to Chobham.   The very spiders who have built their webs in the hedges must wonder whatever has befallen the summer, for they are choked up with thick dust, in spite of all the rain there has been.   Those dusty gossamers parch my throat with thirst only in recollection.

"We came out upon a desolate moorland tract, where before us gleamed forth white in the sunlight the distant lines of tents, with a strange poetical beauty suggestive of the tents of the Israelites.   Tent-life, especially for your dear sakes, being very interesting to Annie and me, we looked into many of these tents, wondering whether your abode presented at all a similar picture.   Before one officer's tent was planted a little garden, and at the door was placed a rustic seat, which, from its enormous height, made us think its possessor must be one of the Amalekites.   The booths of the sutlers, built of straw, and the straw-and-heather-constructed sentry-boxes were most picturesque.   Mr. and Mrs. M'Ion, Mr. Fairholt, Mr. Ansdell, Annie, and I were the most adventurous of the party; for, leaving the carriages and Mrs. Hall, the Lady Mayoress, and the Lovers posted upon a heathery mound, crowded with other carriages and spectators, watching the distant evolutions of the soldiers—whose firing resounded mournfully across the heath, and the white volume of whose smoke floated softly over the dark hills—we hastened into the very thick of the battle.

"Here, from a much better mount of observation, we saw the columns of the infantry swiftly descending the slopes before us, and advancing in dense bright-coloured masses towards the imaginary enemy.   The Highland regiments especially added to the picturesqueness of the spectacle. After due heroism shown by us at the cannon's mouth, we retreated to our carriages, not, however, before Annie and Mr. Fairholt had noted every artistic effect; for, unlike many modern artists, he is sensible and unaffected enough to be enthusiastic, and not too *gentlemanly* to enjoy the beauty and pleasantness about him. Then, all the party covered with dust, our very eyes dust-bins, we returned to enjoy the munificent cold collation at Firfield."

"*Aug.* 23.—Last Sunday we had another holiday. We were driven by Joseph Todhunter in the tax-cart to see their new house at Willesden. We felt vastly like some respectable butcher's or baker's family ; and we only hope these *respectable* individuals feel ordinarily as happy as we did, rattling along through the pleasant lanes, with the wind rushing through the trees overhead, and poor little old Brach rushing along after us, like a big heap of dust. We sat upon the sunny lawn in Mrs. Todhunter's garden, with the distant church-bells ringing pleasantly ; and Annie sketched the quaint old summer-house, with a tangle of hops and roses at one side of it. It was a delightful day indeed. At dusk away we rattled again *à la* butcher and baker, or rather *à la* greengrocer, for this time we were laden with vegetables."

"*March* 2, 1854.—You will see that war is now really beginning in earnest with Russia. Nothing is talked of here but war. One fleet is gone to the Black Sea, and another is going to the Baltic. Troops are being embarked even in the screw-steamers intended for Australia. Men-of-war, it is said, are to be sent to guard the Australian coast, as Russian privateers are abroad, and it is expected that our rich Australian vessels will be seized. It is said, also, that the overland route will no longer be safe; so that, if this be true, it will put an end to your overland return, for which I am sorry. The whole of this excitement and preparation for war has made me very sad. Greatly have we admired and accompanied in spirit Joseph Sturge and two other Friends who have gone to St. Petersburg to endeavour to persuade the Czar to peace. It was really a very fine thing, and quite worthy of George Fox. If you see the *Times*, you will read an account of this interview, and their address to Nicholas, and his reply. Long live such true men of peace! and I wish all the world thought with them. The prices of everything have become twice what they were when you left England.

"The 'rapping spirits' go on rapping, and people listen to them. I myself think it delusion ; but really we hear extraordinary things, and we see sensible people believing so gravely, and in many cases it has produced such beautiful and sincere religious faith and trust, that we do not know what to say. Bulwer is most eager on the subject. Decanters rise up from his table without hands, solid substances suspend themselves in the air."

On May 15, 1854, I went to stay with Mr. Bladon at Uttoxeter, and was joined the next day by my daughter Annie. The little town looked to me but slightly altered, yet somehow old and shabby; the country pleasant, especially the hilly crofts. The vegetation, however, neither so fine nor so early as I had expected.

To MARGARET HOWITT.

" *Uttoxeter, May* 21, 1854.—Lots of folk have called on

us, and we might go out every day to dinner and evening parties, but we have set our faces against it; and Mr. Bladon is very good, and lets us do as we like. We will, however, be civil, and even grateful. Last evening a rich silk manufacturer of Macclesfield called, with his wife, on us. He has settled in the neighbourhood; is a fat, jolly Conservative, whose work-people are emphatically *hands*, and who thinks 'Mary Barton' a dangerous, bad book. He had been to the Royal Academy. He said he could not, for the soul of him, tell what to make of Holman Hunt's 'Light of the World;' whether it was good or bad he did not know. He looked at it for half an hour, and was never so puzzled by any picture before.

"We were at Mrs. White's of Barrow Hill the other morning. She has a celebrated collection of old pictures, which Mrs. Jameson, amongst other connoisseurs, has been to see. Some of them are really good, others indifferent. Mrs. White was in the grounds when we arrived, and came to us in an old, old bonnet, a coarse old woollen shawl, and a gown worth about ten shillings when new. She is not only very rich, but highly intellectual; and were she not so great a lady, would be regarded here as a heretic, for she is a Unitarian.

"Your aunt Anna comes to-morrow, and she will enjoy the oddities as much as I do. It often bores poor Annie, and no wonder. We went out to tea, for instance, and she was shown, for her amusement, a set of small copperplates worth sixpence, a French plum-box, a paper hand-screen, and 'Leighton on the Epistles of St. Peter.' "

"*June* 2, 1854.—I wish you had been with us on Wednesday, when we went to call on the new Vicar and his sister. They have just got into the nice old Vicarage; and he has bought up all the old carved oak chairs and tables and a sideboard out of the houses of the country-people."

ANNA MARY TO HER UNCLE, RICHARD HOWITT.

"*The Hermitage, June* 18, 1854.—We have been for the last several weeks at Uttoxeter. You may believe it was very pleasant to be there and revisit the old scenes. Especially was it pleasant for my mother meeting my aunt Anna there, and for them to wander through their old haunts and talk over old memories.

"A poetical little incident also occurred. When we had been in Uttoxeter a few days, my mother suddenly remembered that she had not heard the chimes play as usual since she had arrived; those sweet melodious chimes, which had so delighted her and my aunt when they were children. What had become of them?

"Every one then began also to ask what *had* become of the chimes. People remembered then that for years they had been silent—silent ever since the church had been repaired many years back. Mr. Joseph Bladon, at whose house we were staying, and who is about the most influential man now in the little town, together with the Vicar—who also had never heard the chimes, being come to the place only within a short time—soon had inquiries made. Then the first Sunday morning after our arrival, in honour of my mother's visit to her old home, the chimes recommenced their sweet music. They had quite passed out of people's memories, but were still in perfect order, only requiring a new rope.

"We shall send you in a day or two a copy of 'The Artist's Düsseldorf Album,' in which you will find a poem

of yours printed.   My mother was asked to translate the
German poems, and also to procure a few original English poems ; and as the time was very short, we sent one
of yours which we had, and greatly liked.   Please read
in the Album a poem called ' Sister Helen.'   It is by
Gabriel Rossetti, an artist friend of ours."

THE SAME TO THE SAME.

" *Oct.* 22, 1854.—I send you the delightful information
that my father and dear old Charlton are on their homeward voyage.   They were to start on August 1st.   My
father has been in Sydney and Van Diemen's Land, and
was very well when he wrote."

MARY HOWITT TO HER SISTER.

" *Nov.* 16, 1854.—Our beloved voyagers are not yet
returned, though we have been listening for their ring at
the gate almost for several weeks.   But our impatience
outran possibility, as they will not, in all probability, be
here before the end of next week.   This we know from a
letter which we received on Monday from William, written
from Rio Janeiro, where they had put in for water, vegetables, and supplies.   I am glad that they touched at
Rio, as they have thus a little peep of South America, and
according to his letter, they are extremely delighted with
the natural features of that fine country.

" We now never are both from home, for we cannot
bear the possibility of their arriving and finding us not
here to welcome them.   It is strange that, while I long
so earnestly for William's return, I yet dread it.   I fear
seeing in his beloved face traces of anxiety, of hardship
and time.   I fear, too, lest he should see them in mine,
as assuredly he will ; only I think our joy will hide our

WILLIAM AND MARY HOWITT AT THE HERMITAGE.

wrinkles.   Life is such a sad history that one's very happiness is mingled with pain and fear.

"Anna, my beloved, is it possible that you may come to the neighbourhood of London?   I hope it may be so. Would it not be beautiful if the evening of our lives were spent in near and dear intercourse, as was our youth? I do not know anything which would give me greater pleasure."

On Thursday, December 7, 1854, at about two o'clock, my dear husband and son arrived at The Hermitage safe and sound, looking so well that it was a great joy to us. At the same period my brother-in-law, Daniel Harrison, settled with his family in the neighbourhood of London; making me thus enjoy a full measure of domestic happiness.

MARY HOWITT TO HER DAUGHTER MARGARET.

"*The Hermitage, Aug.* 9, 1855.—Annie went with Barbara to Glottenham, and had just begun to feel better, when, lo! it was discovered that a poor woman was ill of a fever in a neighbouring cottage, and at five minutes' warning off they set to Hastings, and are now located at Clive Vale Farm, near Fairlight; the same farm where Holman Hunt painted his sheep."

ANNA MARY HOWITT TO HER MOTHER.

"*Clive Vale Farm, Aug.* 10, 1855.—We have just had breakfast.   Our little parlour-window is wide open, with the sunshine streaming in, and the vast expanse of distant sea and undulating green hills coming close up to the strip of cottage garden.   We were very much amused by finding the traces of Holman Hunt's painting in great

spots of green, blue, and red, and traces of oil and tur-
pentine upon a picturesque, little, stout oak table, which
we had chosen also for our work ; and thus quite uninten-
tionally we have trodden in his steps."

" *The Hermitage, Aug.* 21, 1855.—We had a very
pleasant evening at Miss Coutts's. She and Mrs. Brown
set off to-morrow, and will not return before the end of
October. She has had a great annoyance about the
extension of Highgate Cemetery. A few years ago, she
told me, she offered to buy this very land now purchased
by the cemetery company, and reaching down to Swain's
Lane ; she was intending to make it beautiful gardens, to
be secured to the public for ever. At that time the proprietor refused to sell ; and she naturally feels ill-used
not to have had the first offer, when he was inclined to
do so, and before the cemetery company was allowed to
purchase it, for a purpose injurious to the health of the
increasing population.

" Of course, I said, as I felt, that hers had been a noble
and excellent idea, and asked her if I might 'speak of it.
She replied, ' Certainly.' I then added, ' But do not give
up the idea. It is by such beneficial acts that your name
will be preserved to the nation. Let me beg of you to
purchase Parliament Hill and convert that into a public
park.' She answered, ' That is Lord Mansfield's property.
However, I shall think of it.' My heart blessed her for
those words, but I merely said, ' Yes, dear Miss Coutts,
do, for such an idea is worthy of you.' I told her, too,
how beautiful that hill would be with a grand white
marble statue standing upon it, with the background of
blue sky. ' Very beautiful,' she said, in her quiet way."

THE SAME TO THE SAME.

"*Aug.* 22, 1855.—The purchaser of this property intends to pull down all the cottages below us and build a row of villas in their stead. If, however, he leaves this house standing, he may as well retain us as tenants as take new ones. It would be a real grief to me to leave the neighbourhood of Miss A. B. C., for she is a noble creature."

"*Brockham Lodge, Aug.* 26, 1855.—Here we are, my dearest Annie, with our kind friends, William and Elizabeth Bennett. Every object within-doors, every lovely plant without, stand just where they did two years ago. A new fern-house, it is true, is erected. and a chaotic wilderness is being formed, and an exquisite new clematis covers a portion of the greenhouse. But these are only perceived at a second glance.

"It being First-day, the family is gone to meeting, your father with them. It is the midst of corn-harvest; the fields being either clear of corn or filled with shocks ready for carrying. How exquisite was your account of the harvest-field after the storm, and the resemblance which it bore to the bowed and afflicted nation! It was to me a grand poem."

"*The Hermitage, Sept.* 4, 1855.—When we walk in our favourite Highgate fields towards Hampstead we often see Mr. Tom Seddon and his pretty little wife. We did so yesterday, and walked together. He wants to finish his Eastern sketches, and asked us where he could find rocks and old thorn-trees, which he might use for bits of his olive-trees; and where he could find a level burnt-up country for a Syrian desert. We advised him to go to the little inn at Rowsley for the old rocks about Haddon Hall and Stanton. He said that 'Lear had advised the same.' I suggested he could find strange, weird old trees about Hurstmonceaux. He replied, 'So, too, had Lear told him,' and that Lear was painting down there this very summer. He cannot turn his thoughts at present to other subjects than the East."

"*Dec.* 4, 1855.—Of course, your father and I entirely approve of Barbara's scheme for petitioning Parliament for an alteration in the law as regards the property of married women; and we are glad that she is getting her grand scheme into form."

"*Jan.* 8, 1856.—Yesterday I went to Stratton Street. Miss Coutts was at home, and most kindly received me. We sat and talked over Mr. Brown's death, and Mrs. Brown's grief and beautiful resignation; and then she came in. I am always affected, somehow, by the sight of a widow's cap; and to see that bright face so sad, and surrounded by the plain, white, folded muslin, quite touched me. We talked about death and eternity. Both believe in the immediate life after death, and that the spirit of a departed beloved one may be ever present, though unseen, unfelt; only they do not believe in the influence of the spirit through dreams or material manifestations. It was, some way, very sweet, and I had great peace in this part of my visit. Miss Coutts showed me a miniature which Sir William Ross has done of Mr. Brown since death from the bust and his remembrance of the face; but it is not quite right.

"We then talked of this proposed movement to secure to married women their own property and earnings.

They both agree that it is quite right. Miss Coutts, who understands the subject thoroughly, said that she believed some changes would be made in the laws regarding women and the management of their property; but as to supporting the petition, she must fully consider it, and can say nothing just at present.

"I mentioned that Mrs. M. and Mrs. N. stood at the head of its supporters. She replied, that 'if it were so the cause would be greatly damaged.' I was extremely astonished. 'These ladies,' she continued, 'hold such free opinions with regard to marriage that people would naturally be suspicious of the intentions of the whole thing.' I answered that 'I was quite unaware of their entertaining such opinions, that Mrs. M. had had the sorrow of a very bad husband, and therefore she might have a right to speak.'—'Yes,' said Miss Coutts, 'I know it. I am acquainted with Mrs. M.'s books, and think highly of them; just lately, when a subscription was raised for her, I had a pleasure in giving something towards it. But you must excuse me saying it, your name ought never to be joined with those of Mrs. M. and Mrs. N.' I again looked astonished, and wondered to myself what these ladies would say if they heard this. Mrs. Brown asked what Mrs. N. it was? 'The mother of that wild, mad young Lady ——,' was the reply.

"Now, amazed as I am to find myself set up above Mrs. M. and Mrs. N., I do think it most needful to have an eye to the moral status of the persons supporting this movement; and that in the fields of science and literature signatures such as those of Mrs. Somerville and Mrs. Gaskell should be obtained."

"*Jan.* 9, 1856.—We went last evening to the Seddons'.

Mr. Tom Seddon is in very good heart. He has sold one of his pictures to Lord Grosvenor. He showed me a sketch for another of his commissions. It is a sort of halt in the desert at the hour of prayer. He is going again to the East to paint a picture at Damascus. His brother, the architect, has received a commission to restore Llandaff Cathedral, so he is in Wales. They all seem very happy, and send lots of kind messages to you."

Anna Mary Howitt to her Sister Margaret.

"*March* 13, 1856. — The petition about married women's property has already been announced in Parliament. It is spoken of as the petition of Elizabeth Barrett Browning, Anna Jameson, Mary Howitt, Mrs. Gaskell, &c. The London signatures are within a small number of three thousand. Westminster are two thousand. Various little incidents of interest have occurred, such as a very old lady on her death-bed, who asked to be allowed to put her name to the petition, and thus wrote her signature for the last time. Yesterday evening, as it was growing dusk, Octavia made her appearance, looking so bright and happy. She had been taking her Ragged School children a walk in the Highgate fields; and dismissing them, came here. She helped mother to paste the signature sheets, which have all been sent in to-day."

The Same to the Same.

"*March* 17, 1856.—Sir Erskine Perry says that, contrary to his expectation, the petition was received very respectfully in the House of Commons, without a sneer or a smile. Lord Brougham made a capital little speech in the Lords on presenting the petition, paying Mrs. Jameson and our mother each a very nice compliment, to which there was a 'Hear, hear.' He especially called Lord Lyndhurst's attention to the importance of the question. It will be capital if, through this women's petition, the law gets amended." *

On December 19, 1856, we learnt with regret the death, at Cairo, of the gifted young artist, Thomas Seddon; and on the Christmas Day, Holman Hunt called to consult with Anna Mary about her little memoir of his deceased friend.

Our daughter had, both by her pen and pencil, taken her place amongst the successful artists and writers of the day, when, in the spring of 1856, a severe private censure of one of her oil-paintings by a king among critics so crushed her sensitive nature as to make her yield to her bias for the supernatural, and withdraw from the ordinary arena of the fine arts. After her marriage in 1859 to her contemporary and friend from childhood, Alaric Alfred, the only son of our valued associates, Mr. and Mrs. Watts, they both jointly pursued psychological studies.

In the spring of 1856 we had become acquainted with several most ardent and honest spirit-mediums. It seemed right to my husband and myself, under the circumstances, to see and try to understand the true nature of those phenomena in which our new acquaintance so firmly believed. In the month of April I was therefore invited to a séance at Professor De Morgan's, and was much astonished and affected by communications purporting to

---

* The only change brought about by the petition was in the law of marriage and divorce.

come to me from my dear son Claude. With constant
prayer for enlightenment and guidance, we experimented
at home. The teachings that seemed given to us from
the spirit-world were often akin to those of the Gospel ;
at other times were more obviously emanations of evil.
The system was clearly open to much abuse. I felt
thankful for the assurance thus gained of an invisible
world, but resolved to neglect none of my common duties
for spiritualism.

The Hermitage being doomed to destruction, we quitted
it in 1857 for another house at Highgate, pleasantly
situated higher up on the same ascent, and called West
Hill Lodge.

CHAPTER IV.

WEST HILL LODGE.

1857–1866.

OUR new home at Highgate stood back, facing its old-fashioned sloping garden, which was hidden from the high-road by a thick screen of clipped lime-trees; and it possessed from the flat accessible roof a magnificent survey of London and its environs. It was to us a pleasant and attractive abode, yet we willingly vacated it for months at a time. My husband's life of free, pleasant, healthy adventure in Australia had stimulated his innate love of Nature; and, although a sexagenarian, made him henceforth always ready to start off to the mountains, the seaside, or the Continent, fulfilling, wherever it might be, his literary occupations in the quiet and refreshment of fine scenery. It appears to me a delightful, most privileged existence that we were thus perpetually permitted to enjoy God's glorious works on earth, as a foretaste, I humbly trust, of still more sublime ones in heaven.

From 1858 a series of sojourns in Carnarvonshire began, which, interluded by visits to various parts of England, France, Switzerland, and Germany, remained, until we reached Italy and Tyrol, our chief source of rural profit and delight. The Chester and Carnarvon Railway had already brought along the sea-coast of North Wales an influx of tourists and wealthy settlers, demanding and introducing the necessities of advanced civilisation. This tended to develop the resources of the beautiful land, whose valleys and mountain-sides are inhabited by an isolated people, proud of their traditions, history, literature, and language, and jealously guarding themselves as much as possible from the introduction of new customs.

WEST HILL LODGE.

We sympathised with our "Saxon" friends and acquaintances in their desire practically to ameliorate the condition and remove the prejudices of their Cambrian neighbours; with the latter, in their passionate love of their old language—the last remnant left them of their cherished nationality—and in their strong religious aspirations. We familiarised ourselves with their distinct habits and customs, and their belief in second-sight, good and bad omens, presentiments and apparitions.

We find a mention of our first stay in North Wales in the following letter from Anna Mary Howitt to her uncle Richard, dated "The Mill Cottage, Aber, near Bangor:"—

"*Aug.* 28, 1858.—Although we are not amongst the grandest Welsh scenery, we have mountains and a wonderfully beautiful valley, traversed by the rocky bed of a torrent, a regular chaos of huge stones. We have the sea near, and heather and exquisite flowers starring the pasture-fields, hill-sides, and glens ; and we have gurgling brooks, and many an old remain of the Past—Druidical, Roman, and Mediæval—so that there is a great variety to be enjoyed.

"We are located in a regularly romantic cottage, close to the mill of this little village of Aber. It belongs to Mr. and Mrs. Birley ; and she says that my aunt, Elizabeth Howitt of Farnsfield, has been here. Is it not curious how people are linked in acquaintance all over this world !

"We are much struck by a certain resemblance to Germany in the look of the villages, and even of the people. We only wish that some great Welsh writer would arise, and do for beautiful Wales what Scott has done for his native land, or even what Auerbach has for German peasant life in his 'Tales of the Black Forest.' Alas ! this difficult Welsh language is a terrible bar to any English visitor conversing with the country-people ; and unless a person can talk with them, there is no writing well about them. It is a Welsh man or woman born and bred who should be the chronicler of the strange, wild, simple and affecting stories to be met with in the cottages and farm-houses of these solitary valleys and hill-sides.

"It is curious how very little English is generally spoken amongst the common people, and this very fact has preserved much that is peculiar and primitive in the race. It is difficult, too, unfortunately, to find, so far, at least, as our experience has gone, people of the middle class who are interested about the peculiarities and language of their country. You have to hunt after the bits of picturesqueness, for very few of the educated care for them, regarding them as vulgar. We are intending to make the acquaintance of the Methodist preacher, who lives at the neighbouring Methodist village of Bethesda. He *speaks* English, which not all Methodist preachers here do. As he is one of the people, and goes amongst them, we hope from him to hear something quaint and interesting. Mr. Williams, the clergyman here, a Welshman born and bred, takes some interest, for a wonder, in the old legends and superstitions of the race. From him we have heard a few particulars, which only make us long for more. He, however, only tells us about the poor church-goers, and that is quite the minority here.

"You will be glad to learn that my father has begun writing a book he has long talked of, 'The Man of the People.' He has read us the chapters already written, and we are deeply interested in it. Mdlle. Bremer is also sending my mother the sheets of a new tale, 'Father and Daughter.' So that you see both play and work go on here ; the one giving relish to the other."

Richard Howitt was at this time living in the deepest seclusion on his little farm at Edingley ; yet, as the most inspiriting thoughts came to him in isolation, he seldom felt solitary. The young clodhoppers helping him at his work thought him a strange man; and one of them observed to the housekeeper, "He fancied Mester completely *lost*, for when plucking the orchard fruit he would give no reply, and often pause as if going asleep."

If silent and meditative, he was active and eloquent in the service of the care-worn and oppressed. When elected guardian of the poor by a large majority, blue and white flags fluttered gaily from the cottage windows, and for more than an hour the church bells of his village were merrily rung. An immense reader in a wide range of literature, he would start off, after the perusal of any poetry or prose that was brilliant, earnest, deep, sincere, or admirable, to impart the rich treat to his sister-in-law, Elizabeth, the widow of his elder brother, Emanuel. She dwelt in the adjacent village of Farnsfield, where was also the home of her stepson, Leaver Howitt, and his numerous family.

Anna Mary Howitt again writes to her uncle Richard, this time from "Thorpe, near Ashbourne, Derbyshire:"—

"*May* 13, 1859.—You will be surprised to see the above address. We are located for some weeks in a roomy, comfortable cottage, in this quiet, old-world, well-to-do village of Thorpe, close to lovely Dovedale, in which we live nearly the whole day long. We came away very suddenly from home, as Florence Nightingale, who, I regret to say, is very much of an invalid, wished my parents to let her our house, for she wanted a quiet healthy place near town. We came away at almost a day's notice, bringing our work with us, and settling down in these cosy but primitive quarters.

"We have been both to Ilam and Tissington, and about a good deal, for Mr. Watts-Russell and Sir William and Lady Fitz-Herbert are most kind and attentive to my parents. You would write a ballad about the old baronial hall of Tissington, and the holy well-dressing in the village on Ascension Day; and Ilam is equally poetical and charming."

WILLIAM HOWITT TO HIS BROTHER RICHARD.

"*May* 16, '59—The Dale is much finer than I remembered it, and stands well the comparison with other scenery that we have visited. Trains bring lots of people to Ashbourne; and the Dale is crowded on Sundays and holidays, otherwise quiet enough. If all the Waltonians that haunt the Dove, however, caught fish, there could not be much left. Yet I see some fine ones flounce up occasionally, but I let them alone, having 'other fish to fry.' It is wonderful how much the country has become cultivated since I saw it before. All the corn-fields are now on the top of the highest hills, where there only was heather, and where the people thought oats would scarcely ripen. Now it is nearly all wheat; and oat-cakes are almost exploded. We sometimes get some baked as a luxury."

Later on, the writer proposed that his brother should pay us a visit at Thorpe. It was a cross-country journey, that could be made partly by train and partly on foot. He himself would walk twelve miles to meet him at Pentrich. This village was associated in our minds with an incident that had occurred to a friend of ours a few years previously. He had heard one night, when passing a cottage in a row, the drone of a ranter's prayer inside, the words of which became a proverb in an artistic circle : " O Lord ! Thou knowest I am a poor lad from Swanwick ; Thou knowest I can't read ; but blessed be Thy name, I can see the pictures."

Richard Howitt gladly accepted the invitation. He wrote to his brother :—

" *May* 27, 1859.—There is a church at Pentrich, for, if you remember, it was for it that John Lister proposed to have a Parson and Pulpit cast at the Butterley Iron-works.* *That* will be the most certain place to meet at, for what or how many public-houses there may be I don't know. If you leave Thorpe by eight o'clock, I shall be at the churchyard by the time you get there. I say *at*, for *in* is, in these enclosing days, a question to be asked. Ours here is locked up, Heanor is, and Pentrich may be."

After this much-anticipated meeting had been successfully accomplished, and a delightful visit paid us by Richard Howitt, my daughter Margaret and I made a charming excursion into North Staffordshire. We started on June 9, going by train from Ashbourne, reached at noon Alton Towers, and were soon walking in the sixty acres of gardens as if in fairyland ; everywhere beautified by brilliant and delicately hued flowering rhododendrons. Now it is a Dutch garden, very trim and formal, with its orangeries, fountains, and patterned borders in the midst of fine gravel. Now it is a French garden in the style of Louis Quatorze,

---

* This "cast-iron parson" had been mentioned by William Howitt some fifteen years earlier to Thomas Carlyle, who, much tickled by the idea, soon used it in print.

with temples, statues of nymphs and satyrs, and long alleys bordered with flowers. Now a Swiss wilderness, where in the old times, our guide tells us, "women worked in the Swiss costume. My lady had two suits from Switzerland every year for each woman. They did not wear them out of the gardens, because the lads would hoot them. This did once happen to a venturous gardeneress. After that the dress was alone assumed within the park palings." Here again, though the women in Swiss attire are absent, the rhododendrons blaze forth in close communion with masses of golden broom and gorse. Now we are in a Chinese garden, with its artificial sheet of water, bell-hung fountain, and pagoda, its carved bridges, its quaint groups of tall cypresses or yews cut into queer bell-shaped forms crowning circular terraces, and which, when kept in perfect order, was a living picture of garden life in the Celestial Empire.

Most grand palaces and ancestral homes have an old time belonging to their history; but the fair demesne of Alton Towers, dating back but half a century, had risen up in my childhood with surpassing magnificence. Hundreds and thousands of pounds had been lavished upon it. Silver and gold and precious stones, the most elaborately perfected works of man embellished it. The castle and grounds formed a miracle of art and beauty, destined, it seemed, to last until time should be no more. The great Catholic family to whom it belonged seemed to promise equal durability. Strange vicissitudes had, however, occurred. Fierce winds of adversity had shaken to its foundations the ancient house of Shrewsbury; all its honours were stripped and scattered abroad. The seventeenth Earl had died unmarried, on August 10,

1856. The direct line had thus become extinct. The lawyers, like eagles, had gathered round the spoil, and great had been the contest, involving not only titles and lands, but religion. On June 1, 1858, the claim of the Protestant Earl Talbot of Ingestre to the Earldom of Shrewsbury had been allowed. On June 8, 1859, the day previous to our visit to Alton, his right to the Shrewsbury estates *versus* Hope Scott and other Catholics had been decided in London. The verdict had not, however, reached either the village or castle ; and we found doubt, anxiety, and general fear prevailing.

Passing into a vast court, we noticed on a lofty tower the tattered hatchment flapping in the wind. We entered, through an arched doorway, the gorgeous Catholic chapel, and were led onward by a pale-faced young man, with an anxious, depressed countenance, and who could not speak without sighs. To him each ornament of the sacred chapel was, as it were, a bit of his own soul. He pointed out the grand pictures, the jewelled crucifix, the holy emblazonment of the altar, the purport of each gorgeous painted window. Next he drew our attention from the rows of kneeling angels, from the saints and the Blessed Sacrament enshrined in the fair and costly altar, to the grand organ in an opposite upper gallery. "To think," said he, "that it has been silent all these years."—"You love music then ?" we answered. "Better than anything else in this world," was his reply.

"But Mass is celebrated here," I remarked, "though there is no family."—"Only Low Mass," he said, with a mournful cadence, "and therefore no music."—"Do not you yourself play the organ ?" we asked. "Yes, when I have any one to blow for me. There is a servant who does so when he can be spared, and a man in the village who can come sometimes in an evening. It is a splendid organ, with three sets of keys."—"Will you not play for us?" we asked. He looked at us with his melancholy eyes, as if measuring our worthiness; then answered, "Yes, I will."

We left the chapel and ascended two flights of stairs. The first landed us on a level with the gilded gallery, in which the pious family and their friends of old had prayed before their Saviour; the next brought us face to face, as it were, with the mighty slumbering soul of music, which that sad young man was about to awaken. Of course, if he played to us, we must blow, and mounting upon a low step, first one and then the other worked the heavy iron handle which gave breath to the leviathan. The next moment after commencing, the lofty chapel, from the highest centre of its roof to the lowest level of its floor, seemed throbbing and heaving with tempestuous swell of the most wonderful melody. Hard work it was to blow, yet light indeed for such repayment. Not more astonishing than the pulsing, surging torrent of harmony which pealed forth into the silence was the total change in the young man's being.

No longer dim-eyed, dreaming, and melancholy, he sat there an inspired musician, with flushed and up-turned eye. So might a brother of St. Cecilia have appeared. First he poured forth a low, mournful symphony, as if all the surrounding images of angels were lamenting the sorrows and humiliation of the Church. Anything sadder, grander, more heart-rending, could not be conceived. It was as if expression were here given to the immense woe which made our Lord weep over Jerusalem, and as if the young man felt the long silence of the organ, the decadence of the old Catholic line, the threatened spoliation of the chapel, and all the uncertainty of the future were bound up with the sorrow of the Divine Master. Then followed another strain; above the lamenting voices of angels was heard the triumph of the Eternal Church, which no time, no change could overturn; the jubilant utterance of thousands, and tens of thousands, whose garments were washed white in the blood of the Lamb, and who came forth from great tribulation and suffering, from poverty and contempt, to be crowned kings, rejoicing for ever and for ever.

It was a wonderful inspiration. Pearly drops stood on the musician's brow. His eyes were uplifted as if he gazed into the celestial regions of which he prophesied, and a smile of indescribable beauty played round his parted lips. Thanks seemed poor payment for this surpassing entertainment. He did not appear to expect them. Hastily wiping the keys and closing the organ, he walked before us downstairs without a word. I wished from my heart that the Catholic heirs might come into possession, the old faith and worship be maintained, and he be chosen organist.

We took the train to Froghall, walked to the rude moorland village of Ipstones, and there slept. The next morning we proceeded on our way to Apsford, the home of my paternal ancestors, and of which we had deeds dating back to the time of the third Richard. In fact, to visit it was the chief object of this little excursion. On we went, through a district which was unquestionably moorland half a century earlier; large desolate fields enclosed with stone walls, poor land covered with marsh ranunculus and cotton-rush. Here and there the surface was broken up into high ridges, around and upon which were massed, in fantastic confusion, piles of grey rocks. The sky was grey, and melancholy brooded over all, like the spirit of an old northern ballad.

At length we found ourselves at the edge of a deep, wide valley, broken up into little round hills, splintered with crags and shaggy with brambles, bilberries, and birch-trees. A shallow stream slowly tracked its way along the bottom of the chaotic valley. Ascending the other and much smoother side, we found ourselves in the fertile pasture-fields of an old stone-built farmhouse, standing, with its out-buildings and barns, among aged elm and ash trees. This was Apsford. The farmer's wife, in a clean cap with bows of white satin ribbon, opened the door, and cheerfully invited us in. It was a large room into which we entered, with a bare brick floor, yet comfortable and characteristic, with its handsome clock, large cupboard, and broad benches in the wide chimney. In the window stood a splendid arum in flower, and two or three very fine calceolarias. Of our ancestors we could learn nothing. The present farmer had bought the place twenty years previously from "Mester Cotterill, who bought it from the Squire, and beyond this none of their writings went."

After leaving Apsford we walked many miles along the limestone high-road, which, looking backward, we could trace like a loosely waving white ribbon bleaching in the hot afternoon sunshine; then wandering into a more secluded and verdant district, we reached the slumberous village of Caldon, lying under Caldon Low, the highest point of the round, green hills. We were bound to a neat grey stone house, the home of George Wolliscroft, who had been for many years a trusted, confidential clerk of my father's.

In an upstairs sitting-room an old man reposed in an arm-chair near the window, which was gay with scarlet cactus and white geraniums. He was attired in a large, long coat and picturesque wideawake. Invalid habits had accustomed him to his hat until it had become a portion of himself. The broad brim cast a soft shadow upon his handsome countenance and well-chiselled features. We had never been in that house before, yet a strange feeling came over my mind, as if some time or other, in or out of the body, I had been there; had gone up the flight of steps into the small, pleasant parlour; had seen the old patriarch in his tall-backed chair, with his little table and big Bible before him. How was it? Whence come these glimpses as of a past experience in that which is but now occurring? Whence do they come, and what do they indicate?

A whole generation had passed since George Wolliscroft and I last met. We looked, as it were, over the ocean of Time. We talked of many voyagers—some gone into port successfully, others yet far out at sea, driven by storms, and of others who had suffered total shipwreck. The sun of peace shone calmly on the old pilgrim, the billows broke softly at his feet, his soul was surely anchored on the Rock, Christ, and he calmly awaited his call to Eternal Rest.

The shades of night were just beginning to fall as we reached the beautiful, prosperous village of Ellastone, where we intended to sleep. Here all seemed festive. The villagers were standing at the doors of the rose-embowered cottages. The church bells were ringing, till the very air seemed full of melody and rejoicing.

"And why are they ringing?" we ask. "The news has come from London city that the Earl of Shrewsbury has won!"

This was not the little Viscount Ingestre of my childhood, but his next brother, for he had died quite young.

In October 1859 Anna Mary became the wife of Alaric Alfred Watts. By this marriage we gained a most excellent son; the ties of intimacy with our old friends, his parents, were drawn closer; and we continued to enjoy constant personal intercourse with our daughter, for her husband settled near us.

In the spring of 1860 my husband, Margaret, Sister Elizabeth—for the faithful caretaker of my children had become a member of an Anglican sisterhood—and I stayed at Well House, Niton, just within the fringe of beauty and picturesqueness which borders the south-east side of the Isle of Wight.

In our rambles under the clematis-festooned cliff, on the rocky, broken meadow-ground, and by the sea-driven woods, we were occasionally accompanied by Sydney Dobell, who, suffering from rheumatism of the heart, had passed the winter in the island. He idolised Nature after a microscopic fashion; hunted amid a million primroses for one flower that combined in the hue and shape of petals and stem the perfection of seven; rapturously studied the tints of the sparrows' backs, assuring us no two sparrows were alike; and descanted on the varied shades of grey in the stone walls. Yet even this fatiguing minuteness of observation trained the eye to perceive the marvellous perfection, beauty, grace, and diversity of colour and form in the tiny handiworks of the Almighty Creator.

On Saturday, April 21, having heard from Charlton that he was coming down that day to speak with us on business, and should walk from Cowes, we met him three miles from Niton, on the Newport road. The same evening, when going with him to Black Gang, and returning by the shore, we were much affected by learning his desire shortly to emigrate to New Zealand, as an opening had just occurred for his settling with some beloved and highly valued friends of ours in the province of Canterbury. The quiet content and delight with which his mind rested on the plan showed it to be the occupation he yearned after. We had prayerfully to weigh the proposal over and over again through the long hours of the night before we could accept the idea. By the morning his father and I both felt it to be right, and that it would be blessed.

Charlton, we resolved in our minds, was a born naturalist, and possessed every taste and quality needful for a settler in the wilds. As a quaint child, he had made the most extraordinary disclosures about his pet bees, guinea-pigs, and bantams. At fourteen he had especially enjoyed the voyage to Australia, for the sake of the whales, the mollemoke he caught, and the little fly-catcher, which out at sea had spent one day on deck.

Notwithstanding his deep human affections, he was never alarmed by the solitude of the Bush. He was never fatigued, never discouraged—the harder the life the better. On his return from Australia, with his customary industrious, uncomplaining spirit, he had made himself useful, for upwards of five years, in London commerce. But indefatigable in his exertions, he was silently nourishing the hope of eventually emigrating,

and had kept himself in training.   Besides daily thread-
ing the grimy, thronged streets on business, he walked
to and from the City, laboured in the early morning or
evening hours of summer in his large kitchen-garden ;
in winter chopped wood, learnt to make his own clothes,
and never, if he could avoid it, slept in a bed, but on the
floor, rolled in a blanket or his opossum rug.   Yet there
was no exclusive regard to his own advantage : he offered
his hard-earned savings to a suddenly embarrassed friend,
took his fresh vegetables to the old women in the alms-
houses, restored a poor stray dog daubed scarlet by house-
painters to its natural colour and self-respect.   In short,
was always helping, in a practical way, his fellow-creatures.
Thus, as we reviewed his natural, wholesome tastes, his industry, self-denial, and steadfastness of purpose, we were
forced, albeit with a pang, to share his conviction, that it
was right for him to go.

In the summer he studied farming in Lincolnshire
with some kind relatives, who reported him "a desperate
worker, up at five to milk, never a moment idle, and talking to the children in such an amusing manner, that they
hung about him like burrs."

He sailed in November 1860, and after arriving at
Christchurch, encountered equally with our friends unexpected difficulties and disappointments.   Still affecting
all primitive modes, and wishful to redeem a neglected
property in a bay near Lyttelton, he dwelt for some time
in a slab-hut on the slope of a clearing by a mountain
torrent ; surrounded by a happy family of cats, dogs,
and bipeds, for he had acquired the Maori faculty of
calling about him the native birds.   He wrote to me
in December 1861, that, "though he did not express
much, he thought constantly of us, and liked to imagine

what we each were about, as he cleared the bush-land, set potatoes, and made butter. Altogether it was very pleasant."

He was, in fact, enchanted with the sublime mountain and forest scenery, and the different varieties of animal and vegetable life in New Zealand, the Switzerland of the Pacific. It so happened that the solid, hard-working qualities he displayed, and his freedom from all colonial vices, had been observed by members of the Provincial Government, and in August 1862 he received, to his surprise, a summons to Government House on important business. It was to engage him to command an expedition to examine the rivers Hurunui and Taramakau, in the northern part of the Canterbury province, for the purpose of ascertaining whether they contained gold. He hesitated to accept the congenial offer, for "what if he made a mess of it?" until urged to do so by clear-sighted friends.

In September he began following up the Hurunui, one of the innumerable rivers flowing directly east or west from the lofty central chain of Alps which traverses the Middle Island from north to south. These streams, owing to the great fall into the sea, have a most rapid current, which will often sweep away a man, where the water is not more than two feet deep. Charlton, therefore, to assist wayfarers, erected flags as signals at all passable fords, and huts for shelter along the horse-track, which he cut from the head of the river through the hitherto undisturbed Bush over a saddle of the central range.

He next pursued the Taramakau through dense forest to the western beach; coming upon intimations of gold just at the expiration of the three months allotted to the expedition. With the exception of a fortnight, rain or snow had fallen daily, making camping out very cold, and the men, less inured than their leader to exposure and drudgery, refused to exceed the term. The exploration had, however, been conducted with so much energy and perseverance under great difficulties, that on his return to Christchurch he was selected as the most fitting person to take charge of an expedition to open up communication between the Canterbury plains and the newly discovered gold and coal district on the west coast; especially as the road which he had made led more than half-way thither.

This duty was faithfully performed under constant hardships and discouragements. But a few miles remained to be cut, when, at the end of June 1863, after personally rescuing other pioneers and wanderers from drowning and starvation in that watery, inhospitable forest region, Charlton, with two of his men, went down in the deep waters of solitary Lake Brunner; a fatal accident which deprived the Government of a valued servant, and saddened the hearts of all who knew him.

MARY HOWITT TO HER DAUGHTER MARGARET, THEN RESIDING WITH MDLLE. BREMER IN STOCKHOLM.

"*West Hill Lodge, Nov.* 16, 1863.—It is with a very sad heart that I write to you at this time. Dear Mdlle. Bremer will have prepared you for the sorrowful news, which seems incomprehensible; and to our grief for his loss is added our anxiety for you. But the great Comforter is with you as with us; and for how very much we have to be thankful! Few bereaved families have more. Charlton had been instrumental in saving several lives, and if there was no human aid near to save him when in peril, there were angels' hands to lead him up to a higher, safer existence. Thank God that he has been given us to love and rejoice in; that he has done good work; that he has saved life, not taken it; that he has been a pioneer through trackless wastes, opening paths for civilisation and peaceful human existence! There is not a spot or stain upon his memory. Publicly and privately he has been a true, noble Christian. And is it not sweet and lovely to know that his home letters were found in his swag on the lake shore. It shows how he treasured them; and then comes the satisfaction that we were permitted never to fail him in letters.

"Your poor father is very much cut up, and looks very sad; yet he feels all these sources of consolation, and thanks God for them. In some small degree I was prepared for the terrible news. Last Saturday the saddest sense of bereavement possessed my soul. I was persuaded that we should have news of dearest Charlton's departure. I was so distressed that I almost felt unable to do my work. But I forcibly put the feeling aside as fancy. I could not do it wholly. In the evening, looking at the photographs of you, my four dear children, my depression increased. I thought how good Charlton had always been, and I could not remember one instance through his whole life in which he had caused me sorrow. This comforted me, and was doubtless given to me for consolation. On Monday morning dearest Annie came with a letter from your cousin, Edward Howitt, bringing the terrible news. In the afternoon dear Mrs. Todhunter arrived with all the official papers, and a letter from one of the town authorities of Christchurch, saying that all would be done to show honour to his memory."

What a mingled skein of sorrow and joy is human life ! A month after the crushing intelligence of Charlton's sudden removal, at the age of twenty-five, reached us from New Zealand, we were cheered by the news of our son Alfred's happy prospects in Australia. For years we had followed his movements with the deepest anxiety; in 1859, as he successfully executed an arduous journey to the district of Lake Torrens, where, in an arid region of parched deserts, bare, broken, flat-topped hills, dry watercourses, and soda-springs, whose waters effervesced tartaric acid, he, his men, and horses were consumed with thirst; in 1860, as he opened up for the Victorian Government the fine mountainous district of Gippsland, which included the profitable gold-field of the Crooked River; and in 1861, when heading the Government relief party intended to render assistance to the missing discoverer, Robert O'Hara Burke.

Here I must pause to remind the reader that Mr. Burke, an Irish gentleman, furnished with the best-supplied exploring expedition which ever issued from a colonial capital, had been appointed by Victoria to accomplish the great task of traversing the entire Australian continent from south to north. After long suspense, news had reached the Victorian Government that, impeded by the very ample outfit and by the dissensions and disobedience of his officers and men, Burke had from stage to stage dropped behind him, by fragments, detachments of his men, camels, horses, and supplies; and from Cooper's Creek, taking with him an under-officer, Wills, and two men, Gray and King, had pushed on for the Gulf of Carpentaria, and had not since been heard of.

On September 13, 1861, Alfred and his large party came to Burke's depôt at Cooper's Creek, and found papers buried in the *cache*, informing them that Burke and Wills, after reaching the Gulf of Carpentaria on February 11, returned on April 22, and were terribly disappointed to find themselves (although after date) abandoned by those whom they had left in charge of the depôt. A search, which was immediately commenced for the missing explorers, ended in the discovery of the sole survivor, King—a melancholy object, wasted to a shadow, who had been living for upwards of two months with a friendly tribe of aborigines. Weakness, or overjoy at his rescue, made conversation with him difficult, but he was at length able to explain the course of events.

Gray, who had been accused of shamming illness by his companions, had died of exhaustion on the return journey. The impetuous Burke, after reaching Cooper's Creek, and when, being without provisions, their strength gave way, taking the narrator with him, had made a desperate attempt to push on for aid to the cattle-station at Mount Hopeless. He left the gentle, submissive Wills behind, with a supply of nardoo-seed, which, pounded into flour and cooked as porridge, afforded a slight nourishment. Burke, succumbing in the effort, told King when he was dying to put his pistol in his right hand, and leave him unburied as he lay. After obeying the injunction, the survivor returned to Wills, whom he found a corpse, with the wooden bowl near him in which he had prepared his last meal of nardoo; and of which, poor fellow! he had written it was not "unpleasant starvation."

Wills breathed his last in a native hut, erected on a sand-bank, and King had carefully covered the remains with sand; but as Alfred discovered that they had been disturbed, probably by dogs, he carefully reinterred all the bones that could be found, read 1 Corinthians xv. over them, and cut an inscription on an adjacent gum-tree. He found Burke's skeleton in a little hollow, lying face upwards in a bed of tall, dead marsh-mallows, and shaded by a clump of box-trees; under it a spoon, and at its side the loaded and capped revolver. He consigned it to the earth wrapped in the British flag, and cut an inscription on a box-tree to indicate the spot.

We next heard of our son being employed in 1862, by command of the Victorian Government, to bring the bones of the two ill-fated explorers to Melbourne for public interment. He returned with his sacred charge through South Australia, and although impeded for many weeks by rain and floods, in the summer month of December safely reached Adelaide. There he received an enthusiastic welcome from the citizens, and enjoyed the hospitality of Judge Boothby, the fast friend and political ally of my husband, dating from the Nottingham days. Under his roof "Howitt the Explorer" felt singularly at home; and learnt to appreciate, during a fortnight of public demonstrations, whirl, and excitement, the grace and domestic virtues of his future wife. Ministers of state and crowding thousands attended the remains of Burke and Wills to the strains of the Dead March in "Saul," first to the barracks, where they were temporarily deposited; thence to the steamer *Havillah*, which conveyed them to Melbourne. In that city they were buried with pomp and solemnity, on January 21, 1863.

It was the joyful intelligence of Alfred's approaching union with Maria Boothby, and his settled post under Government in his favourite district, Gippsland, which had, the following December, so much soothed us in our bereavement. A happy and most useful future seemed in store for him; and this promise, under a merciful Providence, has hitherto been fulfilled.*

A few passages taken from the voluminous family correspondence will now sufficiently indicate the manner of life led at West Hill Lodge.

MARY HOWITT TO HER DAUGHTER MARGARET.

" *May* 23, 1861.—On Sunday your father and I went to the Batemans', of Clapton, as a farewell visit to them at The Elms. Then, when they were gone to chapel, we went to the Freiligraths', and had a very nice call. I am quite charmed with Kätchen, now in her sixteenth year, a sweet, artless, lively young creature, a blending of the girl and the woman. I want to make her acquainted with your cousins; they would be delighted to know her.

" On Monday your father, Annie, Alfred, and I went to a very grand evening 'At Home' at Mrs. Milner Gibson's. Such a crush, such a jam of carriages in the street, such a crowd on the pavement to see the arrivals! Everybody, almost, was there. Gentlemen in ribbons and stars; ladies blazing in diamonds, in silks that would stand on end, and gossamer dresses like

---

* " *Le jeune Howitt, l'heureux explorateur,*" as the Count de Beauvoir calls him in his work on Australia, has since that period been successfully employed in other public undertakings. He has, in connection with his duties as Gold Warden in Gippsland, devoted much attention to geology. He has likewise published with a friend, the Rev. Lorimer Fison, a learned work on some of the Australian aborigines, entitled " Kamilaroi and Kurnai."

spider-webs; ambassadors white and black. Yes, black; for he of Hayti was there. We saw actually almost everybody we knew—the Dickenses, Thackeray, literary people without end, and lots of Members of Parliament. The M——s were there; and when I saw Emily, with the same face that I had known so well of old, I felt, notwithstanding her estrangement from us, a great kindness spring up in my heart towards her. I went to her and offered her my hand; but with concentrated scorn and contempt she turned away, saying, 'No, she would not shake hands with me.' I have sometimes thought, when praying 'Forgive us our trespasses, as we forgive those who trespass against us,' that I never had such to forgive, for all are kind and good to me. I walked quietly away, and thought that here at least was one to be forgiven.* In writing don't speak of this, because it would be very painful to your father to know what had occurred."

Mrs. Alfred Watts to her Sister.

"*June* 10, 1861.—Yesterday Adelaide Procter was with us for the afternoon and evening—the second time that she has been to see us lately. I like her as much as I like her poetry. I mean to bring her and Julia L—— acquainted, for they are quite sisters. Miss Procter believes all that is most holy and wonderful in spiritualism, for all fervent Catholics more or less experience the same. This has brought us very near in the spirit. Many of the most wonderful teachings which I have received spiritually, I find, are received by the most introverted Catholics. Is it not interesting? She and Julia are made to know each other."

---

* The lady, who was then labouring under a misapprehension, later evinced a spirit of conciliation.

"*June* 20, 1861.—We went to a great pre-Raphaelite crush on Friday evening. Their pictures covered the walls, and their sketch-books the tables. The uncrinolined women, with their wild hair, which was very beautiful, their picturesque dresses and rich colouring, looked like figures out of the pre-Raphaelite pictures. It was very curious. I think of it now like some hot, struggling dream, in which the gorgeous and fantastic forms moved slowly about. They seemed all so young and kindred to each other, that I felt as if I were out of my place, though I admired them all, and really enjoyed looking over Dante Rossetti's huge sketch-book.

"On Saturday afternoon the Hon. Mrs. C—— came to inquire of me about spiritualism as we understand it, because from the religious point of view she can alone accept it. She stayed about three hours. She is seeking for an inner life, for a closer communion with the Saviour, than she finds in the outward forms of the Church of England. She begged that the Marchioness of Londonderry might come also, and hear what we had to say on the same important subject. It was arranged, therefore, that she was to come on Tuesday, I thinking that if it was our dear Lord's will that these great ladies came to such a poor little fountain as myself, He would supply the water, and therefore I left all in His hands.

"On Tuesday I was so tired that I could do nothing but read Mdlle. Bremer's work preparatory to translation. In the afternoon Lady Londonderry came. I had to tell her of our higher experiences and teachings, all of which seemed to interest her. Her eyes filled with tears as she looked at Annie's drawings. She knew her 'Art Student,' and was evidently a lover of art. She stayed

about two hours. She was leaving for the Continent
the next day, but asked to be allowed, on her return,
to come again, and also that a friend of hers, a priest,
might come and have some talk with us."

"*July* 10, 1861.—Annie and Adelaide Procter had a
very pleasant and most interesting visit, the day before
yesterday, to Julia at Hampton Court. Julia was ill,
and suffering, but she and Adelaide made in the spirit
a wonderful compact of love and unity. I fancy great
good will grow out of this visit.

"Adelaide Procter gave Annie many beautiful and touching particulars of Mrs. Browning's death. She did not
appear to suffer much, and became quite conscious before
her departure. She spoke to her husband very calmly
of the beautiful land to which she was going, and which
she already saw. Everybody is especially sorry for her
little boy, who has never been away from his mother's
side. I cannot myself doubt but that her loving spirit
will be permitted to watch over him, now with even
greater yearning and affection than before."

To Mrs. Alfred Watts.

"*Penmaenmawr, Oct.* 6, 1861.—Yesterday was a busy
day to me, in this way. I had been very anxious to write
the poem I had promised Adelaide Procter for the 'Victoria Regia.' I was afraid I could not manage it. However, in the night my mind was filled with a subject
which came very clearly, and yesterday I wrote it. I
hope it is good, for I have a great desire to stand well
amongst the women."

"*Oct.* 13, 1861.—We have had a wild, bright autumnal

day, clouds scudding over the mountains, the tide very
high, the sea the colour of bottle-glass, ruffled and
crested over with spray. I have such pleasure in watching the features of the sea. Your father is reading at this
moment 'The Co-operator,' a year's volume of the paper
published by the co-operative people in Manchester, who
seem to be doing wonders. They have now a capital of
two millions, a cotton-factory, shops, and mills, and are
really making great headway. It is a fine movement,
and he is, of course, extremely interested in it, because
he was one of the earliest advocates of co-operation.
He now seems to see a remedy for a great many evils
under which the age and the race are growing. It
is a wonderful step forward in the right direction. I
expect, now that the 'History of England' is just com-
pleting,* and your father more at leisure, that he will
work for it. I so thoroughly believe that the *smallest*
events are ordered by a Higher Power, if we will only
let It be our guide, that I open my mind to the idea."

"*Farnsfield, Nov.* 23, 1861.—My dearest daughters,
we are, you see, at your aunt Elizabeth's, where we
have had a most kind reception. It was regular winter
at Heanor; from the windows a wide white landscape
and the bright sun shining golden on the tops of the
bare and the half-leafless trees. Your uncle Francis and

---

* William Howitt had been engaged for several years by John Cassell on a
"History of England." Lord Brougham, at the opening of the Social Science
Congress at Glasgow, and in reference to the paper-duty, said, "John Cassell's
'History of England,' in penny numbers, circulates 100,000 weekly." He
also characterised it as a history "in which the soundest principles are laid
down in almost every instance. The interests of virtue, of liberty, and of
peace, the best interests of mankind, are faithfully and ably maintained
throughout."

VOL. II.   K aunt Maria gave us a most cordial welcome; and we went to meeting with the dear people."

To Charlton Howitt in New Zealand.

"*Feb.* 19, 1862.—Tell us everything about yourself. You do not, or you would not have left us to hear of your heroic conduct at the Kays' in the fire, when you rushed in, with a wet blanket over your head, and saved all that was saved. Mr. Joseph Kay told us of it at Miss Coutts's the other evening. And Sir James Kay Shuttleworth was so full of you and your noble conduct, and steady, hard-working, trustworthy character, that he wished it were possible for you to join his brother.

"For ourselves, dear Charlton, we are a solitary old couple just now. Meggie is at Penmaenmawr, and is gathering together the material for a three-volume story which I have engaged to write for Mr. Blackett. Your father is still busy on his 'Lex Magna' or the 'Great Law' of the supernatural which pervades the universe. The subject becomes to him more and more interesting the further he advances. I am just now commencing the translation of another work of Mdlle. Bremer's, Greece and its islands. Last year I translated her 'Holy Land.'"

The Same to the Same.

"*March* 12, 1862.—We spent recently a very pleasant evening at Dr. Blatherwick's, with our neighbours, Lord and Lady Dufferin. You know who they are. He is one of the Queen's equerries, and a great favourite at Court; and she—his mother—is the sister of the Hon. Mrs. Norton and the Duchess of Somerset, who was the

Queen of Love and Beauty at the Eglinton tournament. They are most agreeable, with all that charming ease and grace of manner which belongs to their class. She was very merry about their gipsying frolic on Bookham Common, when they encountered your father, and got put into a book. She says that Lord Dufferin, who was then about eleven, was dressed up as a little gipsy girl; but your father did not see him. She persists that he gave them eighteenpence. He says 'no;' but she says 'yes.' So how it was I cannot tell. Lord Dufferin interested us very much by telling us about his travels in Nubia and amongst the Druses. Still more so about the discoveries of his friend Cyril Graham, who has come upon the most wonderful cities in some remote deserts on this side the Euphrates. They are so immensely old that nothing is known of them, and they are shunned by the Arabs as haunted. Some Arabs told him about a vast city called 'The White City,' built by the daughter of the King of the Panthers. After much persuasion he induced some Arabs to accompany him to the place. Far, far away, many days' journey in the desert, they came upon what, in the distance, looked like a low range of white hills. It was the walls of 'The White City.' All was apparently in perfect preservation. The gates in the walls stood half-open—huge white stone gates on their ponderous stone hinges, as if the inhabitants had only just passed out of them. It was the same with the substantial white stone houses. But there have been no dwellers there for thousands of years.

"One of the most beautiful features in Lord Dufferin's character is his attachment to his mother. He has unbounded admiration for her, and she, a lovely, most gifted woman, has the same for him. He told us that when he came of age his mother wrote him some very beautiful lines ; and as he wished to show his love and respect for her, and in order to do honour to these verses, he determined to build a tower on his Irish estate to contain them.   Accordingly he built at Clandeboye what he calls 'Helen's Tower.'   To make it still more worthy, he asked Tennyson to give him an inscription for it.   Tennyson did so by return of post.   He repeated these lines to us.   I am sorry I can remember but four of them, which, if not literally these, are very like them :—

> ' Helen's Tower, here I stand,
> Dominant over sea and land.
> Son's love built me, and I hold
> Mother's love engraved in gold.'

"Then it goes on to say that the Tower, being only ' stone and lime,' would perish by the hand of Time, but mother's love was immortal.

"Lady Dufferin and Lady Jane Hay were here the other afternoon.   After their call, your father met them again in Millfield Lane, where some rude lads had been throwing stones, not only at each other, but at them. He could not leave them unprotected amongst the young savages, and at their request escorted them home."

To Mrs. Alfred Watts.

"*Pen-y-Bryn, Aber, May* 20, 1862.—Please let our maids fetch my Bible from my seat in the Congregational Chapel—it is an old one that I greatly value ; and remember me very kindly to them, and say I hope they go regularly to chapel.

"I shall think of you most lovingly to-morrow, when you have your visitor.   It will be made agreeable to you, I believe, and all the sting and bitterness be removed.

Be very quiet; let your guest talk, resting with a prayer in your soul for God's holy peace. We are reading of an evening a very excellent essay on the ' Miracles of Ecclesiastical History of the Early Ages,' by John Henry Newman. I am sure these Roman Catholics are very near the truth. Ask Adelaide Procter if she knows it, and do give my love to her."

To CHARLTON HOWITT.

" *Pen-y-Bryn, May* 23, 1862.—Here we are again in Wales; and I shall get Annie, who is coming to us, to make a sketch of this nice old place for you.

"I am glad to tell you that Miss Meteyard, who always behaves so nobly to her relatives, is getting on in the world. It is really most pleasant to think of her enjoying a little sunshine after all the shadows which she has had in her life. We have been instrumental in her obtaining £1000 for her biography of Wedgwood. The MSS. from which she is writing it have been lent her by a gentleman of Liverpool, who met with them in a very curious way. They had been sold as refuse-paper to a marine store-dealer, who had an attic full of them. He could do nothing with a great portion of them, as they were not suited to sell to butter-and-cheese-men. They proved to be the private papers, ledgers, and journals of Wedgwood, the great genius of the Staffordshire Potteries. They were invaluable, yet to the marine store-dealer they were rubbish, and he was glad to part with them for a small sum."

Pen-y-Bryn, which we were occupying during the early summer of 1862, was a very old, dilapidated, but picturesque, ivy-covered farm-house, standing on a pleasant knoll, facing the Menai Straits and Anglesey, with wooded mountains at the back.

Our landlord, Mr. Jones, was a tenant farmer, and a widower with a grown-up son. Winifred, their middle-aged cook and housekeeper, was good-tempered, loquacious, Welsh to the backbone, with bright, brown eyes, a keen intellect, and very communicative. Until Mrs.

PEN-Y-BRYN.

Jones's death, she told us, she had been housekeeper at the Castle Hotel, Conway, where she left two hundred tongues in pickle. By the bye, it was a mistake to call Pen-y-Bryn the identical palace of the princes of North Wales, that had stood on the round green mound by the village; or to say that from the topmost window, now partially closed, in the old tower, Llewellyn had shown his faithless wife the body of her Black William hanging

on a tree in the garden. No; the present house was
built in the French style by one of King Henry VIII.'s
agents, who had dealings with France.

Winifred was an industrious reader of her weekly
Welsh paper, and a long way ahead of us in politics.
The revised code of education had just come into operation, and she feared its effect on the Welsh schools. "In
a debate in Parliament," she remarked, "the member for
Bangor,—shame on him!—had set light by the Welsh
tongue, but her paper had given him an excellent dressing. Then there was 'Essays and Reviews,' one of the
seven writers being the Rev. Dr. Rowland Williams, a
Welshman. She wondered would he be suspended. She
too found the Bible admitted of great differences of in-
terpretation; she nevertheless stuck by the miracles, but
did not push the supernatural so far as to believe in
apparitions. King David had settled the point when he
said he should go to his dead child, but it would not
return to him. Still less did she pin her faith on the
knockers who were said to be heard in these parts wherever treasure was hidden. She was, however, no sceptic,
as every Welsh reader might see in her printed essay on
'Time, the Creature of God.'"

Returning on this occasion to Aber, after an absence
of four years, we perceived that if the Welsh are capable
of long resentment, they are equally so of long gratitude.
As we were desirous of hiring a horse, two young men
named Roberts begged us "to accept the use of their
pony for some days, out of respect." Asking an explanation, the brothers said, "They would take no money for
several excursions, because we had earlier shown sympathy
when their cow died, and had been in the habit of talking to their old mother." I could cite other instances

corroborating an assertion made to us by Dr. Norton, an experienced English physician settled in Wales, that "the Welsh are the most grateful people he ever knew."

An Englishman of high position, who did much to promote the progress of agriculture on his Welsh estates, and to infuse into the kindly but lymphatic race a spirit of improvement, good management, and general alertness, had lately bought considerable property at Aber, including Pen-y-Bryn. He was not aware—so his new tenantry believed—of the head gamekeeper encouraging an enormous increase of rabbits, which ate up the pasturage, until the cattle had to be driven from field to field in search of grazing ground. The rabbits were the keeper's perquisite, and he meant to kill them off for market before his master came for pheasant-shooting in autumn. From the end of June the cruel system began of catching the rabbits in toothed traps, which, after being set, were never visited under twenty-four hours.

Mr. Jones and his son, as tenants, were afraid to meddle with the proceedings of the keepers, although the latter set five traps, to the great danger of the shepherd-dogs and lambs in the paddock behind Pen-y-Bryn, where not a rabbit-hole was found. Nor was it long before we were suddenly awakened one midnight by the terrible howls of a dog, evidently caught in one of these traps. It proving impossible to rouse the Joneses, William threw on part of his dress, ran up the field, and released the victim, a handsome shepherd-dog and general favourite, which, though recognising its deliverer, snapped in its agony and bit his arm.

This misadventure brought matters to a climax so far as our stay at Aber was concerned, more especially as two of the under-keepers called on my husband to desire him to keep up his own little dog Prin, a creature ignorant of game. He could not stand this injustice, so we quitted picturesque Pen-y-Bryn, which, if the truth must be told, was much infested with rats, and when shut up at night, considerably musty, fusty, and dry-rotty.

We went back, therefore, to another favourite haunt, Penmaenmawr, and took up our quarters in Plas Isa, a new house, loftily situated, where we had the unmarried sister of Charles Darwin for fellow-lodger, and where we enjoyed a glorious view of open sea, the fine promontory of the Great Orme's Head, rocky Puffin Island, and the flat, wooded shore of Anglesey.

Our stay at Pen-y-Bryn and the incident with the trap had the beneficial result of drawing public attention to the cruel system of trapping carried on in game-preserves. My husband, who had its abolition much at heart, wrote eloquent letters on the subject in the *Morning Star*, which was the principal cause, as stated by the Secretary, that the Committee of the Royal Society for the Prevention of Cruelty to Animals, offered a reward of £50 for an improved vermin-trap to supersede the cruel ones generally used. One hundred models were sent in, and the Committee invited him to give them, with other competent judges, the advantage of his experience in the examination of these traps.

In this inspection, on May 24, 1864, he saw a great number of admirable inventions, but none likely to supersede the old rat-trap in use by millions all over Great Britain and Wales. Most of the inventions, such as the coffer-trap, the pit-fall, and weight-fall, had been in existence in some form for centuries, but none could compete in cheapness, lightness, and efficacy with the old rat-trap,

which, easily set, fixed its steel fangs in the leg of any
vermin, from a fox to a mouse, and though causing excru-
ciating agony, preserved it alive. The publicity given by
my husband's knowledge of the rabbit cruelties occasioned
many humane and influential individuals, amongst them
notably Charles Darwin and his wife, to work vigorously
for the abolition of the system of torture, and on various
estates it was promptly prohibited.

A glance at some of the correspondence of this period
must bring this long chapter to a close.

MARY HOWITT TO MISS LLOYD JONES.

" *West Hill Lodge, Oct.* 29, 1863.—Thank you for
your last kind note, with its news about yourselves
and dear old Penmaenmawr, of which I am so fond.
Once more I have begun my work " (the novel laid in the
neighbourhood of Penmaenmawr, and called " The Cost
of Caergwyn "), " and I hope now, with God's blessing, to
bring it to a speedy conclusion. But I still want your
help, and am more obliged to you than I can tell for the
aid you have given. I wrote to Mr. Newman Hall, when
he was at Llandudno, to ask Mr. Parry some questions
for me, as I think he told you ; and, after all, it seems I
was indebted to you for some of the answers. Please tell
me how the announcements of preachers at the chapels
are headed. I need this in Welsh in the true form. I
have seen such placards, which seem to me to begin, ' *Y
Parch* Silas Richards,' and so on.

" The regular autumn storms appear to be commencing
with us. We have had for the last two days a wild west
wind, which has howled and raved round the house and
down the chimneys like a regular fury. How grand it
must be with you ! I have been living in your country,

however, all this summer; I have had all seasons in it; and very pleasant it has been to me."

To Margaret Howitt.

"*Scalands-Gate, April* 9, 1864.—On Tuesday it was bitterly cold, with sleet, but I had written to Mrs. Burgess, the wife of the gamekeeper in Barbara's house, to say we were coming; and so come I did with Sarah. She was very melancholy, never having been above four miles away from home in her life. However, she got here safely, and wrote word to Cook that the country is a garden of prim-roses.

"On the platform I met dear Bessie Parkes. She was going to be at 'Brownes.' She was accompanied by the good old nurse who had attended her night and day through her illness. This illness was caused by her sorrow at Adelaide Procter's death. All that she had done for months was with reference to this beloved friend. She went here and there to gather up information to impart to Adelaide, whose great solace in her long illness was being talked to. She could listen for hours, and in this manner forget her pain. She did not entirely keep her bed until a day or two before her departure. She sat up, wearing a pale blue jacket, with her hair beautifully arranged under a little cap. She looked scarcely changed by her sufferings; and a very short time before her decease she received from the biographer of the Curé d'Ars a little souvenir of the holy priest, with which she was enchanted.

"When we reached Robertsbridge station Bessie ex-claimed, 'How do you do, Burgess, and how are your wife and the babies?' giving the gamekeeper her hand. Then she turned and greeted a smiling little old man with white hair. He was her attendant from Brownes, whilst Burgess had come for me. Yesterday I again met Burgess and a man wheeling a barrow-load of heath. I joined him, and walked back with him through the plantations. 'I have been to fetch the heath Madame wished for,' he said. I asked how far they had been. 'Half a mile farther than you met us. I could have got it much nearer, but Madame had some liking for that place ; and I am always glad to please her in everything.' So Burgess and I walked through the woods, and talked about trapping rabbits and 'varmint.' I am glad to say he generally takes rabbits by the snare 'which catches them round the neck, you see.'

" Barbara has built her cottage upon the plan of the old Sussex houses, in a style which must have prevailed at the time of the Conquest. It is very quaint, and very comfortable at the same time."

WILLIAM HOWITT TO HIS BROTHER RICHARD.

" *Scalands-Gate, April* 19, 1864.—I have joined Mary amongst the South Saxons awhile, to smell the primroses on the banks and in the woods. We are occupying for a few weeks the cottage of Madame Bodichon—Barbara Leigh Smith that was. She and her husband spend the winters in Algiers, and do not return till towards the end of May. The country is a hop-growing one, and is pleasantly diversified with hill, dale, and woods, which are now chiefly kept for growing hop-poles, and many of them have very little timber in them, but the walks through them are most pleasant. This house stands on a hill in the midst of one of these woods. In the openings are various kennels of pointers, retrievers, and beagles, which are used in the shooting season by Madame Bodichon's brothers

and brother-in-law, General Ludlow.   They give us plenty
of dog-music.

"The district is a thoroughly farming one, and has a
queer sort of dialect.   The peasants call daffodils Lent-
lilies, and wood-anemones snowdrops.   Wood-peckers
they call Gellie-birds, and the blind-worm the deaf-adder.
This property is three miles long, so we can range about
without fear of trespass.   We have had the pleasure of
Annie's company last week.   She knows the neighbourhood, having been here once or twice before with Barbara
in their maiden days.   Bessie Parkes, too, is making a
little sojourn at a house belonging to Ben Smith, just a
nice walk from us over the fields."

MARY HOWITT TO HER DAUGHTER MARGARET.

"*Scalands-Gate, May* 8, 1864.—Mrs. Todhunter has
been with us, and I hoped she enjoyed the little visit as
much as we did her society.   The whole landscape is now
diversified with all that sweet variety of vernal greens,
which to my taste is more beautiful than the richer
tints of autumn.   Then the wonderful beauty of the earth
covered with blue-bells, the budding woods, and above
them the blue sky; only the earth is bluer than sky.   How
lovely the woods are! always reminding me of Dante Rossetti's colouring.   The nightingales, blackbirds, thrushes,
the shouting cuckoos, and little mole-crickets keep up an
everlasting singing and chorusing in the air.   I hear at this
moment a loud-throated nightingale warbling forth from an
amber-tinted oak-tree that rises from a sea of young birches,
chestnuts, and horn-beams.   Oh! it is delicious."

TO MRS. TODHUNTER.

"*May* 12, 1864.—I have been to-day to hunt out the

ruins of Robertsbridge Abbey, and am quite pleased with what I have seen. There are some fine remains built into a farm-house. The grand old crypt of the Abbey is the dairy and larder, now filled with a wonderful display of the good things of this earth. The garden was full of flowers, with rockeries made of old carved capitals, corbels, and saints' heads. A deaf and dumb gardener was mowing the grass with a machine. I thought of you on my walk, and wished you had been with me, for you would have enjoyed it, as I did. We shall be positively here till the 18th."

Aldborough, especially interesting as the home of the poet Crabbe, was visited in the autumn of the same year. Pitchcombe, in Gloucestershire, as well as France, Switzerland, and Heidelberg, were resorted to in 1865. In the following year, after staying at Penmaenmawr, we removed from West Hill Lodge, intending to settle once more in our favourite old neighbourhood of Esher, for we were still enamoured of its commons and fir woods.

Until our new home could be ready for us, we took a furnished house in the row of villas built on the site of our former picturesque residence, The Hermitage. Here we remained from November 1866 to the spring of 1867. At this time my husband was engaged on his topographical work, "The Northern Heights of London," descriptive of Hampstead, Highgate, and Islington.

CHAPTER V.

THE ORCHARD.

1866-1870.

WE rented in the autumn of 1866 the cottage of our friend Sister Elizabeth, in the parish of Claygate, near Esher. We altered and somewhat enlarged it, laid out an extensive flower and fruit garden, called our new home The Orchard, and imagined we should never rove again.

Fleeming Jenkin, the late lamented electrician, and his wife, two remarkably bright, clever young people, were amongst our fellow-parishioners; and universal regrets were mingled with warm congratulations when his acceptance of a professorship at Edinburgh deprived the neighbourhood of their society.

At first my husband and I luxuriated in our large garden. We trained our plants with the greatest love, and under the healthy influence of mother-earth had neither of us felt better for years. Secker, the gardener, though a crotchety old man, was an admirable coadjutor, mowing and sweeping the smooth lawn with untiring diligence. He implied great satisfaction at all the young birds being spared in the nests; and mentioned how, when one of his hens deserted some ducks' eggs, he hatched them himself in his bosom. Lord Bacon says: "God Almighty first planted a garden, and indeed it is the purest of human pleasures;" and we believed him.

But weeks and months passed on, and we grew less satisfied. Perhaps after all it was a mistake to treat tenderly
all those birds who swarmed in the big chestnut-tree by
our chamber window, chattered from daybreak, demolished
the peas wholesale, and grew so audaciously familiar that,
to quote Secker, "he saw two wrens brow-beating the
kitten." Perhaps the manual labour, the burden of the
garden, and other petty vexations troubled us because
we were growing old.

The manner in which our life in The Orchard passed
is indicated in the following passages from letters :—

Mrs. Alfred Watts to her Uncle, Richard Howitt.

"*Feb.* 21, 1867.—Alas! now, for me, I suppose that
at the end of next week my dear people will. have
migrated to Esher. Glad shall I be for them, but most
sorry for ourselves, as the gap they leave behind them
will be dreadful. It is pleasant, however, to think of
them watching the opening of spring in their lovely
neighbourhood, and of all the walks they will have
through the old scenes. I do not like the situation as
well as West End Cottage, which is on the other side
of Esher; but their home will be very picturesque and
elegant. It is within a short walk of the gates of
Claremont Park."

The Same to her Sister Margaret.

"*The Orchard, Aug.* 25, 1867.—We are curious to
know how you passed your first Sunday in Scotland.
Sabbaths I should rather dread there, for my own part.
Yesterday—Sunday—was a beautiful sunny morning.
The dear Pater went to the station to meet Prince George
of Solms, who duly made his appearance by the 9.30

train. Mother and I, as we sat in her room, saw them walking across the green. We all of us walked about the garden and talked. Then we sat in the drawing-room and talked. After four o'clock we went to Claremont, which Prince George was especially anxious to see, that he might describe it minutely to his Queen, who dreads the thought of residing at Claremont, from the belief that she should die there. We walked all through those

THE ORCHARD.

lovely poetical grounds, sat on the mound beneath the observatory, and by the lake-side. All looked most beauti-ful—far more so than Prince George expected. Yet he felt a great melancholy about the place. It had to him a funereal character. Certainly it was full of a solemn poetry—something very peculiar, especially about what I call the 'Enchanted Island.'

" On Saturday a very interesting Swedish gentleman was here. His uncle was chamberlain to the King of Sweden. He had himself, being very pious, joined the *Läsäre* sect, and found many worldly disadvantages accrue therefrom. He had therefore gone to the United States, entered the army, and fought on the Northern side in the civil war; serving for six months in the same division as the Orleans princes. They were very friendly with him, and invited him to visit them at Claremont. He was in ten battles, and was severely wounded in the leg, which gives him a slight halt. He became acquainted with members of the Society of Friends in America, and after the war, had become so thoroughly convinced of their principles, that now nothing would induce him to raise his hand against any man, not even to save his life. He has come to England to settle among Friends. He journeyed down to Esher to call on the French princes, but found, to his surprise, that they had quitted Claremont. Then he came on to us."

Mary Howitt to her Daughter Margaret.

" *Sept.* 2, 1867.—We find little Raphael Weldon one of the best of children. Secker is mowing the grass at this moment, and he, harnessed like a pony, is drawing the machine. The Pater calls him 'Young Meritorious,' and he is quite pleased with his name."

" *Sept.* 3. — Yesterday afternoon we took Raphael with us to call on the Hertslets; and in coming back along the lane we met two gentlemen, one of whom claimed us as an acquaintance. It was no other than Josiah Gilbert, the son of one of the authoresses of 'Original Poems,' &c., and nephew of Isaac Taylor. He belonged to our Nottingham days. He is, you may remember, an artist. He is a very superior man, is a member of the Alpine Club, and has, in conjunction with his friend, G. C. Churchill, explored a new and most interesting mountain district called the Dolomite Country, and which now, through their graphic descriptions, will doubtless speedily become the haunt of other Englishmen. He and his companion, Mr. Bevan, came back with us to tea."

"*Sept.* 5.—My dear niece Mary and my great-niece little Agnes are now with us. The latter and Raphael are the best of friends, and their ringing laughter comes to us in the garden, through the open window, as they sit in the dining-room painting the Stars and Stripes and the Union Jack for each other's amusement.

" Agnes is a little free-spoken American, full of fun and *dash*. Raphael is more silent and contemplative. They sit painting pictures together for hours at a time. I feel quite proud of them both."

" *Sept.* 9.—I am going to take the children this afternoon to Claremont. I shall sit and read *Good Words* while they play about.

" *Evening.*—We have been to Claremont, and were caught in down-pouring rain. It began to rain coming back just as we were passing the house. We hastened to the lodge, where the gatekeeper lent us his umbrella. Great fun it was to the children. They laughed all the way home, and seem none the worse for the wetting."

" *Sept.* 21.—I had, on Saturday a letter from the Secretary of the Religious Tract Society, enclosing a tract entitled 'A Sermon on the Welsh Hills.' It was the sermon I made Christmas Evans preach in the 'Cost of Caergwyn.' It had been submitted in manuscript to the Committee, much liked by them, and ordered to be printed. The *author* being written to, it came out that it was taken from a novel of mine; and a copy of the book being obtained, was found there almost verbatim. An aged friend of the Secretary, who had heard Christmas Evans preach forty years ago, was able to vouch for the genuineness of the sermon, but instead of his rewriting it from memory, the Society preferred printing, with permission, my version.

"Of course, I have given permission for them to use the sermon, which they say will evidence the Saviour's love to thousands whom my book will never reach. I suppose the aged friend believes he actually heard this sermon of my invention preached by Christmas Evans. It is odd if I should unwittingly have imagined circumstances that actually occurred more than half a century ago."

To Madame Bodichon.

"*Oct.* 15, 1867.—It is several months now since we heard that you were ill. It made us very sad, for we had always connected the idea of perfect health and power with you, so that we could not reconcile ourselves to the thought of your being an invalid. We were all in the confusion of our removal into the country, with workmen in almost every room, the whole garden to make, and everything to do, so that I had hardly a minute to spare for anything but the demand of the moment; therefore I did not write to express the sorrow and anxiety which we felt. Then we heard you were better, and we supposed quite well and returned to Algeria. Now, on the contrary, we find you are still delicate and in England; therefore I at once send you this to express our sincere sympathy, and beg of you to take such care and to use such means as are necessary to restore you to health.

"Again, I say, it makes me very sad, for it is another instance in which the noble-minded, energetic woman yields under the force of that mental and physical exertion which her better and larger knowledge and awakened activity have made, as it were, a necessity of her being. That my dear Annie broke down under the strain upon her naturally delicate frame did not seem to me extraordinary; but that you, dear Barbara, should now be ordered into a state of rest does seem very sorrowful; and my best and most affectionate desire is, that you will be wise and rest, and thus regain your blessed health, and with it all your glorious natural powers and full ability again to work.

"You can imagine how surprised we were to hear of dear Bessie Parkes's marriage with M. Belloc. None wish her happiness more sincerely than I do, for she is a fine creature, and deserves it as much as any."

To Mrs. Alfred Watts.

"*Oct.* 29, 1867.—The leaves are falling, the flowers fading, and every now and then such lovely days occurring that really it is quite heavenly. Margaret and I are busy converting all the old apparel we can lay our hands on into little frocks and petticoats, and all sorts of small garments for the poor in the neighbourhood of the docks. Young Mr. Grimm, at Claremont, who seems most benevolent, has begged one of the women-Friends here to collect all the relief of this kind that lies in her power for these poor half-starved, half-naked people. So we

are doing our small endeavours, and have as much
pleasure in our little hoard as if it were something very
valuable."

To the Same.

"*March* 7, 1868.—Our Dorcas Meeting here went off
very well. There were about a dozen ladies, and a good
deal of work was done. It is the Dissenter class which
composes this benevolent society; and the Mothers'
Meeting held every Monday at the Friends' Meeting-house
seems quite a success. It is astonishing, however, what
little poverty there is in the neighbourhood. If the
husbands were sober all would be well-to-do. It is the
same at Hersham, which forms one parish with Walton.
The poor there have many bequests, 'The Beggar's
Gift' being a most curious one. It seems that some two
hundred years ago a beggar came down in these parts
begging. He was flogged in the parishes of Wandsworth
and Kingston. In that of Walton he was well treated.
Shortly afterwards he died, leaving a will, by which he
bequeathed a whip to the two parishes which made him
feel it, and to Walton all his wealth. This now brings in
for the poor of Walton and Hersham £200 a year, being
house property somewhere in London.

"Your father was troubled that people did not say all
that might be said for Epping Forest being kept open.
Fifteen or sixteen years ago the Chief Commissioner of
Woods and Forests announced in Parliament his intention
to bring in a Bill that session for the enclosure of Epping
and Hainault Forests. Dickens and he were appalled at
the news, regarding such a destruction as an irreparable
injury to London; and consequently your father vigorously
pleaded for the preservation of Epping Forest in the

pages of *Household Words*. He therefore again, like a brave soldier of the right, wrote a letter for the *Daily News*, which I confidently hope did good to the cause."

" *March* 12, 1868.—I give myself the birthday pleasure of writing to thank dearest Alfred and you for your most acceptable and beautiful remembrance of this day. Oh! how I wish I might be re-born; might advance into a higher, better state! One seems so much to stop in the same state. But then one does not see the growth of the tree or the flower, only from period to period that it has developed. So I suppose it is with the soul; it progresses towards the light with imperceptible advance. I hope it is so.

"I am, alas! again very dead as regards my ballad-writing. I suppose it is, in the order of things, a time of rest after labour. I feel as if the fountain were dried up, just as I did before. Mr. Clarke has omitted one month of the series in his *Christian World Magazine*, so that he does not want another before June. This made me feel no necessity to write, and then the spirit died out of me. I shall wake up again before long. In the meantime this fine weather has set me gardening, and greatly have I enjoyed it."

"*Sept.* 19, 1868.—All our guests are now departed. Your aunt Anna's visit was delightful. I think we employed the time well. I read over to her the chronicle of our ancestors and of our early life, and had notes and suggestions from her for future guidance; so now it waits my leisure to put its multitudinous contents into some degree of order, which I hope to do in the winter. The house seems very dull without your two cousins,

Agnes Harrison and Agnes Alderson.   Sweeter girls never were."

"*The Orchard, Nov.* 6, 1868.—Here it has been most exquisitely beautiful this autumnal weather, the trees looking truly as though they had been cut out of gold and coral. We have taken some lovely walks, and often wished you could have been with us. Last Monday afternoon my mother and I went to West End Cottage, now The Cedars. We seemed to be walking in a magnificient gallery of pictures, for at every turn there was some exquisite combination of colour and form. All was bathed in a translucent sunset light as we returned, and the trees looked inky black against a greeny-blue sky, flecked rose-colour; or they were magically crimson and golden, whilst the fields were emerald. A halo of glory seemed flung around everything, it flamed upon the distant casements of cottages, and turned even the pigs crunching acorns beneath the oaks into poetical swine. It was as if we had stepped into a Paradise, and saw all things transfigured.

"I had never been over the old Esher home since we left it, though I had seen its outside several times. It was curious to go through the rooms, full of past memories, and to find them smaller than in recollection, whilst the trees and shrubs outside had grown much taller and bigger.

"We are reading aloud in the evenings Maria Webb's 'Penns and the Penningtons.' My parents will send it you, should you not have read it, for it is well worth perusal.

"Our good friends, Mr. and Mrs. Oldham—she Eliza

Sutton of the early Nottingham days—have left their pleasant home in Gloucestershire and come to reside near my parents. They occupy a cottage with a garden standing upon a hill, about three miles from The Orchard. The whole walk thither is charming, through bowery lanes."

The Same to her Sister Margaret, who was attending their Uncle Richard's Sick-bed.

"*Feb.* 1, 1869.—Tell dear uncle I never enjoy anything that I do not wish he could enjoy it with me; and many letters are written to him in my heart which never reach him. The snowdrops he sent me through you are still fresh, and make me think of so many sweet vernal things. I went on Saturday to Julia, who is suffering much pain, and spoke to her of our dear Poet-Uncle; and Julia, to my surprise, knew him. She had seen him at our house on his way to join you in France. She has often recalled him since; for he had repeated verses so sweetly from Jean Ingelow and Burns. I had quite forgotten that she called that afternoon. How one rejoices when one's friends know and like each other!"

On February 5, 1869, Richard Howitt breathed his last. His tenants and his poor neighbours, according to country custom, one by one visited their old friend and champion, as he lay robed for the tomb; and as they stood beside the coffin, each one laid his or her hand in blessing upon the cold brow, in the belief that this "laying on of hands" gives rest to the dead. His relatives accompanied his revered remains, in a mist of soft rain, across the district of old Sherwood Forest to his grave in the burial-ground of the Society of Friends at Mansfield.

MARY HOWITT TO HER HUSBAND.

"*Feb.* 12, 1869.—I am thinking of one and all of you at the funeral. With us it pours with rain; but be the weather ever so dismal, I hope, as indeed I am sure they will, that both Annie and Meggie will attend their uncle's remains to Mansfield. I remember so many little traits of his character, which touch me deeply; and in no way, as far as I am concerned, shall his memory fail of respect."

TO MRS. ALFRED WATTS.

"*March* 17, 1869.—I have vastly enjoyed Mr. Morris's poems; and thus it is a pleasure to me to think of him in his blue blouse and with his earnest face at 'The Firm,' and to feel that he is a great poet. I am glad that we had the fairy-tale tiles for the fireplaces from Morris & Co.; their connection with this modern Chaucer gives them a new value and interest. Morris is not before Tennyson, but he stands very near him in the living reality of his old-world pictures, and in his exquisite painting of scenery; the flowers, the grasses, the 'brown birds,' every individual object and feature in Nature is so lovingly and so faithfully portrayed. Tennyson's poetry is the perfection of art and truth in art. Morris's is Nature itself, rough at times, but quaint, fresh, and dewy beyond anything I ever saw or felt in language. I shall try to tell Mr. Morris what a joy and refreshment it has been to me.

"If nice mild weather comes to bless us, I shall walk over to the Oldhams' before long, and take them 'The Earthly Paradise.' Perhaps I may go on Sunday and dine with them; I enjoy their simple farinaceous diet so much, and I think they are really pleased when those who appreciate it partake with them."

"*May* 31, 1869.—I do not think such miserable May weather was ever known; so intensely cold that one is obliged to wear winter clothing and have fires in every room. On Saturday there was such a bitter frost that scarlet-runners and tender summer growths are nipped, and everybody mourning over their gardens. The last tolerable day here was Wednesday, the Derby day, when we arranged to go over to the Oldhams' for an early tea, and then walk to the Epsom road and see the folks returning.

"We did so; and very much amused we were. We took our seats on a bench by the roadside. There are several in that locality, probably put down for this purpose. We had the bench to ourselves, with the exception of one man, so nothing could be more comfortable. The whole road was crowded with people, like ourselves, come to be amused; mostly on foot, sitting and walking about, and some in carriages drawn up at the roadside. At about half-past five the people began to return, in every possible description of vehicle, from the grandest four-in-hand to the costermonger's cart; nearly all half-drunk, merry and wild as could be, many in green veils and blue veils, with wooden dolls stuck all round their hats, and with dressed mechanical dolls in their hands, which sneezed and laughed and made all sorts of noises; or with pea-shooters, through which they shot peas at the people as they passed. Those shot at the Pater he collected, brought home with him, and has planted, to see what his winnings at the Derby turn out. Some had on false noses, others women's hats; the women wearing the men's. One man in a carriage wore a woman's night-dress and a mob-cap, as ridiculous as possible; some were biting big loaves of bread; others had bladders in their hands. All were laughing and shouting. The man

who sat on the bench by us said, 'They have no *wice*
in them, only fun.' Your father and Mr. Oldham, two
old men with white beards, seated side by side, were an
everlasting source of amusement. Sometimes they were
lovingly saluted as 'Father' or 'Grandfather;' sometimes they were pitied—'Poor souls! because they had
no father!' There were hundreds of sporting, betting
men in white hats with or without veils; hard, worldly,
cold, business faces of the most repulsive character. One
set of these men sitting in the body of a drag were playing at cards. It was altogether a strange revelation of
a life with which one thanks God one has nothing to
do; and one wonders what will become of these souls in
the other world. What a revolting hell it must be to which
they naturally gravitate! Nevertheless we vastly amused
ourselves. We counted upwards of five hundred carriages
in about two hours. And the women in them! Eight out
of ten were fat, jolly women, used to jovial living. Many
of them we imagined to be butchers' wives and landladies.
It was very diverting, but having once seen it, we shall
never care to go again. "

To William Howitt.

" *Beckenham, Sunday afternoon, July* 4, 1869.—Louie
and I went this morning to a very pleasant church at
Shortlands, a new locality sprung up in a lovely woodland district about two or three miles off, really delightful, and where Mrs. Craik has built her beautiful new
house. I extremely enjoyed both the drive and the service
in the little church.

"Last evening I was greatly interested by a call on
our relatives from young Mr. James Macdonell. He
wonderfully attracted me, because he is up in every

question of the day, and gave me a most hopeful idea of the better class of young men in this younger generation. Every reform that you, dear William, ever desired or worked for seems to be the object for which they are striving. He told me of the marvellous spirit of reform in every shape to which many of the Oxford undergraduates are devoting themselves: the abolition of primogeniture, and the separation of Church and State, among the rest. He said that the influence of Friends' doctrines and opinions was at this time very great; that it was operating amongst these Oxford men. He seemed to know a great deal about Friends' books, and of them as an ancient people. We live in our quiet corner, and know nothing of what is going on in the world."

To MRS. ALFRED WATTS.

"*Beckenham, July* 9, 1869.—Your aunt Anna and I had a very nice call on Mrs. Craik in her new house. It was her first open afternoon, and there were, of course, a good number of people there. The house, which is, I suppose, of the time of Henry VII., is perfect within and without. You can see that to the architect, who is a young man, it has been a perfect work of love. He has followed one uniform plan, and therefore everything is consistent, down to the rather thick dull glass in the windows, which Mrs. Craik likes because there is no glare of light. These windows are very large, but are without Venetian blinds, the sun being kept out when needful by Holland blinds, which draw on a wire with rings; they are most old-fashioned. The scarlet serge curtains also draw over the windows in the same way. There are window-seats cushioned with scarlet in every window. The fireplaces and all the little nooks and

quaint devices are lovely, and would enchant Edward
Bateman. The whole house is carpeted with grey felt,
on which bright rugs and bits of colour produce beautiful
effects. The colours of the paint are most quaint and
original; in the entrance-hall blue-grey, with dull red
walls. I can imagine nothing pleasanter than building
such a house and furnishing it.

"Little Dorothy is the embodiment of health and in-
fantine beauty, fair and rosy, with beautifully moulded
limbs, long fingers, and golden-tinged hair. She can just
run alone, has the most winning ways, and if she had
determined to show herself off to advantage, could not
have been more fascinating than she was. I do not
wonder at the Craiks' love for their little darling."

To William Howitt.

"*Mayfield, near Ashbourne, Aug.* 25, 1869.—All is
bright and peaceful here, and I wish you could now have
joined Margaret and me instead of later in Wales, and
thus have seen how truly Christian a life our dear young
relatives are leading, heard all their views, and all their
experience in co-operation, of which they are warm supporters, and discussed with them social and political
questions, in which you and they think alike.

"The other evening the Rev. Alfred Ainger, the
Reader of the Temple, was here; well versed in all the
literature and topics of the day, most courteous and
pleasant; and just off to Heidelberg, to which place he
said your writings first introduced him.

"Yesterday evening we were at 'Swinscoe wakes;'
that is to say, at an entertainment of tea, a penny-reading,
and music given on occasion of the wakes in that primitive, high-lying Staffordshire village, which, after a long

ascent from this Idyllic spot, lies in quite another climate and region with stone walls and bare hill-tops.

"Mr. Okeover, he being the landowner of the district, was present with his wife, her sister and brother, Lord Waterpark, three of their little daughters, and the French governess; a most interesting and excellent set of people. Of course, Mr. and Mrs. George Mackarness from Ilam were also there, for we were invited by them. I always feel a great charm in this clerical-county life: the pious and refined dwellers of the Parsonage and the Hall trying to benefit in all ways their people, and to elevate them by cheerful means. Hence this entertainment was made as pleasant as it could be; the rich mingling with the poor, simple folks in the most beautiful manner.

"Truly there is to me something most fascinating in the lives and homes of some of these clergy. You know what Ilam is, with its surrounding hills, woods, model village, its peaceful church and affluent Hall and Vicarage. Equally beautiful and perfect is the clerical home, school, and church of Denstone. On one hand stands the church, always open, in the midst of a lawn-like graveyard planted with evergreens, and kept shorn with the mowing-machine; and on the other the Parsonage and its garden, a true paradise, and all around the most peaceful, pastoral Dove scenery. I never felt such a sense of divine calm as I did at Denstone, since those Sundays when we were at Thorpe, and we went over to service at Ilam. I do, of a truth, believe that in such places we are granted a perception of Heaven."

To Mrs. Alfred Watts.

"*Penmaenmawr, Oct.* 1, 1869.—I write at the Pater's dictation the following:—'There has been a great excitement amongst us to-day. This morning Mr. George Mackarness went with his brother, the vicar of Honiton, to bathe. On their way they called for their letters ; and the vicar of Honiton, opening his in the bathing-machine, found one was from Gladstone wishing to make him Bishop of Oxford. After breakfast the brothers John and George Mackarness started off to discuss the proposal on a walk round the Great Orme's Head. Mrs. George Mackarness came to us, and we celebrated her brother-in-law's promotion by an afternoon's excursion together to Aber.

" 'On the Penmaenmawr platform, as we were just getting into the train, all in the midst of a crowd of tourists, going and coming, an elderly clergyman burst out of a carriage, followed by two stylish young ladies. Mrs. Mackarness caught sight of him, and there was a cordial greeting. He was on his way to Ty-Mawr to call on the two vicars of Honiton and Ilam. There was hardly time for explanation, as our train went off with us, leaving him in a state of bewildered consternation.

" 'We found it to be the horse-fair at Aber, which you may remember. The approach to the village was crowded with stalls and all kinds of stall trumpery. In the midst of a lot of *Taffies* and *toffies* the smiling visage of Mrs. Birley was visible. She was accompanied by little Fanny and the two South American children. She gave us an enthusiastic reception, conducting us to the Mill Cottage, which looked really lovely, with roses and creepers right up to the eaves.

" 'On our return, at the Aber station there happened to be two little black ponies, which had been sold at the fair, and were going over to Ireland. They had had nothing to eat and nothing to drink. Mrs. Mackarness and your mother insisted, therefore, upon their having both water and hay, for which they paid a shilling. The poor little things were so frightened that they would neither eat nor drink. The hay, however, was put into the truck with the ponies by a gentleman ; and the purchasers hoped that they would consume it between Aber and Holyhead. At Penmaenmawr there was the same clergyman and the two pretty young ladies, who, after a bootless errand, were now in a great hurry, of course, to find seats in the train. The guard whistled impatiently, but for all that the clergyman rushed forward to shake hands with " Mistress Mary Howitt," exclaiming, " I too am of Ukseter ! " Again the whistle, and we fearing he would lose his train, he was hurried into the nearest carriage, and whirled away, a mass of wonderment, friendship, and cordiality.' "

Penmaenmawr, where we have stayed until the hills were sublimely white, had never lost its stimulating effect on me. How I loved the rugged sea-washed mountain— the natural beacon and name-giver of the district—which, overshadowing the long, stony village, is being blasted, undermined, and hewn into blocks, to be shot down long tramways to the jetty, and then borne slowly through the water in little vessels to England ! How I respected the grave, earnest quarrymen, clad in buff moleskin waistcoats and trousers, similar in colour to the outer coating of the rock, and in blue and white striped shirts of the same tone as its freshly-hewn inside ; often with splendid faces of the rough, stony kind, and hair and beards like rock-growths of the gold-brown hue of late autumn ferns and heather ! Men of fortitude and piety these miners, who to the utmost of their ability support the temperance

movement, their schools, chapels, and ministers ; the latter
belonging to their own class, and often dating their
spiritual vocation from early work-days in the quarries !
How deeply, too, was I thrilled and affected by the grand,
inspirational sound and the rhythmical cadence in the
minor-key of the Welsh praying and preaching in the
chapels !

Very gratifying were the courteous attentions of
English and native residents, the occupants of pleasant
villas and cottages studded over a fertile region in the lap
of the hills. Very enlivening, also, did we find the intercourse with the little community of visitors, which often
numbered bishops, deans, and their families, and who,
brought together in rambles and picnics by the ready
offices of bright, energetic Miss Lloyd Jones, parted after
a few weeks' acquaintance with mutual good wishes.

I cannot make this slight survey of our Welsh experiences without calling to mind the beautiful home of an
interesting and amiable family. Mr. Sandbach, of Liverpool, whose second wife is a Welsh lady, after purchasing
Hafodunos, an extensive, high-lying estate in Denbigh-
shire, finding the tenants half-starved owing to their
rude, inefficient agriculture, speedily bettered their circumstances by employing the men in draining, road-making,
enclosing, planting, and building. He himself heartily
enjoyed the superintendence of his many improvements,
which included the erection of a beautiful church, excellent
farm-houses and cottages, and his own mansion, constructed with plenty of gables and a lofty tower by Gilbert
Scott. The hall stands on a terrace overlooking a most
charming glen, where tulip-trees, great magnolias, hem-
locks, and other pines from America mix with native oaks
and beeches ; where ferns from all parts of Great Britain,

Ireland, Switzerland, and New Zealand grow with curious hardy plants from the Continent, and a winding walk leads to the old kitchen-gardens, with their clipped yew-hedges. The interior of the house is in exquisite taste; no paint is allowed, the woodwork and the furniture being of pitch-pine, red cedar, or dark bullace from Demerara, whilst the capitals of the columns leading to and on the grand staircase are deftly carved with roses, lilies, snow-drops, and other British flowers.

The first Mrs. Sandbach was a poetess, and by birth a Miss Roscoe of Liverpool. Her portrait, finely and classi-cally chiselled full-length in bas-relief by Gibson, adorns the vestibule to the room of statuary. This is specially devoted to the works of the same great sculptor and Royal Academician, and contains the fine group of "The Hunter and his Dog," the "Aurora," together with the busts and medallions of the Sandbach family. Gibson, the son of a landscape-gardener at Conway, had been be-friended and directed in his art-studies by Mr. Roscoe, the author of "Leo the Tenth," who frequently invited him to Allerton Hall, and placed its literary and artistic treasures at his service; and when the poor student had become eminent in Rome, the connection was still main-tained by the relatives of the early patron.

I feel myself once more with the kind owners of Hafodunos in the autumn of 1866. Agreeable county neighbours drive over for afternoon tea; and in the draw-ing-room, opening on to the terrace, gay with masses of sweet-scented flowers, a noted Welsh painter, quiet, elderly Penry Williams, very modestly exhibits his port-folio of charming Italian landscapes and figures. He speaks of getting back to Rome before the winter comes on, for he expects the Italians will soon be down on the

Eternal City, and destroy the antique and picturesque to make way for modern railway stations and Government buildings.

We visited Hafodunos, and indeed North Wales, for the last time in the autumn of 1869.

"*The Orchard, Jan.* 14, 1870.—Many, many happy returns of the day to-morrow! You have had a good many now, and have given us many happy hours. Many changes have occurred since the days when I carried you, a little creature, on my back over the fields from Nottingham to Heanor, and many of our contemporaries have gone out of the world, so that it seems a part of a former life; but pleasant to remember, for one line of affection has run unbroken through the whole. I trust we may for years continue to love each other in this world, and then continue to look back on the happy past from a more happy present. It has been a great boon of our lives that we have had so grand a reassurance of all the old promises of the world to come; the world of reunions and rediscoveries of those who seemed lost; a world of realities and realisations, of reovertakings and rejoicings! What a Friends' Meeting!—not in silence, but amid the welcomes of all our beloved, and the sublimest sense of that Eternity achieved, which on earth had been a poetic dream, a mystic speculation, a mingled vision of clouds and glories and darkness.

"With all the queernesses of spiritualism and spiritualists, this dispensation has been to us *the* fact of our earth-pilgrimage. Where our forefathers have sailed through fogs and tempests after the lost Atlantis, we have reached land; solid ground, with the great highway visible before us, with the pinnacles of the Heavenly Jerusalem glittering on the Mountains of Life."

Mary Howitt to the Same.

"*The Orchard, the eve of my St. Anna's Day.*—You must have a few loving words from me on the auspicious day of your birth. That is a formal expression, but as it means especially happy, it is right, for it was a fortunate and a happy day which gave you to me as my dear daughter and friend. What an age it seems since you were a little child, and used to sit with me in the Nottingham drawing-room, and we read the Gospels together, and I used to read you my poems, often written from thoughts suggested by you! Some of those Sunday evening readings remain most livingly in my mind as little bits of Heaven, when illumination seemed almost to come down from above to us. I remember how 'Thomas of Torres,' in 'The Seven Temptations,' was the fruit of our reading together the parable of the man who built the barns and laid up the treasure, and then his soul was called away. I wonder whether you remember those times, and how you illustrated 'The Seven Temptations,' with heads of all the characters? Many other heads you designed, amongst them a Judas, which I thought marvellous. How distant, yet how beautiful, tender, and peculiar are the memories of those times! May God, in His mercy, sanctify the present and all future time on earth to us by gentle, loving deeds, and by our ever coming nearer and nearer to Him!"

My husband and I wanted to see Italy before we died, so we let The Orchard for twelve months to some desirable tenants from Lady Day 1870. With a prayer in our hearts that the Divine Spirit might accompany us, we quitted

our home in the evening of March 24, and proceeded
to London to pay farewell visits preparatory to our
exodus.

Mary Howitt to her elder Daughter, from Beckenham.

"*April* 3, 1870.—I hope, whenever you can, you will
come and see our dear relatives. It will be a joy to them
and a refreshment to you. There is a holy spirit of
domestic affection in the house; all are so good and
kind. Your aunt seems feeble, but looks better in the face.
Mr. James Macdonell and his sister arrived by the same
train as we did. The evening was very pleasant, and
your father was interested in Mr. Macdonell as a fitting
representative of the new age. Dora Greenwell sent me
by him her volume of poems and the most affectionate
message, 'wishing to see me above all women in England.'
I am some way sorry she should feel thus, especially as
she lunches here next Tuesday. You will understand
my shrinking sense of gratitude. It is always affecting
to me to see how much love one gets. Oh! if one did
but deserve it more."

"*Tuesday, April* 5, 1870.—Miss Dora Greenwell and
Mr. Macdonell came to lunch. We found her very agreeable. Later in the afternoon she went up to town with
William and myself. I was very sorry to part with my
beloved ones at Beckenham. May the merciful Lord
preserve them!"

We started on April 13 for Switzerland and Italy;
anticipating with the rapid flight of time soon to find
ourselves back in old, much beloved England, and in
the society of our cherished relatives and friends. But
this was not to be.

CHAPTER VI.

IN SWITZERLAND AND ITALY.

1870–1871.

ACCOMPANIED by the eldest daughter of our friend, Mr. William Bodkin of Highgate, and by Emily Burtt, a great-niece of my husband's, he, Margaret, and I crossed from England to Belgium. There we visited the green, quiet field of Waterloo, and were joined in gay, flourishing Brussels by our warm-hearted friends, Walter Weldon, F.R.S., the indefatigable projector of most valuable chemical discoveries, his wife and their gifted little son Raphael. They purposely paid a flying visit to the Belgian capital once more to see us.

WILLIAM HOWITT TO MRS. ALFRED WATTS.

"*Gersau, Switzerland, April* 23, 1870. — We have been either posting along, or when stopping in towns constantly tramping about, so that there has been no chance of much writing. Here we have been climbing hills and steaming up the Lake of the Four Cantons, so that my feet are very much delighted at my hands doing the work for a few hours.

"I have no doubt your mother has told you of the Todhunters' arrival. We went with them the day before yesterday to Brunnen, the next village on the lake, where we have found a very nice *pension*, to which we remove next Wednesday. It is a little way out of

Brunnen. The garden goes down to the lake. Opposite rises Seelisberg, with its little chapel and big *pension*, so warmly recommended to us by Mr. Boyle of Kidderminster. We, however, prefer a less-frequented resort. Behind is the Axenberg, on which is perched a large new hotel. The house is small, but with every modern convenience. It was only opened last year. It belongs to and is kept by Fräulein Agathe Aufdermauer; in plain English, Miss Upon-the-Wall. She is a short, stout lady of about fifty, clever, well educated, speaks, I am sorry to say, English, and has, in her brother's house in the village, entertained Fredrika Bremer, Hans Christian Andersen, Bulwer, &c. I think we shall get on with her; and we shall have a great St. Gothard dog to take care of us.

"Our young companions are very good, bright, and pleasant, fond of flowers, and delighted to be in the country. You would hear, of course, of the enjoyable time we had in Brussels with the Weldons, who we expect would visit you last Sunday. With them we went to the Wiertz Gallery. On our first entrance I was quite startled, and did not think I should at all like the paintings, they appeared so huge, so wild, and so fantastic. But by degrees I began to see a great mind and purpose in them. 'Napoleon in Hell' is a grand lesson, and well conceived. You have not said a word too much of Wiertz. Little Raphael came and took my hand as we left the gallery, and said, 'Mr. Howitt, I think Wiertz could not be a good man!' I asked him why. He answered, 'I think he could not be a good man, or he would not have painted some things there.' I told him he might naturally think so, but that a vast deal was to be allowed for his education. No doubt Wiertz thought all was right, and that many of his pictures contained great and useful lessons. His father came up and added, that when Raphael was older he would see those lessons more clearly than he could do now.

"It seems amazing to hear of your dull, hazy weather. From the moment that we set foot on the Continent we have had nothing but clear skies, and this week very warm days. With all our great struggles and vaunted triumphs of reform in our British Parliament, the condition of the people at large is deplorable, and not to be named with that of the Swiss peasantry. It is horrible to remember Seven Dials, Bethnal Green, and all the scores of square miles of such places in London and other overcrowded centres, whilst we see these poor in their cottages amid their fields and gardens, and the children playing amongst green grass, pleasant trees, and flowers. Here and in most parts of the Continent, if the lower orders are poor, their poverty is ameliorated by the enjoyment of fresh air, the comely face of Nature, and the absence of those violent contrasts of splendour and squalor, of superabundance and destitution, that meet us on all hands in England. Our country is, in fact, the Sisyphus of the nations, always straining itself to roll away the crushing rock of debt, and never succeeding ; always on the verge of reform and relief, and never accomplishing it. Like its climate, its political and social condition is most frequently gloomy, hazy, and discouraging."

THE SAME TO THE SAME.

"*Pension Agathe Aufdermauer, April* 29, 1870.—On Tuesday, whilst Emily and Nelly went to Lucerne on some little errands, we three ascended on foot the Rigi-Scheideck from Gersau. It took us six hours, going very leisurely, and making many and long rests; for it is steep all the way. We had a splendid view from the summit of the whole amphitheatre of the Bernese Alps; and descended in three hours by a different path. Our way up and down was amongst green slopes, scattered over with chalets, where the owners were cultivating their patches of potato-ground or watching their cattle. Here and there were pine-woods, deep clefts and precipices, and the beds of streams strewn with huge rocks of pudding and other stones. Some of the slopes were as white with small white crocuses as any fields in England with daisies; others were yellow with king-cups; and there were millions of oxlips, but paler and more slender than ours. The little gentianella was abundant, and frequently in brilliant masses. The *Trollius Europæus* was all over other meadow slopes, but only in bud. We found patches of pink primulas and auriculas. Near the summit grew large and splendid bunches of the yellow auricula. The blue and red hepaticas were not quite over; and the cherry-trees, which grow all the way up, were on the lower slopes in blossom.

"The hotel porters were carrying up on their backs each a hundredweight of provisions, sugar-loaves, potatoes, &c. We asked if they were not tired. They said, 'No; they could carry up twice as much at a time;' and we were told below that this was true, but that they ruin their constitutions by such attempts. However, these men, whom we met three-parts of the way up, passed us before we were down, jodelling and very jolly. Some of them had been up twice that day. So much for habit.

"We are here situated exactly at the turn of the lake into the Uri-See. Opposite to this branch is the Mythenstein, with the inscription to Schiller upon it.

We have a number of copies of his 'Wilhelm Tell' in the house, and shall be able to study the play amid its scenery.

" On Sunday we witnessed an election for the canton of Schwyz. It was in the open air, before the *Rathhaus*. There was no drunkenness, no rioting, no bribery, and no long speeches ! It was the very model of an election. The *Amtmann*, the *Landamman*, and the *Rathsschreiber* stood at a table, and the *Amtmann* read out the names of candidates. They and their friends made a few re-marks each, all to the point ; any one who chose could make an objection. Then the choice was decided by a show of hands. It was all over in about half-an-hour. Herr Müller of the Gersau Hotel was re-elected as one member, which he has been for years.

" We became quite familiar with the village children of Gersau. They ran up to us, with the right hand put out, not crumpled up to beg ; and were always merry when they saw us again. One day an angry woman kept scolding a little boy of two years of age and twitch-ing him along after her. Your mother, as she always does, began noticing the little fellow, saying to the woman what a nice boy he was. The effect, as usual, was instantaneous. The mother caught up the child, kissed it, wiped away its tears, and seemed delighted. The little fellow looked at us with large dark eyes. We patted his cheek and kissed him, at which he set up a great crowing of delight, which lasted as long as we were in sight.

" All the children are educated, both boys and girls from six to twelve ; and then go two years longer to the Sunday-schools. This is the reason that they are so nicely-behaved. Now mind, this part of the country is wholly Catholic, yet the education of the people is universal. Any parents neglecting to send their children to school are severely punished. Observe also that the country is well cultivated, and the trade and manufactures are flourishing. None of the charges of bad cultivation, of want of manufacturing zeal, and prohibition of education apply to Switzerland. Of course, there is no religious difficulty in this canton, as all are Catholics; but where all are educated, the people must be enlightened beyond any great slavery of priestcraft."

THE SAME TO THE SAME.

"*Pension Agathe Aufdermauer, May* 11, 1870.—Yesterday we had an invasion of fresh inmates, but only for one night. It was Richard Wagner, the great composer, with a handsome young lady, legally or by courtesy his wife. She is Liszt's daughter, and was married to the brilliant pianist and composer, von Bülow, who is the best interpreter of his father-in-law's music, and that of the man who has wronged him. The young King of Bavaria being obliged to send Wagner from Bavaria, as he attended more to music than his regal duties, the musician settled at Lucerne. The King, however, made a visit to Switzerland to see his favourite, and privately took up his quarters at Brunnen. In this way, and because Fräulein Aufdermauer is very musical, she became acquainted with Wagner, who now brought his belongings for a birthday celebration to her house. There were four little von Bülows or Wagners, who with their parents kept the house alive, seeing that one and all were very merry and musical. To-day they are gone back to their villa at Lucerne.

"On Sunday there was quite a display in Brunnen.

It was a procession of the Working-men's Unions of Lucerne and all the places on the lake to Grütli and Tell's Chapel. They came up with the steamer, which had at its prow a blue-and-white flag, at its stern the great red banner, with the white cross in the centre, of Switzerland. They brought with them an excellent band of music, and took in here the Brunnen, Stein, and Schwyz Unions, with another band; then went on to the Grütli meadow and Tell's Chapel. They landed here on their return, and after dispersing for some refreshment, formed in procession to march to Schwyz, where they were to dine. There were about three hundred of them, with their banners, scarlet and gold for the most part, belonging to the different Working-men's Unions of the four cantons. There was one of a 'People's Improvement Society.' They marched off to Schwyz with music and flying banners. Each man had a sprig of some green tree or bush in his hat. In front marched about half-a-dozen boys, dressed in the ancient Swiss costume and carrying the '*Wappen*,' armorial shields of the four cantons, bright with red and blue and yellow. One lad represented William Tell, with his cross-bow and the apple in his hand. You may suppose the stir in Brunnen. On their return in the evening the steamer was waiting for them. They were sufficiently jolly with beer and sufficiently dusty. This compact of working-men all over the Continent is a sign of the coming time, and is already larger than the cloud seen from Carmel by Elijah.

"The most lovely scenery here, to my mind, is the great broad valley of meadows and orchards extending from Brunnen to Schwyz. Not far from Brunnen runs down from the Frohnalp a green promontory into the centre of the valley. On it stands boldly up, and visible from far down the lake, the Convent of Ingenbohl, where, as you have told us, the Shelleys once fixed themselves. What was then a ruinous château is now an immense mass of buildings. From the hill on which this convent stands you command the whole view of the elysian valley. On one side shines out the lake, with the white houses of Brunnen; on the other, Schwyz, with its monastery, great church, *Rathhaus*, and a whole region of scattered houses amid the blossoming trees on the great green slopes at the foot of those wonderful and stupendous bare rocks, the Mythen. Up they stand, gigantic twin-pyramids, soaring into the clear air nearly six thousand feet. Round the valley rise the green hills, orchard-like, with their little chalets. Higher rise the steep slopes covered with the now light, green foliage of the beech-woods; higher still, the dark pine-forest; higher still, the eternal mountains. The bottom of the valley is one great green meadow, luxuriant with grass and flowers. All round you bloom the purple orchis, the blue forget-me-not, the golden trollius, and here and there the tall white narcissus. When I look over this wondrous scene, through which run the Muotta and the Schleywasser, clear as the air itself, I am vividly reminded of the description of the Promised Land given by Moses in the eleventh chapter of Deuteronomy.

"On Sunday morning your mother and I walked up to the convent hill, and sat down above it, having this magnificent scene lying wide before us. The air was full of the harmony of the bells of the convent, of the parish church just below, and of churches on the hills; as they ceased, the lighter, lower chime of the cow-bells came up from the meadows. It was like a bright dream of Heaven, of beauty, and of peace.

"As we passed the convent in going up, the nuns were sitting in their ample garden on the upper side of the edifice, in groups under shady trees; and some of them, who were only divided from us by a thin acacia-hedge, rose and bowed to us very courteously. At noon we saw a great procession of them advancing from the convent garden up the *Kreuzweg*, or Way of the Cross, to the Chapel of Calvary on the hill above. Along this steep path at regular intervals are erected fourteen shrines, having each a good painting illustrating the various stages of Christ's passion and crucifixion. At each of these the procession stopped and repeated the customary prayers. It consisted of seventy nuns in all, in their black habits, the white edges of their caps shining under their black veils. As they advanced to each shrine one nun read out a prayer, and all responded with a murmur of voices that came up pleasingly to us. We had taken the opportunity to look into the little Calvary Chapel at the top of the ascent, under the edge of the pleasant beech-wood. It was neat and plain, with two rows of deal forms, just as in a Friends' Meeting-house. The almost only striking object was a large and good picture of the Mater Dolorosa, in a scarlet bodice and dark flowing skirts. She held in her right hand one of the nails from the cross, and by her sat an angel with the crown of thorns on his knee, which she was stretching forth her left hand to take up. Besides this, a plain altar, some framed prayers, and a wreath or two of *immortelles* constituted the ornaments of the chapel. Such was our Sunday morning excursion."

THE SAME TO THE SAME.

"*Pension Aufdermauer, May* 18, 1870.—This Agathe

Aufdermauer is a very extraordinary woman. She has a large head, and an amazing deal in it. She is well read in German literature, and is astonished to find English people who know so much about it as we do. She and I get on amazingly on spiritual subjects, for she is delighted to find that we believe so much that the Catholics do. I tell her I am a Catholic in all the ancient doctrines of the Church, but am not papistical. In all the affairs of life she is clear-headed, able, and active. She bought the ground and built this house, surmounting innumerable difficulties. Everybody knows her for miles round, and everybody speaks in the highest terms of her."

" *May* 19.—My ideal of an Alpine spot is Bürglen, the birthplace of Tell! Surrounded by the mighty Alps: meadows that are masses of the richest floral colouring: people in happy groups sitting amid the luxuriant grass under spreading pear and walnut trees : rushing, hurrying streams of foaming glacial water, turning saw-mills, and forges : chalets amid their meads or perched on every airy height up to the very top of the pine-clad hills : all the little steep, stony lanes crowded with piles of huge pine-trees, which have been sent down the galloping, rioting pale river, or down timber-slides, waiting to be split up by the ever busy, hungry saws that are driven by the irresistible mountain stream. Here and there the little wayside tawdry shrine, with its daubs of paintings and puppet-show Madonna and Child, with their tinsel crowns and country-booth paraphernalia; yet precious to the poor, tender, care - worn souls, especially women, with huge loads on their backs, and often still heavier on their hearts : yes, in most abominable taste, but most gracious to the tired, life-weary creatures that kneel there and cross themselves, already too cruelly crossed by the world. How the slender, red spire of the church on the hill, close to the chapel, built on the identical spot of Tell's house, beckons you on, with a silent but eloquent voice, saying as plainly as possible, 'Come up! come up! and see the eternal mountains, the sublime pinnacles, the dreaming snows, and pale glaciers. See all these soaring, climbing forests of pine, and the torrent dashing in mad transport down the rocky ravine.'

"When you speak of all these sights and sounds of life and beauty to the inhabitants, they shake their heads and say, 'It is not a glorious land. You should see it in winter, so fierce and stormy, so cruelly stern, so buried in snows, so short in its daylight, so long in its darkness. And even now, how much more beautiful would plains be than these steep fields and towering rocks!' Where is the Lost Paradise of earth?"

The Same to the Same.

"*May* 20.—We went yesterday by invitation to the Convent of Ingenbohl. Mother Maria Theresia Scherer, who has been the Mother-General of the Sisters of Mercy of the Holy Cross since 1850, received and conducted us over the establishment. The Sisterhood, which has now extended from Switzerland into neighbouring lands, was founded by Father Theodosius Florentini, a Capuchin monk, priest, and professor of theology. He was so deeply grieved by the rampant materialism of the age, that he conceived the idea of raising up a band of noble-hearted religious women to contend against it, in the careful education and employment of children, in supporting the helpless poor, and ministering to the sick. He went to Rome, and obtaining the Pope's sanction, his order

rapidly grew, women joining it from all parts of Switzerland, from Würtemberg and Bavaria. Possessing immense
faith and indomitable perseverance, he went about, himself
often penniless, and bought castle after castle, estate after
estate, saying that 'God had commanded us to love and
serve Him with all our hearts and souls, and our neighbours as ourselves, and he was sure He would not desert
the great work.' An enormous machinery of practical
benevolence Father Theodosius had brought into operation
in the course of twenty years; when he died, in 1865, at
the age of fifty-seven.

"Mother Maria Theresia Scherer is the fourth woman
who entered this now numerous order, which contains
members of all classes of society. To those who have
been peasants, working in the gardens or fields is no hardship. We saw a healthy-looking nun digging the ground
to set beans. She talked to us pleasantly, without an idea
that her occupation was in any way derogatory to her
profession. We were shown in the house a good library
of religious works, and the little wooden cross with gilt
ornaments presented by the Queen of Prussia; for the
Sisters in the late war nursed in the armies of both Prussia
and Austria. I need not say what enchanting views present themselves from every room. The Mother-General
walked with us in the garden, which was pleasant, but
with the neglect of the grass so common to German ones.
It having a fine crop of dandelions gone to seed, I plucked
one to amuse several young girls, scholars, who had been
allowed to join us, saying, 'Let us see what o'clock it
is.' I knew, having looked at my watch just before, that
it was exactly ten minutes past ten; and blowing it, the
time tallied. The Mother-General, with the care of a
hundred and sixty institutions on her shoulders, took my

joke in the most cordial way, and was quite merry over some more of my nonsense.

"On our return we visited the Orphanage, which is nearer the village. We found the boys and girls at dinner. They seemed to have an abundance of very nice food, and their healthy and happy looks spoke enjoyment of life. The elder girls were going in the afternoon with their new mothers, the nuns, on a ramble through the woods up to Axenstein, and the little ones were to be taken to the convent, where the Mother-General was going to amuse them.

"I am now reading the history of all the places of pilgrimage in Switzerland. What an extraordinary thing is Roman Catholicism! The system is one of the sub-limest schemes of priestcraft and spiritual domination that was ever conceived. At the top all is rotten, but at the bottom God, who overrules all things, has caused it to strike its roots into the soil of the common humanity, and send up shoots and crops of an active, a holy, and an indefatigable beneficence such as present Protestantism knows nothing of. Everywhere Catholic women are in-structing, collecting orphans from the streets and abodes of death, working for and employing the poor, tending the sick and the contagiously diseased in the palace or the poorest hut, and going about with the simple air and the friendly smile, as if they were only doing the most ordi-nary work, and felt themselves but unprofitable servants.

"When Florence Nightingale went forth to nurse the wounded soldiers in the Crimea, she did only a most commonplace deed, for the Catholic women of all ranks had been doing it everywhere for ages. That was not the merit of the thing. The greatness and vital merit of it was, that she introduced the good Samaritan of Catholicism to the proud Levite of Protestantism, and induced him to 'go and do likewise.' It was as splendid a triumph over prejudice and pharisaic ignorance as ever was won by man or woman, and has not yet borne all its destined fruits."

MARY HOWITT TO HER ELDER DAUGHTER.

"*Brunnen, Sunday morning.*—We went last evening, after tea, into a remote valley with the great mountains round it, through the most exquisite pasture-fields and under blossoming fruit-trees, on and on into an ever deeper, stiller, lovelier region, till at length we came to one of the solitary chapels which are so common here. Oh! how lovely they are!—the truest poems. The chapel walls were white as snow, with a dark red, picturesque little spire, and on the front a fresco picture of St. Xavier healing the sick. A young peasant-girl had just gone in to trim the lamp before the altar, and now stood in the dim twilight of the church, with a sort of silent reverence, as we entered. The interior walls were hung round with pictures and tablets, testimonies of Divine help; many of the incidents being represented by rude oil paintings, under which is the little narrative of help or cure. An old-fashioned man in a blue coat sits at a table, cramped in all his limbs by rheumatism, and suddenly the chamber is filled with light. St. Xavier appears with the cross in his hand, in answer to the long-uttered, faithful prayer of the afflicted, and at once the fettered limbs are released; and the man, lifting up his arms, and stretching forth all his fingers, cries aloud a wonder-stricken thanksgiving to the saint. Again, a solitary traveller in Italy is attacked from behind by a robber twice as big as himself. He cries to the saint, who at once opens Heaven and appears in such terrible majesty that the terrified robber drops his weapon and takes to flight.   All this sounds absurd, but to my mind the faith is not absurd.

"This little chapel, the scene in which it stood, the soft twilight which filled it, the young peasant-girl, who in leaving the chapel pointed out to us the holy water, affected me very deeply.   I did not let anybody see me, but coming out of the chapel, I dipped my finger into the holy water and crossed myself; praying that God would give me the right faith—a faith as sincere as governed the poor peasant hearts that have recorded His mercies to them."

To Sister Elizabeth.

"*Pension Felsberg, Lucerne, July* 4, 1870.—Our leaving Brunnen was quite a sad affair.   Poor Fräulein Aufdermauer cried for days before we left; and all the people in the *pension* went down with us to the boat to see us off. We had no end of bouquets and a delicious cake to take with us ; and some of the people had tears in their eyes as they bade us good-bye.   Here, at this new *pension* in Lucerne, the guests are much stiffer, and it does not seem likely to me that we shall ever get on the same terms with them.   We were like one large affectionate family at Brunnen.   Here we know very few.   We have our rooms in an elegant Swiss chalet, standing apart from the larger house, with the most glorious view imaginable over the lake, with mountains stretching out before us like the grandest picture.   We shall remain here about a fortnight, and then move off to Zürich, which, though not by any means in as fine scenery, yet is an interesting old town, where we think it would be well to remain perhaps for another fortnight."

At the beginning of July the Swiss felt no further anxiety than that rain should come to feed the corn and perfect the wonderful promise of the vintage. Then disquieting rumours arose that the candidature favoured by Prussia of Prince Leopold of Hohenzollern to the Spanish throne would cause a rupture between France and Germany. My husband, who believed his English papers, cherished the hope that peace would be maintained. We proceeded on July 16, in very sultry weather, to Zürich, and deplored in its vicinity the increasingly parched aspect of the soil and the shrivelled crops, but still dreaded no sudden social blight from war. We took up our quarters in an old-fashioned *pension* in the suburb of Fluntern, above Zürich. At midnight came the much-desired rain, pelting down amid vivid lightning, with but little thunder, yet attended by a tramping of feet and a curious movement in the country-road outside. Then followed a loud knocking at the street-door. It proved truly a rude awakening to us, for now we learnt that war was actually proclaimed by France to Prussia, and that the Swiss Confederation having ordered the active force of the militia to the frontier, our landlord, with other householders, was required to lodge for the night soldiers arrived from a distance.

The next day, a Sunday, we saw on the Zürich drill-ground the preparations for departure. A private distributed wallets to a line of his comrades. Young sunburnt peasants in regimentals sat resting on their knapsacks, or strapped the Swiss arms—the silver cross on the red field—to each other's coat-sleeves in a brotherly, helpful way, which would have extended from Prussia to France, and from France to Spain, if Europe were truly Christendom. In the evening the perpetual rub-a-dub-dub of drums and the shrill sound of fifes ascended from the gas-lit city to us on the heights of Fluntern.

At this crisis we naturally pondered what we should do. We had no desire to retrace our steps to England. This proved fortunate, as there speedily arrived English and American tourists, madly fleeing, with or without their luggage, from the Rhinelands. We could not move on to Italy, which was itself preparing to rise. We determined, therefore, to await the issue in Switzerland ; and presenting some letters of introduction to Zürich inhabitants, gained thereby a valued friend in Madame Daeniker.

With all our new acquaintance the war was, of course, the one absorbing topic. A nameless apprehension seemed to have settled on men's minds in Zürich ; and one locksmith, we heard, worked night and day, making iron coffers to contain the money and valuables his customers wished to bury. My husband remarked to an artisan, who was seated under a tree, gazing down on the populous city and the lake, with its fringe of prosperous villages, " What a noble landscape ! and how well, after the rain, the vines, corn, and potatoes look ! "

" Yes," replied the man gloomily ; " only there's war ! "

We visited the museum of the Antiquarian Society, containing remarkable lacustrine remains, collected by Dr. Keller, chiefly at Meilen, on the Lake of Zürich. The custodian, a little dried-up old woman, seemed herself lacustrine, such knowledge had she of the prehistoric lake-inhabitants, and of each shrivelled, cindery apple, grain of wheat, scrap of fishing-net, or spear-head. Whilst we carefully inspected the model of a pile-dwelling, military music sounded without, and the street became suddenly alive with blue coats and bayonets. Tears filled the eyes of the aged woman as she watched

this fresh battalion tramp by and cross the bridge, on
its way to the frontier. "Better no war! Better no
soldiers!" she cried, shaking her head. "Yet it's the
same old story from the beginning. When Cain was
wroth, he rose up and slew his brother Abel. The
Lacustrines lived on piles in the lake to be safe from
their enemies; and in my time I have seen the French
once in Switzerland, twice in Germany, and then driven
back to Paris."

The Protestant population of Zürich deplored the war;
but being persuaded that the Prussian rule was wise and
good, conducive to morality, general education, and human
advance, warmly espoused its cause. In fact, we found
political refugees, such as Professors Kinkel and Behn
Eschenburg, who had earlier been imprisoned by Prussia,
now offering her their most loyal support. A tall, slim,
elderly Dane, who was sanguine enough to anticipate
that the outcome of the present campaign would be the
avenging of his native land by Napoleon, was amongst
the few individuals who remembered Prussia's former
aggrandisement, and imputed the war to Bismarck. My
husband and I first met him and his compact little wife
in a wood. They were walking to and fro intently conversing in Danish; but whenever they crossed our path
they made us low bows, which seemed very polite. We
learnt later that they were vainly seeking for the wife's
shawl, which had slipped off his arm.

The next Sunday they and we had simultaneously fled
to the many vine-clad arbours of the *pension*-garden from
the noise of dancing and singing in the *salle-à-manger*.
They explained to us, in the course of conversation, that
they were our fellow-boarders, but lived alone, as the
husband, who was an author named Müller—not a clergy-

man, as we had supposed from his black suit and white necktie—needed quiet for his literary labours. Telling them our name as an interchange of civility, they asked inquiringly, "What, William and Mary?" On the morrow we visited them in their cool little parlour to facilitate, if possible, their homeward movements. The war frustrated their plan of revisiting Italy, where they had been on their wedding-tour thirty years earlier; and only anxious safely to reach Denmark, they proposed journeying through France to England, and crossing from Hull to Copenhagen. This led to the production of a great parchment, signed and sealed by Christian IX., King of Denmark, King of the Goths and Vandals, in which His Majesty claimed free passage for "Frederik Paludan Müller, Danish author, Knight of the Danebrog," &c.

We mentioned to our neighbours at the supper-table what a distinguished man lived below.

"What! the old Professor?—the old *Theolog?*" exclaimed a weakly-chested Prussian medical student, who, unable to fight for his country, aided her cause by superintending the occupation of lint and bandage-making, daily carried on by the lady-boarders.

"What! Paludan Müller, who wrote the beautiful poem, 'At Vœre,' in which a child, puzzled with the strange mystery of existence, asks his mother what it is To Be?" demanded a fair-haired Norwegian, studying at the University.

"No other," we replied; and the next morning the courtly, gentle poet received a perfect ovation.

Frau Henriette Heine, the widow of Heinrich Heine's first cousin and fellow-student, was staying at the *pension*, and sympathised with France. Two middle-aged Jews and their wives, respectively from Carlsruhe and Baden-

Baden, professing no sentiments of *patrie* or *Vaterland*, smiled and were quiescent about the war, which was driving most of the guests at table frantic. The majority consisted of other Jews and refugees, presided over by a tall, stout, dark man in grey, also belonging to "the nation." He spoke most modern languages, had been much in England, had great concerns in Spain, important transactions in Germany, and twenty-three relatives in the Prussian army. Day and night he thought, spoke, and dreamt of the war; and, flaming with indignation, eloquently denounced Napoleon as the arch-troubler of the world.

In the general European excitement false rumours, of course, abounded. Thus, on Sunday morning, August 7, we were mysteriously followed out of doors by the *Knecht*. He was a big red-faced fellow, with curly hair, who went about with the sleeves of his pink shirt rolled up, revealing a pair of hairy arms like those of Esau. Putting his finger to his nose, he dismally whispered, " Awful news! The French have massacred twenty thousand Germans, the Crown Prince among them!" Awful, indeed, if true. But at the *table d'hôte*, in the midst of a joyous hubbub, we were jubilantly greeted by the man in grey with—" Glorious victory! Great defeat of the French! The Crown Prince has led his troops with flying colours! Hurrah!"

The words " Prussians! Wörth! Victory! Wounded French! Fallen French!" echoed through the house while daylight lasted. When the church-clocks of Zürich had long struck ten, and the *pension* had retired for the night, a lamp in the garden shed its light on the ruddy locks of the *Knecht*, who, now happily well-informed, see-sawing his sinewy arms up and down, held forth to a party of Zürich tradesmen, still lingering over their beer; and the everlasting chorus, in a high-pitched key, "Prussians! Wörth! Victory! Wounded French! Fallen French!" entered the room through the closed Venetian shutters.

On the morrow the rattle of vocal artillery, the rolling echo of cachinnation and of fun at the expense of France never ceased. We could picture the same simultaneous exultation in every hotel, inn, and coffee-house in Germany and the Protestant parts of Switzerland. We could still more vividly picture all the beautiful country from Saverne to Strasburg and Basel, which we had seen in April, peaceful, smiling, rich in growing crops and fruit-blossoms, backed by blue romantic-looking mountains, and full of happy, busy people, now devastated by fighting armies, and strewn with the bodies of the wounded and the dead.

When all was fair and affluent in Nature around us, the purple grapes ripening and the golden grain garnered, came the news of the German victories at Metz. It was the sudden collapse of the great French campaign; just as the army of Xerxes had melted away like mist before that of Greece, or Sennacherib's disappeared before the avenging hosts of Israel.

There was now no longer any fear for Switzerland; and on August 22, the eve of our departure for Ragatz, we saw three soldiers, who had returned from the watch on the frontier and were billeted for the night on our landlord, smoking their pipes in peace and contentment. The vague possibility of Napoleon the Third avenging the wrongs of Denmark passed from the minds of the Paludan Müllers, when they and we learned at Ragatz on Saturday, September 3, the astounding intelligence that the

Emperor had given himself up to King Wilhelm, and MacMahon surrendered with his entire army. On September 20, Napoleon's earlier advice to Cavour, "*Frappez vite et frappez fort*," was fully acted upon. Victor Emmanuel's troops entered Rome, and at the same time the astute abettor, disappointed in all his hopes, went into exile. The vicissitudes of war now opened to the Paludan Müllers a safe passage home through Germany, and to us every facility for reaching Rome.

The public mind was still in a most feverish state of sensational curiosity; we therefore felt it quite a relief, before leaving Ragatz, to speak with an old herdsman on a mountain-top, where, in rain and sunshine, he had spent the summer alone, fattening oxen for the butcher, and conning his Catholic Prayer-book. "He did not occupy himself," he said, "with kings, emperors, and their battles. The world's tumults were not his concern. He had to do his duty by the beeves, and fit his soul for a better world!" We admired the lean old rustic, who, guided by a high aim, evidently gleaned real satisfaction in his monotonous, abject existence.

The following is part of a letter written by William Howitt to his elder daughter from Zürich :—

"*August* 3, 1870.—I must tell you about your mother's and my visit to the institution for healing by prayer founded by Dorothea Trudel at Männedorf, on the Lake of Zürich. The establishment consists of four houses, situated in a lane. As we approached we saw people, who were evidently patients, sitting about on benches, and were told at the principal house that Herr Zeller, the present proprietor, was engaged till two o'clock. We could, if we liked, wait for him.

"We preferred to walk up the village to the church standing on the hill above us. The road led us between vineyards, past the nice white Parsonage, its garden a blaze of balsams. From the churchyard we had a splendid view of the hilly slopes above, the scattered white houses of Männedorf and those of Wädenswyl on the opposite shore; and the fine alps of St. Gall, Glarus, and Schwyz to the east. Nothing could be more delightful, nothing could give a more vivid idea of the pleasant places which God has created on this earth.

"Going round the handsome, well-kept church in search of shade, we found seats, and one of them already occupied by several young women in black dresses and white caps. We asked what was their service, and learnt they were Deaconesses, and had the charge of an infant-school to enable the mothers to go out to work in the fields, or better, to employ themselves at home.

"A little beyond was the cemetery, much resembling a Catholic one, only without holy-water stoups and crucifixes, but having little black crosses at the head of each grave. The gates were locked, as were the doors of the church. How odd is this characteristic of Protestantism! Not in England only, but in the very countries and towns on the Continent, where the inhabitants are of both faiths, the Catholic churches and cemeteries stand open and the Protestant ones are closed. The Catholics trust the public, but the Protestants cannot, so far as their churches and cemeteries are concerned; although walks and gardens are recommended by printed notices to the care of the public, and grapes, apples, and other tempting fruit hang close to your hand by the highways, and no man touches them. There must have been something hard and exclusive in the original leaven of Protestantism.

I have noticed that the Fathers of the Reformation, Bullinger, Calvin, Zwingli, &c., as painted by their contemporaries, have faces keen as the east wind, hard as the rock, and most uninviting. This sour severity they sent to Scotland by Knox, and transmitted it to the iron-souled Covenanters. That was a departure from Rome, but by no means a returning to the spirit of the Prince of Peace and Love, to the warm and liberal south of Heaven and of the soul. This is a curious fact.

"We managed to get the keys of the cemetery from a boy gathering the pastor's pears, and he showed us the grave of Dorothea Trudel. It was in the row of others, and in no way distinguished from the rest. It had its little black wooden cross, and this inscription in German :—'No. 41. Dorothea Trudel, born October 27, 1813, died September 6, 1862.' Some ivy was wreathed round the cross, and the small periwinkle bordered the grave. Your mother plucked a few leaves for you.

"We returned punctually to Herr Zeller's at two o'clock. All the doors stood open. Nobody seemed about. Your mother went, therefore, on a tour of exploration, and learnt that Herr Zeller was still engaged with a patient. We were shown into a small square room, very simply furnished, containing a harmonium, an open desk, a Bible, and several pious books, a white porcelain stove, and upon it a plaster group of a guardian angel and a child.

"At three o'clock Herr Zeller entered the room, a rather short, youngish man, in a grey coat, having no look of a clergyman, which, however, he is, for he preaches, and sometimes in St. Anna's Church in Zürich. He told us that he himself had come there as a patient to Dorothea

Trudel for a complaint in the head, which had been pronounced incurable, and which sometimes amounted almost to insanity. He was thoroughly cured, and remained and devoted himself to the work. He is obliged to have several helpers, men and women; and most of the latter had first been patients. He has about thirty cases of bodily disease, and the same number of mental; the charges being five francs each for the poor and ten francs for the wealthier patients weekly. 'This did not by any means cover the expenses, but the Lord sent money liberally.' He had also opened an establishment for children across the lake at Wädenswyl. The method pursued in both institutions was prudent sanitary precautions and dependence on the apostolic means of anointing with oil and prayer and laying on of hands. Sometimes he said the cures were instantaneous, sometimes slow, sometimes not at all. He appears a very candid, straight-forward man. He has other patients, who board in the village. Amongst these is an English lady who is suffering from melancholy."

Mary Howitt to the Same.

"*Bellagio, Oct.* 6, 1870.—Beauty is the law of Nature in this Italian country and clime. The one drawback is the shut-up-ness everywhere. There are no fields, merely vineyards or the beautiful grounds of villas, one and all enclosed by high white walls. It is true that beauty is visible above these walls: wild tangles of vegetation among the olives and fig-trees of the vineyards: roses and creepers, now gloriously scarlet and golden, falling over the walls of palace gardens, cypresses towering aloft like spires, tall magnolias, oleanders, and myrtles—very forests of them. Of these you get glimpses, but nothing more, from the dusty high road or the hot, paved paths. Nevertheless all is to me a series of glorious pictures, suggestive of Turner, of Leslie, of Leighton. Most lovely it is, but most tantalising; after the freedom of Switzerland, a great change most depressing to your father. He maintains that Italy is essentially the land of the painter, not of the poet, who, bird-like, requires the freedom of the fields and woods. There is truth in this. Across the lake, at the exquisite Villa Carlotta, I felt in a manner I had never done before the perfection of Art founded upon and aided by the beautiful in Nature — Nature, which makes the very pellitory on the white wall a drapery of beauty, which turns every mildew and damp stain into delicate colouring, and lends a nameless, indescribable poetry to the very decay and neglect which meet you everywhere."

The Same to the Same.

" *Nov.* 5, 1870. — We have been three days in Venice. It is far finer, far more astounding, far more pictorial and romantic, than I had ever imagined. The weather is glorious, the sky deep blue, and the sunshine quite hot. As all Venice is built to keep off the heat, the narrow, narrow streets are cold and dusky, but the sunshine lies broad and bright on the Grand Canal, on the piazza of St. Mark's, and all the open spaces. Every five minutes, almost, we are thinking of you and dear Alfred. Italy is, of all countries, that which he would love most. Since we have been here we have done nothing but shopping, with the exception of the dear old father, who strolls about, admiring and wondering at the strange old grandeur round him; turning into St. Mark's, when he is tired, to rest there; coming out again to see the pigeons fed, and buying a little loaf or Indian-corn and feeding them himself."

November 22 found us in Rome, and speedily estab-lished in our "own hired house," as St. Paul, great Teacher of the Gentiles, had been eighteen centuries earlier. We were located on the summit of one of the seven hills, at a corner of four converging streets, each visibly terminated by an historic monument : to the north by the Egyptian obelisk and piazza of Trinità de' Monte ; to the south by the lofty campanile and basilica of St. Maria Maggiore, stretching across its ample and elevated piazza, marked by another noble obelisk. To the east we had the Porta Pia, and the still open breach through which the Italian troops, two months earlier, had entered Rome. They had, by this deed, broken down the lofty garden-wall of the Bonaparte villa, trampled over and damaged the beautiful grounds, which we found gardeners putting in order. To the west, but a few paces from our door, extended the long side façade of the Quirinal palace, abutting on Monte Cavallo, with its Egyptian obelisk and famous group of Castor and Pollux reining their horses.

The keys of the Quirinal were still at the Vatican ; the doors had, however, been opened by a picklock, and troops of workmen were busy inside pulling down and building up ; whilst under the colonnade of the inner court were temporary heaps of old timber and wains-coting.

The preparations were made in the hope of the speedy advent of a reluctant and perplexed King, doomed to share with his *vis-à-vis* at the Vatican a capital that recalled merely papal or republican memories. The

Emperor Constantine, on becoming Christian, had found it advisable to remove the seat of government to Constantinople; and through the long succeeding centuries, Rienzi, the French, and "Young Italy" had each proclaimed the patrimony of the Popes a republic, not a monarchy. The thought oppressed Victor Emmanuel; he dreaded to sleep in the violated home of a deprived Pontiff, who was still charming the faithful by the meekness and patience with which he bore his sorrows.

On December 22 Rome was officially declared the capital of Italy. Yet the arrival of the King was constantly postponed. Many of our acquaintance said, indeed, that he never would come. Silence and gloom prevailed. There were no great Church functions, few strangers, and much discontent in the minds of hotel and lodging-house keepers. On Sunday, Christmas Day, it rained piteously; on Monday with increasing violence. On Wednesday the Tiber, having risen to a terrific height, most destructively inundated the lower parts of the city. On Friday the muddy, yellow waters had sufficiently subsided for people to be released from their terrible captivity; but wherever the flood had been, cellars and lower storeys were submerged. In the middle of the streets mud lay ankle-deep—thick, slimy mud, that adhered like ointment to everything it touched, and left a yellow stain behind. The scene of ruin was indescribable. In the Corso, grand plate-glass windows were obscured with mud, and panels of finely painted doors bulged with water. Anxious-looking shopkeepers and weary servants were splashed with the mud they were sweeping from within-doors on to the pavement. On Saturday, at four o'clock in the morning, we heard, as we lay in bed, a distant shout and a roar as of driving carriages. Up we jumped, and looking from our windows, saw, in a sudden illumination of Bengal light, the long-expected King, amid shouts of "*Evviva il Re!*" flash past in a state equipage, followed by other carriages and torches. It was the disaster of the flood that had brought him so suddenly; but after visiting the distressed portions of the city and leaving money for the sufferers, he departed the same night, New Year's Eve.

In February occurred the maddest Carnival that had been seen in Rome since 1848. Our niece and our young friend, after enjoying it amazingly, left the last day but one of the Carnival, under suitable escort, for England; and the evening before their departure, went with Margaret and some of our acquaintance to drink at the Fountain of Trevi, that they might come back to Rome. In their absence we sent down our old woman-servant, Rosa, a peasant from Rimini, to the landlord, who dwelt below, with the request that the street-door might be left ajar and the oil-lamp on the stairs not extinguished until the *signorine* returned.

What, then, was our surprise and horror, when Rosa rushed into the drawing-room, shrieking that "the *birbone* (rascal) of a landlord had *bastinaded* her;" therewith pointing to the marks of a cane across her face. She was pursued by the perpetrator, a man of a melancholy countenance and black hair and eyes. He, livid with rage, was followed by his handsome young wife in a great flutter. Our servant denounced them for claiming our charcoal ashes for their *bucato*—the buck or lye for their clothes to soak in ; they, her, for shutting a door in their son's face. This in their eyes was a tremendous offence ; nevertheless we managed politely to get the couple back to their own premises. Rosa was beyond us. Screaming and weeping, she threw open a window, and shrieked her wrongs into the street. This led to the speedy arrival of two policemen, one of whom remained pacing up and down before the house, much to the surprise of the party returning from the Fountain of Trevi.

We were not wholly unprepared for this outburst of hot Italian temper on the part of our *padrone*. He had more than once, without the least provocation, suddenly appeared on the verge of a towering rage ; then, conquering his passion, would send up flowers or newspapers, as if to remove any disagreeable impression. The morning after the assault he wrote a letter to my husband, "asking pardon for the scandal, but requiring us to dismiss our wicked servant, who was an offence to his excellent consort." As Rosa, notwithstanding her curious habit of drinking our lamp-oil like water, suited us admirably, and as inquiries in the neighbourhood confirmed our suspicions of our landlord's excitability, William appealed to the British Consul.

Mr. Severn, the artist, the devoted friend and nurse of Keats, held this post; and my husband, calling at the Consulate, found him occupied at his easel, in a studio approached through a suite of lofty rooms hung with paintings, and in person reminding him of Coleridge in the decline of life : the somewhat corpulent tendency, the black velvet waistcoat, a certain similarity of features, and the head slightly thrown back in talking. On hearing of the fray he said—

"I've known Italians die in these furies, in what they call a *Rabbiatura*. It is best to cow such people, who are generally poltroons. Fifty years ago the

Roman eating-houses were much worse than now. Dear Keats and I had such wretched dinners sent in, that he told me one morning 'he had hit on a plan for us to be better served.' I wondered what he meant to do, for I knew no Italian in those days, and Keats, though quick at learning, not enough to discuss the merits of a dinner. The *trattore* brought the food, as usual, in a basket. Keats lifted the lid, and perceiving at a glance the quality of the fare, without a word took each dish to the window and emptied it into the street. The cook never charged us for the dinner, and gave us a good one ever after.

"I did not forget that lesson. After poor, gentle, vivacious Keats was dead of his consumption, our *padrone*, fearing infection, burnt the furniture, for which he sent me in a tremendous bill. After it had been discharged, he summoned me a month later to pay for the broken crockery. On going to the house where we had dwelt, at the right-hand corner of the Spanish steps ascending to the Trinità de' Monte, he showed me on a table a pile of broken plates, cups, and saucers, which he must have ransacked the neighbourhood to collect. Feigning a great rage, with one fell swoop I dashed all the bits to the floor, and the affair was settled."

Mr. Severn effectually silenced our *padrone*, notwithstanding the ominous postscript to his final bill: "He meant to be legally indemnified for all the damage we had done—*chi rompe paga.*" This sentence, placarded at the time about Rome in pink, blue, and yellow, had greatly puzzled us. One reading of it was, whichever, King or Pope, broke the peace would have to pay. It might have some such covert meaning, just as, in 1873, the words in large letters, "*Abbasso Verdi*," were no opprobrious term for the composer of *Il Trovatore* and other popular modern operas, but signified "Down with *Vittorio Emanuele, Re d'Italia;*" the word Verdi being employed for an acrostic.

The conduct of our later landlords seemed swayed by combined feelings of liking for their tenants and self-interest. We never again met with such an instance of unbridled, fierce, and turbulent irascibility. But then this *padrone*, who has since been elevated to the rank of a *cavaliere* by the Italian Government, was notorious for his violence. When we were located in charming new quarters, the rector of a college, now a bishop in America, was charged with a message to us from an Italian priest, to the effect that, having dwelt above us, he should have personally expressed at the time his sympathy in our annoyance, but for the molestation it might have entailed on his landlord's family, who were the second-floor tenants of our *padrone*. My husband next read in his Roman newspaper that the female servant of the same *padrone*, having on one holiday exceeded her leave of absence, was accompanied back by a policeman, who threatened to punish her master if he attempted to maltreat her.

The good offices of Margaret Foley, the gifted, generous-hearted New England sculptress, and her tender-spirited young friend, Lizzy H——, had procured us a much better home than we had earlier enjoyed. It was with these and some other valued friends that William and I celebrated our golden wedding, on April 16, 1871, by a memorable excursion to Castel Fusano.

Starting from our dwelling in the Via di Porta Pinciana—so called from the closed gate where the blind

Belisarius is said to have sat and begged—and passing through the Porta di San Paolo, which he rebuilt, we drove over the solitary Campagna, green with spring grass and leaves, for fifteen miles. Then, leaving, to our right, the ancient walls and castle of Ostia—a place so endeared to many devout souls from its pathetic association with St. Augustine and his dying mother— we proceeded a couple of miles to Prince Chigi's park, Castel Fusano. There, in one of the avenues of huge stone-pines, we deposited our wraps and provisions, and greeted by a nightingale and gathering masses of fragrant flowers, we wandered on for another mile to the Mediterranean.

No words can describe the beauty of the scene. A causeway paved with blocks of lava led from the back of the ancient castellated mansion, on its lawny meadows, between woods of arbutus, phillyrea, of flowering daphne, cistus, myrtle, and heath twenty feet high, carpeted with crimson cyclamens and overshadowed by the solemn ilex, cork, and pine, to a somewhat desolate beach of shifting sands, held together by tufts of sea-wheat and the eringo, with its blue-green, thistle-like foliage. It was wonderful to be where in all probability the Christian philosopher, Minucius Felix, and his friend Octavius walked from " that very pleasant city, Ostia, . . . tracking the coast of the gently bending shore ;" and although, after a lapse of sixteen centuries, all now was solitary and deserted, yet, just as then, " the sea, always restless, even when the winds are lulled, came up on the shore with waves crisp and curling."

We had a merry collation in an avenue of stone-pines near Prince Chigi's fine old casino ; then, after wading to our waists through a sea of flowering asphodels to gain

a clear view of the Pontine Marshes, drove back in a
summer-like evening to Rome.

It had been a fine April morning fifty years earlier
when William and I, with our nearest relatives, walked
to Meeting, all the little town of Uttoxeter looking
on. I wonder I did not feel very nervous. We had
some of the Friends to dinner—a better one than usual ;
if I remember rightly, a cook was engaged for the occasion from the White Hart. Then William and I and all
the young people strolled in the garden and up to the
Bank Closes, a nice little home walk. After our return
rain fell. We had more Friends to tea ; all those who
had not been invited to dinner. Afterwards the sun came
out, and we left in quite a splendid sunset. I remember
so well how bright the evening was after the rain, and
have often thought it was like our life—marked by April
showers, with a lovely calm sunset. From the period of
our arrival in Rome, I may truly say that the promise in
Scripture, " At evening time it shall be light," was in our
case fulfilled.

CHAPTER VII.

ROME AND TYROL.

1871–1879.

Our tenants in England were desirous of continuing
their lease of The Orchard, and we to stay on in Italy,
where the climate had something so soothing, so exactly
fitting to old age. I prized in Rome the kind, sympathetic friends given to us, the ease of social existence,
the poetry, classic grace, the peculiar and deep pathos
diffused around; above all, the stirring and affecting
historic memories; for every stone and monument spoke
of famous classic or Christian deeds, of the blood of
martyrs and the virtues of saints. It was a locality which
led me to perceive how, in a manner, each person makes
his own heaven or hell. To some of our intimate friends
Rome was truly, in the words of Dante—

> " The holy place wherein
> Sits the successor of the greatest Peter ; "

the centre of triumphant Christianity, sacred as Jerusalem until the Crucifixion. To others it held the position of pagan Rome to the early Christians—a centre
of cruelty, abomination, and duplicity, its sanitary shortcomings being a type of its social condition. To me it
was a city of habitation after long wanderings in the
wilderness ; to my husband—who did not unreservedly

share my enthusiasm—it became, as well as to myself, the finishing-school of our earthly life.

In the June of 1871, accompanied by Miss Foley, we went for the summer to Tyrol, where we were quite providentially led, in the neighbourhood of Bruneck, to an old mansion called Mayr-am-Hof, which, though

MAYR-AM-HOF.

evidencing a slow decline, stood up massive and grand at the farther end of the gradually ascending village of Dietenheim. It was a long building, with lofty roof and dormer-windows, plastered and painted after the Palladian style in effective designs to represent Grecian pilasters, circles, and other ornamentations, and pro- tected by much fine ironwork that grated the windows

or swelled out in jutting balconies. It had a back-
yard and farm-buildings of no mean order, seen through
a stately but somewhat ruinous entrance, conspicuously
surmounted by a fresco painted dull red and white,
like the rest of the building. The subject, in harmony

ENTRANCE TO THE BACK-YARD.

with the religious faith in Tyrol, represented the Virgin
and Child attended by St. Joseph ; a guardian angel and
its human charge ; St. John Nepomucen, protector against
floods ; and St. Florian, against fire.

We learnt from a tall young peasant, with a refined

countenance and the most self-possessed manners, that
the place belonged to his father. The family merely
occupied a portion, and the rest was empty. We expressed a desire to inspect the interior, and were courteously conducted upstairs through a great stone hall into
a saloon of vast dimensions, with a fine embossed ceiling
of stucco, and lighted by eight windows. We were
shown an adjoining room wainscoted, having the char-

THE FRESCO.

acter of an oratory; and recrossing the hall, a spacious
chamber, possessing a long interior latticed casement,
screened by an old-fashioned chintz curtain with a kneeling bench under it, and opening like a squire's pew into
the old chapel. We were taken, on the second floor, into
three vacant rooms occupying the broad southern gable-
front, the centre one having a balcony which commanded
a splendid view up and down the Pusterthal.

Although the rooms were almost bare, they were furnished with beautiful views, had noble proportions and well-scrubbed floors; and the whole place, from its uniqueness, space, and dignified decay, so appealed to our taste that we esteemed ourselves fortunate to be accepted as tenants. Our landlord, who had never let rooms before, was Anton Mutschlechner, best known as the "*Hof-bauer*," a spare man in a brown homespun jacket faced with green, unless it were some great Church festival, when he donned the long Noah's Ark coat in which he was married a quarter of a century before. He was a quiet disciplinarian, given to hard toil and pious meditation. In 1809 he had been a funny little Tyroler boy, whom the French officers then quartered in Mayr-am-Hof petted and caressed. They were otherwise terrible and alarming lodgers, who burnt cartloads of wood in the great stoves, damaging, cracking, and ever after rendering unserviceable the elaborate pile of white faience in the saloon.

We vastly enjoyed our Robinson Crusoe life at Mayram-Hof, where a godly routine of prayer and labour hallowed the entire household. Margaret Foley, a born carpenter and practical inventor, set to work, and so did my husband, and made us all sorts of capital contrivances. Thus, with fine weather out-of-doors and a roof over our heads, we lacked nothing. Behind the house a common gently sloped upwards, surmounted by an old crucifix and two lime-trees. There we sat evening after evening to watch the wonderful sunset after-glow on a group of strange, rugged dolomite mountains. They filled up the eastern end of the valley, and became indescribably beautiful and strangely spiritual as they flushed crimson, melted into deep violet, faded a

ghastly grey, then were shrouded from view by the pall
of night.

Substantial Mayr-am-Hof, so attractive to us in its
venerable decay, grew from a retreat for a few weeks
into our permanent summer home.   Leaving hot weather

THE STOVE OF WHITE FAIENCE.

and ripe cherries in Rome, we have hastened thither at
the beginning of May to find the sparkling snow lying
thick and low on the mountains; the trees leafless, but a
green flush on the giant poplar, and the cherry-blossoms
ready to burst forth.   The fleeting hours, however, soon

brought us sultry summer heat, interspersed with heavy thunderstorms. Then came calm, cloudless autumn days, when the fir-trees stood out black against the intense blue, fathomless sky, with here and there a mountain ash or a wild-cherry dyed gold or crimson; but all other foliage suggestive of July. Next came November, with gloomy heavens, withered scattered leaves, wild winds and rattling casements, making us thankful to cross the bare, brown plain to the railway station, *en route* for benign and radiant Italy.

Resuming now the chronological thread from April 1871, the following passages from letters tell the story sufficiently.:—

MARY HOWITT TO HER ELDER DAUGHTER.

"*Casa Overbeck, Rocca di Papa, May* 30, 1871.— Here we are very comfortable and well, the father cheerful as the day is long; but it is decided that we act on the original plan, and go on in a fortnight to Tyrol. Mr. Carl Hoffmann is a good young fellow, and has done all he could to make us comfortable. He apologised once for seeming to make so free with us, but said he felt at home with us from the first moment; there was something about us that reminded him of his grandfather Overbeck, whose memory he greatly reveres. He arranged everything for us to go to the flower-festival at Genzano the day before yesterday. We had five donkeys, and nothing could have been pleasanter.

"On Friday the 26th we walked to Hannibal's Camp, which is a meadow platform of great extent above the volcanic heights of Rocca di Papa. There we were met by a little troop of lads, all rags and tatters, with bare, dirty feet, and either bare-headed or with old round-crowned hats, which tumbled almost over their noses. On they came in single file along the narrow channel of the rock-road, shouldering stout sticks for guns, and under the command of a little active urchin with white paper bands on his arm and the air of a general. We had to step aside to make way for them, when at once a halt was called. The juvenile troop was marshalled on a broad shelf of rock, and quick as lightning went through their evolutions. They shouldered, grounded their arms, fired, charged, fired again, and twice, at the command of their officer, fell flat to the ground, and so fired, taking aim at the village of Marino, lying far below, four miles off, on the edge of the Latin plain.

"The eldest of this little company was eleven, the youngest probably seven, yet all had the most perfect self-composure and every movement was agile and graceful. But this was no other than a tiny Papalini troop, true to the Holy Father, and ready, as they thought, to fight for him. The worst of this Italian peasantry is, that all are beggars. The Roman Church has so long taught that alms-giving is a cardinal virtue that it has converted the people into suppliants for charity; so now our brave little Papalini troop had no sooner gone through their manœuvres than their leader stepped forward, and stretching out his small dirty hand said with an air of coaxing beggary, '*Dateci qualche cosa.*' But we never give to the beggars, so we parted somewhat disgusted with each other.

"When, however, we were advancing up the steep Rocca di Papa street with our train of donkeys, on Sunday, we soon found ourselves attacked by the *dateci qualche cosa* tribe; and amongst them the small officer of the former evening, with his stout stick which had served then for a gun still in his hand. He was there, all smiles and courtesy; and with something of the old martial character, declared himself now to be our defender. Turning to Carl Hoffmann, he said, 'I knew these creatures would tease you with their begging; so I have come to attend you to Genzano, Signor Carlo.'—'What a clever little lad that is!' we remarked. 'He is an old acquaintance of mine,' replied Herr Hoffmann; 'he is Ernesto, the *Maestro di Casa*, as you will find before long.'

"We went to Genzano through the great chestnut woods which clothe these hillsides. Above us, and now left behind, was the white convent of the Passionists on the lofty Monte Cavo, where until the time of Cardinal York were the ruins of the great temple of Jupiter. Here and there through openings in the woods we saw below us the far-spreading Campagna; beyond, the green wooded heights of Albano and Castel Gandolfo; and beyond, all the silver belt of the sea. The path was so narrow through the woods that we advanced in single file, with bushes of golden broom bending beneath their weight of flowers, and with such a mass of blossoming plants below, bordering the way-side, as could only be equalled in an English flower-garden: balsam-like archangels, vetches of the loveliest and most varied growths, laburnums, sweet mignonette, roses, white masses of arenaria, rockets, asphodels, now just over, wild sweet peas, columbines, cytisus. We thought the flowers beautiful in Switzerland; they are still more so in this finer climate.

"On we went for four or five pleasant miles and

village, Rocca di Papa, is the funniest place you can
conceive. It is built up the face of a great rock, house
above house, looking from below a dense mass of buildings. The streets are too steep for carriages, and in many
places a succession of steps. It is the filthiest village
imaginable; and the population, about three thousand
persons, are as thick on the ground as rabbits in a warren.
In an evening they are all out in the streets, so that you
have a full view of them. They are a most Irish-looking
population. The men dress exactly like Irish, in rough,
coarse bluish coats, breeches, and old sunburnt hats, with
tapering crowns and slouching brims. The women, however, are very different, dressing in bright colours, red,
lilac, and yellow, with a square piece of white linen on
their heads, or else a coloured kerchief."

MARY HOWITT TO HER SON AND DAUGHTER-IN-LAW.

"*Dietenheim, Tyrol, Aug.* 6, 1871.—We had a great
desire to go up to the Alm or Alp, that we might be able
to understand the life of these simple people thoroughly.
The *Hof-bauer* begged that we would do so, and make
ourselves quite at home with the best they could offer us.
We accordingly invited Maria, the daughter, to accompany
us. She is a tall, buxom young woman of about four-
and-twenty, full of good-humour, and was highly delighted
with the invitation.

"We went in the *Stellwagen* to the village of Taufers;
and engaging a man at the inn to carry up our personal
belongings and our ample provisions, we set off on foot
up a magnificent valley, ever ascending through ancient
woods of larch and spruce, and by the side of a tumultuous
river which comes down from mountains ten to eleven
thousand feet high. This steep road, which no carriage

can ascend, is traversed by the herds of cattle, that come here in the early summer and return in the autumn, their hoofs being able to find foothold on the rock; and it is curious that, so delighted are the cattle to go thither for the summer after the winter's confinement in the stall, that they make the journey with a kind of joyful impatience, going on still more eagerly as they approach the end; and when they have reached the accustomed alp, rushing to the higher summit as if they could not sufficiently enjoy the luxury of the change. These are the cattle which have already been on the alp, the new-comers are often at first timid, and have to learn how to walk upon and climb amongst the rocks. When, however, the summer is nearing to its close, they seem to long for their warm stalls, because the nights and mornings are bitterly cold and early frosts nip the grass; so they appear delighted to return, and rush on with the same eagerness the nearer they approach the old home, each one turning with joyful haste into its own accustomed stall, which they never mistake.

"When we had walked about five hours, and were getting very weary, we reached the village of Rein or St. Wolfgang, standing on the edge of a very watery little plain or central valley, into which many streams flow. Here we turned into a lesser valley, the Bachenthal, a perfect paradise of an Alpine valley. Just then it began to rain, and we had to walk along narrow paths, through mowing grass full of flowers, on and on till, when it was quite dusk, we came to a châlet where the *Hof-bauer's pächter*, a tenant farmer, lives. The *pächter*, with his men, was at supper when we arrived; the wife was busy in the little kitchen baking cakes to be eaten hot with their milk. If we had been comets of the sky we could not

have made much more excitement among them. What was to be done with these new-comers, these outlandish people? But Maria set all right. In the room where the men were at supper we had, later, our evening meal, one of these men meantime hastening off for Jakob Mutsch-lechner, Maria's youngest brother, who was higher up the mountain, at the *senner* huts. The farmer's two children—lads of about eight and ten—crept to the top of the big stove and looked on with wonder as we ate our supper. When it was about half over, Jakob, in his shirt-sleeves and his jacket loosely thrown over his shoulder, made his appearance. He is a perfect gentleman in manners, and made us right welcome.

" We slept in the barn, which was half-full of new hay, sweet and clean ; and were speedily wakened by a storm of thunder and lightning, deluging rain, and a wild wind that seemed as if it would tear off the very roof. Here was a prospect for us ! The thunder and lightning passed over, but the rain continued. No matter, we would lie in the hay till it was fine. In the morning Maria brought us coffee in a brown earthenware pot, and hot milk in a brown, broad, open dish, from the house through the rain. We sat in the hay, and made a capital and very merry breakfast. By eleven, the rain having ceased, we set off for the *senner* huts. Again it was ever ascending, as if into the very bosom of the great snow-covered mountains, through a region of rocks and woods, with intervals of the greenest, finest pasture. Presently the woods opened, and standing upon a wild, stony hillside, the magnificent mountains shutting it in on all hands, we came upon a group of *senner* huts, which delighted your father, as they bore a striking resemblance to a rich Australian station. There were, I think, fourteen separate buildings, all of wood, in the picturesque Tyrolean style; five were dwellings, and the rest cattle-sheds and barns. Our people's huts were the highest of all, and we had a long climb over rocks before we reached them, Jakob coming down to meet and bid us welcome. He and good old Franz, the *senner*, occupied one hut, half of which was the dairy, where stood pans of rich milk and cream. Jakob is the herdsman; he has to count up the cattle daily and bring them in; the oxen, however, of which there are seven yoke, lie out all the night. Franz is dairyman.

"No sooner had we arrived than the latter appeared with a frying-pan, and having taken the thick cream from five pans of milk, proceeded to make cream-pancakes, which proved to be a most dainty dish, although made over a fire of logs in the kitchen, where there was no chimney, the smoke issuing through long slits in the wall. Your father and I sat on wooden stools and watched the cooking process, he interesting the old *senner* and Jakob by stories of Australian life and travel, which the present scenes brought back livingly and pleasantly to his mind. In the meantime the two Margarets had set to work at a cold collation in the dairy. But I assure you the cream-pancakes were better than anything we had taken with us. Besides, it was the right dish to eat in a *senner* hut; and in return we gave these mountaineers of our ham and cold fowl and almond-cake, which were as great luxuries to them.

"After our dinner Jakob went to attend to his herdsman's duties. Franz, a right good old Tyroler, who has been many years in the service of this family, and who, in his old leathern breeches and bare knees, his Tyrolese hat, green waistcoat, and broad leathern belt, is a right pleasant sight to see, had no sooner cleaned and washed his frying-pan at the long trough made of a hollowed tree-trunk, which holds a supply of the finest running water, than he was at our service. We wanted to go up to the glacier, which we imagined (as it looked now so near to us, lying in the bosom of the great Hochgall, ten thousand feet high) to be within a walk; but it proved to be at some hours' distance, and thus unattainable. However, Franz took us to the wild waterfall formed by the torrent which comes down from the glacier; and never in my life do I expect again to have a walk through such scenery, so wild and chaotic; through such old, old woods where the giant trees stand up, scathed and bleached by lightning and storm, like towers, or lie tumbled in the wildest, dreariest confusion, amongst giant rocks, like the remains of some old world. I thought what English word expressed the character of this scenery. I could only think of chaotic desolation: the German word *schauderhaft* gives some idea of it. Through such scenery we went till we reached the wild, foaming water which came down from the glacier, and crossing this by an Alpine bridge, we found ourselves in a lovely green pasture, scattered over with rocks, running into lofty mounds and sinking into fairy-like glens, out of which rose lofty fir-trees of the finest growth; and all round rose up the craggy mountains, and high above the cold, icy glacier.

"We reached the *senner* hut about five o'clock, had a right pleasant tea, and so back to our hay-barn. It was a calm, still night, and in the early dawn we heard the *pächter* 'denzelling' his scythe—that is, beating the edge fine on a little iron anvil, a work which the mower does each morning preparatory to his day's work. By this it was evident that the morning was fine; and by six o'clock the sun shone through the chinks in the wooden walls, and looking through the door, I saw the little goat-herd and the goats ascending the craggy rocks which directly faced the barn. Your father had been out for a walk, and came in to breakfast with flowers stuck in his hat Tyrolean fashion. He had been out gathering them and reading his Roman newspaper, which comes to him every day. Again we visited the *senner* huts ; and the following morning set off on our homeward way. The descent seemed to us quite as fatiguing as the climb, perhaps even more so, because, the road being flagged with rude stones, we came down by irregular steps."

" *Via Sistina, Rome, Nov.* 3, 1871.—October in Tyrol was a season of pastoral festivity, when the cattle returned from their various alps or summer pastures, with their barbaric crowns, embroidered neck-belts, bells, and garlands—the roads being filled with these sleek, well-fed herds, with the lesser flocks of goats and sheep, like the migrating wealth of the ancient patriarchs. On they came proudly, the very cattle conscious of their own dignity and worth, attended by the no less conscious *senner* and his subordinates, all in their Sunday best, and hats decorated with mountain flowers. A truly Idyllic show of cattle slowly passing through villages to their home-pastures.

" '*A Roma!*' It was very pleasant to make this reply to the hurrying porter, who, snatching up an armful of our numerous smaller impedimenta at the crowded railway station of Florence, demanded whither we were bound. It was fourteen days since we left the happy Tyrol. We had travelled leisurely, visiting Padua and Bologna ; and had lastly lingered for eight days among the art treasures and the kindly people of Florence. 'If you are for Rome, make haste and secure your places!' said a friendly voice, 'for the crowd which is going is immense.'

"So it was. A detachment of the thirty thousand Government officials, high and low, and their families, whose exodus from Florence to Rome has left so many houses vacant in the one city, and elated the hearts and whetted the cupidity of landlords in the other, was unquestionably on the move this morning. Thus two unusually crowded trains arrived at Rome from Florence at the same moment, we of the express, and the ordinary train, which had preceded us from Florence by two or three hours, and both bringing in such crowds of people, with interminable piles of luggage, that it was nearly an hour before we could receive our own and depart.

"Rome is indeed becoming a busy and a populous city; and our friends, as we proceeded homeward, gave us to understand the almost impossibility which it had appeared a week ago that quarters could be found for us. New streets were being laid out, and new houses had been built; but who that knew their date would venture into them this first season? Margaret Foley had, however, found a cosy little home for us in the Via Sistina."

To MRS. ALFRED WATTS.

"*Nov.* 5, 1871.—Oh! if only Alfred and you were here I should be ready to say, 'Let Henry Chorley's words about us be true. Let us all live out our lives in this kindly and beautiful Italy, to which surely God has given all the charms of the earth.' As it is, however,

I feel at times as if even gloomy England, with its drab atmosphère, would be pleasanter if one could only sit down by the fireside with you. But we will leave all to God, for He will do that which is best for each of us ; and we do not know, any one of us, what He designs by us or what He has in store for us. Please give my affectionate regards to Henry Chorley when you see him next ; and you can tell him, if you like, that though I hold much of the old Catholic faith, and though I am convinced that within the walls of many convents many souls live in close communion with God, yet no one believes more firmly than I do in the anti-Christianity of the Papacy, and that we are watching with the intensest interest the progress of events, which will, we trust, bring about its downfall.

"I must now give you an idea, if I can, of our locality. Looking up the street, the piazza of the Trinità de' Monte immediately opens out before us, with the distant heights of Monte Mario, where the sun now sets, and the evening skies are beautiful. Just opposite to us is the old palace of some Queen of Poland, a rather dingy-looking place, with traces of grandeur about it. It forms the division between the Via Sistina and the Via Gregoriana, which unite in the piazza. Grand old painters have lived about here—Poussin, Claude Lorraine, Salvator Rosa. The old house of the Queen of Poland was built by the artists Taddeo and Federigo Zuccaro ; and when Bartholdy, the Prussian Consul, lived in it, he employed Overbeck, Schadow, Veit, and Cornelius to cover the walls of an upper chamber with frescoes from the life of Joseph. These art-brethren of St. Luke also dwelt at one time near here, at the top of the Via St. Isidore, in the monastery of that name. It is an Irish Franciscan institution,

and its church is dedicated both to St. Patrick and St.
Isidore. Opposite to the monastery of St. Isidore is the
little church of Maria Riparatrice, where candles are
ever burning, and at all hours a nun kneels before the
altar, her sky-blue and white robes flowing around her;
an immovable figure, in uninterrupted prayer or adora-
tion. It is a wonderful sight. Of course, there must be
a relay of nuns for this severe service, but apparently
it is ever the same—the same blue and white flowing
garments, the same attitude."

"*Jan.* 25, 1872.—We have been to the Hôtel
d'Angleterre, to meet, at the invitation of Mr. and Mrs.
Betts, Dr. Manning and Dr. Davis of the Religious
Tract Society. They received us most kindly, Dr.
Manning explaining that his mother was, in the very
ancient Uttoxeter days, a schoolfellow of mine, Mary
Bakewell, and that she often spoke of me as 'little
Mary Botham, who used to sit upon a box and tell
stories; in fact, romances without end.' Of this romanc-
ing I know nothing; though, from our dear father being
anxious that we should have 'a guarded education,'
Anna and I did sit on a big box near Mrs. Parker, and
the other children generally on seats in the room. Of
course, I remember Mary Bakewell; she was a big girl
and very nice, one whom I admired, and of whom I
retain a most distinct and pleasant remembrance. These
two gentlemen next proceeded to business, requesting
me from Dr. Macaulay to furnish a series of papers on
Italy to the *Leisure Hour.*

"Yesterday afternoon Meggie and I drank coffee with
Frau Hoffmann—such excellent coffee, that we smelt
it before we reached the door; such delicious little cakes

and bread, cold water, and fine linen. What a treat
we had afterwards in looking over some of the multitudinous sketches and studies of Overbeck! Such exquisite bits of drapery, flowers, and foliage, drawn in
pencil, just like yours, with such conscientious care and
love—hundreds of them. It was a real feast of delight,
and she so old-fashioned, living only in the memory of
that '*lieber Vater*,' and wishing that Carluccio (her
son Carl) would but work as hard as his grandfather.
It poured with rain, but we sat with the window open,
looking into the grand old Barberini gardens, with a
great plaster-group of the Saviour blessing St. John,
almost filling up the room behind us; and after the
coffee-tray was removed, the table was covered with
these studies and sketches of the blessed Overbeck."

"*Jan.* 29.—Mr. and Mrs. Edward Flower, of Stratford-on-Avon, are now in Rome. He is a grand old
man, with the head of a Jupiter, very philanthropic, and
most humane to horses, being the most determined foe
of the bearing-rein. With his cheerful wife I have
been drawn into a pleasant bond of fellowship from her
connection with the Society of Friends.

"Yesterday Mr. Flower invited Meggie and me to drive
with him and his niece to vespers at St. Peter's. It
was a long time since we had been there, and we enjoyed
it greatly. We sat in the choir chapel and heard the
beautiful music. Then we drove, like any other worldly
people, to the Pincio, following the King's carriage; and
Mr. Flower, who evidently enjoys these things, had quite
a child's pleasure in seeing the King, ugly man though
he be, and taking off his hat to him; then, later on,
meeting Prince Humbert, who at the first glance of

Mr. Flower took off *his* hat to him, and again a second time. At first Mr. Flower could not understand these salutations. Then he suddenly remembered that the gentleman driving with the Prince was his Master of the Horse, to whom, five years ago, when Mr. Flower was last in Italy, he sold a splendid horse for two hundred guineas. Some time afterwards, in Florence, he met again this official, who told him how delighted the Prince was with the horse, and that His Royal Highness had given it the name of Flower. I was foolish enough to enjoy driving round and round the Pincio, as the rest of the world did, till the sun had sunk behind St. Peter's, and warned the invalid Mr. Flower that it was time to return. We met the dear old father entering the Pincio gardens, but, bless his heart! he never once looked at the gay throng, and all our joint efforts to win a sign of recognition from him were in vain."

"*Feb.* 6, 1872.—Yesterday Mr. Flower was here, and began talking about Joel Churchill, whose adventures with the bear, you may remember, was one of your father's standard stories to you when you were children. Joel Churchill was one of the settlers in America with Morris Birkbeck and Benjamin Flower, the father of our friend, who himself ran wild in the woods till he was nineteen, full of health and strength and all kinds of practical knowledge. By his own wish he, at that age, returned to England, for he remembered a little girl, with whom he had played when a child, and as he grew to man's estate he knew that he loved her. I never heard a more beautiful story than Mr. Flower's. He married the little girl he loved, and became a very prosperous and wealthy man. Two-and-twenty years later he paid a visit to the old backwoods' settlement, which then had grown into vast prosperity; and there still was Joel Churchill, living on the outskirts of civilisation, in his bed, shaking with an ague fit, and his door guarded by a bear, which he had taken young and trained as his watch-dog. Mr. Flower says that Thackeray used to come to him often for these old stories. They both belonged to the Reform Club, and if Thackeray could get him into a corner, he would beg him to relate something about that wild fresh life of the Far West. After his return from America as a youth, he was much with his cousins, Sarah Flower and her sister, and fully appreciates their memory."

"*March* 3, 1872.—One of the most interesting features here, to our mind, is the Scandinavian Society, comprising Swedes, Danes, Norwegians, and Finns. None of them are rich, the sculptor Jerichau and his noted wife, the painter, being the most so ; the whole style of these foreigners is the purest simplicity combined with culture and hospitality. Their love of the sunny South is, as you know, intense. They are devoted to art in its three branches, music, painting, and sculpture. They associate amongst themselves, and Fredrika Bremer's cousin, Mdlle. Aline Bremer, from Finland, is a sort of aunt to many of them. Young Tegnér, the grandson of the great poet, and called Esaias after him, belongs to this little community this winter."

MARY HOWITT TO HER HUSBAND, THEN IN ENGLAND.

"*Casa Hoffmann-Overbeck, Rocca di Papa, May* 26, 1872.—We are most comfortable here—could not be more so. All is so still ; were it not that the great

Gothic-shaped clock in our sitting-room has been set going. It reminds me of some very self-sufficient country-woman come on a visit to you. She makes a bustle with every movement, she smacks her lips as she eats, she sups her soup with a noise, she breathes loud, and has a way of sighing to herself—great big sighs that startle you with the idea that something is wrong; and when she has the least trifle to say she mouths and makes a great fuss. That is the way with this clock. I can never cease hearing the tick-tacking; every now and then the inside jerks and rumbles. But the beginning to strike is a thing never to be forgotten. Notice is given ten minutes before that it is about to begin, and then it purrs and buzzes, and at last blurts out the hour in a way to frighten you. It needs winding up twice in the twenty-four hours, and with this attention, and if you can put up with its oddities, it is not a bad clock."

"*May* 29, 1872.—It is deliciously pleasant. As I lift my eyes I have the most magnificent view before me, Rome lying clear, as if mapped out in light. It is exquisite. The nightingales never cease singing or the cuckoo shouting. Below, on the slopes of the hill, where the young chestnuts are shooting up thick and green after last year's charcoal-burning, a long line of men and boys are hoeing their potatoes and singing their melancholy songs in chorus. I love to hear it. I fancy that singing must come down from the time of the old Sabines. It is wonderfully wailing and pathetic.

"Frau Hoffmann went to Rome on Saturday; and on Sunday, Herr Knudsen, the Dane, the Jerichau girls, and

their governess set off through the woods to Albano,
where Alberto Paulsen, the grandson of Thorwaldsen,
was to meet them from Porto d'Anzio, where he had
been quail-shooting. The Rocca di Papa party faithfully promised Mademoiselle Gotschalk, Knudsen's aunt,
to be back by eight o'clock, by which time in these
southern latitudes it is quite dark. Most especially
did she lay this injunction on them, as Carl Hoffmann,
when he was here the other day, told her it was better
not to be out late at night or unprotected in the lonely
woods. A nice dainty supper was cooked for them
by 'Mamsell,' Mademoiselle Gotschalk's companion, but
they never came. Hour after hour passed. There was
nothing for it but for everybody to go to bed. The
next morning, soon after our breakfast, we heard such
a tramping upstairs and such a talking. Soon after
Mademoiselle Gotschalk came into our room to relate
the yesterday's adventures. Young Paulsen had driven
from Porto d'Anzio, accompanied by a gendarme who
had been ill of fever and recently bled. In the midst
of the woods they had been attacked by brigands, who
took from Paulsen two hundred and fifty lire and his
gun. There was no use making any resistance, because
the gendarme was frightened out of his wits and as
white as a ghost. On reaching Albano, Paulsen was
met by the Jerichau girls and young Knudsen; and was
there not an excitement! They went to the police-
station, and attended by five carbineers they all set
off along the road to Porto d'Anzio to call at every
wayside *osteria* and give notice, so that, if possible,
the culprits might be detected. They returned to
Albano late at night. The gentlemen went off to
Rome early the next morning, and the girls brought

here the strange news.   Later we saw Sophie, the
youngest of the Jerichaus, who is about eleven, swing-
ing; and she shouted to us, 'May I come in and
tell you about the robbers?'   She is a charming girl,
full of health, strength, and character; fresh, bright, and
genuine.   She is just such a child as George MacDonald
would delight in describing.   She was, you may believe,
in a great state of excitement about these bandits.   It
was such an adventure to her."

MARY HOWITT TO HER ELDER DAUGHTER.

"55 *Via Sistina, Rome, New Year's Day*, 1873.—
We have celebrated the day by driving to the Ponte
Nomentana, and there leaving the carriage, strolled on
the Campagna and gathered flowers—large staring
daisies and a bright little purple geranium.   Your
father gladdened his eyes with the flocks of larks that
kept rising before us merrily twittering, but not yet singing, and with the flocks of sheep which grazed here
and there, watched by the shepherds and their dogs."

"*Jan.* 22, 1873.—We are so interested in 'Ginx's
Baby.' How clever it is! What a satire it is on the
religion, legislation, and philanthropy of the age! God
help us all, and send us a revelation of the true light!
Something stronger than the Gospels and the Gospel-
promises, and more tangible. I thought at one time
that spiritualism was going to give us this; but it has
so much shoddy and humbug about it, that even such
as we, who believe in it, reject its outer seeming. Yet
perhaps its very ugliness and seeming untruths are but,
as it were, the manger-birth of the Saviour, a stumbling-
block and an offence. You see, 'Ginx's Baby' has

set me thinking. I look all round, and I perceive that everything is wrong, all out of joint, with an attempt, or it may be a *pretence*, to get right, and no good comes of it? The evil is so mighty, who is able to stand in the combat against it. The ghost of our *Journal* is called up before me. We got wrong; I see that as plainly as possible; but then there are so many things that make the best-intentioned get wrong, and that nothing sooner than a great success. God help the world! It is made up of poor creatures. Even the rich and powerful cannot stand firm against the temptations of riches and power."

" *March* 3, 1873.—There are so many sides to Truth, if people would only look at them. I am reading the 'Life of Père Besson,' that good, pure-lived Dominican artist. What a beautiful revelation it is of the higher class of the Catholic priesthood! No George Fox or John Wesley, no George Herbert or Jeremy Taylor, no Bunyan or Baxter, were any of them purer, truer, or more faithful followers of Christ. There are thousands of noble Christian Catholics. If it were not so, the Roman Catholic faith could not have survived to this day. If the Protestantism which is now being introduced into Rome by the sects were mild, tender, and loving as the Spirit of Christ, it might worthily replace the evil it seeks to uproot; but the spirit of these little conventicles is, in my humble opinion, not what God will give the success of reformation and regeneration to. In the Protestant Episcopalian churches here, there is so evident an imitation of the outward ceremony of the Church of Rome, the officiating ministers calling themselves priests, that it seems to me offensive. I suppose the educational bias is strong in me; and though I love whatever is beautiful, and am sure that the beautiful belongs to Heaven, yet the more devotional part of my being is called forth by a simpler style of worship. Yesterday, however, I went to the English Chapel to hear the Archbishop of Dublin (Trench) preach, and saw Emerson there. He has been, with his daughter, up the Nile. This evening we are to meet them at Miss Clarke's.

"Did I tell you that Sir William Fitz-Herbert and his daughter are here? She is no longer the child, but the young woman. It reminds us of the flight of time, and how many of the kind and intelligent hearts that welcomed us at Tissington have ceased to beat. It casts a sad charm around that stately and retired home."

"*Rocca di Papa, May* 20, 1873.—Dear old father has sent you a half-comic but very hideous picture of this mountain town, which is baptized in Papacy, and has been for many hundreds of years. We must, however, have patience with these poor, dirty beggars; the Catholics believe they open a door for us to Heaven by giving us an opportunity of relieving them. Rocca di Papa is nevertheless a most enjoyable place, and in the Overbeck house we have spacious rooms, and plenty of them, good air, and glorious views. Jonas Lie, the Norwegian author, and his family arrive to-day. They are to have the storey below us, as they had last year."

"*May* 24, 1873.—I must tell you about Ernesto, the '*Maestro di casa,*' as Carl Hoffmann called him the first year we were here. He is our little running footman, coming daily to clean the boots and do odd jobs, and is as sharp as a needle with two points. He is working out four lire which will be paid to-morrow for a pair of boots for him. He wears an old brown felt hat, which is so big that it is either over his nose or at the back of his head, so that his shoulders may hold it on. Last year Margaret and I determined he should go to school. But nothing would persuade him to attend the new municipal school, established by Government. He would not go even to please us, saying, 'Nothing that was good was taught, but a great deal that was wicked. However, he could learn to read,' he added, 'for a *soldo* (halfpenny) a week; and a big lad, a friend of his, would teach him to write. The man who would teach him lived almost at the topmost house in the village.'

"Thither, escorted by Ernesto, we went, up and up the black rock-stairs of the village, over the very house-roofs and chimneys, as it were—such a climb!—to a sort of rock-terrace, where a man of about forty was making wooden hay-forks. He was the good friend who would teach him to read. The wife brought us out chairs, and we sat down. The man was quite willing to undertake the task of instruction. He reprobated strongly the municipal school, which 'had no better way of teaching a child his letters than by having them painted on a wall and pointing them out with a stick. He knew better, and should teach Ernesto from the book.' We asked him, would he be kind enough to read us something from his book. 'Certainly,' he said, and went into the house and brought out a big old Dictionary. 'Had he no reading-book?' we asked. 'Certainly.' Then he brought out a book of devotion, and calling Ernesto to him, desired him to spell the first word—a long word, of which the lad knew hardly half the letters. So we saw what Ernesto could do, or rather could not do. Then the man himself read a few lines. There was no doubt but that he could read. As to his teaching, or rather Ernesto learning, that remains doubtful. However, the lad protests that he goes up every evening and has a lesson."

"*June* 22.—Yesterday morning I took my camp-stool into the little wood to finish a shirt for Ernesto. Presently the church-bells sounded the 'Angelus,' and I thought of all our mercies with a grateful heart, and longed to become very dutiful to our Father in Heaven. Then I heard good Madame Börch, the Norwegian, with her sweet musical voice, give a peculiar call through her window down to the studio below, where her husband, the sculptor, was at work, to intimate to him that dinner was ready. I stitched away at my poor Ernesto's shirt, and towards one o'clock I knew that the Börchs had finished their dinner, for I heard the lovely voice of the wife singing in their small kitchen, which adjoins their one room, as she washed up the dishes and put the things by. This is nothing to tell, but to me it was a pleasant little idyll. Then your father strolled down with his white umbrella, sat down on the flowery grass, and talked pleasantly. Before long we saw Meg's figure on the balcony looking through Mr. Carl's telescope, which he has fixed for our use. Next we heard her give a signal for us. Our dinner was now ready. I had just about finished the shirt. Such a nice little shirt, with plaits laid down the front like a gentleman's. In the evening the ecstatic Ernesto received it, and never, surely, did you see such a face of joy. He is now learning English, so he said very properly, 'Thank you, ma'am;' and to-day he does not wear his waistcoat, that all the world of Rocca may see his splendid new shirt."

"55 *Via Sistina, Jan.* 4, 1874.—This is the first time that I have written '74, for though I sent you a scrap on New Year's Day, I did not date it; and since then I have written no letters, though I have several yet on my conscience, and also on my heart; as I have been trying these last two days to put dear, good Mrs. Gould's annual report of her schools for poor Italian children into a nice form, to wind up with a graceful 'begging clause,' which I find very hard work, and got so disgusted with it yesterday afternoon, that I laid it aside till to-morrow, when it *must* be done."

"*Jan.* 6.—There is to be an entertainment at the Marionette Theatre for the benefit of the Crêche. The dear old father takes a great interest in this proposed diversion, and has bestowed tickets on several individuals, to whom the attention has been a real kindness, as it has brought a ray of gladness into their poor solitary lives. Our own treat will be to take with us the dear, bright, simple-hearted children of the novelist, Jonas Lie, and his sweet little wife Thomasine.

"Yesterday afternoon, when I had finished, to my no small relief, the report of her school for Mrs. Gould, I put on my best bonnet and best gloves, and set off in the first instance to call on those two excellent and agreeable women, Dr. Elizabeth Blackwell and her sister. From them I went to Miss Brewster's afternoon reception; went in at the lower door of the Palazzo Albani, past the old fountain with the Gorgon's head grinning above it, up a winding staircase till I came to a door, out of

which velvet-clad, perfumed ladies were coming; and so
in through a couple of nicely furnished ante-rooms to the
larger apartment, where she sat, in black velvet and an
Indian scarf over her shoulders, receiving her visitors.   I
soon saw a nice white-headed gentleman of my acquaintance, attached to the American Embassy, though himself
an Italian.   So we began to talk—he to tell me of the
Roman college for ladies, which will be inaugurated to-
day, with an Italian poetess, a very remarkable woman,
Signora Fua Fusinato, at its head; exactly similar in
character and advantages to the female colleges in England.
It interested me greatly, yet not so much as to prevent
my seeing what went on around.

"I observed a gentleman seated before a pretty, black
Japanese screen near the fire.   I was wondering who in
the world he could be; for his face, scored with lines and
markings, had a great play of expression, and he exhibited
a considerable expansion of white shirt-front, a crimson
silk kerchief tied round his neck, and the glitter of a
heavy gold chain and of jewellery, when unexpectedly
he was introduced to me as 'Mr. Miller.'

"'Joaquin Miller,' I instantly replied, understanding at
once the character of the man.   Although I had risen to
leave, we sat down together.   He said, 'The first people
I wanted to see in Rome were Howitts; yes, I wanted to
see *them*.   I was taken, when in London, to look at the
house they had once inhabited at Highgate—a pleasant
house standing apart from the road.'   Then he went on
to tell me of a solitary American lady, married to a
Frenchman in Rome, who had begged him to make her
acquainted with 'Howitts.'   He had her address folded
up in his little purse, and seemed very anxious to do
her this service.   We spoke of his dear friends, the

Rossettis. 'Dante,' he remarked, 'was a fine fellow—a true Saxon.' He was much interested by Rome, although he confessed ignorance of its history. The snowy Apennines, as he saw them from various points, charmed him beyond everything else.

"I asked where he was located. 'He had gone first to an hotel,' he replied; 'but it was so dear that he, a poor man, could not stand it, and he moved off.' He would not reveal his whereabouts, affirming he told no one. 'He lived among the plebeians, had a room with a brick floor, and a brazier to warm him. He cared nothing for fine furniture, but he loved the people.' 'The Italians,' I rejoined, 'were a good, kind-hearted race.' He expressed pleasure in hearing me say so, as some of his friends prophesied he would be stabbed and robbed of his rings and gold chains. I suggested it might be hardly wise to exhibit such tempting objects to the very poor. To this he replied, 'He had lived amongst the poor and the so-called wicked without ever being robbed of a cent; the only den of thieves he knew was hotels. He had never locked or bolted a door in self-defence, and should not do it in Rome.' Then he expatiated on his life as a boy, his sorrows and wild adventures—'Poor father, who was so unfortunate, and mother, who was so good'—his being stolen by the Indians, but never being a chief amongst them, as commonly reported; his journeys in Nebraska and down the Wabash, with much more, giving me glimpses of a romantic existence, in keeping with his queer flexible countenance and crimson neckerchief. His first name is really Cincinnatus, not Joaquin."

"*Jan.* 23.—We have Mr. George Mackarness, the newly-chosen Bishop of Argyll and the Isles, and our

little friend Evelyn, now shot up into a young man,
here in Rome. As the Bishop possesses quite a rever-
ential love for the old painter Overbeck, we have arranged
that he goes over the Monastery of St. Isidore, where
Overbeck and his art-brethren led such poetical, devoted,
half-monkish lives. Fra Ippolito, a lay-brother, and
himself a humble artist, equally reveres the hallowed
memory of Overbeck. He will welcome our friend and
take him to the Superior. Meggie and I saw last
summer, before leaving Rome, as much of the monastery
as women are permitted to see. The Bishop will now
describe to us the cells once occupied by the band of
artists, and the rest of the sacred interior."

Sunday morning.—I have been to the English Chapel
to hear the new Bishop preach. He took as his text,
'Now we see through a glass darkly, but then face to
face.' The sermon transported me to Ilam, its exquisite
church and its village congregation."

"*Jan.* 31, 1874.—The excursion planned for the Bishop
of Argyll and Evelyn to Rocca di Papa turned out quite
a success. The sun shone, the glorious landscape displayed all its manifold charms. Everybody was in good
spirits. First came the walk up Monte Cavo, and the
cordial reception given Carl Hoffmann and his male companions by the friendly Passionist monks. Then down
through the woods to the chapel of the Madonna della
Tufa, where the hermit was so long saying prayers for
all the party, that they thought they must leave him to
finish by himself. So down through the quaint, queer
volcanic village to Casa Overbeck, in sight of the most
glorious sunset. Next the brilliant after-glow, gorgeous
over the Mediterranean ; and so across the Campagna in

the clearest, brightest moonlight; and back in Rome by seven o'clock.   It was a perfect day: they all say so."

"*Meran, Tyrol, May* 25, 1874.—I wish you could have a peep of us in this beautiful place and in our most comfortable quarters.   I am quite amazed, and I hope thankful to the dear Providence, which seems so constantly our guide; for if we had imagined an ideal place, we could not have found one more completely to our taste than this.   Here is the most glorious Tyrolean scenery: lofty mountains with their snowy heads, and lower green mountains, with vineyards clothing them to their knees; in the rich valley the famous little town of Meran, formerly the capital of Tyrol, and near to which lies the most ancient Schloss Tirol, that gives the name to the whole land, and is considered almost as its palladium.   Picturesque the old town is as heart can desire, with a splendid costume yet worn by the men: green waistcoat, jacket faced with scarlet lapels, black breeches, and white stockings, with a somewhat broad-brimmed hat, with either scarlet or green cords wound round its somewhat high and peaked crown.   Amongst the women there is much less costume.

"Meran is one of the most frequented spots in the Tyrol as a winter residence for invalids; also for its grape-cure in the autumn, the whole district being one great vineyard, and the grapes of the finest quality for eating.   The suburb of Obermais is full of the most elegant villas, built in the loveliest style, standing in the midst of gardens full of roses—and such roses!—with creepers of the rarest and most beautiful kinds wreathing the balconies and verandahs; hotels and *pensions* all of the same character.   It is a perfect fairy-land."

To Miss Leigh Smith.

"*Mayr-am-Hof, Oct.* 3, 1874.—If a sadness and desolation falls upon the womenkind of this house when we are gone, so it was but a Nemesis by anticipation that we all have been in a melancholy condition from the very time you left us. Everything assumed a garb of sorrow and depression; the supper that evening was like a funeral feast, and old Moro groaned under the table. Rain came down from the sky, and has continued almost ever since; the first little gleam of sunshine being this morning, when my husband and Annie, his faithful attendant, have gone out. But again all looks grey. You evidently took the sunshine with you; and I hope it has remained with you, and that you have been able to accomplish your visit to that pleasant Meran, which I can never think of but as bathed in golden sunshine.

"We accompained you in thought on your journey, fearing, however, that the cloud which has settled down outwardly and inwardly on Dietenheim might, seeing that the moon changed yesterday, extend even as far as Bozen. We will hope not, and that the sunshine you carry with you, whilst it forms an actual sphere of life and light around you, may have power even to influence the weather; and that, gloomy as the weather is here just now, it is but typical of our state of mind, which, however, is beginning to mend. For instance, dear Peggy last night sat down to carve her Madonna, after half-an-hour's work on her wooden image of Moro, and covered the table with heaps of chips and shavings, whilst Lizzy put a little life into us by singing some of her old songs; so I think we are sliding back into the comfortable groove of our daily life; remembering you and dear Isabella as the patriarchal families would remember the visits of angels, something to rejoice over in the past, and to look forward to with joy and hope in the future."

To Mrs. Alfred Watts.

"55 *Via Sistina, Dec.* 18, 1874.—Your father has been out again and again with the Pattons. What child-like, sweet people they are! she just the same as the Abby Hutchinson of thirty years ago. We have had a talk with them about the negroes. They say, what I feared must be the case, that freedom will alter greatly the character of the negroes. They will now endeavour to become like the whites, and to forget what they were in bondage. Even of their songs they are beginning to be ashamed; yet some of these I think most lovely. There is one especially of which the Marchesa di Torre-Arsa spoke to me last night with perfect delight, and she knows what good music is. I will try to get the exact words, but the burden of it is, 'We have not long to stay here; —steal away to Jesus!' You shall have the words, and must imagine the sweet, plaintive, yearning melody.

"Will Garibaldi come to Rome? Strange indeed will it be if the old walls contain at the same time the Pope, the King, and the former Dictator."

"*Dec.* 30, 1874.—Last evening we had the Pattons, and in the middle of the evening our fat Louisa, opening wide the drawing-room door, ushered in a young man in a long cloak and a black fur cap. He gave your father a letter. It was from Daniel Ricketson, of New Bedford, introducing his son Walton. This was he, and we made him heartily welcome. There is something amazingly fresh and attractive about him. He had arrived that morning. It was wet, but no matter. Off he set to see the wonders of old Rome; went to the Forum, which can only be entered on certain days. The custodian stopped him in his descent. The man having a book in his hand, young Ricketson inquired what he was reading. 'Oh! he was studying English.'—'Good,' said the American. 'Come, let us sit down, and I will give you a lesson.' He taught him for half-an-hour. After that they were capital friends, and he saw all there was to be seen.

"I wish you could have beheld his astonishment when the Pattons stood up side by side to sing, before leaving, some of their sweet Jubilee hymns, and his delight to find that she was no other than Abby Hutchinson. Right glad was he to meet her and her husband—old abolitionists, like his father, who had kept open the underground railway.

William Howitt to his elder Daughter.

"*Jan.* 25, 1875.—Mrs. Gould is going to bring out a book written by different people, to be printed at her new school-press. Adolphus Trollope and his wife, and Mr. Marsh, the American Minister to the Quirinal, have all promised contributions. Mrs. Marsh hopes to get something from Gladstone; and I dare say there will be a good many things from American authors. Your mother is going to write an introduction narrating Mrs. Gould's efforts in Rome to educate the children of the poor. I have written my contribution, called 'Progressive Steps of Popular Education, and a Pioneer Working-School,' which is that of Captain Brenton, the martyr of the juvenile outcasts of London.

"Garibaldi arrived in Rome yesterday afternoon. He was drawn by the people in triumph to his lodgings. They were wild to have a speech from him, and clamoured with their ten thousand voices. He came on the balcony and simply said, '*Giovanotti! Buona notte!*' and so retired."

MARY HOWITT TO HER ELDER DAUGHTER.

"*Mayr-am-Hof, Sept.* 15, 1875.—We had a delightful excursion to Taufers with Josiah Gilbert, his sister, and Mrs. Angus. Everything was looking its best. Mr. Gilbert knows all the country, and had been there before, but he wanted his companions to see the old castle, standing up grandly with its background of glacial mountains. At the castle, however, we found every door locked. The people were all out at work in the fields; so we prowled about, and finding one wainscoted room open, with its old benches round the walls, there sat and 'had high discourse,' as Mr. Gilbert said; we talked a good deal of nonsense, your father being as merry as the rest. We then slowly walked back again to the inn, where our dinner had been ordered. In going up to the castle Mr. Gilbert and I had conversed together; and my heart not only sympathised, but had been filled with joyful thanksgiving that sorrow such as he had experienced could so beautify and elevate a life.

"It was altogether a season of friendly intercourse; and we arranged in driving back how we were to wind up with a right pleasant evening. He was to get his sketch of Mayr-am-Hof made before tea. Then at seven the zither-player was to come and play and give Mrs. Angus a lesson. They were to see the handsome cow-bells and crown; and go back to Bruneck, no matter how late, by full moon. So we had arranged; but hardly had we reached home, when, behold! a carriage stopped at the gate, and out stepped a grey-bearded man, with a most sad countenance. It was no other than poor, brokenhearted Dr. Gould, come hither from Perugia to find comfort from us if he could; his wife dead only about ten days, and he brought down to the brink of the grave, as it were. Here he was, and when he was not expected, and when the mood of the whole house was rejoicing! However, there was nothing for it but to receive him kindly. The guest-chamber was made ready, and he took possession of it. His nerves are unstrung; he can talk of nothing but his wife, whom he loved tenderly and was most proud of, and by whose sick-bed he has watched night and day for many months, through one of the most awfully agonising maladies that I ever heard of."

"*Sept.* 22.—Our poor guest! How sad it is to make an idol of any living thing which death may remove! Yet I have such compassion for him. I walk out with him, and let him talk as much as he will about her. He is now sitting on the sofa at the upper end of the room, reading a handful of letters. He often reads me these condolences; many of them beautiful letters, extremely well written, fit to print; and I wonder at the number of well-educated people there are who have the gift of expressing themselves eloquently, gracefully, and with so much deep feeling. I don't wonder at the poor man weeping over them. They would half-break my heart, I verily believe, if mine were the sorrow and my friends wrote thus to me."

"55 *Via Sistina, Jan.* 12, 1876.—What the fate of Mrs. Gould's school will be in the end seems now a curious question. I think your father has told you of the wicked theft and dishonesty of some of the people left in charge of her school by Mrs. Gould; more particularly of a young woman whom she had educated to have care of the *Kindergarten*, and in whom she and her husband had great confidence. This teacher has most basely repaid their faith and trust. She is now gone off, and the school and the Home, greatly diminished, are in the hands of a Waldensian minister and his wife. They have taken charge of the work for a month; but a serious difficulty has occurred. One child, a boy of about fourteen, refused to go to the Waldensian church, and left the Home. This made a commotion. He was a favourite pupil of poor Mrs. Gould's, and her husband took up the matter warmly. A public meeting had been appointed and invitations sent out to everybody interested in the subject, to consider the propriety of the Home and school being placed in the hands of the Waldenses. Then occurred the bother of the papal boy taking himself off, and a very strong party in consequence showed themselves in opposition to the Waldenses. This was the Mazzinian party. Madame Mario and an Englishman, a wealthy Jew named Nathan, declared themselves ready to rescue these poor children from the persecuting hands of the narrow sectarian Waldenses and make this a great Mazzini school and printing-press. Mr. Trollope appeared at the meeting as their advocate.

"Poor Dr. Gould urged us to attend the meeting, but I never intended to go ; and when your father heard, the day before the meeting, of this proposition, he thought it was much the best that he stayed away. Mrs. Gould was eminently religious; faith and love to the Saviour and loyalty to King Victor Emmanuel were the most prominent principles inculcated. She herself was a member of the Waldensian Church.

They are the only body likely to carry on the institution in the spirit of its foundress. This one obstinate boy had better be removed and restored to his father and the priests, rather than the whole work should be broken up on his account. That is my present feeling."

" *Albano, March* 4, 1876.—We yesterday had a charming little outing with Mr. Young of Kelly. We drove to Rocca di Papa, and went up to the old Overbeck villa, where we knew that Carl Hoffmann was not, but that his queer woman-servant, Marianna, who has the learned pig, was there; and very welcome she made us; brought us apples and walnuts, old grapes dried almost to raisins; and received in return five lire from Mr. Young, and all the remains of the lunch—a regular dinner. I was so glad to have another peep at the pleasant place, and to see again my favourite picture by Overbeck, of himself, his wife, and little Alphonse; the portrait, too, of Pforr, his dear art-brother, in a sort of Raphaelesque dress, and a cat rubbing against his elbow; also the little old painting of 'Shulamite and Mary.' I looked at these three small pictures—all of which belong to such a lovely part of Overbeck's life, and which are so intimately connected with the time when Meggie and I were there alone—and the hallowed past came back again. I wonder, when we are in the other life, whether bits of our earthly experience will come back to us with the same sweet, tender reality and interest.

" Everybody hopes that Mrs. Gould's school is now definitely taken by the Waldenses; though there is no doubt that they are rather narrow in their religious creed and life."

"*March* 8, 1876.—I must tell you that Mr. Young has pleased Peggy and me very much, by giving, without a word from us, fifty lire for a poor, bedridden old woman, whose two daughters—needlewomen—not so long since were burnt to death by the upsetting of a paraffine-lamp. It is a very sad case, which Peggy has taken up; the poor mother, who is left, being totally penniless and helpless. She is ill, and probably may not last long. So now, as Peggy and I were driving with Mr. Young and his eldest daughter to Castel Gandolfo, he out with his big pocket-book, and gave Peggy this fifty lire, telling her, if the poor woman outlived that money, to apply to him."

"55 *Via Sistina, March* 27, 1876.—Last evening we spent with the Youngs at Peggy's. Mr. Young then told your father that it was a cause of concern to him that Garibaldi's two little girls, about nine and ten, were being brought up in a very rude and careless way; and that, as he knew those in Scotland who would gladly find the money for them to be carefully educated, if their father would only consent to the plan, he wished the proposal could be made to Garibaldi in some way which would ensure his acceptance of it. Mr. Young also wished your father to go with him to the General, and with this good object in view, he felt he could not refuse. The first thing this morning, therefore, he went to call on a friend of Garibaldi's, to ask how and when it would be possible to see him, and whether there was a likelihood of his accepting the offer. But the individual was in bed; so your father left a note, and I hope we shall have an answer before long.

"It seems that it is Mr. Young himself who wishes

to provide for these children, and has arranged with a Scotch lady to undertake the management of them."

"*March* 29, 1876.—Garibaldi's friend said that Mr. Young had made a magnificent offer, but that, in fact, only one was Garibaldi's child, and the other was the child of the mother before Garibaldi took her. This threw a new light on the matter. Then came the great religious difficulty. It was not to be expected that Garibaldi, who hates priests of all sorts, and who does not believe in Christianity, I fancy, would be willing that his child should be brought up in the Scotch or any other Church; and, of course, Mr. Young could not engage to bring her up without any religion. The friend was very anxious that no cold water should be thrown on the scheme, wishing Garibaldi to have the offer. More revelations of the domestic relations were, however, made; and Mr. Young considered it quite necessary to let the scheme lie over for reflection, saying that he must write to the Scotch lady and acquaint her with the facts. I should think the proposition will evaporate."

To Mrs. Todhunter.

"55 *Via Sistina, Rome, Dec.* 20, 1876.—On Monday William entered his eighty-fifth year, and it was altogether a most pleasant day to us all. The weather, however, was not very fine; therefore we did not make the little excursion which was intended to the Tre Fontane, the convent erected on the spot on which it is believed that St. Paul suffered martyrdom. But it was not in honour of St. Paul that we purposed to go there on the 18th, but to see the good Trappist Brothers, some of whom are rather friendly acquaintances of my husband's, and always make him and those who accompany him heartily welcome. They are great growers of the Eucalypti of all kinds, and he has furnished them with a good deal of seed, which our Alfred has collected for him in his mountain district and elsewhere in Australia. Every now and then, therefore, when we want a pleasant little holiday, we drive over to the Tre Fontane, see the plantations of Eucalyptus-trees, have a talk with the friendly Trappists—who are allowed to talk, certainly, when strangers visit them, however silent they may be at other times—and receive from them at parting a small draught of their Eucalyptus liqueur. On Monday, however, we could not go, but instead spent part of the day very pleasantly with Margaret Foley, who is now our next *floor* inmate, having removed into the apartment below ours; so that we are all under the same roof, and go backwards and forwards at pleasure. Our evenings we spend mostly together. We have thus, in company, just finished ' Macaulay's Life and Letters.' What a fine character he was as a man : full of the rarest intellect, with the most affectionate heart! I do not know any biography which has delighted us more."

To Mrs. Alfred Watts.

" *Palm Sunday, March* 25, 1877.—This is a Sunday which I remember so well in your Munich life, when you took a long country ramble; the scenery you described always comes back to me on Palm Sunday. With Palm Sunday, too, you commence your narrative of the great Christian tragedy of Ammergau; all of which is sweetly engraven on my memory. In Rome it is a great day at St. Peter's, even in these times of

non-celebration; and if all things were consonant therewith I should have gone to that basilica to-day and seen
the commemoration of the Lord's entry into Jerusalem.
It is to some but a formal affair; to me it is a venerable relic, and I like those things: the procession of the
priests outside the closed church-door; then the sub-deacon
knocking at the door with the staff of the cross; its being
opened, and the procession entering singing, '*Ingrediente
Domino in sanctam civitatem.*' It pleases my imagination at all events. And the blessing of the palms; and
their distribution, the big ones to the officiating clergy
and other dignitaries, and lastly the little ones and
the broken branches of olive given to the people. The
whole is a memory of old, reverent things. It is typical
of a higher, grander ceremonial, which is, I dare say,
taking place spiritually all round us; and not in Rome
alone, but throughout the world: Christ's spirit poured
out and His gifts distributed to hundreds of thousands,
though none may know of it but themselves and the
Divine Donor.

"Yesterday, in the afternoon, I went out to try to find
people who would take tickets for Madame Ristori's
reading on Tuesday evening for the benefit of the 'Gould
Memorial School.' I had not at all a successful cru-
sade. None were inclined to put their hands in their
pockets, excepting dear Margaret Gillies, on whom
I called; and after that went no farther. She was just
finishing her picture, and was worried at the last, and
wanted to go to good Mr. Glennie to borrow a sketch
of distant scenery in the neighbourhood of Rome; the
bad weather not permitting her to go out sketching for
herself. When her things were all put aside and left
for their Sunday rest, we took a little carriage and

drove to the Glennies', down into the very centre of
Rome; and had such a cordial reception, such a nice
call: tea made for us, and dear Margaret given the pick
of his rich portfolios for a bit of Latin or Volscian mountain, blue and dreamy in its sunny distance. Then, en-
riched with two most serviceable sketches, and charmed
with their genuine kindness, we went down their many
stairs, to find there had been a deluge of rain; and I
bethought myself anxiously of the father and Meggie,
gone to gather flowers in the beautiful Borghese.

"Here I found them, very cheerful, but somewhat
wet. This, however, was speedily rectified, and we sat
down to enjoy your welcome letter. We all wish you
a most pleasant and happy time with the Cowper-
Temples at Broadlands. I hope you will remain with
them and Sister Elizabeth over Easter Day. There are
so many sacred, sorrowful anniversaries before that day
comes. What a right thing it is to keep them with
befitting reverence! I wish we had been brought up
in a faith that had these holy observances. What a
mistake Friends made in regarding nothing but First-
Day, and that in such a dead manner! I am too old
now to begin; yet I do seem to feel a very great want
of higher religious life in myself. I would, it seems
to me, give anything for a sense of the Divine life
within me. I hope, therefore, amongst the good people
of Broadlands, that you and dear Alfred will know a
strong influx of Love and Wisdom.

"Remember me most kindly to the Cowper-Temples,
for whom I have a great love and regard. They are
amongst the angels of God now on earth, who celebrate
the second coming of their Lord. Oh that we might
all be of that glorious band! How I long to feel

myself recognised by Him! I do not as yet. But I love all His children, wherever I recognise them; and the Cowper-Temples are of the number. Our love to dear Eliza. She is one of the Lord's servants and dear children."

To Miss Leigh Smith.

"*Dietenheim, Oct.* 26, 1877.—We have lately had a very sad and anxious time, and have so still. Our poor Peggy returned from Innichen in the same ailing condition. She was better one day, and severely suffering the next; until this day fortnight, when she was taken with congestion of the brain; in fact, a stroke of paralysis. The Bruneck physician regarded her condition as very serious, and ordered us to write to any near friends or relatives she might have, and that, if she had outward affairs to settle, it might be done. But dear Peggy had made her will, and we were amongst her nearest friends. Happily the most sad effects of the attack abated in a few days. Her sufferings, however, from the root of the malady being an affection of the spinal cord, are inconceivable; and she has a pain in the head, making her, at its worst, wish for death rather than life. Indeed, her constant prayer to be taken, if consistent with God's will, wrings our hearts. Truly her patience and endurance of this awful agony are wonderful and most touching. In this condition she cannot be removed to Rome. We have therefore decided to go from here to Meran for the winter. That good Dr. von Messing, whom we mentioned to you when here, and whose wife you saw, will be there to receive her professionally. We have been fortunate to get some very comfortable rooms where William, Meggie, and I were three years

ago, when we went to Meran for a short time. One
of the great comforts to us in this season of sorrow and
anxiety has been the kindness of the Sisters of Charity
here, who have, one of them, come each alternate night
to sit up with our poor patient; Meggie and I, between
us, taking the other."

To Mrs. Alfred Watts.

" *Meran, Nov.* 16, 1877.—Our dear sufferer has many
alternations of better and worse. She begins to look
very like that touching sketch of Keats in his last illness,
which you know so well; the face thin and the eyes
large, but with such a meek, patient, pathetic expression; and she is so gentle and affectionate, so like an
obedient, loving child. The final parting with her will
be a sad, sad sorrow.

"It is a most beautiful morning, the mountain-
summits shining out like alabaster, and lower down in
this ever-varied valley the autumnal colouring of the
trees yet remains. It is most exquisitely beautiful. I
wonder whether Alfred and you will ever visit Meran.
I hope you may. If this is to be Peggy's last resting-
place, it will ever be sacred to us; so I think in some
future time you will be here. The peculiar landscape
is much more striking and beautiful at this season than
in spring, when all is green.

"You will be glad to know that our little apartment
in Rome, which I feared might be despised, and so hang
on our hands, is now let. Bishop Tozer and his sister
have taken it, and entered upon it yesterday. It is very
pleasant to us to know that such extremely good people
are occupying the place, which, humble as it is, has been
our happy Roman home for five winters. Is not the

dear Heavenly Father good to us? I hardly knew how sufficiently to give thanks yesterday, when the news came."

"*Friday, Dec.* 7, 1877.—All is over. Very peaceful. But we are very sad."

"*Dec.* 12, 1877.—For the first time since dear Peggy's departure do I to-day feel a little consoled. It is a most beautiful morning, and we are presently intending to visit the grave. I wish you could go with us. Then you would see in how lovely a spot our poor sufferer lies. We are now beginning to receive acknowledgments of the announcements sent out. I will give you a few words from the letter of an Episcopalian clergyman received this morning :—'Impelled by I know not what motive, I had closed the Sunday service this afternoon with the prayer from the Burial Office : "Almighty God, with whom do live the Spirits, &c.," and coming straight from the church, received your letter a few minutes after I reached my room, so that it seemed as if unconsciously I had offered it for her who now rests from her labours.'

"Is not this consolatory? And it is in keeping with the whole history of Peggy's last illness : the coming of Dr. von Messing to Dietenheim, the physician that she wished to consult ; the nursing order of Sisters of the Cross from Ingenbohl established in Meran ; the affectionate attendance of her faithful Francesca, and of good Frau Walter ; the coming here of the English chaplain, just a week before his services were needed—everybody and everything as if appointed by angels. The lovely day of the funeral ; the kindness of strangers in following the remains to the grave ; the unknown eleventh wreath laid there, as if by an angel—all these may be accidental circumstances, yet I am sure you will understand how doubly sweet and welcome they are, if accepted as evidences of Divine approval and co-operation."

" *Jan.* 4, 1878.—Your father and I have just come back from a very pleasant walk right into the country ; amongst picturesque houses and such ancient orchards and park-like fields scattered over with grand old Spanish chestnuts. You might fancy it England in the reign of one of the Edwards or Henries. I feel it the time and character of that little story I wrote years ago for Messrs. Chambers, ' Steadfast Gabriel ; ' whilst the old castle of Rubein is just as it would have been in the days of ' Jack of the Mill.' Outside this castle—which is one of many—stands a venerable Spanish chestnut, on the ancient bole of which is placed a little shrine of the Virgin ; and in front of the tree, on a sort of mound, are benches and a table for the convenience of wayfarers or simple worshippers. There is a wonderful repose in the character of the country ; no hurry, driving, or bustling along. All seems so peaceful and still in the quiet old lanes, with their low stone fences, up which ivy grows, the whole dating from centuries and centuries ago."

WILLIAM HOWITT TO HIS ELDER DAUGHTER.

" *Meran, Jan.* 20, 1878.—I am deputed to write to you whilst the other two are gone to church. I suppose you have in England been deluged with accounts of Victor Emmanuel ? It is curious to me to remember the number of times that I have seen him driving on the Pincio, when scarcely a man would lift his hat to him ; and the number of times I have heard Italians say as Prince Humbert drove past, ' He will never come to the throne !' Miss Clarke writes to us that one day 78,000 people came into Rome by rail, and the next 70,000 for the lying in state. The editor of the *Popolo Romano* has not been able sufficiently to express his admiration of Victor Emmanuel. He says no such death has occurred since those of Titus and Marcus Aurelius. He sets him on a par with Scipio, Fabius, Maximus, &c. They cannot well go further unless they put on the front of the Pantheon, ' *Divo Victorio Emanueli.*' "

Mary Howitt to the Same.

" *Feb.* 23, 1878.—Day after day races on, and no sooner has a week begun than it is ended. Yet how full of events is the time ! Just looking at ourselves, month by month ever since we came here some occurrence has gone near to our hearts or awakened our interest to the highest degree. On December 7 Peggy died ; on January 9 Victor Emmanuel died ; on February 7 the Pope died : and through it all lay the terror of war ; the uncertainty what the nations would do. Of course, with us it is a mingling of important world interests and our individual petty concerns ; yet all is interwoven into our daily lives, forming a strange, startling, momentous epoch. The European agitation seems now terminating very peacefully ; God over all, and bringing mankind, I trust, into the harmony of peace and good-will. We have taken a deep interest in the election of a new Pope ; knowing, too, how curiously and uncomfortably the Cardinals have been immured in the cells temporarily contrived for the purpose in the

Vatican. On Thursday afternoon, as your Father and Meggie were taking their walk, he, I believe, was wondering how the Cardinals were getting on, and whether they had nearly brought their work to a conclusion; when Meggie, lifting up her eyes to the lofty church-tower just then come into sight, exclaimed, 'The Pope is elected! See there the white and yellow flag with the cross-keys and the papal mitre!' So it was; where the black mourning flag for Pius the Ninth had hung, now was reared aloft the flag of rejoicing proclaiming the fact. Your father was almost as excited as Meggie. Away they went to the Post, to hear who was elected; but before they reached it they saw a placard at the street-corner announcing that Cardinal Pecci was the new Pope—was Leo XIII. Now, you must know that Pecci was the very prelate whom your father would have chosen; a right good man, whose life you will be sure to have read before this. Home they came full of the good news; and Meggie, bidding me put a shawl over my shoulders, hurried me off into a verandah at the back of the house in sight of the church-tower, and bade me look up and see. There it was, the white and yellow flag; and best of all, Cardinal Pecci elected Pope!"

WILLIAM HOWITT TO HIS ELDER DAUGHTER.

"*Rome, April* 28, 1878.—The weather here is quite summer. This morning, as I was on the Pincio, the gardeners and custodians saluted me very smilingly: '*Fa caldo, signore. Pare comincio del' estate.*' This greeting was the result of my telling them the other day that the female swan, which had begun laying, and had but a scrap of a nest on the ground, near the hut by the little lake, wanted more straw; that swans made huge nests, and unless she had more straw the eggs might spoil, which would be a pity. The next time I went, I saw she had got and appropriated her straw. They all know me well by sight, but now they think that I am a cute old fellow, who takes an interest in their affairs, and are amazingly civil."

My husband, with his unworldly nature, led the same unsophisticated life in Rome as in the quiet surroundings of Dietenheim. In the mornings, when children of all nationalities, under the surveillance of attendants, played in the broad sunlit paths of the Pincian hill; and in the afternoons, when a gay, fashionable throng drove, strolled, and listened by hundreds to the music, he walked alone, unless joined by some sociable acquaintance. He admired the fan-palms standing out clear in the sunshine, whilst snow was still visible on the Alban and Sabine ranges; noted the beds of roses, bay, and laurustinus, full of life and vigour; listened to the pleasant, familiar warbling of the little tit-mice; observed the arrival of the chiff-chaff a month earlier than in England. He spied out in the thick bushy boughs of the pines, cedars, and evergreens many goldfinches, some warblers, and a grand old blackbird that sang in good English; and canaries, some intensely yellow, others of a greenish hue, from mixing, he supposed, with linnets. To its death he was familiar with the stealthy Pincian cat.

At Mayr-am-Hof one of the main attractions to my husband was his gardening. He carried it on in a field allotment, and in the former baronial kitchen-garden, which, neglected for half-a-century, was divided from the mansion and farm-buildings by the road and a rude old wall surmounted by a fence, long unrepaired. It was a strip of terrace-garden, containing a primitive shed for bees and some unpruned fruit-trees with straggling naked branches. In the sloping orchard below better specimens, however, lingered on, and tradition dis-

MAYR-AM-HOF FROM KITCHEN-GARDEN.

tinguished one apple-tree as having, by its fine growth and prolificness, called forth the admiration of the Empress Maria Theresa.

William indefatigably dug with his English spade— a unique and expensive tool in Tyrol, which is the land of clumsy husbandry—planted, tied up, watered, and cut off dead boughs or leaves. I enjoyed sitting near him, reading, knitting, and in the summer of 1876 working

at a huge cabbage-net intended as a protection against
the legions of butterflies.

A little tawny owl sojourned for a series of summers
in a cavity of the venerable poplar, now defaced by
decay, which raises its massive trunk outside the closed
entrance-gate.   It slept by day, but became briskly

THE CLOSED ENTRANCE-GATE.

sociable on the approach of night.   It would then dili-
gently converse with my husband in the gloaming, per-
sistently answering his hoot with a monotonous cry,
that had an alert gravity about it bordering on the
ridiculous.

When, notwithstanding annoying incursions of the
burrowing mole-cricket, the practised old gardener stood
still in perfect amazement at the growth of his redun-

dant New Zealand spinach, his wide-spreading "Royal Albert" rhubarb, his exuberant tomatoes and towering spikes of Indian-corn, there came the hoopoe; in ruddy buff, black, and grey attire, with "crested plume, long beak, and sharpened as a spear," as if out of Ovid's "Metamorphoses," and uttering its hollow "hoop-hoop," sought its insect food in the rotten wood of the old trees or the spongy soil of the orchard.

A host of confiding swallows inhabited the eaves of the house, warbling in the early morning on the iron-work of the balconies, skimming in and out of the open windows, and, as the season advanced, bringing their young into the upper corridor, to essay from the top of the old cartoons of sacred subjects, or from the cornice, and pediments, the art of flying.

This upper hall assumed by degrees the character of a plainly furnished ante-room, where we could dine, or the servants sit at their needlework. Indeed, that portion of the house which we rented had gained gradually a more clothed appearance, from our bringing inexpensive carpets and draperies from Rome, or buying them in Tyrol; and engaging a carpenter to make chairs, tables, and cupboards after our design; our landlord, the *Hofbauer*, giving the wood. When curtains excluded the glare of the sun from the three-windowed recess in the saloon, I beguiled many hours there, in the attempt faithfully to reproduce with my needle on crash the apple-blossom of the orchard, the crocus of the meadow, the crimson carnation—almost the national emblem in Tyrol—and other flowers of the locality.

The *Hofbauer*, perceiving our love of the old place, and being desirous to show his regard and retain us as his tenants, acted contrary to his firmly-rooted antipathy

to innovations and needless expenditure, and began signalising our arrival by a series of surprises, that on more
than one occasion filled us with blank dismay.   He
replaced old hexagonal panes by modern square ones,
stencilled the walls of the saloon to imitate a first-class

THE UPPER HALL.

waiting-room in a Tyrolese railway station, and had the
dull green panels and gold mouldings of the doors
coarsely painted over to represent satin-wood and ma-
hogany, and the finely-wrought ironwork of the locks
obliterated.   It was a real injury—something that grated

on one's nerves and set one's teeth on edge. It was all
the more painful from being a worse than useless effort
on his part to please.

Fortunately, a few old doors in a side-corridor, with
classic subjects painted in distemper on the panels,

PEEP INTO SALOON.

and arabesques on the frames, much faded by time,
but having a stamp of ancient grandeur that suited
the physiognomy of the house, had been overlooked.
We pleaded their merits, and they remained. Thus
has experience taught us never to desire signs of

care and improvement about the weather-stained old
place.

Our quiet industry at Dietenheim was at times most
agreeably diversified by the visits of valued friends.
Hither, amongst others, came on a second visit, in the

ONE OF THE OLD DOORS.

summer of 1878, Miss Freeman Clarke, bringing with
her the result of much patient wanderings about Italy
and even Tyrol, in her collection of exquisite pen-and-ink
drawings of the various scenes of Dante's exile. She
had long been a resident in Rome, and closely associated

with our life there, but was then bound for a new home in Georgia. We wished her God-speed with sorrowful hearts, for we knew, in all probability, we should not meet on earth again. It never entered our minds that such would be the case with another welcome guest who left us at the same time. This was the large-hearted, nobly-endowed young writer, James Macdonell, a son-in-law of my beloved sister Anna. His lucid, rapid thoughts, expressed in easy, polished language, had charmed and enlivened our little domestic circle.

CHAPTER VIII.

THE HOME IN MERAN.

1879–1882.

DURING the last seven years of my husband's life we occupied small but pleasant quarters in the Via Sistina, close to his favourite Pincio. The back windows looked across a little garden of luxuriant Southern vegetation, filled with scattered fragments of old Roman friezes and statues, to the frescoed walls of the house in the Via Gregoriana, which had been occupied for many years by our old friend, the American actress, Miss Charlotte Cushman. Above its quaint tiled roof and picturesque *loggia*, we surveyed the slopes of the Janiculum and rejoiced in those brilliant sunsets which Claude Lorraine had loved to paint from his near-lying studio windows; until, alas! Miss Cushman having long since returned to America, and her Roman dwelling passing into other hands, it was transmogrified by the addition of two storeys and a flat roof, which blocked out our long stretch of the Janiculum ridge, dotted with stone-pines, and prominently terminated to the right by the mighty dome of St. Peter's.

I have always desired to retain each precious thread of friendship, never letting it wholly slip through my fingers, although it may be years since I held it first. This made me most highly estimate our residing in Rome, whither all roads seemed truly to tend, bringing us in contact with an infinite variety of old friends and acquaintances. Each season we felt more at home in the great centre of learning, art, and religion, notwithstanding the ruthless spoliation carried on under the guise of needful advance; and in the annually changing society of winter visitors we always found ourselves meeting earlier associates.

After the temporal downfall of the Pope, or of "Mastai-Ferretti," as a plain man-Friend of our acquaintance deemed it right to call him, the Evangelical bodies were eager to show their sympathy and interest with Rome, from the belief that her political situation must impel her to seek the alliance and support of Protestants; and it was to me like a strange resuscitation to behold intelligent, highly-cultivated Quakers, whose forefathers were connected with my earliest recollections and family traditions, walking amid the original scenes of those engravings by Piranesi, which had so deeply stirred my youthful imagination.

There were other Evangelical Christians, more or less in unity with Friends, who included a visit to Pius the Ninth in their Roman sojourn, and even went up the Scala Santa on their knees. There were others who, for conscience' sake, went even farther. We had a very pleasant call in the spring of 1876 from the widow of John Bright's youngest brother, Samuel, accompanied by Thomas Richardson of Jarrow, author of "The Future of the Society of Friends," and Edward Robson of Sunderland; and she told us that, of the four Quaker brothers, the Lucases, three had gone over to Popery; that some of their sons were now priests; and that Samuel Lucas, editor of the *Morning Star*, was the only one who remained a Protestant.

My husband's life-long advocacy of peace principles brought us in contact, in November 1873, with Mr. Dudley Field, Mr. Richard, M.P. for Merthyr Tydvil, and other gentlemen selected to promote international arbitration instead of war. Mr. Richard had, I believe, earlier carried the resolution in Parliament by an accident; for had there been an ordinary house, it would have been negatived by a large majority. His having so done, however, and thereupon receiving an address in support of his views signed by a million working-men in Great Britain, made a profound impression on the Continent. In Rome, Mancini, Professor of International Law, carried the motion unanimously in the Chamber of Deputies. Mr. Richard and his colleagues were cordially welcomed by the citizens; and an enterprising milliner, turning the sentiment of the moment to the advantage of her trade, introduced the *Chapeau Richard*, or Arbitration Bonnet. It was of soft grey silk, fastened on one side by a dove of oxidised silver, with an olive-branch in its beak.

Although William and I never cared for dinners or late evening parties, and avoided so-called " society," with its petty jealousies and struggles for precedence, we thoroughly appreciated that agreeable interchange of heart and mind with friends and neighbours which yields present delight and fills the memory with enduring satisfaction. Possessing no predilection for the Church of England, we yet highly esteemed many of its ministers, and were on excellent terms with the clergy in charge of the English Chapel in Rome. Thus, on our first arrival we had agreeable intercourse with the then chaplain, Mr. Shadwell, and his family. I next remember Mr. Grant holding the same post. He was

from Yorkshire, and full of good-heartedness and true
human sympathies. There were, besides, two younger
clergymen—one a desperate Radical, who took to my
husband as holding the same views ; the other a smooth-
faced Ritualist, full of self-control and devotion, who
remains in my mind as a young evangelist. From my
heart can never be effaced the impression made by the
Christ-like minister of the Gospel, the Rev. Somerset
Burtchaell, who, more than missionary to the Jews
in the Ghetto, was a universal peace-maker. We
mourned much his premature death, which occurred
in Jerusalem. The Rev. Henry Wasse, the present
chaplain, came from solitary, remote Axe Edge, in Derbyshire. He was as a boy fond of William's "Rural Life
of England," and quoted with true relish and perfect
pronunciation the anecdote given of the farmer who
said to his guest at table, "Ite, mon, ite!"—*Guest:*
"Au have iten, mon. Au've iten till au'm weelly
brussen."—*Farmer:* "Then ite, and brust thee out,
mon: au wooden we hadden to brussen thee wee!"
He knew the Mackarnesses and other friends of ours.

Here I would record that the concourse of English
visitors to Rome brought, in the Easter of 1871, the
incumbent of the village church which I had attended
when we dwelt at The Orchard ; a guileless character,
whose one thought was how faithfully to do his duty
both to God and man. It was quite a joy to us that
he came. The next spring we met again, at first
accidentally on the Spanish steps, the Unitarian minister,
Dr. Sadler, and his wife ; he whose thoughtful, poetic
sermons had soothed and stirred my mind when we
dwelt at Clapton and St. John's Wood. Later on came
the Rev. Thomas Stooks, a good friend of ours, and who

had been the incumbent of St. Anne's, Highgate Rise, when we dwelt in that locality. How pleased were we to see once more, and that in Rome, our old acquaintance of Nottingham, Philip Bailey, the author of "Festus," who had come with his wife from their island home in Guernsey for a six weeks' tour in Italy. In March 1873 the gentle and refined Mr. Edward Clifford and his sister were in the Eternal City. They sang together beautiful hymns and spoke much with us of Broadlands and Sister Elizabeth.* In 1876, at the Christmas season, Professor Boyd Dawkins quite captivated us by lively descriptions of his exploits in old bone-caves. In the spring of 1879 came our literary co-worker and much-esteemed friend, the deservedly popular author, Dr. Samuel Smiles, and his wife, ever his true helpmate. We also found among the established residents the Countess Gigliucci, with whom, when Clara Novello, some reader may remember we had enjoyed travelling many years earlier.

Among the very numerous Americans whom we had the pleasure of meeting were, in the season 1870–71, the two clever daughters of the philosopher, Amos Bronson Alcott. The one, Louisa, who already had attained celebrity by her " Old-fashioned Girl " and "Little Women," found time, amid much sight-seeing and company, to write in Rome her "Little Men;" the other, May, meanwhile devoting herself to landscape-painting. Moncure Conway, when preparing his lectures on the "Natural History of the Devil" for delivery at the Royal Institution, paid a flying visit to Rome in the

----

* Mr. Clifford has since personally rendered signal service to the late Father Damien, apostle of the lepers, in Molokai.

spring of 1872. He supposed that Rome must offer him rich contributions for his demonology, but, if I remember rightly, in this he was disappointed. 1873 brought the Bayard Taylors. He was changed since last we met from a handsome young bachelor of slender person and equally slender means into a powerfully built, middle-aged man, evidently enjoying the good things of this life, and that best earthly reward, a sensible, agreeable wife ;—she was of German origin. In February 1874, Mrs. Adeline D. Whitney stayed, with her husband and daughter, at the Hôtel de la Paix. She was in person, manner, and conversation just what the author of "The Gayworthys" and other good, womanly books ought to be. And although we have never been granted the privilege of seeing face to face the home-abiding poet Whittier, the bond of sympathy and mutual regard was drawn closer in Rome by kindly messengers bringing us his verbal and written greetings.

I have already referred to the very interesting Scandinavian society in Rome. Finns, Swedes, Norwegians, and Danes economised together, and each spoke at their common club-room in his or her native tongue. They were rapturous over Italy, and reluctant to leave, and at the same time they yearned for their Northern moors, their beech and pine-woods, their mountains and fjords. Once at home the majority grew restless to return, and an old Northern poet, dying in Rome in the winter of 1871–72, rejoiced that he drew his last breath in so heavenly a clime. At the same time young Runeberg, the chief sculptor of Finland and the son of her greatest poet, was mourning with his wife the loss of their two young children, who now lie buried under a cypress-tree in the Protestant cemetery. The last of these little ones

was laid in the earth on the fourth anniversary of the
Runebergs' life in Rome. Altogether it was a most sad
story, and to see the heart-broken young couple wandering forth in their desolation through crowded streets and
ancient ruins made my heart ache.

In our valued friend, the mother of Mr. Osborne
Morgan, we had an agreable link with Scandinavia and
North Wales, as she had spent many years of her youth
in Sweden, and took a keen interest in all pertaining
thereto. On one occasion, when she was calling on me,
charming Anna Hjerta—now Madame Retzius, of Stockholm—a beautiful specimen of a Swedish woman, entered.
It proved, in conversation, that her mother and Mrs.
Morgan had been friends in their youth. This further
led to Anna's mentioning that her mother was closely
related to the unfortunate Karl Wilhelm Jerusalem,
whose suicide was the cause of Goethe publishing his
romance, "The Sorrows of Young Werther;" an act
which had caused the Jerusalems much just indignation.

Madame Jerichau, the clever painter of portraits and
genre, who was likewise present, remarked, turning
to Mademoiselle Hjerta, "It is curious. You are a
direct link with Werther, and I am an indirect link with
the heroine, Lotte; for when I was first in Rome, in
my young days, Kestner, the then *chargé d'affaires* for
Hanover, and who was her son, wanted to marry me."

It is not much to relate, yet the coincidence carried
me instantly back to the far-off days of my childhood,
when the universal astonishment and admiration caused
by the passionate, sentimental romance reached even to
quiet Uttoxeter, shattering the domestic happiness of
Humphrey Pipe.

Mrs. Morgan and her two daughters constantly

wintered in Rome; and the Sandbaches came one season. Mr. Penry Williams, whose fifty years of residence in Rome was festively celebrated, much to the hero's surprise, by some appreciative friends in December 1876, dwelt at 42 Piazza Mignanelli, surrounded by his admirable sketches and glowing oil-paintings of Italy and her *Contadini*, which he showed in his accustomed quiet, unobtrusive way. Miss Rhoda Broughton may also be classed in the Welsh list, from her residence in the Principality with her married sister, who accompanied her to Rome in the early part of 1874.

In Rome our connection with the Antipodes was brought prominently before us. Not only Mr. G. W. Rusden, of Melbourne, but other Australians just arrived from Naples or Brindisi on their way to England, dropped in to see us. An accidental visit, moreover, to the studio of a sculptor named Summers made us acquainted with the artist of the monument erected by the Victorian Government to Burke and Wills, and which commemorates in statuary the offices performed by our son.

In the spring of 1877 we had the joy of welcoming our faithful friend, Miss Margaret Gillies, whose affectionate and enthusiastic nature luxuriated in a sojourn at Rome. It was a time of exquisite happiness mingled with pain, for our beloved and gifted friend, Margaret Foley, was then already treading the Valley of the Shadow of Death in sickness, weariness, and agony, which were to end, the following December, in death.

The friendship of Baron and Baroness von Hoffmann was a great blessing to this poor sufferer and ourselves, and cast a golden effulgence over my husband's closing hours. He delighted to wander with them in familiar converse about the extensive grounds of their beautiful

home, which possesses the grandest view of Rome that
I can recall. It embraces much of the imperial city,
the cupola of St. Peter's, the vast Campagna, with its
engirdling mountains; a landscape scattered over far
and wide with ancient aqueducts, dull red and ivied
walls, ruins, temples, churches, monasteries, presenting
an epitome, as it were, of classic and Christian Rome.
Old box-hedges, or rather walls, neatly clipped, bound
the gardens, alleys, and approaches to the mansion, and
send forth in the sun their peculiar odour. Ancient
statues of old Romans, broken friezes, torsos, and sarco-
phagi, all genuinely pagan and characteristic spoils of
the soil, flank the sunny terraces and the dark avenue
of wide-spreading ilexes; whilst an old stone seat, em-
bowered in luxuriant foliage, and facing Monte Cavo,
marks the spot where, according to the inscription, the
Apostle of Rome, kind St. Philip Neri, "conversed with
his disciples on the things of God."

Scenes are these of beauty and plenty; nay more, of
awe-inspiring devotion. On this self-same Cœlian Hill,
the very pearl of Rome to English Christians, St. Gregory,
from his home and monastery, sent to our heathen forefathers, through his most willing missionaries, headed
by St. Augustine, faith, baptism, and Holy Writ. Here,
in other hallowed precincts, hearts have bled and
prayed, and hands have worked for Britain. It is a
locality once possessing the house of the Christian lady,
Cyriaca, in whose portico the deacon Laurence distributed alms; and still possessing the rude retreat of
the great abolitionist of slavery, St. John de Matha,—
a locality, in fact, where, from the time the sacred grove
of the Camenæ skirted the hill, saints have left their
impress. As I think of this my soul echoes the melo-

dious verses of my friend, Madame Belloc, commemorative of the Cœlian Hill.

The last visit my husband ever paid was to his favourite associates on this Cœlian Hill in January 1879. He appeared quite well up to the middle of the month, when he caught a cold that brought on bronchitis. He had, however, unconsciously to himself and others, been suffering for some months from a valvular disease of the heart, which the bronchial attack revealed. On Monday afternoon, March 3, 1879, he expired.

MARY HOWITT TO HER ELDER DAUGHTER.

"55 *Via Sistina, Jan.* 27, 1879.—Your father had been slightly indisposed on Wednesday, but he took his little walk on the Pincio as usual. On Thursday, however, he felt so far from well that I proposed to ask Mr. and Mrs. Purdie and Miss Trelawny and her brother to defer their visit to us ; but he would not consent to that. They came, and he was so lively and seemed so much to enjoy himself, that we thought all was right. In the night, however, he was taken with extreme difficulty of breathing and inability to lie down. As soon as possible a physician was sent for. Under his good care he has most satisfactorily progressed, and now looks quite like himself again.

"People are very kind in sending or coming to inquire after the dear father's state. This morning we have had a long call from the Rev. Mr. ——, who has been interesting us very much by giving us an account of a visit he paid to the King and Queen the other day, when he took them the letter recently published by the dignitaries of the Church of England. They had a long conversation on the present state of the Catholic Church in Italy, and on the public religious feeling in general. Queen Margaret is a strong Catholic. King Humbert is a Catholic, but takes, as he himself says, 'his religion mildly.'"

MRS. ALFRED WATTS TO MADAME BODICHON.

"55 *Via Sistina, Rome, March* 9, 1879.—I am deeply grateful to our Heavenly Father for the marvellous manner in which He has comforted and sustained our darling mother through these long weeks of greatest anxiety; and now, in the first sharp surprise of her bereavement, her peace of mind, her joy in the belief in my father's peace and joy, are marvellous to behold. Indeed, we all feel a strength, nay, even, strange as it may sound, an inward joy, which is not of this earth.

"My father bade us in departing to *rejoice with him*, not to mourn, and we seem to lie in the reflex of his bright hope. He met the approach of Death with the same brave heart that he had ever shown throughout his career. His intellect was bright to the very end, and his whole spirit merged into intense love—love to God, love to man, love to all created things. The innermost tenderness of a most tender heart bloomed forth and exhaled itself in a perfume as of Heaven itself.

"He sent his love and his blessing to all his friends; so I give you your share. We all felt very much indeed your writing that kind letter yourself. God bless you, dear Barbara, and make all lovely days of old be transfigured again into yet better days. God's hand is for ever outstretched, and there is no end to His bountiful gifts and heavenly outpourings to all the creatures who love Him. He may transform us, but the transformations are only into lovelier, more subtle and exquisite forms. And our days end not here."

THE SAME TO MISS MARGARET GILLIES.

"*Rome, March* 10, 1879.—When Mr. Duncan was here, my beloved father was sick unto death; but we knew that you would so take it to heart, that we dared not then let you know. Dear Octavia, too, came; and how sweet and noble-hearted she is! She knew, and said she would break the news to you. We are aware what a severing of an old, old friendship this must seem to you. Yet it is but a seeming! Love is an immortal creature, Time and Death render her stronger and grander; and only when we enter behind the veil may we see how glorious she has become through trial and pain.

"When dear Alfred and I arrived here three weeks ago yesterday, we found our beloved father looking but little changed in his countenance; only a shade thinner and paler in the face. But so ethereal-looking! He was very quiet. He was not permitted by the doctor to speak much. He was sitting in the dining-room, in his easy-chair, propped up with pillows. He wore his crimson-lined, dark-blue dressing-gown and a little black silk cap.

"A fearful hemorrhage had come on when the bronchial symptoms had lessened, and it was the fact of this hemorrhage, and the news sent us by Meggie of the heart being affected, that made Alfred and me set off at an hour's notice. What a journey we had! And how all seemed a terrible yet beautiful dream as we rushed across France and Italy! Italy always has, some way, been to me the *ideality of grief;* and she put

on her mingled robe of terrible beauty to greet us on
that journey. I scarcely expected to see my father
alive. But how much consolation, how much store of
golden memories, were to be given us during the fortnight that we were all blended into one heart and soul,
as it were, in this crucible of suffering Love!

"I found my beloved mother wonderfully calm and
sustained, and my dear father love, meekness, and
patience; the servants, good, fat Louisa, and that
faithful Gaetano — you know them — most devoted.
Father inspired the strongest esteem in a wide circle
of friends. All sought to minister to him and my
mother. Indeed, during this time we all feel that
ours has been a very banquet of love. Prayers went
up daily both here, in Tyrol, and in England; most
tender, fervent prayers for him. I believe that very
many Catholics prayed for him, and even had Masses
said for him in some of the churches here. A very
cloud of prayer, like incense, was always ascending;
and the prayers had their fulfilment, in the tenderest
state of mind, in his gradually relaxing hold upon
this outer sphere, in his yearning for the higher life,
in a perfectly internal state of peace, and in the gentle
termination of a sickness which might have been terrible both from length and intensity.

"This day week — Monday, March 3—at half-past
three o'clock in the afternoon—we all round him, good
Dr. Nevin having been to see him, and having read
with deep feeling the 'Prayers for the Sick'—the end
came! It came fully expected by us all, longed for
by him. He must in some mysterious manner have
had an intimation of the very hour of his departure,
because, asking some one to tell him the hour, and

learning that it was one o'clock — 'Only one!' he exclaimed in a tone as if greatly disappointed. 'Then I have yet some hours to struggle!' His breathing was much oppressed; and after blessing us all—'all his friends, and all the world!'—and bidding Dr. Nevin good-bye, he did not speak again, except to say rapidly and with a joyful sort of impatience, 'Lift up my hands! Lift up my hands.' This my mother and I did, standing, as we were, one on each side of his bed. His hands were heavy and cold like marble. His eyes were closed. Death had set his seal upon the beloved white face.

"Two days after this, with every honour that his friends in Rome could show to his mortal remains, he was laid in one of the sunniest of spots in that most beautiful of all burial-places, the Protestant cemetery here—'That place,' as Shelley said, 'to make one in love with death.' His dear chrysalis reposes, beneath heaped-up garlands, near to the grave of Gibson. You know the spot, and can picture it all. There was a beautiful service, arranged by kind Dr. Nevin for the occasion; and the choir from the American Church was present, singing lovely hymns in the Mortuary Chapel, and then over the grave. Every one sought to do his memory honour. Again, I say, we can only bless and praise God; praise in the beginning and praise in the ending.

"Is it not singular that precisely at the same hour and upon the self-same day, at the old home of his childhood in England, my father's younger and last-surviving brother, Francis, long an invalid, passed away? They have become, so to speak, twins in the new birth."

My beloved husband was wont to say, "There was no cause to lament such exits. The ripe fruit must drop, and now and then a night's frost severs the young fruit too from the tree." Most true! for on March 2, consequently the preceding day, our much-prized young kinsman, James Macdonell, was snatched away by death, at the commencement of a most promising literary career.

Mr. Augustus Hare, now so indelibly associated in literature with Rome, attended, with other sympathisers, my husband's mortal remains to their last resting-place in the cypress-shaded Campo Santo, the strangers' burial-ground, which, just within the circle of mighty Rome, is guarded by the ancient tower-crested walls of Aurelian and the blackened white marble pyramid of Caius Cestius.

The old Romans, amidst the funeral games of gladiators, solemnly bore, with inverted torches, the ashes of their beloved to sepulture on the Appian Way. It seems to me I have in these pages led the reader stage by stage to the tombs of my departed. It must be so in the reminiscences of a very old woman, who has survived the majority of her kindred and contemporaries. Yet is not the life of each one of us a Via Appia from the cradle to the grave? Well for us when we have not to ask, as Peter had of Him he met on that sacred way, "*Domine quo vadis?*"

MARY HOWITT TO HER ELDER DAUGHTER.

"*Rome, March* 25, 1879.—Hardly had Meggie gone with you to the railway station than the postman brought the important document announcing to me the grant of a pension. I was so overjoyed and astonished that I knew not what to do. My first thought was to get a little carriage and drive to the station, and gaining admittance to you, convey the blessed intelligence before you started. But the fear that after all I might be too late calmed me down; and giving thanks with all my heart, I waited as patiently as I could till Meggie returned, when we set off to the telegraph-office and despatched our telegram to you at Turin; which was a comfortable outlet to our excitement. And, dears, does not this grant seem most wonderful, quite like God's own blessed work? It is so readily given, so kindly, so graciously, for my literary merits, by Lord Beaconsfield, without the solicitation or interference of any friend or well-wisher. I do not know how sufficiently to give thanks."

THE SAME TO THE SAME.

"*April* 3, 1879.—Did I tell you that Octavia Hill and her friend, Miss Yorke, are again in Rome? They move from their hotel to an apartment in this street this afternoon, and in about a week or ten days Miranda comes. They took us yesterday to the Villa Livia. It lies seven miles from Rome, on the old Via Flaminia, where you and I drove one afternoon past Poussin's rocks and Domenica's tomb, and past the meadow of white narcissus. The villa was excavated about sixteen years ago, and has some very remarkable and beautiful frescoes on the walls of one of the rooms; something in the style of your Morris's paper, all a thick wood of branches and leaves, through which you see birds and butterflies and tall flowers rising from the ground. I thought I should never tire of looking into the sylvan, flowery scene. We had a most pleasant excursion.

They returned to dine with us, Miss Yorke and Meggie bringing with them quantities of flowers. The Judas-tree is now in bloom, one mass of crimson pea-like blossom covering the boughs before the leaves are out, excepting just leaf-buds at the top of the branches. It is a splendid tree, but not common as yet in England."

To Miss Margaret Gillies.

"*April* 13, 1879.—Dear Octavia and Miss Yorke are very comfortably settled near us, and yesterday Miranda arrived; therefore Meggie and I went over in the evening to welcome her. They all seemed so happy and bright, that we were drawn into their cheerful spirit, and told our bits of experience of Roman life; and everything seemed to take a comic turn. But oh! when we got out of the house into the street, coming home, we felt as if we must cry, not laugh; and so I have felt all day. I cannot bear having people here, we so sadly miss dear William, and all his pleasant, interesting stories, and the sympathy he had in everything that went on round us. You do not know, and yet I am sure you do, how deeply I feel my loss. But I will try not to dwell upon it.

"We had a letter from Mr. Duncan the other day, which made us unhappy by his saying that you were not well. Every way and on all sides we hear of nothing but death and suffering. It is a strangely solemn time. You know, I suppose, that dearest William's death was accompanied, so to say, by that of his sole surviving brother, two years younger than himself, who died at the same time, to the minute: and of our dear nephew by marriage, James Macdonell, who died suddenly the day before. Three deaths of our nearest and dearest male relatives in two days! Now, in one week we have lost three dear and faithful old friends : one of them beloved as a sister by Alfred and Annie ; one, Mr. William Oldham, two years my husband's senior, wonderfully hale, and with all his mental faculties clear, but who never got over the shock of William's death, and thus soon followed him. The third was Miss Meteyard, poor old 'Silverpen,' our faithful friend for thirty-five years ; one who had sympathised with us so tenderly and lovingly in our great sorrow.

"Now, please, dear Margaret, take care of yourself, and do not work too hard. Mr. Duncan says he is probably coming again to Rome. I hope he may bring us a better account. He has such a true interest in you, and is so kindly sympathetic, that, as you know, we like him much ; and so did dearest William.

"You have thought very often and very affectionately of us and our return to England. I shall never now, so far as I can see, desire to return there as a home ; for since William's mortal remains are laid in the beautiful cemetery here, there is a space reserved for me by his side, and I wish to die in Rome. We are leaving this little apartment, and our furniture will be stored in the premises of a good friend till our return from Tyrol. We go back there—a most sorrowful going back !—for the summer ; so that it will be November before we are once more in Rome. We shall then hire on lease some suitable dwelling."

To Mrs. Alfred Watts.

"86 *Via Sistina, May* 12, 1879.—I think we shall be very comfortable in these spacious lodgings for the remaining fortnight of our stay. This house, you know, is exactly opposite our old home, and we have flitted across the street to-day. There are great goings on at the Vatican in the creation of the new Cardinals. It makes quite an excitement in the clerical world. We only get very passing glimpses of the important proceedings. For instance, about two hours ago, after leaving No. 55 for the last time, just as we stepped out of the street-door we had the edification of seeing a very sombre-looking carriage-and-pair drive up. It brought back Dr. Newman from the Vatican. That most interesting old man, on alighting, tenderly embraced another son of St. Philip, one of his attendants from England, and who, in the Oratorian black cassock and white collar, had been standing for some time on the pavement, evidently awaiting his return. Then they passed lovingly together under the large arched entrance just below No. 55 ; for Newman is located in our close neighbourhood, in the house where Signor Vertunni, the landscape-painter, lives. I have a great desire to hear him ; only he will not preach anywhere ; at least, so it is said.

"Now I shall leave my writing and take the pamphlet on 'Buddhism in China,' and read by the fire, for it is so cold, with the rain falling, falling, and our little apartment opposite standing quite dismantled."

The Same to the Same.

"*Rome, May* 21, 1879.—I have lent Mrs. Terry the Buddhist pamphlet. She too takes an interest in the subject, as her son, Marion Crawford, a young fellow brought up at Oxford, has somewhat suddenly turned his attention to Sanscrit, for which he found in himself a great capacity. He has now gone to Bombay, and he writes to his mother about the wonderful wisdom and the pure morality of the Zend-Avesta; and how, when people understand what the teaching of that theology is, boys and young men will not be corrupted by the immorality of classical learning and literature, to which so many years are devoted. Now, when Mrs. Terry brings it back, I shall have the extract from your letter for her. But, dear Annie, I want to ask whether you think the children of Israel being carried into captivity to Babylon upwards of five hundred years before the Christian era might not indoctrinate those Eastern sages with the wisdom which God gave through the Israelitish prophets, taking with them the grand prophecies of Christ, the Son of a Virgin, the Prince of Peace, &c. The recluses and hermits of the Buddhist faith are but an earlier version of the hermits of the Thebaid. I suppose all this has been worked out and made clear by some of the many minds which are now turned to these subjects."

THE SAME TO THE SAME.

"*Meran, June* 12, 1879.—I thank you very much for the touching little intimations of the spirit-world which you sent me. I wonder very much whether good Catholics would accept anything of the kind. Would Father ———, for instance, sanction dear Julia having tokens of love and recognition from her spirit-mother? We know they recognise such tokens when they come to their saints; yet they regard them as snares of the Evil One when they come to those outside the pale of their Church. We are just now reading Cardinal Newman's 'Callista,' a lovely, pure, and noble story of the early Christian times.

"To-morrow afternoon there is going to be another

little excursion. The Woodward Scotts and their dear children, Mary and John von Messing, Meggie and myself are going to drink coffee at the rural inn belonging to the Cistercian monks. It is a romantic spot, well known to your dearest father. The house stands on a slope by a fine spreading Spanish chestnut-tree; below stretch well-kept meadows and gardens, filling the breadth of a narrow valley planted with fruit-trees. A straight path from the Cistercian farm-house and inn leads to a beautiful and venerable little church, as old almost as the hills, and dedicated to St. Valentine, the first apostle of Christianity in this region, and who dwelt here. A few years ago it was restored in the Munich style; and a large fresco over the chancel represents the Saint preaching to the half-savage inhabitants of this neighbourhood."

THE SAME TO THE SAME.

"*Dietenheim, July* 15, 1879.—Now let me thank you for your kind appreciation of 'The Seven Temptations.' I am so glad that in re-perusing it you found it good. The publication of that book was such a painful blow to me, or rather to my authorly pride and conceit, that I never really got over it. Nobody, reader or critic, seemed at the time to think anything of it, excepting Mr. W. J. Fox, who gave a most kind review of it in the *Monthly Repository*. It was called in the *Literary Gazette* 'blasphemous,' and everywhere, as I remember, rather scoffed at. I have never had the heart to read the book since. If it be a good book, then I am thankful, for it will be recognised in Heaven; and the writing of it was a delightful enthusiasm of poetic fervour and of hope. But, dearest, it has all been discipline. I do not complain ; it has been good for me. I was very ambitious in those days ; and I am glad to think that I had my disappointments and my crucifixions."

" *Dietenheim, July* 20, 1879.—And so poor William M—— is gone ! The other world will soon leave us with very few old friends in this. I had always a peculiar, tender regard for him ; and the friendship that was broken in this world of blunders and mistakes will be, I believe, renewed and perfected in that next wise and loving world. Then I hope I may take his sister to my heart, and that she may return the love I so freely give her."

To Madame Bodichon.

" *Dietenheim, Sept.* 2, 1879.—You, dear Barbara, belong to those peculiar old times which live in my memory and my heart like the sweet poetry of life, which one must not expect to continue on to old age. But how bright and lovely it is in memory ! And the sorrows and disappointments of later life never dim it.

" We are come, you see, to our old summer home, where eight summers in dear William's companionship had been so happily spent. Some of our friends wondered at it ; but there was no home to us like this, where he had been so happy, and where remained only tender and lovely memories of him.

" We stayed, by the way, at Meran, where there is an excellent physician. As I was out of health, we thought it best to see him first ; and we have decided now to spend the coming winter there, instead of returning to Rome ; thus, if I am spared, avoiding the long journeys to and fro."

To Mrs. Alfred Watts.

" *Dietenheim, Sept.* 26, 1879.—No heavenly intimations come to me as yet; and I feel so painfully that I am unworthy. I formerly shut my heart against spiritualism. I even said to your dear father, ' Don't come to me after death, for I should disbelieve you. I should remember the false, deceiving spirits that have come, and reject even you as false.' How bitterly I repent it now! I have asked in prayer that my sins might go beforehand to judgment; and I think all have been brought to my remembrance, from the very days of my childhood; and I seek for repentance, and pray for a sign of acceptance. If I were a Catholic I should ask counsel from my confessor. But God, if He would condescend so far, could do more for me than man. I will not trouble you with these things. Only, the remembrance of the past, and of my own perverseness and my own shortcomings, presses heavily upon me at times. If one could only live up to one's mercies. Day by day see how unspeakably great they are ; such a gracious supply for all our wants ; such a surrounding us with good people ; such a making of our daily path not only easy,- but pleasant. Surely, surely all this can be nothing else but an evidence of the Love of God! Yes, it is so, I know. But then I want something more. I want the knowledge in myself that I am accepted. I longed for this in the early days of spiritualism. I heard of the new life that had come to Mrs. C——, and almost envied her the blessing. I wish, now, that we had gone on accepting what came, without criticising and carping. Then perhaps a fuller measure had been given to me at last. Your father, though he rejected much, yet held fast by that which was the mainstay and foundation of all true faith—confidence in Christ Jesus and the nearness of the spiritual world. What a blessing it was! I seem to be complaining. In truth, I am not. I am only telling you how I am seeking, as it were, to recover lost ground, and praying in my poor, feeble way for a sign of acceptance."

"*Meran, Nov.* 29, 1879.—To-day dear Julia's present, the 'Life of Ozanam,' has come. I have been reading it this afternoon. It is quite a comfort to me to find him a Catholic. Faber has spoiled me for any religious reading of the Protestant type, however good it may be. Two such works have recently been sent me. I have read them conscientiously; but they do not seem to me to have the true unction of spiritual life in them. In this we shall find it.

"If you should happen to see Christina Rossetti, please to give my kind regards to her. I saw a little poem of hers, some two or three years ago, which uttered, as it were, a cry out of my own heart—to be delivered from *Self*. It was the whole cry of an earnest soul embodied in a few words; a wonderful little outburst of prayer. I think it was in an American magazine, or perhaps *Good Words;* I was so sorry I did not copy it."

To Miss Julia Leaf.

"*Meran, April* 8, 1880.—I wonder whether Annie has told you about a project, which seems to have grown up in a wonderful way of itself, or as if invisible hands had been arranging it; that we should have a little home of our own '*im heiligen Land Tirol.*' This really is a very great mercy, seeing that Tyrol is so beautiful, the air so pure and fresh, the climate so beneficial to health, and the people, taken as a whole, very honest and devout. Our little nest of love, which we shall call 'Marienruhe,' will be perched on a hill with beautiful views, surrounded by a small garden."

To Mrs. Alfred Watts.

"*Meran, June* 6, 1880.—You know that Zillah and Miss Gurney are here; and a very great pleasure it is to us to have them so near us, for we can see their windows from ours, and, if they walk in the hotel garden, can talk together. Dear Zillah will tell you about our bit of land, and about our building that is struggling forward. I say *struggling*, because of the immense blocks of rock that the work-people come upon in clearing away the soil for the foundations. Yesterday we were present at some of the blasting. It is literally erecting a house on a rock."

To the Same.

"*Schloss Pallaus, Brixen, June* 13, 1880.—What a great pleasure we had in your letter and its interesting details! For my part, I am fully persuaded that not the smallest work of love shall fail, in God's time, of its accomplishment; and that, whilst we are mere bunglers in this school of life, our training here, with the Divine blessing, will fit us to produce, in that great hereafter, marvels of beauty to the glory of God.

"You are right in supposing that we are spending a delightful time with Baron and Baroness Ernst von

Schönberg. They and Meggie have now gone a walk; and I am resting in the blue sitting-room, which adjoins my bedroom. If I step out on the balcony, I see the fresco on the wall above, depicted in a bold style in red. It runs along the upper portion of the western front. The subject is a tournament, the figures a great deal larger than life, very bold and grand. The castle, which is under the protection of the Archangel Michael, was built in 1492; so it is old, but has no ghosts. At the present time the large blue iris, with its broad blue-green leaves, which is planted on every space of the indented parapets, is now in full bloom, making the battlements a garland of natural beauty, encircling the old stronghold. I never saw anything like it before; and you would admire it as much as I do."

"*Dietenheim, Aug.* 20, 1880.—To-day is a very great day in Bruneck, for the new Prince-Bishop of Brixen comes on his first visitation, and our little town is decorated and prepared to do all a good child can to welcome and honour its spiritual father. At three o'clock Anton drives us to Bruneck. We are to drink coffee with the Baroness Marie von Sternbach, and then go to the hospital, from one of the windows of which we are to see all the town authorities, in their civic grandeur, whatever that may be, bring the Prince-Bishop into the town. There is an open space before the Capuchin Convent, where I do not know what is not going to be done; only this I know, that little Bertha von Vintler, attired in white muslin, with a lovely bouquet in her hand, is to address him in a poetical speech, which she has been learning

for the occasion, and is frightened out of her small
wits. She is, however, sure to do it very prettily,
and her parents will be proud of her to the end of
their days."

"*Aug.* 29, 1880.—The Prince-Bishop's visitation was
a great success. The Sisters of Charity were most
anxious about his going to the hospital. He himself
they did not mind, but his chaplain, secretary, and
other clergy who might attend him, and who would
stand round in silence, listening to all that was said.
He arrived at the hospital in pouring rain, and, to the
infinite relief of the Sisters, quite alone. He visited
each room and patient, and was pleased and satisfied
with all he saw. As he was about to leave, he said
to the Sister Superior, 'I feel as if I knew you, as
if we had been acquainted in earlier days.' Then
she joyfully replied, 'True enough; we lived for six
months at the same priest's house. You were his
young assistant, and I was learning cooking in the
kitchen.'

"I am very glad that Calmet's 'Dictionary of the Bible'
is under your care. I was seized the other day by a sort
of old love and longing for Calmet, remembering the
time when your dear father bought it, and how we used
to sit at Nottingham, you a little child with us, and turn
over those illustrations of Ashtaroth and Dagon, the old
fish, and the goddess Diana of the Ephesians."

"*Dietenheim, Sept.* 30, 1880.—Mr. Woodall, who has
been to see us on his way to Athens, made himself very
agreeable, as was to be expected, and we took the opportunity of gaining much political information from him on

many points ; the working of the Burials Bill amongst other things. He could also tell us about poor old 'Silverpen,' who, we knew, had the highest opinion of him ; and how her literary affairs have been left."

"*Meran, Dec.* 9, 1880.—I turn to the topics of your letter. You mention Herr Herder. He is getting gradually better. Everybody marvels at it. But prayers were put up for him in many parts of Germany. I never, till I knew as much of Catholics and their life of faith and prayer as I now do, could have believed the same amount of child-like trust existing in the hearts and souls of grave, earnest men and women as I now see is the case. Another instance of cure by prayer, that of the Baroness von S——, is known to us. The visit which your father and I paid to Dorothea Trudel's institution for healing by prayer did not satisfy us. Now I see that amongst Catholics the age of miracles is not past. I look on, wonder, and give thanks ; and I wish many of those dear, excellent people whom we know and love could have their minds disabused of their prejudice against the Catholic faith, which is really the old Apostolic faith. Now, don't think I am 'going over.' There is no fear of that. But I cannot help seeing and feeling that the interior life of the Catholics we know, is very near to my ideal of a pure, simple Christian practice ; intellectual, loving art, loving Nature, but living, loving, and enjoying all things in God. This is a long screed, all grown out of Herr Herder, his illness, and his present betterment."

"*Meran, Dec.* 27, 1880.—Your letters of the 23rd and the 24th came together this morning, both of them bringing news of deaths very different from each other, yet each affecting us deeply. Dearest Julia! what can we say of her removal that you have not already said? It is a glorious change for her. We cannot imagine one greater from that long, weary bed of suffering, that long, living crucifixion, to the glory, the peace, the fulness of existence into which she has entered, and that not as a temporary thing, not as a simple variety and relaxation, but as a perfect state for ever and ever. No more suffering, no more grief, no more change, unless it be into a higher state of blessedness. Happy Julia! We must rejoice for her; and though she is removed from her dear earthly friends, yet many among them feel that she does not lie under the green sod, but is of a truth in the blue heavens of God's life and love, and sooner or later will be amongst the St. Philips and the St. Cecilias, with whom she was so kindred on earth. What a blessed faith is that of the good, sincere Catholic, to whom the glorious other world is only next door!

"We have felt an astonishment, a sort of awe almost, in hearing of the death of George Eliot. What a wonderful change, too, for her! What can the discovery of yet continued life be to those who had not believed in it? Oh how strange it is!"

"*Meran, March* 23, 1881.—Our guests, Anton and Jakob Mutschlechner, are gone. I think they had a nice time. But I fancy their pilgrimage to the home of Andreas Hofer was a disappointment, as I believe it is to all. They seemed so tired when they came back last night, and had seen so little. It is a very uninteresting walk of four hours from Meran to Sand; a most fatiguing one too; and no fine scenery by the way, nor when you get there. The house of Hofer, the Sand-Wirth, is in itself uninteresting, and the room which is shown as his has nothing at all remarkable about it. There is only the chapel just by, where Hofer went daily to Mass, and the place where he knelt is shown. Anton and Jakob were, of course, pleased to have seen it. There is a strong movement now among some gentlemen, headed by our revered friend, Count Fries, to erect a beautiful chapel at Sand in commemoration of the brave patriot. This will be attractive, and repay the labour of going there."

"*Schloss Pallaus, July* 5, 1881.—Here are we, so far on our way to Dietenheim, lodged like two princesses, and in the midst of kindness. Besides ourselves are two lady-visitors. One is French, the other an American, whom we and your dear father knew in Rome. She is a *pervert*, with whom he had what seemed to me at the time a hot controversy on the Catholic faith and people turning to it, and which, I had feared, must have offended her. She says, 'No, not at all!' and that she respected his fervour. She says, moreover, that it was my translation of Herder's holy legend—

> 'Among green, pleasant meadows,
> All in a grove so wild,
> Was set a marble image
> Of the Virgin and the Child,'

in my 'Seven Temptations,' which first, when she was quite young, inclined her heart to the Catholic faith; and that in this way I may be considered the cause of her *perversion*. After we leave comes, this week, Lady Herbert. Our dear friends, Count and Countess Hompesch, are spending the summer, with their two little

boys, Pius and Paul, at an adjacent villa in this hamlet
of Sarns."

PRIVATE NOTES.

" *Dietenheim, Sept.* 13, 1881.—Mr. Weldon joins us,
and seems very happy to be with us, just as we are to
have him."

" *Sept.* 15.—Mr. Weldon, Annie, Meggie, and I left
Mayr-am-hof, and were given more flowers than we knew
what to do with.   Dined at Bozen.   Drove to Meran,
having, as we approached, a nice view of our completed
Marienruhe.   Slept at the Post."

" *Sept.* 16.—After breakfast, attended by Mr. Weldon
and my two daughters, entered Marienruhe, and we were
all much pleased with the rooms and the views."

" *Sept.* 29, *Michaelmas Day.*—We sleep for the first
time in the new home."

" *Sept.* 30.—I write my first letter from Marienruhe to
my beloved sister Anna."

On May 26, 1880, I had laid the first stone of the house
represented in the woodcut.   It commands on its four
sides rich and varied landscapes.   It faces the south, and
there stretches out below it the broad valley of the Etsch
or Adige, bordered by lofty wooded mountains, having
old castles and little churches crowning verdant crags
and summits, and terminating in the bold precipitous
profile of the Mendola, a mountain that marks the
division of German and Italian speaking Tyrol.

To the north runs the valley of the Passer river,

containing the birthplace of Andreas Hofer. It too is edged by mountains. It has a broken, picturesque foreground of vineyards and grassy slopes, shaded by luxuriant Spanish chestnuts, mediæval castles, and capacious châlets; and a background of the Jaufen range, the Mons Jovis of the Romans.

MARIENRUHE.

To the east the view is more limited. It is bounded at a distance of two or three miles by the high porphyry walls that hem in the Naifthal, a wooded gorge dominated by the granite crest of the Ifinger, and characterised by its hermitage and chapel, and the savage nature of its treacherous mountain torrent.

To the west we look into the Vinschgauerthal, the upper Venosta Valley of the Romans. On its northern side a range of stupendous mountains lift their jagged peaks into the intense blue sky. The Muthspitze, the nearest of this giant band, has an elongated spur called the Küchelberg, whereon nestles the village of Tirol; and on the nearest and lowest slopes stands a solitary square tower with battlements. It is called the Pulver Thurm, and rising up amongst vineyards above Meran, immediately catches the eye.

To MADAME BODICHON.

"*Marienruhe, Jan.* 9, 1882.—It was so very kind of your aunt Julia to write, and to give us such full details of Scalands, which is associated in my mind, and in my heart also, with you, in those old, never-to-be-forgotten days, when you so kindly lent it to my beloved husband and myself. I never saw spring come out so beautifully, I think, as in your woods, those young plantations in which that quaint, picturesque house is embosomed. I should hardly know it now, I suppose, judging from what dear 'aunt Julia' says; you must have added so greatly to it. Never shall I forget my delight in the beauty of those clustered pale yellow Banksia roses which grew on one wall, and now, I dare say, cover the entire side of the house. Little did I then imagine that in my old age I should live in a house where, this very spring, they will be planted with other roses to climb up a balcony, and probably in time reach the very roof; for so do the roses and many other creepers in this beautiful climate of Meran. In a few weeks, dearest Barbara, when we receive our small belongings from Rome, we shall place upon the wall of our pretty drawing-room one of your beautiful landscapes. It is Festiniog, with grey rain-clouds sweeping over the mountains. How I wish you could see it, could come and sit down with us and admire the glorious views which we have on every side!"

To Miss Margaret Gillies.

"*Marienruhe, Meran, Feb.* 1, 1882.—A letter from Gertrude, the other day, gave us the happy intelligence

VIEW FROM MARIENRUHE (LOOKING EAST).

of your being so much better, for which we are very thankful. You are so tenderly connected with old, old times that seem to belong to another life, that I have for you a peculiar affection. What a pleasant experience my dear husband had of his first acquaintance with you in London, when the Misses Flower were living, and Mr. Fox was in the bloom of his early fame!

How beautiful it all was !   Not, perhaps, what we should
in after-years have felt in the same way.   But there
was a poetry, a grace, a beauty, and a life about it, that
remained its own to the last.   Then came the time
when I first knew you and dear Mary, with her gentle
ways—how sweet she was !—and all that life at Hillside;
and the wild, single daffodils in the field opposite, all
of your planting.   They did not get double and spoil
themselves, like other daffodils.   I do not think that a
single feature of that time has faded out of my mind.
Good Dr. Southwood Smith and all his clever granddaughters, Gertrude's pony, Snowball; even Collins the
gardener has his place in the group that gave life to that
picture of an ideal home.

"All this, dear Margaret, makes a beautiful portion
of the past, which dwells vividly in my memory, in spite
of sorrows, disappointments, and crosses, which came
like heavy clouds, necessary discipline, and the conse-
quences of one's own mistakes or self-deception; but
which have been permitted to pass like clouds, leaving
behind precious recollections.   Every now and then, too,
in later years, you remain like a ray of light in our
memory.   For instance, those few weeks in Rome, and
the pleasant time together at Albano, when you were
so contented with everything in that ill-furnished but
pleasant house!   How much we enjoyed it I cannot tell
you.   The pictures you painted in Rome and at Albano
I love to remember; our fat Louisa looking, with other
women, out from a window and drawing up a letter in a
basket! and the pretty sketch you gave our dear Peggy
Foley.   I hope I shall not have wearied you with my
review of old times; but as they make up a part of my
affection for you, I must be excused for dwelling on them."

VIEW FROM MARIENRUHE (LOOKING WEST).

To Mrs. Alfred Watts.

"*Marienruhe, March* 16, 1882.—It is perfect summer weather, without a cloud from week's end to week's end. All you say about my low-fits is true; and if it were not that I am so afraid of laying the flattering unction to my soul, as if the Heavenly Father might be satisfied with me because I do my best, I really could have great peace of mind, and even joy, in the sense of the continued Divine goodness; only I know that God's sun shines on the unjust as well as the just. Then I know of a certainty that I have not deserved the blessings with which every passing day is stored, and that, like Dives, I may be receiving my good things in this life. I often try to comfort myself with these lines of Cowper's :—

> 'Sometimes a light surprises
>   The Christian while he sings ;
> It is the Lord, who rises
>   With healing in His wings.'

"Now, if I really were not afraid of the unsurpassed peace and happiness of my outward life, I might bask, as it were, in continued sunshine, rejoicing ever. But then I know myself; I know the awful shortcomings, the actual sin of my long life; and so I get very sad, wanting an assurance of salvation, of forgiveness."

"*Marienruhe, April* 14, 1882.—You will have had my letter by this time showing you that the sad news of your dearest aunt's great illness had reached us. We must now look for the end. Oh! it is very sorrowful. Yet how beautiful, how full of love and good works her dear life has been! One's heart naturally clings so to beloved relatives on earth, who have been ever ready to speak words of love and tenderness. My dear, dear sister and true friend, may it only please our Lord to make me as fully prepared for the great future when my hour comes! Your dearest aunt found a place of rest for her soul, an anchor for her faith, in the Church of England, which was all-sufficient for her. This seems to me a great privilege, even though that which satisfied her never could satisfy me. I am so thankful for her."

"*April* 15, 1882.—The sad tidings has reached us. I cannot as yet realise that your dear aunt Anna has gone. Then I have such an entire confidence in her happiness, in her well-being, that I cannot feel heart-broken. But for the dear ones left behind, what an immense sorrow must be theirs!—she that was so lately with them, so cheerful, taking such a tender interest in that which interested others, watching with such keen delight the coming out of spring buds and blossoms. She enjoyed reading modern books of a sweet religious tendency, not overflowing with the teaching of creeds. Thus, one of her last letters was so full of that charming book, 'Journals and Letters of Caroline Fox,' also of 'John Inglesant.' Her mind had not become old, her heart had never become chilled. I know that my life is poorer now that she is gone; but I will not murmur. I will do my endeavour to follow in her track; to take hold, as it were, of the Saviour's hand—then I shall be safe."

CHAPTER IX.

IN THE ETERNAL CITY.

1882–1888.

Private Notes, 1882.

> "Of outward pleasure, wealth or ease, dear Lord,
>   I do not ask increase,
> I only ask, with Thee a sweet accord,
>   And that the end be Peace."

"*May* 6, 1882.—The last medallions and pictures were hung in the various rooms and on the staircase. All is extremely nice ; too elegant and perfect for one like me. Oh ! my dear Lord, fit me for the reception of Thy increasing mercies."

"*May* 12.—Received a note from the Countess Hompesch that her cousin, Father Ceslas de Robiano, would come with them to afternoon tea. He is a Dominican, who, by order of his superiors, remains on in Berlin, where their monastery has been suppressed. He has suffered no little in the *Culturkampf.* The Hompesches and Father de Robiano duly came. I was deeply impressed by him. I spoke of my great desire for baptism. I hope I did not say too much."

"*May* 14, *Sunday.*—Father Ceslas called in the evening. I again spoke with him of baptism; wishing I could have a direct message from God, that an angel could come and tell me what He would have me to do.

"To this the Dominican replied, 'God speaks by His messengers, saying, "He that heareth you, heareth Me. He that despises you, despises Me." But you would be right in demanding from a stranger his credentials. Mine are the Cross of Christ on my forehead, and the words He uttered to me at my ordination, "As the Father hath sent Me, I also send you." I come from God, and with all the weight and authority of the Catholic Church.'

"I spoke of the great difficulty I had concerning the honour paid to the Virgin Mary, though I should like to love her; and he answered, 'The hatred of the Blessed Virgin in the world is the fulfilment of the Divine Word: "I will put enmities between thee and the woman, and thy seed and her seed: she shall crush thy head, and thou shalt lie in wait for her heel." Why, in Berlin, where I am known, the street-boys, poor little fellows! run after me, crying out to annoy me, "Hail Mary!"'

"He took out his breviary, opened it, and asked, 'May I read you a little prayer which a dear friend of mine, Père Besson, gave me at a very critical moment of my life?'

"I expressed pleasure and surprise that he should have known Père Besson.

"'Ah!' he replied, with emotion, 'he was my dear friend—my brother. He was with me when I took the habit.'

"The prayer of the Dominican artist was written in French, Father de Robiano's native tongue, for he is a

Belgian. He read it very slowly, translating it into English:—' O Jesus, my Saviour, the only physician of my soul, I fling myself with all my weakness and misery into Thy ever-open arms. Humiliated as I am by the sight of myself, I know perfectly well that I am both ignorant and much mistaken about myself. Thou, Who seest in very truth, look mercifully on me. Lay Thy healing hand on my wounds. Pour the salutary life-giving balm of Thy love into my heart. Do for me what I have not the courage to do for myself. Save me in spite of myself. May I be Thine; wholly Thine, and at all cost Thine. In humiliation, in poverty, in suffering, in self-abnegation Thine. Thine in the way Thou knowest to be most fitting, in order that thereby Thou mightest be now and ever mine. Thou art my Master, my Lord, my Saviour, my God. I am Thy poor little creature, dependent alone on Thy merciful charity, O Jesus, my only Hope.'

"After this the question of baptism was decided, and even the day fixed—May 26."

"*May* 15.—Very pleasant letter from Australia. All are well; and my dear eldest grandchild, Charlton, was to sail on May 4 for Europe."

"*May* 19.—Father Ceslas came this morning. I question if I learned much, but the conversation was interesting. I told him I should never know what to say in my self-defence when a Catholic. He advised me ' to leave it to God. He always did so, especially before magistrates; and in Prussia he had been taken up five times.' In my case it will never be so bad. No one will take me before magistrates."

"*May* 22.—We talked together on Everlasting Punishment. I said it was dreadful to imagine millions of souls burning in torments for ever. Then Father Ceslas exclaimed, 'Who said there were millions of souls? Who knows how many souls wilfully reject God at the last? I remember, when my brother and I were studying law, a dear friend of ours studied with us. He had an intense perception of the holiness of God. He was ever thinking that if God was so pure, so just, He could never pass over the least sin. He kept pondering and pondering whether there were many or few saved; with his estimation of the Divine Holiness he kept reducing and reducing the number, so that they· grew fewer and fewer each time we met. At length my brother, who was a generous soul, could bear this restriction of God's mercy no longer. Up he rose in righteous indignation, crying, "I tell you, Heaven is full of scoundrels, murderers, fools, and blasphemers!"'

"I yield to the doctrine of Everlasting Punishment; trusting all to the wisdom of God, which is far beyond my poor comprehension. I know He is merciful, and that all He does is right."

"*May* 25.—The permission arrives from Trent for my baptism in the private chapel, arranged for the convenience of Father de Robiano's brother-in-law and sister, Count and Countess Franz Stolberg-Wernigerode, in Schloss Rametz, where they are staying. I shall have to read the profession of faith in the Tridentine form, commonly called the Creed of Pope Pius IV. It is all right, though it seemed to me a little sweeping."

"*May* 26, 1882.—A very important day to me. I

became a member of the Church of Rome : I hope and trust directly of Christ. It was all very beautiful. Ernst von Schönberg was with me; and the act was performed in the midst of a heavenly human family. Went later with Ernst and returned thanks in the little church of St. Valentine."

To Mrs. Alfred Watts.

"*Marienruhe, June* 16, 1882.—Dear Charlton is here. He is a quiet, well-bred, self-possessed youth; a water-drinker, and never smokes. He is all we can desire. This must satisfy you for to-day."

To Miss Leigh Smith.

"*Marienruhe, Oct.* 6, 1882.—We thank you for so kindly sending us *The Graphic*, and afterwards *The Illustrated News*. We are interested in every incident of your brother Ben's voyage to Franz Josef Land, the loss of his ship, and the return of the explorer and his crew from Nova Zembla. We were glad to have a peep of them in their hut on Cape Flora. But above all were we thankful to see that the brave man himself was so little changed; that, notwithstanding the sufferings and hardships, it was just the same calm, thoughtful face that I remember thirty or more years ago. I am afraid that, with such an amount of health, strength, and unabated vitality, he will be setting out again to the Arctic regions. I hope and trust not, but I am afraid he may. I have always felt toward Barbara, Ben, and you as to none other of our friends, as if in some mysterious way you were kindred to us.

"Of course, dear Nannie, you have heard of the awful visitation of water which has come down upon

poor old Tyrol and the north of Italy. The misery,
ruin, destruction, and general devastation of hundreds
of districts up in the mountains is what nobody can
conceive but those who have been shut up there and
cannot get away. Then think of all those towns,
Verona, Trent, Bozen, Brixen, and poor old Bruneck,
which has, perhaps, lost more houses than any other
place."

To Mrs. Todhunter.

"*Oct.* 13, 1882.—How kind you have been in feeling
anxiety about us here at Meran! But it has been
mercifully spared; for, excepting the breaking up of
the railway and overflowing of the river in the broad
valley which extends on to Bozen, destroying vineyards
and orchards, the town itself, and all its surrounding
hills, with their numerous villages, have been quite
uninjured. Beyond this broad valley, which no doubt
in primeval times was a lake, all is ruin, desolation,
loss, and misery inconceivable. Our poor Pusterthal, so
peaceful and flourishing, like the once-beautiful region
surrounding Trent and Verona, is now a scene of
devastation.

"The whole year has been abnormal in some respects;
so much wet, and so unusually cold; at least, it was so
in Pusterthal. There was snow on the mountains even
in July, fresh fallen, so cold was the weather, with
rain in the lower country. The summer harvests were
got in with difficulty; the later crops must be all lost.
The destruction of bridges, mills, dwellings, almost
entire villages, is so appalling and heart-rending that
one knows not how relief is to come, nor even hope;
because rain still continues; for, though it may clear

up and there be two fine days, electric clouds gather and two days of rain certainly follow.

"This terrible visitation has been foreseen by the really wise for half a century, in consequence of the wholesale destruction of the forests on the mountains. Timber being greatly in demand, Government enforced fines for the total felling of mountain-woods; but the purchasers of timber coming from a distance have paid the penalty, and the peasant-proprietors have sold their wood. The roots of growing woods or forests bound the earth together, the very moss spreading under the living trees and nourished by them, acted as a sponge, and drank up the water of rain and snow; so that all was kept in equipoise. The excess of water now on the mountains has loosened also the old moraines, which had lain there for untold ages, till they had become, as it were, portions of the mountains. These have now slid down, and adding weight and force to the swollen streams, have brought frightful destruction with them. I do not think that any newspaper statements have been exaggerated, although they may have been written in that sensational style which always offends one's good taste, and often makes one disbelieve the narration."

To Mrs. Gaunt.

"*Nov.* 8, 1882.—We are very thankful just now for dry weather, as we have had about ten days without rain; and some of · them very brilliant, belonging to the true character of Meran. The end of October was awful; three days and nights of incessant rain, which again produced floods, and every provisional means to amend the former devastation was again destroyed,

carried away before the raging waters, and much more
ruin and damage produced than earlier. People in
some places were in despair. The military, who had
in the first instance been so helpful, had been withdrawn from most of these quarters, and so the population, doing what they could single-handed, left the rest
to chance.

"In Bruneck, the cemetery was overflowed and the
dead carried out of their graves; the burial-vaults of
families, which had been built as if to last for centuries,
were washed away, almost like houses of cards. Some
families, at the first alarm of danger, removed their
dead. It has been truly an awful time. Dr. James
Young of Kelly, the discoverer of paraffine, has sent
me £100 for the relief of the inundated. May our
dear Lord bless him for it! The Austrian Government,
which is not rich, has sent large relief. But this second
flood has destroyed the work which the Government
grant enabled the various local authorities to effect."

To Miss Leigh Smith.

"*Dec.* 4, 1882.—Thank you for your kind cheque
for poor Welsberg, the condition of which has become
much sadder since the letter I wrote you. I should
like to send you an account which appeared in the
Kölnische Zeitung, by the Baroness Alexandra von
Schleinitz, a wonderfully gifted young woman, who,
with her mother and sister, were at Bruneck at the
beginning of these sorrows; and speaks now of the
misery and desolation there, and above all at poor
Welsberg. She is a calm, intellectual woman, yet she
says that really nothing seems to remain to the home-
less, desolate people but to become insane!"

To Mrs. Alfred Watts.

"*Schloss Pallaus, Brixen, Feb.* 13, 1883.—We have arrived here quite safely after a most prosperous journey; looking, however, with extreme and sorrowful interest at the dreadful havoc caused by the inundations, which has transformed the once-smiling, although grand valley of the Eisack into a gloomy, desolate defile. Baron Schönberg was waiting for his guests at the Brixen railway station, with various conveyances, and we drove by quite a new route to Pallaus; the bridge over the Eisack having been swept away. We came here into Alpine scenery, for within the last few days snow has fallen here abundantly; yet, the wind being in the south, the air is quite mild."

To the Same.

"*Pallaus, Feb.* 15, 1883.—We went yesterday on our Confirmation errand to the Prince-Bishop of Brixen. It was all very beautiful and solemn, but not at all sad. I, the old, old woman, Mrs. W——, and Alice—three generations, as it were—received the rite. The ceremony was in the private chapel of the palace, and when it was over the Bishop received us all in one of his grand yet simply-furnished old rooms. The party consisted of Ernst and Bessie von Schönberg, Mr. and Mrs. W——, Alice, Meggie, and myself, Dr. Mitterrutzner, Director of the Brixen Gymnasium, Father Paul, and Mr. Basil Wilberforce. It is a pleasure to us that Alfred saw Mr. Wilberforce, whom we consider one of our especial friends. Although the weather had been for several days misty and cloudy, the sun was by this time shining. As I was driving with Bessie out of the court of the Bishop's palace, the letter-bag was put into the carriage,

and a most kind, affectionate letter from my dear
Australian children was handed me. It seemed to
come like a recognition of approval and satisfaction
from a Power higher than merely earthly contrivance.
What a warm, loving reply I shall send by the next
mail ! "

To the Same.

"*Marienruhe, Feb.* 24, 1883.—Here we are at home
again. The goodness, care, and loving providence of
our blessed Lord is something untold and unimaginable.
We did so wish you could, at the time, have known with
what cheerful, thankful hearts we all went through those
muddy, flood-destroyed roads at Brixen. It was really a
journey of pleasure ; and those dear young von Schönbergs rejoicing over it, and giving thanks, as all the rest
did. Another thing I must mention is the great kindness of everybody at Meran. Our dear neighbours, the
Miss Pembertons, and good Mr. Marke especially welcome us back most cordially. So, too, our other neighbours. I feel very grateful to one and all."

To the Same.

" *Feb.* 25, 1883.—The whole of the little journey, with
its varied details, was so completely one beautiful succession of harmonious links of love, that nothing could have
been more perfect. Nothing, too, that I ever experienced
or hoped for is so sweet, tender, and real as what I now
feel in my soul. Give thanks for me that there are
times, but only now and then, just now and then, when
I feel the reality of the spiritual life, and even its nearness, with such intense love and gratitude to the Lord
that I could almost weep for joy."

To the Same.

"*Easter-Sunday, March* 25, 1883.—A Happy Alleluia to you! This is the paschal greeting which friend gives friend here in Catholic Tyrol. Father Paul and dear, kind Caroline Schmid came on Easter-eve to wish us it.

"I have been with Meggie and Alice to the parish church this morning, to High Mass. It was very beautiful and stately. The church, which is said to hold four thousand, was quite full, even the aisles, with praying men, women, and children—those dear little observant children, some not above five years old, all attention, and kneeling with small clasped hands. Then the rapt silence and devotion of such an assembly. At the more solemn portions of the service, when all regard the Lord as present, and every man, woman, and child is kneeling, there is not a sound, not a head turned as with curiosity to look about. It was this morning as silent as if nobody was there. This, I think, is the most wonderful feature of Catholic devotion. I, who am so sensitive to outward influences, find this mute attention of all around me most comfortable. Well, having said this much, and again offered dear Alfred and you my salutation of a Happy Alleluia, I will proceed to the next joyful subject, to Raphael Weldon's wedding, which was in the best style of taste; and both bride and bridegroom very remarkable young people. She, with her Girton honours, has a rank in intellectual culture equal to one-half, at least, of the men who leave our universities."

To the Same.

"*April* 6, 1883.—Let me go back to the day before yesterday, when we had our London guests. Mr. Woodall remained at home with me, answering all my

questions about everything in the political and public
world that we are interested in. Of course, he answered
and explained all from his point of view, looking at
everything with much more favourable inferences and
opinions than we probably should. He does not fear
Fenian malice and revenge. It is only an epidemic in
Ireland, he thinks, such as occurs again and again, and
then passes away. He likewise thinks well of the Salvation Army. The results of its labours in the Potteries
seem wonderful. He has presided at its meetings, and
upholds it warmly.

"Well, all the time Mr. Woodall was indoctrinating my
mind on these subjects, Meggie and Alice were in the town
with genial Mr. Harry Furniss, who was photographing ;
not ' versing or prosing it,' but ' picturesquing it everywhere.' They showed him the old Burg, the town-house
of Margaret Maultasch, with all its quaint old furniture,
with which he was delighted. They stopped old men,
old women, children, everything that was effective, posed
them, got up groups instanter ; all were photographed,
and people were delighted. It was the merriest, most
amusing morning. Mr. Furniss lives at the bottom of
the Avenue Road, in a house that was not built, I think,
in our time. He has joined this Royal Commission of
Inquiry into Technical Education, not at their expense,
but his own, and gives a most amusing account of the
very hard work it has been to him. They posted on, and
he wanted to stay ; and they said, ' Now look, Furniss,
here is a magnificent scene for you. Take it all into
your mind, make notes of it, and you'll have a splendid
picture !' But that is not what he wants, but rather
what he has been doing in Meran this morning : getting
true little bits of picturesqueness that abound here, and

which could never be imagined. We wanted him to stay a day or two with us, as he found Meran such a peculiarly pictorial place, and then catch up his companions farther on the tour; but he thought it wisest not to part from them.

"The secretary of the Commission is Mr. Gilbert Redgrave, whose father I had the pleasure of meeting at Liverpool many years ago. He has kindly sent me word through Mr. Woodall that my 'Steadfast Gabriel' influenced his early career.

"Yesterday came one of the most beautiful and affecting letters I ever read. It was a farewell from the Bishop of Argyll, now lying hopelessly ill at Brighton. Reflecting on the very pleasant, friendly intercourse which subsisted for so many years, we feel this grief still more acutely. I am sorry to conclude with so sad a topic."

To the Same.

" *Meran, May* 6, 1883.—We have been to our little church of St. George; and then we went, with hundreds of other people, to see a very great procession of the ' *Schützen-Verein*,' a word which sounds much better than when translated into English—' Sharp-shooters' Brigade.' The Tyrolers, like the Swiss, pride themselves on their skill in shooting, as you know. This was a large general meeting of all classes, and was made an exact reproduction of the peasantry, who at the beginning of this century kept watch and ward, and fought under Hofer in defence of Tyrol and the Emperor. There were several hundred volunteers in various national costumes —which were the same with shades of difference—and in many cases very old, dating from the commencement of

the century; such old breeches, coats, and hats as Mayr-
am-Hof can turn out; and such old weapons, rude,
savage battleaxes, pikes, spears, and halberds; and queer
grotesque weapons like short scythes on the top of poles.
As to guns, they were wonderful. Each district sent its
troop, with their banners, some very old, tattered, and
torn; others beautiful, with their rich old faded colours.
It was quite touching; and every now and then one saw
a something which stirred the poetry within one and
sent a choking feeling into one's throat, so that one could
not say anything for fear of crying. I remember when
many things touched me in this way; but thought I
was now quite too old to feel in this emotional manner.
It was like the old war-horse being excited by the sound
of the trumpet; or rather our poor pony Peggy, at
Esher, going off at a canter when the fox-hunters came
by on Bookham Common. I smile at myself as I write
this, to think of me and my old emotion."

To Mrs. W——.

"*Dietenheim, July* 4, 1883.—Your letter has awoke
the deepest sympathy in our hearts. What can we say
to you as regards Miss ——'s resolute rejection of a
faithful old friend? I can really say nothing, excepting
that assuredly she never needed more the earnest prayers
of her rejected friend. We grieve for you, but it is
Miss ——, poor dear lady! who needs our pity. You
can do nothing but accept the silence she has enjoined
and imposed upon you; and you and your good Catholic
friends must pray for her enlightenment. In this spirit
you will feel no bitterness against her. Indeed, the
only real injury that her rejection of your friendship
could do you would be the awakening of bitterness

and anger in your heart. That you will never feel; but, instead, a tender, earnest yearning for her enlightenment, which, in the Divine Mercy, may have influence upon her, and in any case will bring you nearer to the Spirit of the Lord. You, in this respect, are nearer to the experience of the true disciple than I am. You are called upon to make a sacrifice for the Blessed Lord and His Truth; that is what He anticipates for His faithful followers. Therefore, dear friend, buckle on your armour, as it were, and stand truly prepared for what comes. Be ready for the combat. Give all up to God, and leave the end to Him! We pray that strength may be granted you for all trials, and that the peace of God may abide with you. The Great Helper is on your side. Fear not. Do boldly that which has to be done."

To MRS. ALFRED WATTS.

"*Dietenheim, July* 22, 1883.—We have been to church at the Ursulines'; Anton driving us, as he always does on Sunday mornings. While we are at Mass he fetches our letters, which we then have the pleasure of reading. In yours of to-day you speak of the death of our *Hofbauer's* brother. Your prayer for the dear old soul is quite Catholic; the usual words being, 'Eternal rest give to him, O Lord. Let perpetual light shine upon him. May he rest in peace!' This, I truly believe, will be Onkel Johann's state. How your father and we all respected him! He was seventy-nine years of age, yet his eyes to the last were those of a young man. I never saw such an old face. He had been no reader; he worked with his hands, and knew many prayers by heart. He would hold

his rosary in his hard, withered old hands, and live
over with the Blessed Virgin the entire life of Her
Son, as he watched the cows in the fields, and seemed
to be standing in vacant idleness there. Many peasants,
especially women and children, have wonderfully precious times in the solitary pastures, when tending their
cows and sheep. Very much teaching can be acquired
out of the rosary. This reminds me of your charm-
ingly-painted and beautiful picture which we have of
the old Munich woman in church telling her beads.
It is one of the most tender and lovely old Catholic
faces that I ever saw. I never knew how true it
was to life, and what a depth of religious experience it
expressed, till I knew what the rosary is to the simple,
pious Catholic. I never shall forget the countenance
of a youth of perhaps eighteen who knelt by me one
Sunday in the Ursuline church last summer. He was
an Italian, a navvy, or something of that kind, sunburnt, and with coarse and hard young hands. The
rosary was round them, and the beads passed slowly
through the clasped fingers. He never saw me; he
never stirred. His countenance was beautiful; his soul
was with Mary and her Divine Son, God Himself.
You can understand how I could not help praying
that his prayers might be heard and his soul's devotion
be accepted. Your old woman could be the grandmother of that youth."

In the summer of 1884 my beloved daughter Annie,
unknowing it, came to Dietenheim to die. With no
revelation of the approaching parting, she and I were
wont to sit, at her favourite hour of sunset, on the
upper balcony of Mayr-am-Hof, where she read to

me "The Idylls of the King," or "The Holy Grail"
and "The Passing of Arthur," and finished her water-
colour sketch of the quiet village street. It was a
fair and familiar scene, through which, a few evenings
later, the mourning inhabitants carried her to her final
resting-place in God's Acre. They bore her under the
quaint old archway of the village church to her grave

ARCHWAY OF THE VILLAGE CHURCH.

next to that of poor Onkel Johann, when, in the
hush of Nature, the evening glow illumined the moun-
tain-tops and twilight spread over the valley and lower
slopes.

On the common above both the churchyard and
Mayr-am-Hof, near the old crucifix, where we have all
so often sat to enjoy the sunset, a granite seat for wayfarers had been erected. It was often visited by her in

the beautiful closing hours of her pure and devoted life. It was a memento to her beloved father from our generous friend, Walter Weldon, who has also gone to his rest and his reward.

THE CRUCIFIX ON THE COMMON.

To THE BARONESS ERNST VON SCHÖNBERG-ROTH-SCHÖNBERG.

"*Meran, Dec.* 22, 1884.—Now that the shortest day has passed, I hope the lengthening days may bring your dear sufferer amending health and joy to you all.

"I will not write to you to-day on black-edged paper,

because I should like, if God so willed it, to come to you as a harbinger of peace and joy.

" We have had Mass in our little Marienruhe chapel. Meggie and I have taken together Holy Communion. So it has been a good day to us, and the first thing I do, breakfast being over, is to write to you."

To Mrs. Gaunt.

" *Meran, May 27,* 1885.—We have had an unusually cold and broken sort of winter and spring here. Just now, within the last week, the first settled and true Meran weather has set in. Nevertheless endless grandees and royalties have been here ; and notably the Duke Charles Theodore of Bavaria, brother of the Empress of Austria, and his lovely young Duchess, an Infanta of Portugal. That which makes them especially admirable and estimable is, that he, having naturally a talent for surgery and an intense interest in diseases of the eyes, has devoted his life for some years to the cure of the blind, principally of cataract. He has a hospital for the purpose situated near his palace at Tegernsee. Being himself out of health, he came for change of air to Meran ; but the fame of his healing-power having preceded him, the blind soon presented themselves ; and he, unable to resist their appeal, saw them and began to operate on them. Others came, and still more and more, from all parts of Tyrol, old and young, mothers with their children, tens, twenties, till at last two thousand in all have come to him. On two hundred he has operated, and nearly always successfully. Even old men who have been blind for ten and fifteen years have left the Meran hospital seeing ; two wards there having been set aside for his use.

"His assistant surgeon, and even the gracious young Duchess herself, worked with him ; she often holding the hands of the poor patients, speaking words of kind encouragement to them, and giving the instruments to her husband as he needed them. Anything more angelic or Christ-like than this cannot be imagined. Our Alice, who has been in the habit of giving her services in the Meran hospital, has been the eye-witness of these proceedings ; and every evening we have had the privilege of assisting her to prepare the bandages for the next day's use. This and other circumstances which are not worth mentioning have made us all personally acquainted with these excellent people ; so that the sweet young Duchess, her three little daughters, and her lady-in-waiting have all become our friends, and given quite a grace and beauty to Marienruhe. Such an instance of pure Christian love as that exercised by this royal couple has never before been known in Meran. Yesterday they left, with the blessings of all following them.

"Yesterday, also, we parted with some dear Australian relatives, whom till the week before we had never seen, and whom charmed us by their intelligence, freshness of spirit, and simplicity of taste and manner of life."

To Mrs. W——.

"*Meran, Dec.* 6, 1885.—We have recently had some most welcome visitors, who came for a week to Meran— Octavia Hill's sister, Gertrude, and her husband, Charles Lewes, the son of the well-known writer and the biographer of Goethe. You would have greatly enjoyed, as we did, Mr. and Mrs. Lewes's society. They are very bright, taking an active part in all good and useful efforts for human improvement and well-being. They and her sister Octavia have been working very hard this last summer to obtain for the northern side of London that fine addition to Hampstead Heath, Parliament Hill, with its adjoining land. This was a scheme which we also, when living at Highgate, coveted for the public, and for which my dear husband laboured, but feared it would never be obtained. Now, however, through unremitting efforts and unlooked-for help, it seems likely to be accomplished. All this good news our friends brought us, which caused us, as you will understand, a great rejoicing."

To the Same.

"*March* 10, 1886.—We have now some excellent friends visiting Meran, Mr. Alphonso Clifford and his sister, Miss Constantia. They are most earnest Catholics by birth and conviction, and connected in various ways with my dear old county of Stafford. They often come to afternoon tea. Last Friday they were here, and, to our pleasant surprise, Mr. Wilberforce walked in; just the person we were all wishing for.

"Alice goes on as usual. She is now working away for the strange, solitary, out-of-the-world mountain village of Karthaus. As I understand the situation, it occupies a lofty platform of rock in that remote valley, the Schnalserthal. It was, as its name implies, a Carthusian monastery or Charterhouse, until Joseph II. dissolved it, dispersed the good Brothers, despoiled the rich church and library, and gave up the place to ruin. Now the monastery has become a village, and the dwellings of the Carthusian cenobites those of peasants. The number of inhabitants is between one and two hundred; but there are a few scattered farms on the outskirts and in the bordering glens, which also belong to the parish of Karthaus. The priest is an enlightened man, but the people themselves seem to belong to three or four centuries ago. I never heard, even in other secluded parts of Tyrol, of any as simple and primitive as these.

"Alice first heard of the place from the Sister Superior in the Meran hospital, and learnt that two Sisters of Charity had gone thither, at the desire of the parish-priest, to nurse and tend the sick and poor, and that they, the Sisters, had nothing at all to begin with. Alice went up, in consequence, to lofty Karthaus to visit them, and the result has been, that a six-roomed house there has been purchased for them. It is being fitted up as a hospital, and will, when it is finished and furnished, be a very nice little institution. The Countess Hompesch and other charitable well-wishers have sent up supplies. Frau Perwanger, the bonnet-maker, has been most active and energetic in the good work. She has interested her customers and friends; and this has caused beds and bedding, pots and pans, being sent here, till our ironing-room downstairs resembled a furniture warehouse.

" Everything has now been carried off and up to Karthaus, where Alice has gone, and will return on Friday; leaving all, I expect, in a comfortable state of progress."

To Miss Leigh Smith.

"*Dietenheim, Aug.* 11, 1886.—We owe you such warm thanks for the books. Alfred is delighted with the 'Vulture Maiden' (which describes the life and people adjacent to Karthaus). He thinks it splendid. I am more deeply interested than I can tell you in

'All Sorts and Conditions of Men.' It is the first
by Besant that I have read. It affects me like the
perfected fruit of some glorious tree which my dear
husband and I had a dim dream of planting more
than thirty years ago, and which we did, in our
ignorance and incapacity, attempt to plant in soil not
properly prepared, and far too early in the season.
I cannot tell you, dear Nannie, how it has recalled
the hopes and dreams of a time which, by the over-
ruling providence of· God, was so disastrous to us. It
is a beautiful essay on the dignity of labour."

To Mrs. Oldham.

"*Dietenheim, Aug.* 27, 1886.—Few letters could
touch my heart or be as kindred to my spirit as the
one you kindly sent me a month ago. Alfred Watts
was with us when it came; and he was as glad as we
were to have news of you.

"*Sept.* 4.—I left the above unfinished, and have
since then written no letter, having taken a severe
cold.

"It is quite a comfort to me to know that you are
still at Kingston. Though I have never been to your
house there, our beloved Annie had. But do not
imagine, dear friend, that I cannot understand what
it is you miss, even with the river, the old palace
and the stately gardens of Hampton Court at hand.
You miss exactly that which gave the living charm
and interest to all that surrounds you. I understand
it perfectly.

"We are having here a very fine summer. The
harvest seems to be well got in, and the peasant-

people are all advancing into a state of great expectation and excitement in prospect of five days of magnificent military manœuvres which take place here in the middle of this month in the presence of the Emperor of Austria and his entire staff. He has never been to Bruneck for forty-two years, and then only for one night, on a journey he was making, as a boy, with his two little brothers, Carl Ludwig and Maximilian, under the charge of their tutor, and when there seemed no chance of his ever being Emperor. Military manœuvres of one kind or another take place here every autumn; but those this year will surpass in importance all preceding ones. Twice this old Mayr-am-Hof, which is a conspicuous object on this side the valley, has been made the special point of attack by one party, and consequently of defence by the other; so if now, in this Imperial inspection of the troops, it is used for the same purpose, it will give us an especial interest in at least one day's work.

"We have been reading with enjoyment Mr. Froude's 'Oceana.' We much approve of his very strong desire that our colonies should, like good, faithful, well-trained children, be staunch in love and service to old Mother England. How deeply we feel on this subject I cannot tell you; and I hope and trust that you join strongly in this truly English sentiment.

"I am quite a fixture to the house, as I cannot walk any distance. Still, before I had this bad cold I spent a portion of each day out of doors, sitting under the wide-spreading trees by the old closed gateway, which you will find in this September number of *Good Words*— as drawn by dear Annie—in the last chapter of the 'Reminiscences.'"

PRIVATE NOTES.

'*Sept.* 6.—My cold makes me a complete captive to my room."

"*Sept.* 8.—As I am worse, Dr. Erlacher is sent for, who thinks seriously of my case."

"*Sept.* 11.—Still worse. The doctor comes twice; and Father Flavian said Mass for me in the chapel."

"*Sept.* 16.—I am better. This day the Emperor arrived in Bruneck."

MARGARET HOWITT TO MISS LEIGH SMITH.

"*Dietenheim, Sept.* 24, 1886.—I cannot let another day pass without telling you how much better my mother is. The doctor now speaks quite hopefully; and although, in her present weak condition, there seems little likelihood of an immediate return to Meran, we can now dare to hope that we may take her back before the cold weather sets in.

"We have had the Emperor Franz Josef and four Archdukes in Bruneck from last Thursday night until Tuesday afternoon. On Tuesday morning, he, his relatives, and the military suite watched the sham-fighting for two hours from the fields belonging to Mayr-am-Hof and from the crucifix just above on the common. He allowed the villagers to stand with him to see the manœuvres, and our cook and housemaid being of the company, returned indoors quite enchanted; Josefa pronouncing it 'the treat of a lifetime.' They and Anton, moreover, had the gratification of hearing the Emperor

admire the outside of Mayr-am-Hof, which was made
festive with flags of the Austrian and Tyrolean colours.
He spoke of the house to an aide-de-camp as '*grossartig.*'
The Pusterthalers are doubly loyal, from the sympathy
and the substantial aid given them by their sovereign at
the time of the floods. Knowing, therefore, his liking
for costume, they put on wonderful old attire belonging
to their forefathers to appear before him last Sunday on
the shooting-ground. We can see the spot, with its belt of
fir-trees, across the meadows ; and the weather being as
brilliant as the uniforms and the peasant-costumes, the
glimpses gained at the distance resembled some wonderful ballet. Had my mother only been well, it would
have been a charming episode. She will, however, enjoy
hearing of it when she is better."

Mary Howitt to the Same.

"*Marienruhe, Oct. 23,* 1886.—Restored to health by
the loving mercy of God, I wish gratefully and affectionately to acknowledge your many kind letters of inquiry
and sympathy throughout my late illness. I had no pain,
and I have heard that old people often pass away without
any suffering. However, I know well that I was very ill;
that a medical man came regularly to see me ; that a dear,
kind Sister of Charity attended me in the night, allowing
Margaret or Alice to rest. But oh! how can I tell you
the sweet calm all this time? for I felt assured that I
was about to pass away into the other life, which seemed
to me perfectly natural.

"I wonder, dear Nannie, whether you and Isabella
are acquainted with that little work of Cardinal Newman's, 'The Dream of Gerontius.' It is a great favourite
of mine, and I know all its incidents perfectly. If you

know it you will remember where the dying man
says—

'I fain would sleep;
The pain has wearied me. . . . Into Thy hands,
O Lord, into Thy hands.' . . .

At that passage one understands that the soul leaves
the body. I felt that I was at that stage after I had
received what is called 'Extreme Unction,' a solemn
but beautiful occasion. It seemed to me—only please
to remember that I am not sure whether I was in the
full possession of my mind, for it is all to me like a
wonderful, sweet dream—that I closed my eyes after it
to sleep, but not, as Gerontius, to wake in the other life,
but rather gradually by soft degrees to full conscious-
ness and returning health and an abiding peace of mind.
I was there—old Mary Howitt again—just myself. If
that short illness had not reduced me almost to skin and
bone, with scarcely ability to turn myself in bed, I should
have thought it a dream or some sort of strange delusion.
I am thankful to know it was real. I assuredly believe
that the wonderful power of Catholic prayer, not for my
life, but for the fulfilment of God's will, whether I were
to live or die, prevailed, and that for some purpose or
other I was raised up again. This seems arrogant, does
it not? I feel it so; and yet it is to me so wonderful.
And I like you to know how marvellously the dear
Lord has dealt with me; and what an angel, what
a true Sister of Mercy, night and day, was Alice by
my bed.

"We are not at all surprised by what you tell us of the
changes in Rome. How detestable they are! I fancy
the end is not yet come. I suppose the intention is to
destroy everything venerable and sacred. We are very

thankful that Caroline Higgins, dear industrious soul!
is prospering. Give our love to her, please, and tell her
that she has a very affectionate place in our memories."

To Miss Lloyd Jones.

   " *Marienruhe, Jan.* 8, 1887.—Your letter, which arrived
duly on New Year's Day, gave us great pleasure and
interested us much. There was sorrow and anxiety in
it, as it spoke of the events of the closing year; but
all was made bright and beautiful by the love and
fatherly care of the dear Lord. The greatest sorrow of
all, the death of the precious little nephew, was changed
into a sweet memory by the beautiful spirit of the departed.

   "You mention that Mrs. Goode has sent me a parcel
by post. Can this be two Birthday-books which reached
me ten days before Christmas—new books, intended as
presents from a mother to her children? One was
inscribed 'Leslie Pepys;' the other, 'Guy Leslie Pepys.'
The paper of the parcel was torn; the postmark was
indistinct. There was no letter or card with them, nor
have I received any. We, of course, supposed that it was
wished that I should write my name and date of my
birth in them, which I would gladly do; but where to
return them we have not the least idea. If you can
help us in this difficulty we shall be much obliged."

To Mrs. Gaunt.

   " *March* 21, 1887.—It was just like you not to forget
my birthday; and I think that altogether it was one of
the pleasantest possible for an old woman. It seemed
as if nobody forgot me, either near or remote; and with
quantities of flowers and plants, which will continue

ornaments to our rooms and lovely memorials quite into summer or later. Your dear, sweet violets from my husband's grave will be amongst the fragrant realities for years to come; longer, no doubt, than I shall remain to treasure them.

"It was so pleasant to hear of your doings in Rome and its neighbourhood, going down to Porto d'Anzio and paying a visit to the Villa Livia; two places which we remember well, and which have each their little events belonging to them in our experience. We have an immense love of Rome, which will remain with us as long as we live. In fact, it is very seriously in our mind to spend the coming late autumn and winter in Rome, to go off to the old city, whether for life or death, and where, dear friend, I have a home."

To Margaret Howitt, at Rome.

"*Marienruhe, June* 21, 1887.—Another day is over now; that the longest, and our Queen's Jubilee. I wonder how they have gone on in London and all over England. Our Union Jack is up, and makes a great show. I rose in good time and went to Mass in the parish-church. On my way back, when passing over the Roman bridge, there was Father Paul coming up the opposite path under the trees, looking pale and suffering. He has been ill and confined to his bed, but being able to say Mass this morning, he, a Tyroler Benedictine, remembered our Queen's Jubilee, and made it his intention. He was now walking up to Marienruhe. I could tell him somewhat of the great doings in London; the Queen intending to go through it all like a Queen.

"Count and Countess Hompesch and our other friends and neighbours are most kind in looking in upon me. Dear Ernst, too, has been over. He spent part of Friday with me, and we had a charming time together.

" This morning I have received a deeply interesting letter from the Countess Clam-Martinic, giving touching details of the death of her husband in Prague. It was unexpected, and thus she was at church when he passed away. He kissed his crucifix, spoke the name of Jesus, then her name ; and all was over, without agony or suffering of any kind. I am treasuring up for your return two splendid passages from the Count's will, which were printed in ' *Das Vaterland.*' I think them the most beautiful evidence of a noble Christian that I ever read. What a privilege it is to have known such a statesman !

" Ernst and I both hope that you and Alice have been able to see Father Douglas. May the blessed Angels' be with you ! Have no anxiety about me ; only give thanks for the old mother and grandmother."

To Mrs. Gaunt.

" *Marienruhe, July* 15, 1887.—Yes, dear friend, what a pity it is that you are not going this year to Rome, instead of last ; at least for us ! It will be, as you may naturally suppose, a very interesting winter to be there, and many of our friends will be there also, which will be particularly agreeable. Margaret and Alice seem to me to have managed their business very speedily and satisfactorily, for we shall again be in the old familiar and beloved neighbourhood, just by the Pincio. Fortunately, too, the spirit of new Rome has not penetrated into that neighbourhood as ruthlessly as elsewhere, so that in one way it is almost like going home again.

"I am, as I think you are aware, very fond of Yorkshire, and have a particular regard and love for all the Yorkshire people I have known and proudly call my friends. Therefore it has been a real pleasure to us to become acquainted with Mr. John Lupton and his family from Leeds. The publication of my 'Reminiscences' in *Good Words*, and Miss Linskill's contributions to the same periodical, had led to her and my corresponding, and our becoming much interested in each other. She was travelling on the Continent with her friends the Luptons ; and as they came to Meran, we of course saw them while here. We were delighted to have them ; and what a great deal of talk we had ! How nobly Christian, original, pure, manly and good were all his views of life ! You will know of them, if you do not know them personally. So much for one of the visits we have had this summer in our little Marienruhe."

To Miss Clifford.

"*Meran, Aug.* 26, 1887.—We now can count only a few weeks longer at Marienruhe. However, we shall be, with the Divine blessing, at Rome, and that will be all right. But I confess that to me, old as I am, and now so little accustomed to taking any journeys, it seems rather like a great undertaking. Father Paul, who was allowed to see your very pleasant letter, is now again at Meran, and will take back with him this evening *The Tablet ;* and I must tell you the great pleasure we have had in reading the conversation given in it by a correspondent which the writer had with your excellent brother, Sir Charles Clifford, with regard to the taking possession of New Zealand, and the glorious manner in which the latter opened the path there for the Catholic faith."

To Father Paul Perkmann, O.S.B.

"38 *Via Gregoriana, Oct.* 9, 1887.—I send you a few lines to prove to you how kindly your prayers, and those of others, have been answered for us, in the fullest sense. The journey was good throughout. Our apartment is most comfortable.

"If you could only be spirited here this moment, and sit with me, the sun shining in deliciously, and on the opposite side of the old Via Gregoriana no new building, but a bit of an old garden, with lemon-trees appearing over the wall and blue sky above, you would not think it unpleasant. Thus we feel we have much to be thankful for. I as yet have not been to Mass, but it is a comfort to me in the early morning to hear the bell of St. Andrea delle Fratte signalising the action of the sacred office, so that I can spiritually be present."

To Mrs. Gaunt.

"*Rome, Oct.* 10, 1887.—We are in what was Miss Charlotte Cushman's Roman home, and our dear friends, Nannie Leigh Smith and Isabella Blythe, are coming at the beginning of next month to be inmates of the same old house.

"Now let me thank you with my whole heart for so kindly sending us this very interesting life of Rossetti, of whom we saw a good deal when we lived at the quaint and picturesque little Hermitage. We also saw a good deal of Miss Siddall. She was very delicate, and had certainly a marvellous influence on Rossetti; though I never could believe she possessed the artistic genius which he ascribed to her, for what she produced had no originality in it. Still, she was, in her way, an interesting woman, and his love for her like a passionate romantic Italian story. But it is altogether a strange, melancholy history. Of his later pictures I know nothing. The last of his which I saw was a short time before we left England, at his house in Chelsea, where I went with my

VIA SISTINA AND VIA GREGORIANA, ROME.

eldest daughter to call on him. He was painting beautiful women, it seemed to me, and nothing else, in gardens of roses. His rooms were piled up with heaps of blue and white china, heaps and heaps of it on the tables, and even on the floor."

To the Same.

"*Nov.* 14, 1887.—It does me good to hear that

genial-hearted man, Dr. Vardon, speak of you. This kind physician, his wife, and little children occupy, as you know, the highest apartment in this house; and below the Vardons come Miss Leigh Smith and Miss Blythe, now our dear house-mates.

"What a most sad case is this of the poor Crown Prince of Germany! Anything more sorrowful I cannot conceive. At the same time, I cannot help feeling that a blessing will come out of it. So solemn a warning must have its purpose. I am sure the entire Catholic world prays for him, and that God's Will may be done by this affliction and in all ways. This seems a very grave ending to my letter, but Margaret has just read me the last report of the case; and I write what I have felt upon it, and you probably have felt the same."

To Father Paul Perkmann, O.S.B.

"*Rome, Dec.* 9, 1887.—More rain has fallen for these last few weeks than Romans are accustomed to, and as St. Bibiana, the rain-bringer, now just passed, has come with it very much in her train, they say it will last for more than a month to come. This we are sorry for, as we are now beginning to think about the great English pilgrimage which is to arrive in the first week of the new year, and which even I, the old woman, desire to join, though probably I may not do so. But we none of us as yet have paid our respects to the Holy Father. You will wonder at this, probably. I almost wonder at it myself. But so much is going forward, and those very friends of ours whose advice and co-operation we desire—the von Schönbergs and Cliffords—are not yet here. So we wait till they come."

To Mrs. Gaunt.

"*Dec.* 21, 1887.—I find that our English letters must all be posted to-day, if they are to be in England before Christmas Day. Unfortunately, I have been either over-taken by time (which does pass unusually fast, I have noticed of late) or else have been very lazy, for now at the last moment various letters, which I had intended to make particularly interesting by mention of the wonderful events now daily taking place in Rome, must be cut short, and I content myself with ordinary Christmas and New Year's good wishes.

"However, I will do my best, simply being content if my poor hurried lines only convey love enough to those who, like yourself, dear kind friend, deserve the best I can do in any way.

"I can but wish you were here; for, though you are not a Catholic, you have a large heart and a poetical mind, and can feel the wonderful period this is for the thou-sands who are of this great Church. The national pilgrimages taking place and continuing in the New Year are each very interesting to us, but more especially those announced from England, Scotland, and Ireland. We have just had eighteen hundred pilgrims from France, rich and poor, men and women, chiefly of the artisan and peasant class, attended by priests, and all impelled by an earnest Catholic spirit. Then again another—eight hundred, I believe—from Hungary, also principally poor people, men and women in the national costumes, with grave, earnest, rather sad countenances, likewise attended by priests, and headed by a few of their nobility. It was really most affecting to see them; and so will it be as other races from all parts of Europe come, speaking their here unspoken languages, wearing their costumes, should such remain in their lands ; yet all holding the same faith with the same living tenacity, and all looking up to St. Peter's, as the Jews in olden time to their Temple in Jerusalem.

"It is wonderful, dear friend, to think of this, and a great privilege to be here, and to witness something of it. I, at my age, can do no more, but I am thankful even for that. All this is page after page in the great history of the present day. Not less interesting and valuable to us is the fact that it brings us into personal intercourse with really great and good men whom otherwise we should have no chance of knowing. Then, too, we see the commencement of events and the first progress of great purposes which may before long develop into enduring blessings to the whole human race. It is, therefore, very interesting to be here now, when so much is going forward. You may say, ' But that is only in Catholic circles.' Very true ; but these circles embrace the whole world..

"Rome has always been to us a sorrowful as well as the dearest place of residence we ever had. Here it was that our dear Peggy became one in our family ; and here, day by day, we watched the progress of her fatal malady. My dear husband, who loved Rome, and felt it to be a happy home, here, like a tree losing its leaves in autumn, prepared calmly, if almost unconsciously, for the end. Here lie calmly his remains, awaiting, if God so will, for mine to be laid beside them. You, therefore, can understand why we do not have merry gatherings in Rome, only the visits of a few choice friends."

PRIVATE NOTES.

"*Jan.* 1, 1888.—

> Grant me, dear Lord, for my life's term, I pray,
> A threefold grace to sanctify each day.
>
> Grace so to guide and to control my tongue,
> That none by it may be misled or stung ;
> Grace to detach my mind from worldly snares,
> From trivial talk, or worrying Martha-cares ;
> Grace in adoring love to take my seat
> Like Mary, meek and silent at Thy feet.

The above is my daily prayer for this year, as for the last. May the dear Lord be pleased to hear it, and mercifully grant it. Amen. This has been, in every sense of the word, a glorious and a blessed day. After the wet, dull weather we have been suffering from, the sun shone brilliantly. Margaret went, with Isabella, Dr. and Mrs. Vardon, and Janet, to the Holy Father's Jubilee Mass in St. Peter's. The ceremony was magnificent, harmonious, with the blessing of the Lord over all. Alice also had a beautiful time at the Papal Mass."

"*Jan.* 2.—A change in the weather ; therefore a double mercy that it was fine yesterday."

"*Jan.* 7.—A dull day ; rain and dirty roads ; very dis-agreeable. Bessie von Schönberg comes, and afterwards Ernst. It is very pleasant to see them."

"*Jan.* 9.—A beautiful day. I am most anxious about myself for to-morrow. May the Blessed Virgin Mary pray for me ! We receive our English deputation tickets. Mr. Clifford has most kindly arranged everything for us."

To Father Paul Perkmann, O.S.B.

"*Rome, Jan.* 11, 1888.—I cannot allow myself to

have all the blessings and enjoyment which yesterday afforded me without endeavouring to make you, at least in part, a sharer. For no one, I believe, would bear me more sympathetically in mind during that eventful morning than yourself.

"It was a brilliant day, after wretchedly wet and dreary weather, just as if Heaven were in perfect harmony with the desires of the English pilgrims, to the number of about five hundred.

"Our friends, Mr. Alphonso and Miss Constantia Clifford, are here, you know, and this English deputation was under the conduct of their cousin, the Bishop of Clifton. Yesterday, Mr. Clifford, as a private chamberlain, was in attendance on the Pope, it being considered in order that he, an Englishman, should be so on the occasion of the English deputation, at the head of which was, of course, the good Duke of Norfolk.

"But though on duty and very much occupied, he made time to receive us at the private entrance, where we could immediately ascend by a lift, without any fatigue, into a warm, comfortable ante-room. Here we could rest till the time came for the interview. Various distinguished personages, whose names, high in the Church, were familiar to us, were moving about; and every now and then Mr. Clifford introduced us to them. In a while we were moved on, advancing perhaps through five or six rooms, all of which interested me greatly, nothing striking me more than the wonderful simplicity of the apartments; all similar and wholly without ornament or costly show. At length we were in the room immediately adjoining and opening into the Throne-room, where, it now being ten o'clock, the Holy Father had received the Bishops of the deputation. Here we heard the low, calm voice of the Holy Father addressing the various delegates, who one after the other knelt before him. We were about fifty ladies and a few gentlemen, just the first detachment which had been admitted, as it would have been impossible to receive the full number at once; and we were so favoured as to be in this first detachment. I now discovered, with a little nervous trepidation, that *I*, your poor old penitent, was to be honoured by first receiving the blessing after the delegates. But, to my infinite surprise and thankfulness, though I did feel a little bit startled with a deep sense of my own unworthiness, I felt at the same time very calm and grateful, trusting that our dear Lord would indeed be with me. At length the moment came. My friend, Mr. Clifford, was there, and I was within the doorway.

"I saw the Holy Father seated, not on a throne, but on a chair, a little raised above the level of the floor; and the English Bishops, in their violet silk cloaks, seated in two rows on either side of him. The gracious, most courteous Duke of Norfolk came forward and acknowledged us. This might last, perhaps, two minutes. Then Mr. Clifford led me forward to the Holy Father; Margaret, as my daughter, following with Miss Clifford. I never thought of myself. I was unconscious of everything. A serene happiness, almost joy, filled my whole being as I at once found myself on my knees before the Vicar of Christ. My wish was to kiss his foot, but it was withdrawn and his hand given me. You may think with what fervour I kissed the ring. In the meantime he had been told my age and my late conversion. His hands were laid on my shoulders, and again and again his right hand in blessing on my head, whilst he spoke to me of Paradise.

"All this time I did not know whether I was in the body or not. I knew afterwards that I felt unspeakably happy, and with a sense of unwillingness to leave. How long it lasted—perhaps a minute or so—I know not; but I certainly was lifted into a high spiritual state of bliss, such as I never had experience of before, and which now fills me with astonishment and deep thankfulness to recall. I woke in the stillness of last night with the sense of it upon me. It is wonderful. I hope I may never lose it.

"On leaving the room I received from a monsignore in attendance, with the words that the Holy Father gave it me, a silver medal of himself in a small red case; a present which was made to others of the deputation.

"The Duke of Norfolk, after this, very kindly led me out by another way of exit; and thus we could return home immediately, descending in the lift by which we had ascended.

"Now, dear father, you have a long letter. But to you and to dear Father Ceslas I feel that I owe a debt which I can only repay by little offerings such as this. And it is not often that I have a chance of such a glorious, divine opportunity of thanksgiving."

THE LAST ENTRIES IN PRIVATE DIARY FOR 1888.

"*Jan.* 13.—A very fine day. The Cliffords drove with us to the Villa Celimontana, to call on the Archbishop of Prague, a most noble-looking man, extremely friendly and agreeable. Then we visited dear Lily; and all was charming. On our return, the Princess Löwenstein, her sister, the Countess Fünfkirchen, three of her daughters, and their cousin, a young Princess Liechtenstein, came. While they were with us Mr. Cox of *The Tablet* called."

"*Jan.* 14.—Have had my confession and a pleasant visit from Father Carey. Lord Selborne and Lady Sophia Palmer call; afterwards Lady Eyre and a friend of hers; and later Mr. Wedgwood."

"*Jan.* 15.—A fine day, but so cold I could not go to Holy Communion."

"*Jan.* 23.—Father Carey will administer Holy Communion to me in my room to-morrow morning. I hope and pray that it may be blessed to me, and that I may be made worthy to receive it. Baron Hoffmann came."

My mother was at this time suffering from an attack of bronchitis, which at first confined her to the house; then, as she grew weaker, to her room; and finally to her bed. It seemed likely that the desire of her heart, to attend the Papal Jubilee and then to pass away in Rome, would be granted.

In a note written to an intimate friend from Marienruhe we find her saying :—

"*Sept.* 14, 1887.—We had Mass yesterday morning, and shall again have it next Tuesday, which will be our last. Rather sad it seems to me. Perhaps altogether my last here, for though I am as well as usual, and in some respects perhaps better, yet everything, as far as I am concerned, is done with that feeling. Though I seem to write rather dismally, we are all in good heart."

The last tie with this earth was snapped when the
Holy Father spoke to her of a near approach to Paradise. She longed to go, and yet was sorry to leave
us. From that time her soul remained in a continuous
state of prayer and thanksgiving; her heart and mind
overflowing, as usual, with love and interest for all her
surroundings. On Saturday night, January 28, she
spoke of the total eclipse of the moon, commending
the energy of an elderly lady of her acquaintance who
had gone in the dark on the Pincio, if possible, to
observe it. On the afternoon of the next day she
received the Last Sacraments from the parish-priest
of St. Andrea delle Fratte, with the assistance of Father
Carey; and in so joyful and intelligent a manner as
to astonish the lively young Italian server. He remarked to the parish-priest he could perceive no signs
of approaching dissolution in the "Signora," and received for reply, "It was on account of her great age
and by the advice of the physician."

Later the same evening Father Lockhart, a dear
and intimate friend, came to see her. She spoke with
him in rapture of the blessings she had received a few
hours earlier. That night she conversed much with her
beloved Isabella Blythe, thanked Dr. Vardon and her
devoted nurse for their faithful, unflagging attentions,
and repeated the customary evening prayers with her
daughter. Then she composed herself to rest, and
gently passed away in her sleep at ten minutes past
three on Monday morning, January 30. She had nearly
completed the eighty-ninth year of her age.

It happened, by a kind providence, that Father Luke
Carey, who had spiritually aided and strengthened her
since her arrival in Rome, was the Superior of St.

Isidore, a monastery to which, for various reasons, she was greatly attached; and that the Sons of St. Francis, rich in piety and innocence, and loving poverty for God's sake, could perform for her the last rites within its walls.

On the day of her death various of her friends visited her chamber and prayed by her mortal remains; and thither came, in the afternoon, Father Carey, with one of his Franciscan Brothers, to say their office. In this pious act they were joined by the Rev. Kenelm Vaughan, in whose "Work of Expiation" the deceased was deeply interested.

In the early morning of Tuesday, January 31, she was laid in her coffin. Serenely happy and youthful she then looked; her hands were crossed on her breast, and she reposed amongst flowers. Attended by the parochial clergy, Dr. Vardon, Mr. Marke, and a young Benedictine, she was borne from the Via Gregoriana past the convent of the *Reparatrici* nuns, where she had been wont to receive Holy Communion, to the collegiate church of St. Isidore, and consigned to the care of the Franciscans. Numerous Catholic and Protestant friends and acquaintance were assembled for the Requiem Mass, at which Father Carey was the celebrant.

The morning was wet; but in the afternoon, when the mourners returned to complete the burial, they found the church-doors wide open, and the sun streaming in upon the coffin and its wreaths of flowers; whilst some of the neighbouring poor, chiefly children, had turned into the church, and were kneeling on the pavement in prayer near the bier. The young Seminarists of St. Isidore, Irish, German, and Spanish, in their brown gowns and sandalled feet, each holding a tall lighted taper, filed in long procession from the sacristy, and standing round the bier, headed by their Superior, chanted in a most heart-touching manner, first the *Libera me Domine*, and then also in Latin, " May the Angels conduct thee into Paradise; at thy coming may the Martyrs receive thee and lead thee to Jerusalem, the holy city. May the Angelic Choir receive thee, and with Lazarus, once a beggar, mayest thou have eternal rest." At the end of the office, with their lights burning, they attended the coffin to the hearse waiting to convey it to the cemetery of Monte Testaccio. There, by permission of the Cardinal-Vicar of Rome, the mortal remains of Mary Howitt were reverently interred by those of her husband.

INDEX.

 2 A

THE END.

9 783337 011451